I0716754

THRONE OF BLOOD

RR JONES

APOLODOR PUBLISHING

THRONE OF BLOOD

J.B. Bury, Public Domain, via Wikimedia Commons

CHAPTER I

EDIRNE SARAYI, NOVEMBER 1444

Here in Edirne and everywhere else in Rumelia's South-Eastern plains, the last days of November are losing the battle with winter. The slow-moving Tunca River mirrors the heavy gray sky, and the trees shiver in the sharp wind, clutching on to their last dying leaves.

Just two weeks ago, the battle of Varna, the Battle of the Two Sultans, as many call it, saw the Ottoman Army obliterate the Christians' last crusade. Hunyadi, Christianity's White Knight, ran home with his tail between his legs, leaving behind King Władysław's headless body. The king's head, well-preserved in a casket of honey, now travels from one corner of the empire to another as proof of the sultans' victory.

The celebrations were something to behold. Ali had never seen so many people sharing so much joy, whole flocks of sheep and chicken eaten in one day, or mountains of sweets as big as a mosque vanish overnight.

But that was then, and this is now. Now, life at the palace is back to normal. Sort of. And Ali resumed her daily chores.

She rushes out of the steamy palace kitchen, stumbling under the weight of a silver platter loaded with the best kitchen delights: Amber-like grapes trapping sweetness in their golden light, blood-red pomegranates bursting with flavor, wrinkled salt-cured olives, sesame-sprinkled round flat breads, melty pieces of snow-white feta, and rose water flavored baklava crusted with green pistachios and dripping with honey.

She moves so fast that her loose blue shalwars and her kaftan flutter behind her, but her feet, wrapped in soft velvet slippers with upturned noses, make no noise as she cruises along the white marble hallways to the validé's apartment. Hüma Hatun, Sultan Mehmed's mother, is Ali's mistress and the validé, and Ali's first job is to please her, soothe her, and make her happy. It's not an easy job, especially these days.

Hüma was nothing but sunshine when the victorious army returned. She welcomed home not only her son, young Sultan Mehmed, but also her husband and master, Sultan Murad the Second, whom she hadn't seen in many months. Ever since summer, when he resigned the Imperial throne to Mehmed and withdrew to the heart of Anatolia, hundreds of miles away, to live a life of prayer and meditation dedicated to Allah.

That was last week. But now, Hüma's sunshine faded into a gray winter storm, just like the heavy sky. A week later, she still hasn't seen Murad, and there are rumors he's about to leave again. And, as she's locked in the harem, she can't just pop by to see how he's doing. Like all his other women, she has to wait for his pleasure to see her, and that pleasure has been lacking.

Ali bows deeply and sets the silver platter loaded with deliciousness on the Isfahan carpet where exuberant vines, fruits and flowers entangle. She bows again and turns to the door.

"Ali."

Hüma sits on her podium on a red brocade pillow, drinking from a silver cup. Her moss-green velvet kaftan sets off her snow-white face and fiery red hair. Ever fierce, her green eyes pierce Ali with unkind light. Hüma Hatun is unhappy, and when the validé is unhappy, the universe is unhappy too.

Ali wishes she was elsewhere, like the kitchens, or the Transylvanian forests she came from, or the moon. But she's not. She's right here, a young eunuch-in-training at the Edirne sarayi whose mistress glares at her with killer eyes.

"Yes, my lady."

"What did you hear?"

"I heard that Sultan Murad's Anatolian sipahis and janissaries have been told to get ready."

"When are they leaving?"

"Soon, they say. A couple of days maybe."

Hüma's cheeks turn fire red. "And he hasn't come to see me yet. It's been a week, he's getting ready to leave, and he hasn't been here yet."

Ali shrinks and says nothing. What is there to say?

"Has he been to see Mara?"

Ali nods. Mara Branković, the sultan's fourth wife and a Serbian princess, has had the honor of the sultan's visit. More than once, in fact. And everyone knows it, since here, in the sarayi, walls have ears and everyone knows everything about everybody.

Hüma hurls her cup across the room. The goblet hits the wall and cracks a blue tile, marring the geometric pattern above the door, before crashing to the ground. Ali ducks. "How about that whore, Halime Hatice Hatun?"

There is no love lost between Halime Hatice, Sultan Murad's second wife and the mother of his late favorite son, Aladdin, and Hüma Hatun. Still, she's not a whore — she couldn't be if she wanted to. Here, in the harem, the women are locked in and guarded by eunuchs. Whoring is just as likely as sprouting wings to fly. Still, mentioning Halime Hatice Hatun's virtue at this point seems unwise. Ali nods and makes herself even smaller to avoid being hit with whatever the validé will throw next.

The validé throws nothing, but she jumps to her feet to pace across the room. She moves so fast that her waist-long red curls fly behind her, making her look like a walking green torch.

"Why? Why go see her, when she's years older than me and dark and ugly? And she doesn't even have a son?"

No longer, that is. Halime Hatice's son, Aladdin, the eighteen-year-old şehzade and much-loved heir to the Ottoman throne, died in mysterious circumstances last year, together with his two young sons, making room for Mehmed's succession.

"Maybe that's why," Ali whispers, then wishes she'd kept her mouth shut.

The validé glowers at Ali with murderous eyes. "She's been drinking your potion for more than a month now. And she's not dead yet. How much longer?"

"A few weeks, maybe. If she keeps drinking it."

Hüma laughs a joyless laugh. "Oh, she will. That stupid whore thinks the potion will help her have another son, so she'll be drinking it, since there's nothing she'd like more than to produce a son that would threaten Mehmed's throne. She wants to be the validé, but she won't. Not if I have anything to say about it. A few weeks, you said?"

"Yes, my lady."

"How about the potion for the boy? When will that be ready?"

Ali wishes her master were less prone to murderous rages. Ever since she told Hüma — under duress — about the secret knowledge she learned from her grandmother, Hüma has done nothing but plan who to kill and how fast. First, it was Halime Hatice. Now she wants to kill a boy, and she wants that done yesterday.

Ali wonders how long she'll manage to placate her. She figured out that the boy Hüma wants killed is Ali's friend Radu, a prince of Wallachia and a hostage at the Ottoman Empire. He's Mehmed's best friend, and some say he's more than that. Especially since that night when Radu stabbed Mehmed, and instead of executing him on the spot, Mehmed delayed his departure to war just to keep him safe. Now they're together again and they seem tighter than ever.

"I need some more herbs I haven't been able to find. I'll try again under the next full moon."

"Don't try. Succeed," Hüma says.

Ali bows again. She catches a glimpse of the cross hanging under her shirt glowing red, telling her she's in danger. Like she needs telling. "I will..."

The door opens to let in Sultan Murad.

A MURDEROUS RAGE

Resplendent in a golden kaftan and a silk turban whiter than snow, Sultan Murad sucks the air out of the room with his presence. His handsome face with a dark beard and well-kept mustache looks serene, but his eyes take in Hüma and the room, missing nothing.

He nods, and Hüma's anger vanishes like a snowball dropped in hot water. She crumbles to the floor under his powerful gaze, and prostrates herself, touching the rich carpet with her forehead.

"My sultan. Thank you for honoring me."

Murad is technically no longer the sultan, since he resigned and handed the Sword of Osman, the symbol of power, to his son Mehmed. But he's still the Ottoman Empire's most powerful man. Many in the empire wish he'd take back that sword and send young Mehmed to Manisa to play with his hawks and his horses until he grows up. Many, but not Hüma Hatun.

As Mehmed's mother, Sultan Murad's resignation promoted her from his third wife to the validé. That makes her the mistress of the imperial harem and gives her rights of life and death over everyone inside it. Except for the sultan's other wives and his children, of course.

But the eunuchs and the women know she holds their lives in her soft, bejeweled hands.

Sultan Murad studies her and nods. "How are you, Hüma? Just as beautiful as ever, I see."

Hüma blushes and lowers her eyes, and Ali knows she's happy for the countless hours she spent in the hammam getting ready for this moment.

"Thank you, my sultan. You?"

The sultan nods without a word.

"Congratulations for your amazing victory against the infidels. People say this has been the last crusade. The Christians will finally understand they can't compete with the Ottoman Empire. Not with leaders such as you and our son."

"He's a good son, Mehmed. He'll make a good sultan someday, I hope. And a good leader. But he's got a lot to learn."

"He's so young, still."

"He is indeed. But there's more than that. Remember Aladdin?"

Hüma blushes. "I do, though I never knew him well."

"Too bad you didn't. Aladdin was a great young man and an excellent soldier. With his potential, he would have made a great sultan someday. Too bad he died so young. And in such strange circumstances."

Hüma looks down. "It was Allah's wish. His ways are hard to understand, but always just."

Murad's eyes on her are devoid of love. "Surely you don't think that the death of his two young children was just too? They were only babies."

Hüma shrugs. "There will be others. Our Mehmed will soon be of age to get married."

"I'll look into that. Though I understand he may have other... interests."

Hüma sighs. "He's still so young. But I have no doubt he will do the right thing for the empire. He'll be one of the greatest sultans that ever lived."

"I hope you're right, Hüma. But we both know he's got a long way to go, and he'll need a lot of help. But sadly, he has trouble accepting help and taking advice. That's why I rely on you to help him. Çandarlı Halil Paşa, the grand vizier, is experienced, wise and faithful. He'll do whatever he can to guide Mehmed in the right direction, if only Mehmed will let himself be guided. You need to help him."

Hüma bows. "You are leaving, I understand?"

"I am. We can't leave Anatolia undefended, and Mehmed can't grow and learn with me breathing down his neck. You can't have two sultans in one palace. I'll leave for Manisa in a few days."

"May I join you?"

Murad stares at her like she's lost her mind.

"Join me? Of course not. Your place is here with your son. Make sure he behaves better."

Hüma's cheeks catch fire, but her voice stays soft. "I thought that Çandarlı Paşa and Akşemseddin and the dignitaries will be enough to help and guide Sultan Mehmed. I thought you'd be lonely and..."

Murad laughs. "Lonely? I wish. I have a whole army. And I'll take Halime Hatice with me."

Hüma gasps. "Why Halime Hatice?"

"Because she's a good woman, from a good stock. She's the daughter of Isfendiyár Bey, and she gave me Aladdin, the best son a father could hope for. *Insha'Allah*, she'll give me another. She's still young enough. We have to ensure the empire's succession. Mehmed has no sons, and I have none but him. If we both die, the closest we have to a şehzade is that drunk Orhan that we pay Constantinople to keep hostage. We need a better succession plan.

"Moreover, Halime Hatice is a lovely woman and great company. I'm so sorry to see that she's not well. Apparently, she's been unwell for weeks now and nobody is sure why. I hope a change of air will do her good."

Ali knows that Hüma's brain is about to burst. There is no higher insult to Hüma than her husband, Sultan Murad, taking Halime Hatice with him and leaving her here. Unless it's reminding her that Halime

Hatice is good old Anatolian stock, while she, Hüma, was just a Rumelian slave, paid for with a few cows and sheep. That shouldn't matter, now that she's the validé, but it still stings.

"Stay well and take care of Mehmed. Make sure he knows his responsibilities and treats Çandarlı Paşa with the respect he deserves."

Hüma prostrates herself one more time, and Murad leaves without looking back. His boots clang against the marble floors, further and further, until they fade in the distance. The silence is so deep it hurts. Even the caged birds went quiet.

Hüma sits up and looks behind the footsteps like she can see her lord and master through the thickness of the walls. She wrings her hands, and the heavy emerald Sultan Murad gave her when she birthed his son throws arrows of green fire. Her lips tight, her cheeks burning like she got slapped, Hüma Hatun trembles with anger.

"Ali."

"Yes, my lady."

"Can you make me a quick kill potion by tomorrow?"

"I can't, my lady. You know I need her blood, and her hair, and..."

"Her? Who said I was looking at killing Halime Hatice? If it's not her, there'll be another."

Ali's heart skips a beat. If it's not Halime Hatice Hatun the validé is after, that means she's planning to kill Murad.

That's worth keeping in mind.

CHAPTER 3

ÜNYE, ANATOLIA

Vlad's eyes open to a star-studded sky. The night is dark and quiet, and a cool breeze fills his lungs with the scent of the sea. It's a heady combination of salt, algae, and dead fish. Not quite perfume, but for Vlad, that's the smell of freedom. The small fishing village of Ünye should be the end of the journey he started in the prison-fortress of Tokat. It took him weeks, but he did OK. He planned his escape carefully and executed it well. With one exception.

He glances at the two children sleeping in the ditch next to him. The girl holds her brother in her sleep, like she always does, and smiles at whatever she sees in her dreams. Vlad sighs, wishing he'd left them where they were. But in his heart of hearts, he knows he couldn't have, even though they cost him a whole extra week on the road.

They walked every night and hid through the days. It took them way longer than planned, but they're finally within reach of the sea and the one thing left is to find a ship that will take them to Varna or the Dardanelles.

Or to wherever else, for that matter. As long as they're out of this piss-pit that's Anatolia. Vlad doesn't care, and the kids don't either. He shouldn't have taken them with him, but for the first time in his

10

life, he felt pity. And look what good it did him. They slowed him down every inch of the way. Though, to be fair, they never complained. The boy couldn't, since he's deaf and mute. How can he complain? But the girl didn't either. They walked and walked until their feet bled, their breath shortened and their bones hurt. But it wasn't fast enough.

And God only knows what has happened in the world in the meantime, since Vlad has no way to get the news. When he escaped Tokat, Hunyadi's crusaders were getting ready to board the Genoese and Venetian ships in Varna, sail to Constantinople, and throw the Ottomans out of Europe. But that was weeks ago. By now, for all that Vlad knows, the sultan may be dead and the crusaders might have stormed the Ottoman Empire. That would make him a free man.

Unless it's the other way round. If the sultan crushed the crusaders, they'll catch and kill him sooner or later. What else can they do after all the people he's killed? And he wasn't the sultan's favorite even before. Mehmed's favorite is Radu, Vlad's handsome brother, who'll never grow to be a real man, since he's wired wrong. But his pretty face and soft smile always fool everyone.

Oh well. It is what it is. He'd better leave the kids here and check the port. If he finds a ship that will take them, he'll bring them over. But if they nab him, at least the kids are free.

He gets up quietly, but Sophia opens her huge blue eyes like she's never slept.

"I'll go see what's going on. You stay here," Vlad whispers, even though he doesn't need to. There's nobody around them for miles, and the boy is so deaf he couldn't hear the church bells if he slept under them. That's what a hot needle in your ear will do to you, Vlad thinks, filing that with the rest of his knowledge about the human body and what a skilled torturer can do to it. He's gathered a lot of expert knowledge in Tokat, and he can't wait to put it to good use.

Sophia's hand grasps his sleeve. "We'll come with you to help."

Vlad would laugh, but he doesn't want to hurt her feelings. Help him? The two of them? They'd only be in the way, make noise, and get caught. He doesn't need their help. And he doesn't need to worry about them either.

"No. I'm better off alone."

Her blue eyes tear up. Vlad curses himself, but there's not much he can do. But one thing.

"Here. Take this," he says, giving her the purse he stole from Sevlet Paşa when he escaped. "If I'm not back by sunrise, hide it, but take a few coins and find a fisherman to take you to Varna. Or maybe further north, to Chilia. If you get there, look for me at the royal court of Târgoviște. Ask about Vlad, Vlad Dracul's son."

Sophia's eyes swim in tears. To Vlad, her pain is bitter-sweet. He's sorry she's upset, but he's glad to see her care about him.

He leans over and touches her lips with his. A wave of warmth and sweetness runs through him, so strong it melts his knees. He hates leaving her, but he doesn't have a choice. Their freedom depends on him.

Vlad smiles and touches her cheek with his finger, then leaves without looking back. He trudges and stumbles through the dark muddy fields until he sees a flickering light. When he gets close, he drops to his knees and crawls through the shadows, listening to the waves and the gull's cries and breathing the smell of the sea.

One with the darkness, Vlad crawls forward until he's close enough to count the ships bouncing around their anchors. Some are big, some small. They're Ottoman, Greek and Bulgarian. A few slim sailing ships, two large Ottoman galleys looking like fat centipedes with their dozens of oars, and a few tiny fishing ships loaded with nets that look ready to weigh anchor and get underway.

Vlad wishes he knew more about boats, so he knew which one to choose, but it's too late now. He shrugs and heads to the ship closest to the shore, a small two-masted brigantine with a sharp bow and receding stern that looks abandoned. He reads the Greek letters on the hull. *Agape Mou*, My Love. Nice name for a ship.

As he steps into the water, a hand grabs his kaftan and pulls him back while a sharp blade probes his throat.

"Stop," someone whispers.

The voice is hoarse and rough, with an accent that Vlad can't place. The body it belongs to smells like fish, smoke and old sweat, but it's rock-hard and unafraid.

"What do you want?" the voice asks.

"I'm looking for passage."

"To where?"

"To Varna. Or Chilia. Or the Dardanelles."

"Why?"

"Because I need to get there."

"In the middle of the night?"

"I have some friends looking for me. I'd rather they didn't find me."

"Who are you running from?"

"My sweetheart's parents. They don't like me, so we eloped."

"Where is she?"

"I left her behind while I looked for a ship."

"Can you pay?"

Vlad reaches for his belt, but the knife digs deeper into his skin.

"Let me show you."

"Not so fast, my friend. Lay down."

Vlad does. The rough sand is cold under his cheek, and the hand searching for his money isn't soft. But he's glad he left the bag of coins with Sophia, and only took a few. The man takes them, along with his dagger.

"This isn't enough."

"I have more."

"Where?"

"Not here."

"I want a hundred."

Vlad doesn't have a hundred, but that doesn't matter. No matter what, he'll have to kill this dirty son of a bitch, but only after they get out of here.

"I'll give you twenty-five."

"I'll take fifty."

"For fifty, you take us all the way to Chilia."

"OK."

"I'll be back. Get ready."

The man shrugs and lets him go. He's short and wiry, and smells like he's never heard of soap, but he seems to know what he's doing, and that's the best Vlad can hope for. That, and that he won't betray him as soon as Vlad turns his back.

But he won't. He'd lose the chance to make a lot of money. He'll likely try to kill them at sea and take all they have, but that's par for the course. Vlad will just have to kill him first.

"I'm always ready," the man says. "Don't be long."

Vlad nods. "My dagger."

"What about it?"

"You can keep the coins; they'll be part of the payment. But I need my dagger now."

The man spits to the side and hands him the dagger. Vlad slides it under his belt and leaves. He feels the man's eyes burn holes in his back and struggles to not turn around until he's deep in the shade. When he does, the man is fussing with the lines, getting ready.

Vlad runs across the fields, looking for the kids, but he has trouble. He walks up and down and up again. Still nothing. That darn place looked just like this, but then don't all ditches look alike? Did he get lost in the dark?

He turns back again, and a sparkle catches his eye. He leans over to see better.

Deep in the bottom of the ditch, half-buried in the dirt, a golden coin mirrors the moonlight.

CHAPTER 4
THE DOOMED ESCAPE

Vlad's heart skips a beat. He jumps back, but it's too late. Strong hands, too many, grab him from behind and push him face-down to the ground. Heavy knees press his shoulders, and someone's feet hold his arms down. He's trapped.

He spits out a mouthful of bitter dirt and tries to look up, but a hand grabs his hair and pushes his face back down into the ground.

Someone laughs a silly, high-pitched laugh.

This laugh... Vlad has heard it before. It's Sevlet Paşa, Tokat's governor, who, only weeks ago, was the most important person in Vlad's life. Vlad was so grateful for his teachings that he let him live when he escaped. Sevlet Paşa taught him a lot about the human body, and even more about the human mind. He's an artist of his craft, and he taught Vlad how to control people through pain and fear. That lesson was so valuable that Vlad couldn't bring himself to kill him.

Now he wishes he had.

"Look who we have here! Get him up," the paşa says.

The hands lift Vlad up and turn him to face the paşa, whose round, smiling face glows with joy in the light of his torch. He's having a great day, the paşa.

"Long time no see, Prince Vlad. Boy, am I happy to see you."

Vlad sighs. "I wish I could say the same."

The paşa chokes with laughter. "Oh, my prince. I find it so sad that you destroyed our wonderful friendship. I have to admit that you've been my very best student ever, hands down. I was so proud of your achievements, until the day you chose to disappear, leaving behind a trail of deaths: my guards, peasants, even horses. That made me sad."

The paşa looks anything but sad. He looks overjoyed, in fact, and Vlad wonders why. But whatever the reason is, Vlad knows it won't bode well for him. The paşa trades in pain. Making people suffer is his art, and nobody does it better. Sevlet Paşa enjoys it like a chef enjoys cooking a splendid dinner or a gardener enjoys turning a plot of desert bloom into a garden. But Şevlet Paşa's art makes nobody happy but himself.

"Because of you, prince, I almost lost my job. A job that makes me very happy. To keep it, and maybe even keep my head, I had to bring you back in less than a month. Lo and behold, I got you back. I'm very pleased."

"I'm pleased for you, paşa. What's next?"

Vlad acts like he doesn't care, but he's trembling inside. Going back to Tokat as a prisoner is not something he looks forward to. The Tokat prisoners don't do well. He was one of them for a short while, and that was way too long. But on the other hand, getting executed before his fifteenth birthday doesn't feel good either.

The paşa pulled his lips downwards. "I don't know. It will be up to our enlightened sultan to decide your fate. I personally hope he'll send you back to me — there are so many things that you and I still have to experience together. But I won't hold my breath. I'm afraid that the sultan may decide he's shown you enough clemency. Either way, it's not up to me. You're going to Edirne, and the sultan will decide."

Vlad nods. "I understand. What happened to... to the kids I was traveling with?"

"The girl, you mean? And the deaf-mute? They are fine. Very well indeed. I have to give it to you, my prince: you have very fine taste. The deaf-mute? He's almost priceless. Healthy, good looking, and completely unable to utter or hear a single word. Slaves like that are even more expensive than pretty young eunuchs. You know why? Because deaf-mutes have the rare quality of lacking any empathy. They'll destroy anybody on the sultan's orders, since they can't even hear their cries for mercy. And, since they can neither hear nor talk, they'll never betray what the sultan said or did. What a fine gift! I bet our sultan will be delighted with that boy."

Vlad sighs. This is not news. Deaf-mutes are worth their weight in gold, since so very few survive the change. Cutting their tongue causes so much bleeding they often choke or bleed to death. As for piercing their eardrums, that causes deafness, but also, more often than not, a fever that goes to their brain and kills them. And if it doesn't, they're too damaged to be of any use.

The paşa smiles. His hungry eyes look for Vlad's pain.

Vlad smiles back. His pain is not for Sevlet Paşa's use. As much as he wishes to know, he doesn't dare ask.

But the paşa is good at his job. He's done it for years, so he knows exactly how to read someone's pain and grow it, just like one grows a fire by blowing gently into it. "The girl..."

Vlad's heart jumps. He wants to know, but he'd only give Şevlet Paşa more ammunition, so he acts like he doesn't care. "The girl?"

"She's pretty. In a soft-hearted sort of way. She's not the kind of beauty that would start a war, but there's something warm and welcoming about her."

Vlad knows it. Oh, doesn't he know it! He just can't tell this Ottoman twerp, or he'll try even harder to hurt him. So he shrugs and acts cool.

"I thought about letting her go. After all, she's not that pretty. She won't bring much money on the market."

Vlad's heart skips a beat. He doesn't know what Sophia would do, nor where she could go, but anything is better than being a slave, isn't it?

The paşa's eyes watch him carefully. For him, every breath, every twitch of his nostrils, every flick of his eyelids is a clue to Vlad's feelings. He's a student of human emotions, the paşa, and no matter how good Vlad is, he can't compare to the expert.

"Then I thought better," the paşa says. "She's not that ugly, you know? And it's been ages since I... spent any time with my wives, because I've been looking for you."

Vlad's blood drums in his ears so loud he can barely hear. He yearns to kill the paşa here and now. He can't imagine the things his ugly fat body would do to Sophia, nor does he want to. He just wishes he'd killed him when he escaped Tokat Castle. If he did, he wouldn't have to deal with the heart-wrenching sorrow that chokes him right now. His heart is breaking and there's nothing he can do but watch.

The paşa's dark eyes stare into his, reading the insides of his soul. He sees the hate, the anger, the impotence and the regret of not having killed him, and he laughs.

"But then I thought: There must be a better use for this pretty young girl, the sister of a deaf-mute and the love interest of a Prince of Wallachia than quenching the needs of an old paşa. So I decided against it."

He nods to the guards to bring over the kids.

Holding his sister's hand, the deaf-mute stares in the void. He doesn't understand what's happening, but Sophia does. Her tears run down her cheeks to her chin, then drip on her chemise, which is wet and almost see-through, showing her budding breasts.

"There she is. Isn't she a beauty?"

Vlad wishes he could murder the paşa. "I decided she can have better than me. And you. So I'll send you all to the sultan, may Allah bless his heart. He has no wives and no children, even though he's established himself as the ruler of the world. I think he'll appreciate my gifts, and Allah knows I need his clemency, since you got me into more trouble than I've ever been in. I hope that sending you all to him will let me keep my job, and who knows? Maybe the sultan will be so pleased he'll reward me. I still hope that you and I meet again someday. There's so much more I have to teach you."

The paşa leaves as the guards tie Vlad's hands behind his back.

Vlad smiles. *It will take them weeks to get to Edirne. And every week has seven days, and every day has so many hours. There'll be plenty of time to escape.*

CHAPTER 5
EDIRNE PALACE, DECEMBER 1444

It's a crisp winter morning up here in the wooded hills behind the castle. The air is fresh, and so clear you can see all the way to the mountains, miles and miles away.

After weeks of preparations, Sultan Murad is finally ready to return to Anatolia, and Sultan Mehmed can't wait to see him gone.

He's riding Rüzgar, his favorite stallion, and hunting the Edirne palace grounds with his friend Radu. Güzel, his beautiful hand-raised hawk, sits on his left gloved hand, ready to release, and Mehmed couldn't be happier. He'd be in heaven, but for his father. And he can't put Sultan Murad out of his mind.

Sure, Father is a great general. Mehmed is really grateful that he came back from Anatolia to help him out of the predicament he was in. But now that the Christians are crushed, the janissaries settled and everything else is back to normal, Mehmed feels encumbered by his father's presence. He can't wait for Sultan Murad to be gone, so he can be the sultan again and do whatever he wants without his father's sharp eyes judging him. Having his mother, Çandarlı Paşa and Akşemseddin watch his every move is bad enough.

"But what's the difference? After all, you already know that whatever you say or do gets reported to him anyhow," Radu says.

The ride tangled his honey-blond curls, and his flushed cheeks bring out the blue in his eyes, making him look prettier than ever.

Mehmed sighs. "Eventually. But not immediately. And I don't have to see the disapproval in his eyes. Like this morning, when I told the stable boys to get our horses ready. Father was there, checking on his horse, and he gave me a look. He said nothing, but his eyes said it all. I should stay at the palace and take care of business. Deal with the janissaries, meet the Venetian diplomats looking for a truce, and do all the other boring stuff sultans are supposed to do."

"But we haven't hunted in ages!"

"Father doesn't care. He doesn't think I should waste my time with something as pointless as taking out my hawk while there's any governmental business waiting. And there always is. There's no end to it, ever. And even if there was, he'd still want me to be reading the Quran or learn philosophy or some other stupid..."

The hawk on his glove feels his anger and flutters her wings in response. Mehmed does his best to soothe her. There's no use having an angry hawk. That's why they wear the tiny caps covering their eyes and ears, to keep them quiet and placid in their own black, silent world. "There, now, my beautiful. There now. It's OK. It's all good."

The hawk settles, and Mehmed forces himself to forget about Father and return to here and now. He looks for the dogs, but they're screaming somewhere down near the Tunca. They must have scented prey.

A big hare leaps out of the bushes to cross the open grass that the frost burned to cinnamon brown, the color of his fur. The only reason Mehmed gets to see him is that he's moving. As soon as he stops, he blends into the ground so well he disappears.

Not for the hawk. Güzel screams and takes off, flying high into the sky before letting herself fall like an arrow onto the hare.

The hare hears her just a heartbeat before the iron claws grab him. He tries to leap, but his speed is no match for the hawk's. She clutches him in mid-leap, digs her talons into his sides and flies away with him. Her strong wings flap hard as she struggles to soar, but the hare's old and heavy. Burdened by his weight, the hawk has to fly low.

The scream of the hare reaches them.

"Go, Güzel, go! Isn't she wonderful?"

Mehmed glances at Radu, but he's looking away. Mehmed knows Radu doesn't love hunting; he's only here to please him, but he can't resist. "Look at her! Look at her."

Radu turns his head and looks just as the hare contorts himself in mid-air like an acrobat and slams his back feet into the hawk's belly. The hawk gasps with surprise and lets him go. The hare twists through the air like a cat and breaks his fall in the branches of a plane-tree, then thuds to the ground and takes off.

Güzel screams indignantly. She circles the tree again and again, but the hare is gone.

Mad with frustration, Mehmed joins the hawk in screaming his ire. Rüzgar catches his mood and takes off at a gallop, jumping over the dead trees and narrowly avoiding the others. Mehmed tries to stop him at first, but the crazy speed soothes his rage, so he lets him run off his anger before returning to pick up the hawk.

He takes out a piece of fresh brain from his treat bag and calls Güzel. From high in the sky where she looks no bigger than a fly, the hawk drops to his glove. Her iron claws dig into it, and her sharp cruel eyes glance at him sideways as he offers her the treat. She settles to eat, and Mehmed speaks to her softly to soothe her as he covers her with her hood.

It's barely past noon when they ride back to the castle side by side, with the dogs surrounding them. But, for once, their feelings don't jive.

"I'm sorry, Mehmed," Radu says.

"Don't lie to me. You're not sorry. I saw you. You were rooting for the hare."

He knows he's harsher than he needs to be, but he's tired of everybody being against him. His father, the vizier, the janissaries, even the freaking hare. And now his best friend.

"I'm not lying. I'm not sorry that the hare escaped. I'm sorry you're upset."

"I thought you were my friend."

Radu raises his eyebrows but says nothing.

They ride back in silence. Mehmed knows he's wrong, but he's frustrated and angry, and he can't bring himself to apologize by the time they dismount at the stables.

He looks at Radu, wondering how to mend their fences, when two guards arrive.

"Sultan Murad wants you. Now."

Mehmed nods and follows, wondering if he's still the sultan.

CHAPTER 6

FATHER'S WISDOM

His heart in turmoil, Mehmed follows the guards along the empty marble corridors, wondering if going back to Manisa would be so bad. Truth be told, being the sultan isn't all it's cracked up to be. It's actually worse than being the şehzade. Sure, he had a lot of boring lessons, and Mother and his tutors kept harassing him about his studies, but nothing like now. Now, there's always somebody to tell him what he should do, and what he shouldn't. Starting with Father, of course, but then every single little dignitary in the palace needs him to read this, order that, or sign the other. That's why he needs to go hunting to have a little peace.

Then Mother sends women he has no use for to his bed; Çandarlı Paşa won't stop bitching about those darn janissaries; and Akşemseddin pushes him on his lessons. Mehmed misses the good old days when he could hunt and ride as he liked. He day-dreamed about conquering Constantinople someday, but didn't actually have to calculate how many camels he will need to carry supplies for the troops, figure out where to get enough money to satisfy the janissaries, make sure the pope is busy elsewhere, and figure out how to break Constantinople's five-layered Theodosian walls. All in all, he's quite fed up with being a sultan, he thinks, standing in his father's studio's door and waiting for permission to enter.

His father puts down the illuminated Quran he's reading and invites him in.

"How are you doing?"

Mehmed sits on the visitors' red brocade pillow and crosses his legs.

"I'm OK. You?"

"How did today's hunt go?"

"Not well. The hawk caught a hare, but he was old and heavy so she couldn't fly back up. Then he somehow kicked her, and she dropped him. He escaped."

Sultan Murad smiles. "So, what did you learn from this?"

Mehmed isn't so sure he learned anything. But that's not what Father wants to hear.

"That old hares are hard to hunt?"

"Excellent. That goes for people too. Old hares got old for a reason: They know tricks. And the older they get, the more tricks they learn. They may not be as fast as the young ones, but they're tough and cunning. The same goes for people. I know you don't think much of Çandarlı Paşa, but he's an old hare. You're still young."

"But I'm not a hare."

"Lucky you. The lesson still holds. What else did you learn?"

Mehmed racks his brain for something else he should have learned from today's hunt fiasco.

"That the hare was too heavy for the hawk?"

"Precisely. The lesson is that you shouldn't overreach. Some things are just out of your league. You need to get stronger before you tackle them if you want to be successful. Like Constantinople. I know you're obsessed with it, and I am, too. But it's too early. You're not ready and the empire isn't ready, but our enemies are. Do you think that the Karamanids in Anatolia and Hunyadi in Hungary and even Wallachia's Vlad Dracul, your friend Radu's father, will sit idle and wait to see how you fare? They won't. As soon as you focus all your resources on

Constantinople, they'll hit you in your unprotected underbelly. Just like the hare did to the hawk."

Mehmed nods. He doesn't like to hear that, but he gets it.

"Did you learn anything else?" Father asks.

Mehmed shakes his head. He's done with this nonsense. He's sweaty and tired, and can't wait for his bath and his massage to feel clean and fresh. Then to bed, hoping for tomorrow to be a better day. But he doesn't have that kind of luck.

"OK. I'll tell you a couple more things. One is that the world doesn't stop when you do. You took the day off to go hunting. Did anything happen while you were away that you should know about? That your people should interrupt your hunt for?"

"I don't know."

"Sure, you don't. Because you didn't tell them to let you know. Quite the contrary, in fact. Your people are afraid to disturb you, so they didn't. They came to me instead."

Mehmed waits. Whatever it is, it can't be good.

"Vlad escaped. Your friend's brother, who tried to kill you before, has escaped Tokat. Not today, of course, but weeks ago. Whatever time it took us to get the news. He killed some guards and a civilian, stole a horse and rode away."

Mehmed's blood is about to blow up the top of his head. He's so mad he'd like to crush Vlad into dust and sprinkle him in the wind to never hear about him again. That devil!

"What do you think?" Father asks.

Mehmed sighs. "You were right. We should have killed him then. I'm sorry about my mistake. I'll make sure he gets killed as soon as they catch him."

"Why?"

"Because he's a danger to the empire?"

"How is that true now more than before?"

Mehmed doesn't know, and he doesn't care. He's tired of all these riddles and lessons, and of the feeling that he does nothing right. "I don't know, Father. Why don't you tell me?"

"I sent them an order to spare him at all costs. He may be our key to Wallachia, and through them, to their brethren, the Moldavians and the Transylvanians. And Hunyadi."

"But we have his brother. Radu is…"

"He's your… friend. Nice kid. And maybe the balance to Vlad, when we need him. But Vlad is an unsheathed dagger. He'll destroy whoever he touches, if they aren't careful enough. Have you looked at that kid? He's a force of nature. He's anger and hate personified. We can use that against our enemies, as long as we figure out how."

"I see. What else?"

"I'm leaving for Anatolia tomorrow. That's why I needed to see you tonight. I'll take the Anatolian sipahis and janissaries, and I'll take care of them. You take care of the Rumelians. Remember that you must make them happy if you want them to serve you well. They need to feel blessed to be your soldiers, if you want them to die for you. Pay them on time, praise them, and show them love. It's inconvenient, I know. But that's how you get your men to be loyal."

Mehmed nods, wondering how long until he can have his bath. Murad laughs.

"I can see I made a great impression. Good luck, and remember: I'll let you be sultan and learn, as long as you don't endanger the empire. If you do, I'll be back. Reluctantly. I've done it long enough to know how much fun it is. Heading an empire is a job. A hard job. Call me if you need me."

Murad nods. Mehmed prostrates himself, wondering if it's the last time he sees his father. He's not sure how he feels about that.

CHAPTER 7

YOU LOOK LIKE A GIRL

The Edirne Palace school dormitories are not luxurious, not even for a prince. Especially when said prince happens to be a hostage. And now, in winter, when a wild wind whorls through the cracks under the door, it's bone-chilling cold too. Curled under his woolen blankets in his little cramped room, Radu is glad to have his cat to keep him company and keep him warm. Sari is always there for him, unlike certain sultans that shall not be named.

His deep friendship with Mehmed is not an easy one. Some days, the sultan is like the sun — exuberant, warm and happy, the best friend one could ask for. Then, like today, he's like a storm coming out of the blue.

Radu is always ready to admit he's wrong — after all, he's been nothing but wrong since the day he was born. He's been a disappointment to his father and his mother, and an embarrassment to his older brothers. And pretty much to everyone else but Mehmed, who's always been kind, patient and understanding towards him.

Not today, even though Radu did nothing to deserve Mehmed's wrath. Sure, he was glad to see the hare escape. So what? He did nothing to save him and he didn't make a fuss about it either, but the sultan saw fit to blow his disappointment on him, like the spoiled hunt was his fault.

Still, this wasn't as bad as that night in November when Mehmed had too much wine and touched Radu in ways that friends didn't touch each other. Radu blamed that on the wine, but ever since that, he's been uneasy around Mehmed. He's waiting for the other shoe to drop and wondering when whatever that was will surface again.

That night was the scariest Radu ever lived through. He was so terrified that he stabbed the sultan, an offense punishable by death. But Mehmed forgave him, and after he returned from Varna, they rekindled their friendship. Still, things will never be like they were. In their relationship, there's a "before" and an "after". And, no matter what, this is the after.

Radu sighs and turns to his other side, trying to fall asleep. Tomorrow is a big day: the beginning of the school exams. He'd better be rested and ready. But the sound of steps by his door startles him.

Someone knocks.

"Come in."

It's Ali, his eunuch friend, bringing him a tray of fruit and pastries from the kitchens. He's tiny, Ali, even smaller than Radu. With his narrow freckled face and his mop of curly chestnut hair, Ali looks like a doll. But his eyes, the color of the ocean, are old and wise and they can see into Radu's soul. Besides Mehmed and Sari, Ali is the one friend Radu has in Edirne, but sadly, they don't see each other often. Ali is always working, since he's assigned to Hüma Hatun, the validé. But he stops by whenever he can to bring Radu a snack and, more importantly, a word of encouragement. Ali somehow knows when Radu needs him.

"Thank you, Ali, but you shouldn't have bothered! I'm not hungry."

"Sure you are. You just didn't know it. And, if you're not hungry for food, at least you're hungry for company. And news."

They sit on the Persian carpet with the tray between them. Radu picks an apple, wipes it against his shalwars until it shines, then bites into it. The apple crunches, and the tart juices drip on Radu's chin. For lack of a towel, he wipes his mouth with his sleeve, glad that nobody can see this lack of decorum other than Ali, who doesn't care.

Ali picks up a yellow piece of hard cheese and bites off its corner, holding it delicately between his long fingers. Radu smiles.

"You look just like a girl," he says.

Ali pales. He puts the cheese down.

"Really?"

He's upset, though Radu doesn't know why. "I'm sorry, Ali. I didn't mean it in a bad way. Just that you're so delicate and tiny and graceful…"

Ali's face grows longer and longer, as if Radu told him he looks old and disgusting.

"There's nothing wrong with looking like a girl, Ali."

"If you are a girl. But I'm not. I'm a eunuch."

He says that like it makes him proud, and that boggles Radu's mind. He's been taught from childhood that a man's most precious treasures are his family jewels, but no matter. He needs to get himself out of this.

"Of course. That's probably what it is. I just never spent much time with eunuchs, other than you, and you are very pretty."

He hopes he didn't mess up again. But he doesn't know what else to say, so he changes the subject. "You said you have news?"

"Yes. But don't tell anyone that I told you. It's a secret, and the sultan may want to keep it that way."

"Of course."

"Your brother escaped."

"Mircea? But that's not a secret, Ali. Mehmed already told me. He escaped with his four thousand Wallachians almost intact, even though most of Hunyadi's army was destroyed. He's a good general, Mircea, even though he's only seventeen. My father must be very proud of him."

Ali shakes his head. "No. Not Mircea. Your other brother."

"You mean Vlad? Vlad escaped?"

"Shh! Yes. The news arrived early today. He killed a bunch of guards, then stole a horse and ran away. Nobody knows where. But, of course, that was weeks ago."

"Really? Vlad escaped Tokat?"

Radu has trouble wrapping his mind around this. Vlad, his lifelong nemesis, somehow managed to escape the Ottoman Empire's most famous prison. Nobody ever escaped Tokat; that's why Sultan Murad sent Vlad there when he tried to kill Mehmed. And now he's on the lam.

"He could show up here any day then," Radu thinks out loud.

Ali shrugs.

"Why would he? Don't you think he'll head north, to Wallachia? That's what I would do if I escaped. If he crosses the border, he's home free. Why would he come here and risk getting caught?"

"Why? To kill the sultan. And me."

CHAPTER 8
THE SIKMA

Radu didn't sleep that night. He tossed, turned, and ruminated awful thoughts. Will Vlad come to kill him? Is Mehmed tired of his friendship? Has he figured, like everyone else, that Radu isn't worth loving? And how has he offended Ali? He still can't understand the boy's strange pride in being a eunuch. How weird is that?

He's glad to see the sky fade from black to pretty shades of pink, even though he feels unprepared. Today is a very special day at the palace school: it's the first day of exams for the sikma, the palace school graduation.

Sikma only happens every few years, or after a new sultan's accession. That's when the best and brightest boys in the palace school get their career assignments.

Not Radu, of course. He studies with the others, but how he does on the exams won't make any difference. Whether he passes or fails, he'll go back to school and learn the same things: Greek language, geography, art, music, calligraphy, and so on. Unlike the others, Radu isn't working towards a career at the sultan's court. The Ottomans call him a guest, but he's really just a hostage to get slaughtered if his father strays from his loyalty to the sultan. He already had a close call in the fall, when Vlad Dracul allowed Mircea, Radu's oldest brother, to join Hunyadi and the pope's men in the last crusade. Boy, what a debacle that turned to be! Only Mehmed's friendship kept him alive. If it wasn't for him, Sultan Murad would have sent Radu's head to Vlad Dracul in a bag like the custom required. He's lucky to be alive.

That's why the sikma exams mean nothing to him, but for the hundreds of devşirme boys coming from the vassal countries, like Wallachia, Serbia and Albania, this is a make-or-break opportunity.

Only the best will get a shot at a career in government or in science. Some will become the Ottoman Empire's next dignitaries, since any office at the sultan's court is open to the worthy, up to the office of the grand vizier. Or they'll become engineers, architects, or doctors.

The less successful will go to live with an Ottoman family and work on a farm. They'll learn and get tough before returning in a couple years to train as janissaries and sipahis, the sultan's elite troops. Some day they'll join the standing army that made the Ottoman empire what it is today: spanning two continents, holding Constantinople in an iron grip and crushing the Christians' hope of ever reuniting their faiths under one pope. That's how the Ottomans built their empire: by skimming the best Christian kids and making them theirs.

But for now, they have these exams to go through, and they aren't easy. Today's subjects are math and administration. Nothing that Radu enjoys, though he must be able to count, add, and make sense of the boring business of numbers if he's ever to be voivode.

He sits with the other hundred kids that fill the festivities room, inhaling the examiner's words. The man is the sultan's tax accountant, but, by his pale skin and blue eyes, he must have been devşirme a few decades ago, Radu thinks.

"Selim has a hundred sheep. Three are barren, and the others lamb in spring. Seven of them produce three lambs each, and two-thirds of the rest produce two. The last third has one lamb each. If eleven lambs die at birth, a fifth of the others get taken by wolves, and Selim sells the rest at three coins each, then lends the money to his cousin for a year at ten percent yearly interest, how much money will Selim have after his cousin returns his loan and he buys another thirty-one sheep at six coins each?"

The room freezes. The kids have never heard something like this. They gasp, then start vociferating until the examiner thunders: "Silence. This is an individual exam. You have until this candle burns down. Check your work and make sure to give me the correct result."

The kids stare at each other and shrug. Radu grabs his quill, leans over his paper and starts calculating. He's doing good, but he loses track when he gets to the wolves. Darn it. He shrugs and starts over, glad that his life's fate doesn't depend on Selim's sheep.

He counts and adds, but loses track again. Dang! He glances around to see how the other kids are doing and recognizes the last one to his left. It's Ali's friend, the dark boy who won the Kırkpınar, and he's struggling. He's so bewildered that he doodles on his cheek as he scratches his ear with his quill.

The blond boy behind him laughs. He pokes him in the back and whispers something in his ear, then stands and takes his paper to the examiner.

The man glances at it and hands it back.

"That's not the right answer. Go back and do it again. You have plenty of time."

"It's correct."

The professor glances at it again.

"It's wrong. You missed calculating the interest."

The blond boy shakes his head.

"I didn't miss it. There can be no interest under Islamic law. If Selim is a good Muslim, he can't charge his cousin any interest. He can finesse it with a faith-based profit-sharing deal, like Ijarah or Murabaḥah, but he can't charge interest. The result is one hundred ninety-eight."

The professor stares at him. Radu does too. The boy is slight and not too tall, but the brightness in his face makes you smile.

"What is your name?"

"Here at the palace I'm Isa," the boy says.

"Where are you from?"

"Transylvania."

"How long have you been here?"

"Since last summer."

The tax man nods. "OK. Come see me tomorrow, after the second prayer. I have a job for you."

Isa nods, but he doesn't look happy. Nor does his friend.

When the exam is over, sheep and all, Radu heads on to speak to Ali's friends, hoping they can enlighten him. He still doesn't get why Ali got upset yesterday, but maybe they will.

"It's good to see you again…"

"I'm Kemal. This is my friend Isa," the dark boy says.

"Are those your real names? They don't sound Romanian," Radu asks.

The boys laugh.

"I'm Ion. And he's Codru, which means forest," the blond boy says. "But here, we must use the names they gave us."

"I know. I'm Radu, from Wallachia, and I'm a friend of Ali."

Isa's face lights up. "I haven't seen him in ages. How is he?" he asks.

"He's OK. He works for the validé, and she keeps him busy."

Isa nods. "I bet."

"That was something else what you did there, Isa. I got lost after the first set of sheep."

Isa laughs. "That part was easy. The tricky part was the interest."

"Easy for you, maybe. How did you do it?"

Isa shrugs. "I don't know. Numbers speak to me. I just look at them, and I know."

"I sure wish I could say the same," Radu says.

"Me too," Kemal adds.

Isa shrugs.

"We all have our talents. Mine is numbers. Yours is fighting. I've never met a boy who could fight like you, Kemal. And yours…" Isa turns to Radu. "What's your talent?"

"I have no talent."

"Of course you do. You just didn't find it yet."

Radu smiles, but he knows better.

"Ask Ali," Kemal said. "He'll tell you."

"How so?" Radu asks.

"Ali's talent is to read people's minds and see inside their souls."

"I know. He can also tell the future."

The boys nod.

"Speaking about Ali. I said something that upset him yesterday, and I don't know why."

"What did you say?" Kemal asks.

"I told him he looks like a girl."

The boys stare at each other like they've seen a ghost. Isa clears his voice.

"In Transylvania, where we come from, that's an insult for a man. Like, if you look girly, you're not manly enough. I wouldn't mention that again if I were you."

"But I thought, since he's a eunuch..."

Isa shrugs. "You think too much. You and I, we can't really understand how it feels to be Ali."

"You're right. I didn't think about that. Thank you. Congratulations on your new job."

Isa sighs. "Thanks. I just hope they won't separate me from my friends. I barely ever see Ali. Now Kemal too? It gets lonely."

Radu nods. He understands lonely.

"Let me see what I can do."

CHAPTER 9
THE SULTAN'S WOMEN

It's dreary cold and gray outside, but here in the hammam the air is moist and warm and smells of roses, and the sound of water dripping from the marble ceiling into the cooling pool is more soothing than music.

Lena lies on the warm marble slab, her flesh a soft puddle, and sighs with delight. Hard to believe that she used to hate the strong hands of the slaves scrubbing her, kneading her muscles and shaving her hairs with sharpened clams. But that was long ago. Now, she finds pleasure in the bath, especially in winter. No matter how many red-hot brasiers they keep going, there's still a cold draft from the screen-covered windows.

The women flip her and drip warmed olive oil on her back. Lena sighs once more, feeling her shoulders relax under the skilled masseur's fingers, and inhaling the jasmine scent. It's not the pine scent of the forest at home, but it's not bad. In the years since she's been away from Moldova, she got used to living in luxury, but she hasn't forgotten that this isn't home.

The water gurgles in the cooling pool as someone sinks into the scented water. Lena ignores it until she hears the voice.

"Have you bled this month?"

She sighs, wishing she could disappear. The voice belongs to Sultan Mehmed's mother, the validé. She's the one who sent Lena to Mehmed's bed, hoping for an heir. That was months ago, but there's still no heir. And there won't be, since Lena and Mehmed are just roommates, and she's still a virgin.

Truth be told, Lena might get persuaded, since the sultan is young and handsome and the only man in many miles. But Mehmed, even though he said he likes her, never made a pass. They sleep in the same bed, which is big enough for a small army, then the guards take Lena to her room in the morning. That's an excellent arrangement for everyone but Hüma, who's desperate for a grandson.

"Yes, my lady."

There's no point lying. The servants who watch her will tell Hüma everything she wants to know.

"How come?"

Lena shrugs, praying for something to fall out of the sky and stop the interrogation, but nothing does.

"He's only been back for a few months, my lady, after the Varna crusade. Not even half a year."

"Have you two..."

No. Of course not. That's the whole point, isn't it? The sultan only takes her to his bed because she leaves him alone. He's too busy with the empire's business to deal with some power grabber who'd do anything to be the next sultan's mother. That's why Mehmed keeps her around. He even promised to set her free if she keeps his cover. Another year, and he'll let her go back home to her sheep and her cat Mitzi. But the validé doesn't know this. So Lena lies.

"Of course, my lady. I learned everything from your pleasure courses. I learned how to pleasure him with my hands, my mouth, and everything else, especially my baby funnel. We have been ..."

"Hello, girls."

The curvy body of Mara Branković, Sultan Murad's fourth wife, drops on the marble slab next to Lena, and her throaty voice makes her smile. She's a wonder to behold, Mara. She's been married to Sultan Murad for years, but she's never borne him a child. Still, she's still here in the sarayi, enjoying everyone's love and respect. That's because she's a Serbian princess and came with a valuable alliance, Lena thinks. Then she remembers that Sultan Murad blinded and jailed Mara's brother when he found out he was plotting against the empire. Some even say that Mara's father, Serbia's despot, hangs from a thread, ready to be replaced.

"Hi, Mara," Hüma says. Unlike Lena, she's not happy that Mara interrupted their talk, but she does her best to be polite. Mara has that effect on people. She makes them laugh, and they become her friends before they even notice.

"Am I interrupting anything?"

She's got a heavy accent, Mara, since she was quite old — almost fifteen — when she came to the Ottoman Empire. That was years ago, but she hasn't lost her accent, her smile, or her charm.

"No," Hüma says. "We were just chatting."

"Great. How are you doing, Lena?"

Lena smiles, relieved to have escaped the validé's pointed questions, but wary about Mara's.

"Great. How are you?"

"Phenomenal. Isn't it great to have our husband gone?" she asks Hüma.

Lena chokes.

"Is that how you feel?" Hüma asks.

"Are you kidding? It's like a weight fell off my shoulders. Don't you feel the same way?"

"You don't want him in your bed?"

"God no. What are you talking about? Why should I?" Mara asks.

Hüma looks forlorn. That's not a question she ever asked herself.

"To make you a son?"

Mara laughs, and her low, throaty laugh makes Lena's insides twinkle.

"I need a son like a need a hole in my head. I'm perfectly happy with yours, if you'll allow me a little piece of him. I can enjoy watching him grow and succeed without going through all the gruesome motions, from... you know what, to having a baby. And then spend years bringing him up and hoping he'll live. No thanks. Not my thing. But I'm happy to watch our Mehmed grow into the great sultan he's meant to be."

Hüma smiles like she hears music.

Lena wonders how Mara always knows the right thing to say. Just a few words, and she won Hüma over. She wishes she had that skill. It would come in handy.

CHAPTER 10

TÂRGOVIȘTE, SPRING 1445

The winter's almost over in Wallachia. Much of the snow has melted, leaving behind patches of dark earth waiting for the plows to split it open and fill it with the seeds of the new harvest. There's no trace of green yet, but the warm wind smells like spring and hope.

The men who made it back from Varna have recovered from the ugliness of war. They warmed their wives though the long winter nights, and a bumper crop of children should come in the fall, right after the harvest, God willing, to replace the fallen and rejuvenate the country.

Standing on top of Târgoviște's watch tower with Mircea, Ștefan feels the spring deep in his bones. He breathes in the hope in the air and can't refrain from smiling, even though the three muddy riders at the gate are nothing to smile about. Their proud horses and rich garb speak about noble messengers with important news.

Good, Ștefan thinks. It was high time. The four months they've had to recover from the terrible battle of Varna followed by the awful retreat have been three too many. He's itching for another war to cover himself in glory. And that war should be coming, since the western

Christians, who ignored the Poles' and the Hungarians' calls for help like the Ottoman Empire was none of their business, are coming around. Or so they say.

The riders leave the horses with the stable boys and head inside. Their heavy boots are splattered with mud, and so are their skin-tight breeches that leave little to the imagination. But their velvet cloaks, their gold-embroidered doublets and their fox-trimmed mushrooming hats show them to be rich and foreign.

"Who are they?" Ștefan asks.

"Have you ever heard about Wallerand de Wavrin?"

"No."

"He's Flemish, but he's the Duke of Burgundy's captain general. He brought his seven galleys to the Black Sea to take part in the crusade, but he got there late. By the time he made it, we'd already been defeated. So he started looking for King Władysław of Poland. There were some rumors that he managed to escape after the Battle of Varna and he's hiding somewhere along the Danube, looking for a way to get home."

Ștefan laughs. "That's poppycock! King Władysław is deader than a doornail. You know it as well as I do. You saw his head impaled on his own lance."

"Of course. And I heard that Sultan Murad had it preserved in a casket of honey and sent it to Bursa as proof of his victory. They washed it and paraded it for all the Ottomans to see and rejoice."

"So then…"

"Then what?"

"He won't find him."

"Of course not. But he found us. Let's go see. Father said give them a few minutes, then pop in."

Pop in they do. They sit at the end of the table, watching and listening without interrupting, but there isn't much to hinder. The words are few and the silences long, and it's easy to see that the court of Târgoviște's great room is not what these elegant Burgunds are used to.

The one who looks like their boss talks with Vlad Dracul, but he can't help but steal furtive glances at the trophies on the walls staring him down like he's prey. Mircea and Ștefan don't seem to be much to his liking, either. He glances down his long nose from one to the other as if he expects them to do something rude.

Ștefan wishes he'd brushed his hair and donned a clean shirt after looking after Lena, his mare. She's beautiful and spunky and the apple of his eye, but she still smells like a horse. Oh well. He stares back until the man averts his eyes, then studies him and struggles not to laugh.

The Burgund's pink velvet doublet with slashed sleeves that bloom like cabbages makes his head look small, and the peacock feather in his cap swings in the opposite direction of his pointy nose every time he turns his head from one Wallachian to another.

"Welcome, boys," Vlad Dracul says. "This here is Sir Pierre Vast. He's coming from Buda, where he met our old friend John Hunyadi and his retinue. They advised him to stop by the court of Târgoviște and talk to us about trimming the fat from the Ottoman's holdings along the Danube."

Mircea acts like he doesn't much care, but Ștefan wants to jump out of his skin. He opens his mouth to say something, but his uncle's warning glance freezes him in place. He leans back and tries to look bored.

"Sir Vast comes on behalf of Burgundy's captain general, Sir Wallerand de Wavrin. He and his seven galleys have been looking for the King of Poland all around the Black Sea. He plans to continue searching up the Danube, and he asked us to join them. They'll sail from the Black Sea and plan to meet Hunyadi and his army at Nikopolis in mid-August. From there, they'd start a joint effort to curb the Ottomans. I told him he might talk you into it," Vlad tells Mircea.

"Interesting," Mircea says, pretending he doesn't care. "What would they want us to do?"

"Join them on the ground with our men and bring supplies and local knowledge."

Mircea turns to Ștefan. "What do you think?"

Ștefan chokes under the weight of the question.

"What will they contribute?" he asks.

Mircea's eyes shine with glee. "Good question. Sir Vast?"

Sir Vast stares at Ștefan, who, at fourteen, isn't much to look at. "And this is who?"

Vlad Dracul glances at the kids, and the smile in his eyes doesn't reach his mouth.

"This young man is my nephew, Ștefan Mușat, the grandson of Alexandru the Good. God willing, he'll be Moldova's voivode someday. The greatest voivode Moldova has ever seen."

Sir Vast sighs. "You'll benefit from our knowledge and our war experience. And the pope's guidance, prayers, and blessings. The pope is very invested in this effort."

"Really? Is this the same pope who failed to get us supplies for the Varna crusade?" Mircea asks.

Sir Vast bristles. His narrow eyes measure Mircea, and his thin mouth puckers.

"And, pray tell, who are you to ask such an impudent question?" Vlad Dracul smiles.

"This is Mircea Basarab, my son and heir. He led the Wallachian troops in the Battle of Varna, when your Cardinal Cesarini and your bishops got themselves slaughtered. Mircea tried hard to save their necks, but they were just too stupid to live."

CHAPTER II

BROTHERLY LOVE

Edirne Castle is ablaze with the news. Vlad Dracula, Radu's older brother, is on his way to Edirne. He's the one who tried to kill Sultan Mehmed last year, and then managed to escape from Tokat, the empire's safest prison.

"I can't wait to see him. They say he's a vampire, and he can turn into a bat and fly away whenever he wants," one of the palace school students says to another.

"Nah, that's bull. Had he been a vampire, they couldn't have caught him. But he has dark magic. He's born in Transylvania, and up there, they all do."

"How about Radu then? He was born there, too."

"And you're saying Radu has no magic? Are you kidding? How else did he wrap Sultan Mehmed around his little finger, then?"

"Like really? Did you look at that kid? You don't need no freaking magic when you look like that."

Radu can't take it anymore. He bursts out of the music room to confront them, but they scatter like a flock of sparrows when they see him.

Radu's feet are heavy as lead and his heart even heavier as he heads

45

to the throne room where he was summoned. He's not looking forward to seeing Vlad. As a matter of fact, there's nobody he wants to see less. He has no good memories of the times they spent together. But the crowds can't wait to see him, and they gathered in droves to be there when the caravan arrives.

The throne room is packed. Dignitaries, paşas, aghas — they all gathered to see what happens to Vlad and gauge the direction of Sultan Mehmed's reign. Old Sultan Murad, who led the empire with a steady hand for over two decades, left for Manisa, leaving Sultan Mehmed, young and untested, to rule in his stead, and nobody knows what to expect.

Radu drops on the brocade pillow the guards point him to. He's right by the sultan's podium, alongside the highest dignitaries, and has a full view of the proceedings. He glances at Mehmed, who sits cross-legged on his golden throne big enough for five sultans. The sultan holds the bejeweled hilt of his curved kilij and looks commanding in his mink-trimmed green kaftan, but he doesn't meet Radu's eyes.

Mehmed makes a sign, and the guards bring in a pair of kids. The girl is lovely, in a gentle sort of way. She's blonde and blue eyed and looks oddly familiar. The young boy by her side gawks around with eyes so wide the white shows all around them. He doesn't understand what's happening, so the girl holds him close to soothe him.

The guard bringing them bows.

"They are a gift from Sevlet Paşa, should you choose to accept them, my sultan. The boy is deaf-mute and healthy. His sister is a virgin."

Mehmed looks at the boy, then measures his sister, and his eyebrows go up. He glances at Radu, then turns to the girl and he smiles.

"What a thoughtful gift. I'm happy to accept them. Please give Sevlet Paşa my thanks."

Mehmed nods, and the guards take the kids and bring Vlad.

But this is not the Vlad Radu remembers. The months he's been in jail have changed him. He's older, thinner, and even angrier, if that's possible. His dark eyebrows knit together over his poison-green eyes, his mouth has all but disappeared under a thick black mustache, and the fists tied behind his back are so tight the knuckles turned white.

The guards push him down. Vlad tries to resist, but the men are too strong. He grunts and drops to his knees, then whips his head around as if he's looking for something. *Not me,* Radu hopes, but his hope dies the moment their eyes meet. As always, Vlad radiates hate, and Radu's heart twinges. Vlad hasn't changed much, he thinks. He's still lightning looking to strike.

The guard turns to Mehmed.

"This is Vlad Dracula, Prince of Wallachia. In his escape from the Tokat Castle, he killed three people and a valuable horse. Still, Sevlet Paşa feels he is a precious hostage, and redeemable. He begs you to send him back to Tokat for reeducation. The paşa says he's never had a better student."

Mehmed smiles, but it's not a pretty smile. It's the evil grin of a starving cat finding a fat mouse on crutches. He turns to Radu.

"What do you think I should do with him, Radu? Do you think your brother will ever change?"

Caught by surprise, Radu shakes his head.

"I don't. My brother is who he is. But he is a prince of Wallachia and a valuable hostage. I think you should spare his life."

Vlad glares at Radu, his eyes daggers. There's neither love nor gratitude in Vlad's heart. He wants Radu dead. Not now, but yesterday. Still, he's Radu's brother, and he can't do anything but try to save his life.

Mehmed nods.

"That's just what I expected from you. You are such a loving soul, my friend. You want to save his life even though he tried to have you killed not long ago. You're too generous."

He turns to Vlad.

"Your brother is a forgiving soul, unlike me. I'd love to crush you and kill you right now. Allah knows you deserve it. I'd love to see the color of your blood and send your head back to your father. But I won't. You know why? Because my father, Sultan Murad, advised me to spare your life. So I'll do that, despite my own urges."

His eyes and Vlad's cross like swords.

"I'll let you live. You'll go back to prison, of course. Not Tokat. You liked that too much. You'll have your own special cell in the fortress of Eğrigöz. That should give you time to think. Maybe you'll finally get to understand how lucky are the Ottoman Empire's friends, and how unfortunate their enemies. And maybe you'll plan your future accordingly.

"I hope you'll remember my mercy and Radu's kindness, should you ever find yourself in a position to reciprocate. But I won't hold my breath. I know kindness isn't your thing. Still, I'll be very kind to your friends. The deaf-mute will have the best life somebody like him can hope for. As for the girl, I'll be even kinder to her. I like her a lot. Did you notice how much she resembles your brother?"

CHAPTER 12
TOGETHER, AGAIN

Edirne Palace isn't much into privacy. Meeting someone without being seen or speaking to someone without being heard is about as easy as squeezing water from a stone. That's why the Transylvanians haven't met in forever, other than furtive encounters in some dark doorway to exchange a few words, and never all three. But today Radu let them use his room while he went to the hammam.

They came one by one, Ali from the validé's apartment, Isa and Kemal from their separate quarters at the palace school. The boys live apart since Isa left the janissary barracks to train as an Ottoman administrator.

Kemal is last. He closes the door, picks Ali and twirls her around. He gives her a sloppy kiss on the cheek and hands her to Isa, who does the same. Embarrassed by this rare show of affection, Ali blushes. She doesn't know whether to laugh or to cry, so she does both.

"Good to see you, boys."

"Same here. You've grown so much, and you got even more beautiful. Radu was right," Isa says.

"Radu is just a silly kid, but that was scary. I have to be more careful."

"And do what? Start farting and grow zits like the boys?"

"Not a bad idea. I wonder if any of my herbs could help with that."

"Speaking about herbs, I'm running out of my potion. I only have enough left for a month," Kemal says.

Ali sighs. "I'll make more as soon as I get some blue wolfsbane. I've looked for it everywhere, but couldn't find any. It thrives on rocky mountain soil, like we have at home, and this isn't it. But I'll try to find something to replace it. How are you otherwise?"

"Bored. Nothing happening but the same old. Except for this smart one here." He elbows Isa. "He managed to get promoted and left me wither in the barracks."

"That's great news, though. He can now gather information about the Ottoman Empire's finances, troops and records that we couldn't get before."

"And what good is it if we can't send it back?"

"We will soon. They needed time to lick their wounds after the Varna debacle. But now that it's spring, we should hear from them any day."

"I hope you're right, Ali, but I'm afraid we're wasting our time. We talked about killing both sultans, but Murad left before we could come up with a plan. And killing Mehmed will only bring Murad back. We need to get them both," Kemal says.

"You're right. But I think we could find some help with Murad," Ali says.

"How so?"

"Hüma Hatun is livid that Murad ignored her while he was here. Even worse, he took Halime Hatice when he left, and that drove her mad. She's worried he'll get her with child and threaten Mehmed's throne."

"Wow! Now, that's a plan. Let's have them kill each other and stay out of it," Kemal says.

"I can't. Hüma wants me to brew a death potion for her to send over and have someone feed it to the sultan. Unless she changes her mind."

"Better make that potion before she does then," Isa says.

"She also wants to kill Radu."

"Radu? Why?" Kemal asks.

"Hüma thinks Radu is the reason Mehmed isn't interested in girls. She wants him to straighten and produce an heir to ensure his succession. That's why she wants Radu out of the way."

"So what will you do?" Isa asks.

"I don't know. I delayed her as much as I could. I even thought about killing her, but I don't know if that's a good idea. I know Hüma. I know what to expect from her and how to play her. But with her gone, who knows what happens next?"

"You'll figure something out. You always do," Isa says.

Kemal nods.

"I agree. I have news too. The janissaries aren't happy. They've been expecting a raise since last summer when Mehmed took the throne, and they're still waiting. Apparently Çandarlı Paşa told them he's reminded Mehmed over and over, but he did nothing."

"Why?" Ali asks.

"The empire is strapped for cash. Between the old wars, Mehmed's lavish coronation ceremony and the cost of the Battle of Varna, they're having trouble covering the regular expenses. There's no extra money for the janissaries," Isa says.

"That would be worth sending back, if we could figure out how," Kemal says.

"I have an idea," Ali says, just as Radu, flushed, clean and smelling like roses, knocks at the door and steps in.

The boys thank him and make themselves scarce, but Ali stays behind.

"I'm sorry to interrupt, but I had to come back."

"You were most generous. Thanks to you, we spent more time together than we did since we left Transylvania."

"Any time. Well, not any time, but often. Maybe next week?"

"Great."

Ali gets ready to leave when a thought crosses her mind.

"My prince, are there any smells that you can't stand? Something that turns your stomach?"

"Chamomile. I hated chamomile tea ever since I was a baby. My mother used to force it into me whenever I got sick. Just thinking about it turns my stomach. Fortunately, they don't use it much here."

"What would you do if somebody gave you a drink of chamomile?"

Radu shudders.

"I'd drink it, I guess, if there was no other way."

"Don't. Listen to me: Don't. If you smell anything that makes you think of chamomile, drop it on the ground and spill it. Don't drink it, no matter what."

Radu stares at her.

"If you say so…"

"I do. Even if it's the sultan himself who gives it to you, pretend you're clumsy and drop it. Spill every single drop of it, then pretend to get sick."

"Is there something I should know, Ali?"

"Some at the court are not your friends, and they may try to harm you. That's why you need to avoid anything with chamomile."

"I didn't think chamomile was that bad."

"It's worse. Don't touch it."

Straight from Radu's room, Ali heads to her little kitchen. She puts together the most disgusting herbs she can find and adds enough chamomile to sink a ship.

CHAPTER 13
THE NEW GIRL

Sitting on a gold-embroidered brocade pillow in her luxurious quarters, the validé inspects the new girl. She's pretty, with soft blonde curls, downcast eyes and flushed cheeks.

It's got to be the scrubbing she got in the hammam before being presented to the validé. Unless she's just shy and unaccustomed to parading herself naked, Ali thinks, wondering where she's seen her before.

"Turn around."

The validé examines her perky breasts and her gently rounded hips. "Open your mouth."

The validé checks her teeth like she's looking to buy her. Which, of course, is not the case. As a gift from Sevlet Paşa to Sultan Mehmed, the girl already belongs to the harem. No matter who she was before, now she's a slave in Sultan Mehmed's sarayi, and that's what she'll be until she dies. A tear runs down the girl's cheek, and Ali feels sorry for her.

"What's your name?" Hüma asks.

"Sophia."

"Are you Greek?"

"Albanian."

"How old are you?"

"Fourteen, my lady."

"Have you bled yet?"

The girl's face catches fire.

"Twice, my lady."

Hüma turns to Ali. "What do you think?"

Ali thinks it's none of her business to stare at this poor naked girl, but she's not been around Hüma for all this time without learning to keep her mouth shut.

"I think she's a very promising young lady. She'll be a splendid addition to Sultan Mehmed's sarayi."

"You think he'll like her?"

"I know he will."

Ali was in the throne room, hiding behind one of the monster Chinese vases, when they brought the girl. She saw the way Mehmed stared at her, and no wonder. This girl could be Radu's twin. She may not be as dazzling as Lena, but she's warm and delightful.

Hüma agrees.

"She's nice and soft. Rather like chicken soup. She's not exciting and flashy like some others, but she's the kind of girl a man would return to again and again."

Ali nods, wondering how well the girl understands the Ottoman language. But, sooner or later, she'll have to come to terms with her fate. Here, in the Ottoman Empire, a woman's job is to make children. If this girl gives Mehmed a son, she'll live a comfortable life. She might even be the next validé. If she's barren, and he gets bored with her, she'll become a seamstress, a bath attendant, or she'll train the new girls in the Ottoman language, customs and etiquette, hoping that someday one of her students will become validé.

Hüma nods. She decided.

"From now on, your name will be Gülbahar. That means Spring Rose. They are graceful and soft like you. Your old name, Sophia, is not a good name for a woman. That means wisdom, and, here, in Allah's country, women aren't supposed to be wise. They are supposed to be faithful, loving, and a comfort to their men. That's every woman's second task. Their first task, of course, is to give them sons. I hope you'll work hard and find your way to greatness. I'll help and guide you whenever you need it. You will learn the Ottoman language and customs, and you will learn the Quran, the Holy Book of Islam. As soon as you become proficient, Allah will give you support and guidance. You understand?"

Gülbahar nods, looking at the ground.

"Look at me," Hüma says.

Gülbahar does, through her tears.

"I will be here to help you. Whenever you have a question, a problem, or a need that does not conflict with your goal in life, which is to give the sultan a son, I will help you. Come and ask me anything, anytime."

"Now?"

Hüma is surprised. It's like she didn't think the girl could talk. But she nods.

"What will happen to my brother? He's only eight. He can't hear and can't speak, and he's frightened and alone. I need to take care of him."

"I'll take care of that. Your brother will stay with you until he's ready to be on his own. He'll learn the same things you'll learn. You'll have your own room in the sarayi, and he'll stay with you and learn from you. The better you teach him, the better off he'll be."

Gülbahar falls to her knees.

"Thank you, my lady. I will do anything I can for you to be happy with me. Thank you for your kindness."

Hüma nods, but her eyes are unusually bright, and Ali wonders if she's tearing a little. The eunuchs take Gülbahar away.

"What do you think?" Hüma asks.

"You chose wisely. She'll be the mother of a sultan."

"Really?"

"Without doubt. She is the one."

Hüma looks happier than she's been in ages, so Ali knows it's time.

"I have something for you, my lady," Ali says, handing her a closed bottle of bright green, evil-looking liquid.

Hüma picks it up and stares at it in the light.

"Is this what I think it is?"

"Yes, my lady. The potion you requested is ready."

"Is it going to kill him overnight?"

"Yes. If he drinks all of it."

"What if he doesn't?"

"It depends how much he drinks. If he just has a few sips, it will make him sick, but it won't kill him."

"Thank you, Ali. I'll see what I can do. You have been very helpful to me."

"Thank you, my lady. I live to please."

Ali leaves, wondering what's next. There's never a dull moment with Hüma.

CHAPTER 14
AN ARDUOUS JOURNEY

Vlad couldn't think any happy thoughts throughout the long, painful trip to Eğrigöz. He had two whole weeks to do nothing but think about what he's done, what he should have done, and what he can do now.

That last part is easy. The answer is absolutely nothing.

After his last failed attempt to escape when he almost killed two guards on the way to Edirne, the Ottomans took no chances. He travels in a cart with his hands tied behind his back, and they don't even release him to pee. That's why he's always dirty, smelly, and sore. That fills him with hate against Mehmed's men, and he'd love to kill them all. But killing, right now, is not on the agenda. Staying alive is hard enough.

Sometimes it's hard to remember why. The Orthodox priests at home taught him that the dead go to heaven, where there's nothing but joy and light. They said he'll rejoice in God's love and kindness.

Vlad was skeptical. He wasn't into any of those things, but right now, they sound pretty good. There's been no love and no joy in the many days of traveling tied down in the filthy cart.

The trip to Tokat wasn't that long ago, but it feels like a lifetime. Then, he had a horse to could ride as he pleased — between the guards, of course. Now, he lays in the cart in his own filth. His hands are bound, and he can't even lower his pants to pee. If they were looking to humiliate him, they did a fine job.

For many days now, he's laid on his back, watching the clouds sail across the blue spring sky. He moves a little when his hands get too numb and he can't feel them anymore. But what he mostly does is think.

He thinks about his father, Vlad Dracul, who sent him to the sultan as a token of good faith, and then defaulted. But he's not angry. His father did what he had to. Sacrificing yourself and others to accomplish your goal is fine with Vlad; he gets that.

He thinks about Mircea, his father's firstborn son and heir. Vlad wishes it was him instead, but he respects his brother's struggle. He's a good man and a good soldier, even though they lost the Battle of Varna. Nobody told him, of course, but it wasn't hard to figure out. Sultan Mehmed keeps the throne warm while Sultan Murad chills in Manisa. The Ottomans won, and the crusaders lost. That much is clear.

Vlad hopes his brother is alive, but what if he's not? If Mircea died, Vlad is now the heir to the Throne of Wallachia. Unless the sultans got rid of his father and established a new ruler, like they did many times before.

Then he remembers his brother Radu, and his mind clouds with anger. Radu, clean and dressed in silk, looking pretty and well fed. Radu, showing him pity. That's the most insulting thing. The little deviant acted generous, but Vlad knows he was just toying with him. He must have planned it with Mehmed. Radu played his part just like Mehmed had taught him.

Vlad's hate for Mehmed has no end. More so now that Mehmed has Sophia and her brother, and they are his to use whichever way he chooses to. Just thinking about how Mehmed will use Sophia makes Vlad sick to his stomach. That's the one thing he can't let himself think about. He knew damn well that caring for anyone was a mistake. It exposes you, open and vulnerable, to others hurting you. Vlad won't do that. Never again.

Vlad pushes Sophia and her brother out of his mind and focuses instead on what he'll do when he goes back to Wallachia as voivode. Someday soon, he's sure. Everything he's been through can't be just a waste. God wants him to obliterate the Ottomans. He knows that.

He dreams about planting an endless row of high stakes on each side of the road from the Târgoviște to the Danube, and loading them with Ottoman bodies. Murders of fat, cackling crows will feed on the rotting corpses swarming with maggots. He can almost smell the stench, and it feels good. To Vlad, the smell of blood is like the scent of flowers is to others, and thinking of decay warms his heart.

The cart stops. Vlad lifts his head to stare at the emptiness around. They arrived at the mighty fortress of Eğrigöz, which is nothing but a pile of stones perched on top of a mountain.

The guards drag him and set him on his feet, but he's too weak to stand, so he crumbles to the ground. He, Vlad, the Prince of Wallachia. His legs are shriveled, his pants soaked with piss, and his numb hands tied behind his back.

He struggles up to his knees and looks up. A turban covers the sun.

"Welcome to Eğrigöz. We're delighted to have you. Sultan Mehmed honored us by trusting us with a valuable prisoner like you."

Vlad looks the man up and down, wondering how he can ply him with his wishes. After all, he'd built a good life in Tokat before he escaped.

"Just a word of caution. This isn't Tokat. I've heard you did a great job there, and made yourself almost indispensable. But we're nothing like that. We're only a few - my guards and me - and you are our only reason to be here. We'll do our best to keep you alive, but we'll keep you here no matter what. There'll be no torture sessions, no wine, and no lonely paşa looking for someone to bare their soul to. You'd better get used to being on your own."

He nods and leaves.

The guards take Vlad to a cell inside the mountain that's nothing but stone walls, four feet by four, with a thin layer of straw on the ground and a pitcher of water.

If Vlad thought Tokat was bad, he knows he's about to learn otherwise.

CHAPTER 15

CHAMOMILE

Half a mile down from Edirne Castle, shaded by the old plane trees that lean low over it, the Tunca flows like a thick mass of melted silver, hugging a tiny green island Sultan Murad loves. The sun setting behind the western mountains painted the sky blood-red, forecasting another glorious day, and Sultan Mehmed is in high spirits.

Today's hunt was a success. Thanks to Güzel and the dogs, he's taken a hare and two pheasants, and he couldn't be happier. And he got to spend the day with Radu without worrying about what Father would say. Thanks to Allah, the Most Merciful, Sultan Murad went back to Anatolia, so Mehmed is the sultan again. He can lay down the law and ignore his mother's harassment, Çandarlı Paşa's whining and the janissaries' incessant grumbles.

"I'm thinking we should go for a long hunt. Just you and me with the hawks and a few guards. We could be away for weeks, and I wouldn't have to worry about the darn Venetians and their truce treaty. They want verified and signed, but, believe it or not, they want it ratified by Father, too. In case I change my mind, I guess. Or if he returns to take back his throne. They act like we've broken the truce, not them and their slimy pope, who doesn't shy away from releasing

61

them from fulfilling their sworn oath. Anyhow. You'd get to skip school and the other boring stuff, and we could be together, riding our horses, rambling through the forest, and enjoying the last of the spring while the woods are still green and alive, before the summer's heat scorches the earth."

"That would be lovely," Radu says.

"Great. I told Mother already. I'll tell Çandarlı Paşa tomorrow, and we'll leave on Saturday."

"What did the validé say?"

Mehmed shrugs. His mother hates Radu more than she hates anyone else in the palace, even though he's his best friend. Or maybe just because of that. She wants nobody else but her to be close to Mehmed. But Radu doesn't need to know that.

"Who cares? It's none of her business. Her job is to take care of the women in the sarayi, not the business of the country."

"But she wasn't happy?"

"She kept on and on about my leaving the reins of the empire in the grand vizier's hands; she thinks he's a weasel who can't wait for Father to return and send me back to Manisa. She even said he's been riling the janissaries against me, but that's silly. There's nobody more faithful than our janissaries. They always supported the sultan to their last breath. They'd never rise against me."

"How about we postpone the hunt until you've dealt with the Venetians, and…"

"No! You too? I thought you were my friend. What's the point of being sultan if you can't ever do what you want? We're leaving on Saturday."

Back at the stables, Mehmed dismounts and hands the reins to a stable hand. He rubs Rüzgar's nose and hugs him to thank him for a great ride, like he always does. His eyes bright, his ears pricked, Rüzgar snorts and rubs against him.

Radu takes an apple from his pocket and offers it to Snow, his beautiful white mare. Her huge eyes narrow with pleasure as she crunches the apple between her yellow teeth. Radu gives another apple to Rüzgar, who makes short work of it.

A kitchen servant brings a tray with cold drinks in tall filigreed silver cups.

"Great idea." Mehmed grabs a cup and sniffs it. "Lemon sherbet. Delicious." He takes a sip, then empties the cup and puts it back on the tray.

Radu takes a sip from the other cup and makes a face. He sniffs it. "What the…"

He takes another sip, then drops it to the ground. The thirsty earth sucks up the liquid.

Radu stumbles. He kicks the cup, then crumbles to the ground and curls up, moaning. He clutches his stomach and retches something dark.

His heart racing in panic, Mehmed kneels by his friend. He looks at his pale face, touches his cold, sweaty cheek and shouts,

"Bring Akşemseddin."

He wipes Radu's green lips with his sleeve and remembers when he got poisoned in Manisa. He lays his hands on Radu's stomach and pushes, making him retch.

Radu screams and tries to shove him away, but Mehmed will have none of it. He pushes on him again and again until nothing comes out.

Mehmed takes a deep breath. The boy who brought their drinks stares at them in horror.

"What's your name?" Mehmed asks.

"Amir."

"Who sent these drinks, Amir?"

The boy shudders and falls to his knees, prostrating himself.

Radu sits up looking bewildered.

"My sultan…" the boy gasps.

"Who sent these drinks, Amir?"

"Your mother, my sultan. The validé told me to bring you the drinks as soon as you dismount. She told me to make sure you got the lemon one."

"Are you sure?"

The kid's lips tremble, but his horrified eyes tell Mehmed what he needs to know. The other stable boy returns from the palace alone.

"The honorable Akşemseddin is away for the day and he can't be found."

"Get me Ali," Radu mumbles.

"Who's Ali?"

"Your mother's eunuch."

Mehmed nods, and the boy runs back to look for Ali. The sultan sits by his friend and caresses his soft curls with a loving hand.

"How are you feeling?"

"Better, my sultan. Thank you. I don't know what happened. I think I didn't care for the taste of that drink."

"I guess not," Mehmed says, picking up the cup, now empty, and smelling it. "It doesn't smell like lemon sherbet."

"It's chamomile," Radu says. "I hate it."

A young eunuch rushes in from the palace so fast that his blue kaftan flies behind him. He's small and freckled, with wide blue eyes and unruly red hair falling out of his turban. He bows in front of the sultan, then looks at Radu. He touches his skin, listens to his chest and smells his breath.

"You'll be OK," he says. "You should rest for a day or two, though. Don't eat or drink anything but the tea I'll make for you, and you should be as good as new in a few days."

Radu nods.

"How do you know these things?" Mehmed asks. "Are you a healer?"

"My grandmother used to be. She taught me a thing or two, my sultan. Your friend will be all right, but of course you'll have your own doctor look at him."

"Of course. Where are you from?"

"Transylvania, my sultan."

"How did you get here?"

"My mother sold me. She had other children to feed."

"But how did you become a eunuch?"

"My new master liked to gamble, and he took a chance with me. Fortunately, I was lucky and didn't die."

Mehmed frowns. There's something unsettling about this kid, something he can't put his finger on, but he's not like the others. Then he realizes. "You're white. How come you're assigned to the sarayi? We only have black eunuchs there."

Ali shrugs.

"Maybe because I'm still in training? I was fortunate. Your mother, in her wisdom, chose me to serve her. I do my best to be worthy."

"Good. Then take care of my friend, Radu. He's important to me."

"Yes, my sultan. He's important to me, too."

Mehmed wonders what to do about his mother. Sadly, he can't ask Radu for advice.

Then he smiles. He knows exactly who to ask.

CHAPTER 16
A SECRET ADVISOR

The sunset came and went. The gardens soaked in the last of the golden light, and the wide leaves of the old plane tree dance on the soft breeze, heavy with the scents of peonies and lilac. It's the intoxicating smell of late spring, and Mehmed lifts his nose to inhale it.

He sits on the hidden marble bench under the plane tree. He's been waiting for a while, and starts wondering if she's even coming. But why wouldn't she? Still, the dusk turns to dark, and she's still not here.

Mehmed stands to head back to his quarters when he hears soft steps. A tall shape veiled in black flutters towards him, followed by a eunuch. The eunuch is Ali. Mehmed signals him to go away.

"Hello, Mehmed. Long time, no see."

The voice is low and soft and full of laughter, and Mehmed's heart fills with joy. He didn't realize how much he missed her. He loved spending time with her as a child. She played with him, sang to him, and told him strange stories about Serbia and other foreign places that were unlike the Ottoman Empire but not less wonderful. And she always laughed, unlike anyone else in the sarayi. Mother never laughed. She was always irked by some slight or other, unless she was busy showing Halime Hatice who was boss. Father didn't laugh either, whether because of the gloomy business of the empire, or the sobriety he owed to the Quran. Mara alone used to laugh, sing and play, acting as if life was just fun and games. Then Mehmed got sent to Manisa, and he didn't see Mara since. But she's just as lovely as ever.

"Hello, Mama Mara. I'm delighted to see you."

"Me too, Mehmed. Look at you, all grown up and so handsome. Congratulations on the great victory at Varna. I've been told it was one for the ages."

"Thank you, Mama Mara. But I did nothing but try to interfere with Father's strategy. Fortunately, he didn't let me do it, so we won."

Mara laughs. "You haven't changed a bit, my son. Keep laughing at yourself and others. That's the ticket for a long and happy life. Now tell me, what can I do for you?"

"Let's walk," Mehmed says, worried that someone might overhear them.

They walk side by side along the narrow alleys lined with fragrant rose bushes. And, whether it's the soft evening air, or having someone he trusts to unburden his soul to, everything feels easier to Mehmed.

"It's about my friend Radu, the son of Vlad Dracul, Wallachia's voivode. He's a guest at our court."

"I heard he's a lovely kid."

"Yes, he is. And he's my best friend. But somebody tried to poison him."

"I'm sorry to hear that. How is he?"

"He seems OK. Akşemseddin saw him and said there's nothing wrong with him, but he got horribly sick after he drank something Mother sent to him."

Mara gasps. "Hüma? You think Hüma tried to kill your friend? But why?"

"She... Mother is worried that I spend too much time with him and neglect my duties. This morning when I told her I was going hunting with him instead of waiting for the Venetian ambassadors, she wasn't happy."

"Is that it?"

"She... she thinks I like him too much, and that's why I'm not interested in girls. She wants me to... produce an heir."

"I see."

"Mama Mara, I don't know what to do. I can't just wait and see if she kills him next time. And I can't go tell her to stop poisoning my friends. Not like she'd listen, anyhow."

"How about your father? Can he help?"

"I don't dare tell Father. He... agrees with Mother that I need to focus on the business of the empire rather than spend time with Radu. I don't think he would help."

"You really care about Radu."

"I do."

"Well, it looks like you need to finesse things a little. You need to give your mother and your father what they expect from you — focus on the empire, and start working on producing an heir, if you want to keep your friend Radu safe."

"You think that's enough?"

"I'd have a private conversation with your mother. Tell her you know she tried to poison your friend, and you understand that she's got the best interest of the empire at heart. Promise that you'll do your best to make her happy if she stops harassing you and makes sure that your friend is safe. Tell her that if anything happens to Radu, you'll resign and give the throne back to your father. She'd lose her place as validé, and may get to see Halime Hatice produce the Ottoman Empire's next heir."

"That's rough."

"I know. But if you love him, it's worth it."

"You understand?"

"Of course. Love doesn't always happen in the ways of the Quran. The heart doesn't read. It just so happens that your heart found that Radu is its soulmate, instead of a girl. So what? Whose business is it?"

Mehmed stares at Mara. "How come you understand, while nobody else does?"

Mara shrugs. "My soul also found its hidden ways to love. And it's no one's business who I have in my heart."

Mehmed nods. He'd like to ask further, but doesn't dare. "What should I do if Mother does it again?"

"I hope she doesn't. She won't, if you give her what she wants, which is a grandson. But if she does it again, go tell your father who killed Aladdin."

Mehmed gasps. "How do you know?"

Mara laughs. "Here in the sarayi, everyone knows everything. If you want to keep a secret, keep it to yourself. Whenever you share it, it will come out sooner or later. Keep that in mind, sultan: Three can keep a secret when two of them are dead."

"What would Father do if I told him?"

"He'd kill her. But you don't want that. You'd lose not only your mother, you'd lose a priceless ally. Don't do that unless you must."

"Thank you, Mama Mara. Thank you very much."

"You're welcome. Remember that I'm here whenever you need me. Ali?"

The little eunuch appears out of nowhere, and Mehmed wonders how much he heard. "Three can keep a secret when two of them are dead," Mara had said.

CHAPTER 17

IN THE SULTAN'S BED

By the time Mehmed finally gets to his quarters, he's had a long day. His hunt with Radu was only this morning, but it feels like weeks ago. Then Radu got poisoned and came back to life. Mehmed had a hard time refraining from killing Çandarlı Paşa, who kept harassing him about the janissaries. Then he had the troubling conversation with Mama Mara that opened his mind to thoughts he never had before.

Mara must not care about men. That's why she had no children, and she doesn't give a hoot who Sultan Murad sleeps with. That's also why she gets along so well with his other women, even those who would strangle each other.

In his heart of hearts, Mehmed knows that his feelings for Radu are not right. Many Ottoman men like boys. They take them to bed, use them, then get rid of them when they're done. No big deal, as long as it's done discreetly and not to excess. It's fine to enjoy a boy or two, but not two dozens. And you should neither fuss nor brag about it.

But that's not love. For the faithful, love is all about Allah, the prophet, and his teachings. The empire too, and their sons. And even their wives. Sort of.

Love, romantic love, is not an Ottoman thing. That's the silly stuff of ballads, where valiant knights fall in love with beautiful damsels and strive to conquer the world in their honor. And even then, it's never a man loving with another man. Or a boy. That's why loving Radu makes no sense.

He sighs and shakes his head. He's too tired to think about this tonight. Tomorrow, maybe. He opens the door to his bedroom to find Lena sleeping in his bed.

She's beautiful, with her rose-bud soft mouth, her creamy skin glowing against the blue silk sheets, and her riot of honey-colored curls covering the pillow.

He likes this girl. She's got more guts than most men. She refuses to let others decide her fate, refuses to beg, refuses to let things get her down. She's smart, pretty and funny.

But she's not his thing.

He drops off his sword and his dagger, takes off his kaftan, and squeezes between the sheets, trying not to wake her up.

Her blue eyes open, and she smiles. "How are you?"

"Tired. You?"

She looks at him and feels that something isn't right. "Are you OK?"

"No. Rough day."

"I see. Come here."

She holds him close and spoons around him. Her hug melts the strain of his muscles and softens his tension.

"Lena?"

"Yes?"

"We need to talk."

"Tomorrow. Sleep now."

She holds him like nobody held him before. She falls asleep, her slow, steady breath tickling his ear, but she doesn't let go. Her hug is soothing warmth and kindness, but not love. Her warmth shields him, and he lets himself fall asleep.

They wake up in the morning like lovers. Except they aren't.

"Lena?"

"Yes."

"I need a baby."

"What for?"

"My mother won't settle until I give her one."

"That's too bad."

"Not interested?"

"That wasn't our deal."

"I know."

"I'm not into babies. Not yet."

"So you want to go home?"

"For real?"

"Yes."

"Yes, please."

"I'll miss you."

"I'll miss you, too. But I can't wait to go home, ramble through the woods, and climb the trees to pick apples."

"You can't do that."

"Why not?"

"There are no apples till the fall."

She turns around to look in his eyes, and her face glows with more joy than Mehmed has ever seen in any human being.

"Really? You'll let me go home? Soon?"

"Next week?"

She jumps out of bed and dances half-naked around his bedroom with the endearing grace of a kitten. She's breathtaking, with her pink cheeks, bright eyes, and lustrous hair, and Mehmed wishes he hadn't promised to let her go. He'd love her to have his children, who would be as beautiful and as alive as she is. But it's too late. He promised.

"I'll get to see my mother, and my father, and Mitzi, and the sheep. And maybe Ilie. No, not Ilie. He was old when I left and that was years ago. Then I left him when I ran from the posse..."

"Who's Ilie?"

"Our old horse. He's probably dead now. Poor old thing. I hope Mother and Father are alive though, and Mitzi…"

Her joy vanishes, replaced by worry.

Mehmed hopes her home and her parents are still there, but it's been a long time.

"How long were you gone?"

"Two years."

"It's not that long, two years," Mehmed lies.

Lena leans to kiss his lips, making him feel more awake than he's been in a while, then puts on her shalwars and her kaftan.

"What's the first thing you'll do when you get back?"

Lena stops to look into that day when she'll return home.

"I'll get home. Mother will bake bread, and Father will split wood for the oven. Mitzi may be looking after a new litter of kittens. The chickens will rummage through the yard for worms, and the lilac and the jasmine should be blooming, filling the air with sweetness. I know. I'll go milk Minerva."

"Who's Minerva?"

"Our cow. Have you ever had warm milk straight from a cow?"

Mehmed shakes his head.

"You should try it sometime. It's one of the best things on earth. It's still alive, you know. It's almost white with a hint of butter and it smells like heaven. Next week, you said?"

"Next week."

She leaves without looking back, and Mehmed misses her already.

CHAPTER 18

THE ONE THAT GOT AWAY

Edirne Palace is in turmoil. The rumors spread like wildfire, from the sarayi to the hammam and the kitchens, then the barracks and everywhere else. But nobody believes them to be true.

"That's impossible. That has never happened ever since Osman, the first sultan, and it won't happen now," the Kapı Ağası, the head of the eunuchs, says. "Stop spreading these stupid rumors or I'll tell the validé."

"Yes, Kapı Ağası," his bath attendant says, trying to look contrite, but his eyes sparkle with mischief.

But Ali happens to know that it's true. She heard it from Lena. More importantly, she heard it from Sultan Mehmed himself last night, when Hüma Hatun summoned him to her quarters. "Is it true, what I've heard?"

Mehmed shrugged. "Depends on what you've heard."

"Don't you get cheeky with me, young man. There's a rumor that you're sending Lena home. Is that true?"

"Yes. She's going home in two days."

"But... why?"

"Why not?"

"She's a slave at the harem. There's no reason for her to leave!"

"She's MY slave in MY harem. And she will leave if I so decide."

"But why? If you no longer want her, you don't need to call her to your bed anymore. She could work with the seamstresses or with the bath women and..."

"I want her to go home."

"But that's impossible! That never happened before."

"It's happening now."

"You're crazy! What will the other women say? What will the other slaves think? That they can just leave whenever they please?"

"No. Whenever I please. Tell me, Mother, what got you so upset? It's not like we don't have a harem full of women here! You can't swing a dead cat without hitting a dozen."

"Mehmed, this is not proper. Women don't just leave a sultan's harem to go home. Almost never. Unless a sultan dies, and his son decides, in his generosity, to let his father's women return to their parents. The ones he doesn't give away to his dignitaries, or marries off to forge an alliance. Otherwise, they die here. Why would you let this peasant girl go? And think of her! What good will it do to her, now that she's used to live in the harem? You're condemning her to a life of misery. She'll have to work the fields, shiver in winter, and wear scratchy wool and linen instead of silk and brocade. She'll go hungry and marry some dirty peasant who will beat her and get her heavy with child every year. And then you'll be lucky if her issue doesn't pretend he's your son and come to claim the throne. This is foolish and dangerous. It's bad for her, bad for our other women, and unsafe for the empire. I beg you to reconsider. You don't have to ever see her again if that's your wish."

The sultan thunders.

"My wish is for Lena to go back to her parents the day after tomorrow. Now, do you have any other questions?"

Hüma shakes her head, her eyes swimming in tears. Mehmed's hasty decision upset her, but his shouting at her hurt her more.

Mehmed sees it.

"I'm sorry, Mother, but I made my decision. Lena is leaving. But..."

He takes her hand and kisses the emerald on her finger. "We got that new girl Sevlet Paşa sent. Why don't you send her to me one of these nights?"

Hüma's face lights up. "What an idea. She's a nice girl, even though her education has just started. She seems good-natured and loyal. And she's so caring towards her young brother."

"The deaf-mute. I know."

"I'll look into that. You may be right. She may be more suitable than Lena. Lena is beautiful, but there's something rough inside that girl. She's not soft and malleable like Gülbahar."

"Or like you."

"What?"

"Nothing. You picked a nice name. It suits her."

Mehmed leaves, and Ali can see the wheels turning inside Hüma's head. She'd like Gülbahar ready as soon as possible. Tonight, even. But tonight won't do, because she needs her bath and her epilation and a little of training in what to do and say when she meets the sultan. One wouldn't want to disappoint the sultan! She'll also need someone to look after her brother while she's gone. Otherwise, she'll worry about him instead of focusing on Mehmed's every blink.

"Tomorrow night, maybe. Ali, I need you to spend some time with the boy. He needs to be comfortable with you, and she needs to feel that he's safe. Drop everything and take care of this."

"Yes, my lady."

"Figure out a way to communicate with him. He needs to learn anyhow; he may as well start. Something simple that he can understand and the servants can, too."

"Yes, my lady."

"I don't know who'll make the arrangements for Lena's return. Not me, for sure. But check that she has a safe way back. It wouldn't do to have her kidnapped and sold, or hurt. Let me know if she needs anything."

"Yes, my lady."

"That's it for now."

Ali bows deeply and leaves.

"Ali?"

"Yes, my lady?"

"What happened to Radu?"

"The Prince of Wallachia? He drank something that got him sick. They looked for Akşemseddin to care for him but he wasn't here, so they sent for me. Something he drank didn't agree with him, but he's better now."

"Ali."

"Yes, my lady."

"He drank your potion. And he didn't die."

"My potion? Was it for him?"

Hüma glares at her.

"Cut that. Why isn't he dead?"

"He didn't drink it, my lady. He just had a sip, then dropped the cup, and the potion spilled. He barely touched it."

Hüma nods. "I see. I guess we'll have to make another. But that's not urgent right now. Go take care of the deaf-mute."

"Yes, my lady."

Ali bows and goes to see Lena.

CHAPTER 19
DANGEROUS SECRETS

Lena is beside herself with joy. She twirls around the room like a whirling dervish, picking up a brocade kaftan here, a silver necklace there, and dropping them into the carved sandalwood coffer she's taking with her. The whole room looks like a bazaar — a riot of silks, brocades and velvets in every color of the rainbow. But nothing's more colorful than Lena herself. Her cheeks are flushed, and her blue eyes sparkle with joy.

"He's actually letting me go! Can you believe it?"

She hugs Ali, who hugs her back. "I'm so happy for you."

"I am too. I wonder what to take with me. I can't wear any of these at home, of course, but my aunt sews. She can re-cut them into something I can wear in the village. I'd love to give you some of them, but you're so tiny. And you don't need girl clothes. I wonder what Mother will say when she sees me. Father too. And Ștefan, even though he won't be there, of course... Oh, Ali, how I hope he's still alive..."

"He's alive and you'll see him soon," Ali says.

"How do you know?"

"I just do. Trust me."

Lena hugs Ali again.

"Of course I do. I trust you with my life."

"Thank you. Lena, I need a favor."

"What?"

"My grandma, Mama Smaranda, lives alone in a cabin near Kronstadt. That must be about a hundred miles from your village. I wonder if you could send her a letter from me."

"I'll figure it out. Where is it?"

"Here."

Ali hands Lena a folded piece of paper. Lena looks at it but doesn't take it.

"Read it to me."

Ali unfolds it and reads it out loud.

Dear Mama Smaranda,
I am well. I am in the sultan's sarayi, and I am blessed to
serve his mother, the validé. I am healthy and strong and I
have no complaints but that I haven't heard from you or any
of our friends in a long time and I'm worried about you. If
you ever sent me anything, I didn't get it. I'm also in urgent
need of some Wolfsbane for my potions. Maybe even some
seeds. Please let me know.
With all my love,
Ali

"Is that what that really says?"

"Yes."

"OK." Lena takes the folded piece of paper and squeezes it in her little pouch. "I'll do my best to get it to her. I'll take it there myself if I can. Is she a nice person?"

"She's a lovely person. The most interesting person I ever met."

Lena laughs.

"That's a funny way to talk about your grandmother. Most people never 'meet' their grandparents. They've known them all their lives."

Ali realizes Lena is much sharper than she realized. "We met a little late."

Lena looks around. There's nobody there but for the two of them. She opens the door and looks up and down. Still nobody. She turns around and whispers.

"I trust you. Do you trust me?"

Ali's world tips. Whatever it is, she's afraid. Very afraid. She nods.

"You're not a eunuch. You're a girl, just like me, but younger. And very sharp. But your body is starting to betray you. Your breasts are budding. Your hips are filling. Soon enough, you'll start to bleed. Somebody will notice."

Ali pales.

"Bind your breasts. Make sure that nobody sees you naked. And, whatever you're doing here, your time is running short. You can't hide who you are forever. Get out of here. The sooner the better.

Same with your friends. The werewolf? Tell him I said thanks for watching over me and saving me from the bear. He's a good man. What's his name?"

"Kemal."

"No. His *real* name."

"Codru."

"I'd love to see him again someday."

Ali nods, too overwhelmed to talk.

"I don't know who you're working for. Transylvania, I guess, therefore Hunyadi. I'll be happy to help you. I'm from Moldova, and we're all brothers. We speak the same language, pray to the same God and fight the same enemy."

"What enemy?"

Lena looks at her like she's gone mad.

"The Ottomans, of course. Who else?"

"But..."

"What?"

"The sultan just freed you..."

"Sure he did. After his people captured me and sold me. I've been their slave for years. I'm lucky that Mehmed prefers boys, otherwise I'd be feeding a baby right now. Are you out of your mind? They stole two years from me I'll never see again, and who knows what else? I don't even know if my parents are still alive. And my cat. And Ilie. Ottomans are the scum of the earth. I can't wait to fight them any way I can."

"Why didn't you tell me?" Ali asks.

"Tell you what?"

"All this."

"Why didn't you?"

Ali stumbles.

"I didn't know."

"Neither did I. But now we do."

"Thank you, Lena. Mama Smaranda is very special. You can trust her with anything."

"I'll do my best to get there. I love you, Ali. I hope you make it out of here and we get to meet again. Don't let the bastards get you down and get out of here. Time works against you. Sooner or later, they'll figure you out and it will be too late. Same with your friends."

"Thanks, Lena. One question."

"Yes?"

"How did you know the werewolf was my friend?"

"He smells of soap and herbs. I've never heard of a werewolf smelling like chamomile. And, even as a werewolf, he had that side grin you sometimes have. He was like your wolf brother."

Ali nods and hugs Lena one last time, then heads to the deaf-mute boy, though she's sick with worry.

If Lena figured out she's a fake, who else did? And how long has she got before it's too late?

CHAPTER 20

BRĂILA, JULY 1445

Brăila, Wallachia's largest port, sits on the Danube barely a hundred miles east of Târgoviște's royal court, just before the mighty river veers east to flow into the Black Sea.

Even so, Brăila is neither big nor pretty. It's almost fifty years old, but compared to the world's greatest ports, like Venice and Constantinople, Brăila is nothing but a little fishing village smelling like fish, garlic, and refuse. As for its people, the fishermen, the sailors and the merchants elbowing each other in the port, they come from all over the world, as witnessed by their rainbow of skin colors, strange languages and strange garb, but few of them look rich.

Still, for Ștefan, who's never seen a port before, the tall-masted ships straining against the screaming chains of their anchors are a wonder to behold. And more than any, the glorious galleys of Wallerand de Wavrin, the Duke of Burgundy's captain general.

Wallerand himself sits at the head of his table in the grandest room of his grandest ship, planning the Danube Campaign with Vlad Dracul, surrounded by Mircea, Ștefan, Cardinal Condulmer, the pope's cross-eyed envoy, and a few elegant Burgunds holding perfumed handkerchiefs under their noses.

The Burgunds are all richly dressed in lustrous velvets and gold-embroidered silks. Their doublets have mushrooming sleeves that bloom like cabbages, so their arms look shriveled, and skin-tight tights. Wallerand's pink tights make him look like he forgot his breeches, and his fur-trimmed yellow tunic with deep slits on the sides is cinched so tight at the waist he resembles an oversized wasp. But he doesn't know how silly he looks as he talks to Vlad Dracul with the voice of a victor.

"I have seven galleys. All smooth and nimble, powered by thirty oars each, and aided by large sails. They'll have no trouble sailing up the Danube, especially if God blesses us with favorable winds."

"God will bless us with favorable winds and everything else," the cardinal says, fondling the massive gold cross on his chest. "He knows we're doing his work."

"I sure hope he'll pay more attention than he did at Varna," Vlad says, and the cleric throws him a murderous look.

"How many men can you give us?" Wavrin asks.

"How many did Hunyadi promise you?"

"He promised to meet us up at Nikopolis with an army of two thousand by mid-August."

"I guess I can give you half that."

"No more?"

Vlad shakes his head. "No more. I need my men to protect my borders. I'm still reeling from the losses at Varna last year."

Wavrin glances at him down his thin nose.

"Not that many losses, I've heard."

Vlad looks him in the eye. He knows what Wavrin is saying. He spoke to Hunyadi, who's still spiteful after losing most of his army and his foolish king at Varna, while Mircea brought his Wallachians home.

"Our people are not foolish. Like some others, I may add. But I'll throw in fifty canoes and the men needed to handle them. Plus enough wheat flour to keep the whole army fed throughout the campaign."

"That would be good. We're running short of supplies, since it's been a long time since we left home."

"So I've heard. Are you still looking for the King of Poland?" Mircea asks, glancing at Ștefan.

There's no more king. They both saw him die and saw his bloody head with its frozen eyes still open get paraded above the battlefield impaled on his own lance. That was before the sultan, whichever of them, sent it to Manisa preserved in honey.

"Yes. We need either the king, or proof of his death, since many of our people can't believe he's dead."

Mircea nods. Ștefan wonders why he doesn't tell them what he saw, then realizes there's no point. The Burgunds have made up their mind. Hunyadi must have told them too, but they didn't listen. They started this campaign to look for the king and they want to keep looking. Why would Mircea try to dissuade them when he can use them to hurt his enemies?

"We also have a surprise for the sultan: a legitimate contender to the Ottoman throne. We'll bring him with us, hoping to turn the Ottomans in the forts along the Danube into allies. We'll look like liberators coming to help them get rid of the usurpers Murad and Mehmed. If they turn around and start a movement that spreads through the empire, we could see another civil war."

"Is that so? Who have you got?" Vlad Dracul asks.

"We have Orhan Çelebi, the grandson of Süleyman Çelebi, Bayezid the Thunderbolt's eldest son. He's the rightful heir to the Ottoman throne."

Vlad Dracul nods.

"Oh, I know all about Orhan. They don't call him the Drunk of Constantinople for nothing. That man can party like it's going out of style. But I hate to break it to you: In the Ottoman Empire, primogeniture doesn't count. Unlike in Burgundy and most of Europe, the Ottomans don't care if you're the first son or the seventh. All that matters is if you're strong enough to lead the empire. That's why Mehmed the First grabbed the throne from under Suleyman's ass, even though he was just Bayezid's fourth son, born from a slave. So, for all intents and purposes, your Orhan is no more legitimate heir to the Ottoman throne than my horse."

Wavrin turns a sick shade of purple that clashes with his yellow tunic.

"That's no way to talk. Orhan Çelebi is pure Ottoman royalty and has more rights to the throne than…"

Vlad laughs and waves aside his concerns.

"OK, OK. You and your people made your call. You decided to whitewash this little incursion into a so-called liberation attempt. Why not? I don't think the Ottomans will fall for it, but what's it to me? This is not half as bad as when your Duke of Burgundy and the pope sold that little girl, Jeanne d'Arc, to the English to burn her at the stake. At least Orhan is old enough to know what he's doing."

Cross-eyed cardinal Condulmer crosses himself.

Wavrin sputters: "This is a state business that no outsider…"

Vlad nods. "I get it. Orhan is your problem, not mine. Let's move on and get back to our business. So, you're sure you can count on Hunyadi and his twenty thousand men to be at Nikopolis in mid-August?"

Wavrin nods. "Of course. The Voivode of Transylvania is a good Catholic and a man of his word."

Vlad Dracul shrugs. "I wouldn't know about Catholic. But as for his words…"

Someone knocks at the door.

CHAPTER 21

A CHANGE IN PLANS

It's a messenger. The man presents a scroll, and Wavrin checks the red wax seal.

"It's from Hunyadi."

He breaks the seal and reads, his face growing longer and longer. He reads it again, then hands it to Vlad Dracul.

Vlad reads it and smiles.

"Why am I not surprised? Just as I thought, the brave Voivode of Transylvania isn't ready for battle. He sends word that he can't get to Nikopolis with his army before Saint Mary's Day, on September 8. Maybe later."

Wavrin shakes his head so hard his velvet hat slides to the side.

"What am I supposed to do with my ships and my men until then? That's almost a month later than planned. How do I feed them and keep them busy so they don't get in trouble? That's terrible news."

Vlad Dracul sighs. "It's worse than you think. Our winters are harsh. We never know when the Danube will freeze, but it always does. Then you're stuck. If your galleys freeze in the water, they'll sit like fat ducks waiting for the Ottomans to pluck them."

Wavrin frowns. "When does the Danube freeze?"

"There's no usually. Every winter is different. But, to be safe, you should be back at sea by December."

"So what can we do?" the cleric asks.

Mircea clears his voice.

"How about starting without Hunyadi? We're not even sure he's coming in September. We could, you with your galleys and us with our men, sail up the Danube and pick off the Ottoman forts one by one. By the time we fought, rested and resupplied, we should be at Nikopolis just about the time Hunyadi says he'll be there. That will keep your men busy and get them some loot."

The Burgunds stare at Mircea like he grew a third ear. Vlad Dracul smiles.

"What forts are you talking about?" Wavrin asks.

"Silistra first, then Turtucaia, Giurgiu and Russe. They're all protected by Ottoman garrisons, but they shouldn't be a match for our joined forces. Taking the forts should help replenish your supplies. And you'd get a chance to show off your pretender and see how that works."

"Orhan Çelebi is not a pretender. He's the rightful ruler of the Ottoman Empire who was deprived from his birthright by the pretenders who are Murad and Mehmed," Wavrin snorts.

"Sure. You'll get a chance to see what the Ottomans think about your rightful ruler, then."

Wavrin glares at him down his nose and turns to the cardinal. "What do you think?"

"Not a bad idea. But we need to seek the pope's approval. This is a serious deviation from our plan."

"How long will it take you to get a messenger there and back?" Vlad Dracul asks.

"A month, maybe?"

"That works. That should allow our men to harvest the crops and get ready."

"Good, then. I'll be honored to lead your men into battle," Wavrin says.

Vlad Dracul laughs.

"I bet you would. But you won't. Our men have their leader. Mircea will lead our troops in battle. You will, of course, lead your galleys. Unless you'd like him to?"

Wavrin's face falls.

Ștefan bites his lip to stop from laughing.

"As the pope's delegate, who is the representative of God on earth, our men's leader is the cardinal. I'm at his disposal, and I lead my men thanks to his authority."

"As my representative, Mircea will lead our men. With Ștefan as his deputy."

Wavrin glances at them. "They're just children."

"They're older than they were at Varna. More experienced too. You're lucky to have them, Captain General. I'd be glad to say the same thing to them," Vlad Dracul says.

Wallerand de Wavrin nods without glee, and the Burgunds stare without smiling as the Wallachians step ashore.

They walk out happy to be on solid ground and feel the breeze, even if it smells like rotten fish. When they reach their horses, they stop to glance back.

"Nice ship, though," Mircea says, looking at the oars aligned in three clean rows and the proud mast, ready for the large square sail.

"Yes. Better than its people, I may say. Those galleys are easy to handle, thanks to the oarsmen. With a bit of wind, they can pick up a nice speed. But I'd rather be on a horse. Are you boys ready to head back?"

Ștefan coughs. "Since we're already all the way here... I... I would like to go north to Moldova for a few days."

Vlad stares at him like he's lost his mind.

"Go to Moldova? But why? You want them to catch you? You barely escaped last time. You may not be that lucky again. Your father's still a fugitive, and I lost count of which of your uncles sits on Moldova's throne at this exact moment."

"I have an… old friend I'd like to check on. It's not too far. I thought that since I'm here anyhow…"

Mircea laughs. He knows all about Lena.

Vlad Dracul shrugs.

"Suit yourself, then. You can take five men. Make sure to bring them back alive."

"Can I go with him, Father? You don't need me right now, and I'd like to meet Ștefan's… friend."

"As you wish, both of you. Take a dozen men then. Just don't get into trouble."

CHAPTER 22

EDIRNE PALACE, JULY 1445

It's late in the evening by the time Mehmed finally heads to his bedroom. He spent the whole day working on a plan to conquer Constantinople, even though they all try to deter him: His mother, his dignitaries, even Radu. Çandarlı Paşa more than any. The old man coaxed and pleaded, wringing his bejeweled hands. "Constantinople has been there for a thousand years. Many tried to take it and they all broke their teeth on its walls. There's no way to take it, my sultan. Especially not now."

Mehmed bristled. He's had it with this old timer who won't fight, won't agree with him on anything, and won't even leave him alone.

"Why not? We crushed the crusaders at Varna. They're out of commission, so our western front is finally safe. Father took care of business in Anatolia and got the Karamanids to step back and settle. Now is the time, if there'll ever be one."

"I disagree, my sultan. The crusaders aren't crushed, just delayed. They'll be back at it any day now. As soon as they choose a new king of Poland and Hungary. I bet Hunyadi is already preparing. If you start towards Constantinople, he'll stab you in the back."

"Is this more information from your spy at his court?"

"No, my sultan. I've been waiting to hear from her for a while now, but nothing. I hope they didn't find and hang her. That would be a huge loss. This is just what I figured from their troop movements."

"Sure, Çandarlı Paşa. I know you're wise and very cautious. And I see how this could happen. We'll make sure we're ready for this. In the meantime..."

"My sultan, there's more than that."

"What?"

"Your Uncle Orhan."

"The Drunk of Constantinople?"

Çandarlı Paşa sighed, but he kept his voice soft.

"Your Uncle Orhan is blood of the blood of Osman Ghazi, the Ottoman Empire's founder. He's the heir of your grandfather's older brother Suleyman who got killed in the interregnum. His partisans aren't happy with your father's ascension to the throne, and therefore yours. Some even think he's the rightful heir to Osman's throne."

"So what?"

"There are rumors that your uncle Orhan has left Constantinople and is sailing the Black Sea on some galley."

"He can't be. We pay Constantinople a tidy sum to keep him there. If that's true and they let him go, we'll have to cut their subsidies. Like yesterday."

"Of course. But that won't bring your uncle Orhan back, if he's out, looking for a way to hurt you."

"Don't you see it, Çandarlı Paşa? Everything you told me gives me more reasons to grab the red apple. Our empire can't be whole as long as these filthy Greeks, who call themselves Romans but wouldn't know the Roman majesty if it hit them between their eyes, choke our empire. They control the passage from Anatolia to Rumelia and thus have a stronghold on our troop movements. We can't have full control of our country before we get the Bosporus into our hands."

"But, my sultan..."

"That's enough, paşa. My patience is running thin, with them and with you. We are done. Come back when you have something new to tell me."

Çandarlı Paşa bowed low and left.

Mehmed knows he wasn't happy, but his job is not to make Çandarlı Paşa happy. His job is to protect the Ottoman empire. And for that, he needs Constantinople.

He steps into his bedroom, glad to be done with all the talking, cajoling, negotiating, and all the other crap that's a sultan's job. He's well overdue to lie down with his thoughts and enjoy the silence.

But there's a girl in his bed. Blonde and delicate, with a soft pink mouth and round cheeks, she stares at him with blue eyes as big as saucers. And she looks like Radu's spitting image. She must be Sevlet Paşa's gift.

"Hello."

"I wish you a good evening, my sultan."

"Thank you. What's your name?"

"Gülbahar."

"Lovely name. What was your name before that?"

"I used to be called Sophia."

Mehmed nods, looking for something nice to say to this scared girl he doesn't want in his bed. Then he remembers.

"How's your brother doing?"

A tear runs down Gülbahar's cheek. "He's good. Thank you, my sultan."

"How old is he?"

"He's eight."

"He looks like a bright kid," Mehmed lies, since all he saw was a scared kid looking lost.

Gülbahar smiles.

"That's so observant of you to notice, my sultan. He used to be bright, but since they took away his hearing and his voice, it's been hard to communicate with him. It's like he's stuck behind a thick wall I struggle to get through. Thank you for keeping us together. I'm sure you'll find him very helpful."

"How about you? Are you going to be helpful to me, too?"

Gülbahar's eyes brighten with tears.

"I'll do my best, my sultan. I'm here to bring you pleasure."

Mehmed nods. This poor girl looks scared to death, and the last thing he needs is to get pleasure from her. "How about we get some sleep?"

Gülbahar stares, wondering if he's jesting. He's not.

He drops his weapons and his kaftan and squeezes under the sheets next to her, though she looks like she's waiting to be stabbed.

"Come here."

She turns to him, entangled in the many layers they dressed her in to impress him. He helps her take off her kaftan, then hugs her like Lena hugged him. "Now we sleep. Tomorrow there's another day."

He falls asleep holding her tense body, hoping tomorrow proves better for them both.

CHAPTER 23

BERZUNȚI, AUGUST 1445

Ștefan and Mircea have been riding north for two days. After the scorching heat of the plains, the chill of the mountains came as a relief. The evenings are lovely and soft, and the crisp mornings have a bit of a bite. The incense of the pines cleansed their lungs and souls of Brăila's stench of fish and debris.

"What a lovely country your Moldova is," Mircea says, wondering at the hundred-year-old pines surrounding them. "Your forests smell like churches, only cleaner, without the smoke of the candles and the priests' laments."

"Wallachia is beautiful, too," Ștefan says, but his heart fills with pride. This is his country, with indomitable mountains, rushing rivers, and golden wheat fields swaying in the wind. He's proud to be her son, even if he's still on the lam, waiting for better times to come.

"Sure it is, but it's not like this. Wallachia is nothing but plains going all the way to the Danube, and then it's marshes and mud. And the Ottomans lying in wait south of the river. You never know when they'll cross and come to burn our villages, kill our people, and steal our children."

"It's the same with us. The lower Danube separates Moldova from the Ottomans. And we have marshes, too."

"But look at your mountains," Mircea says, his voice full of envy.

Ștefan agrees. He loves these mountains with their snow-capped peaks stabbing at the clear sky and the flocks of white wooly sheep grazing the green pastures. "We're almost there," he says, looking at the hill he knows so well. They didn't go to the village — too many eyes and ears, and too many running mouths to gossip about the Wallachian riders. They came straight to the sheepfold instead. That's where Lena's father should be, now, at the end of summer. And who knows? With a bit of luck, she may be here too.

They're climbing the narrow footpath up the hill when Ștefan hears the dogs. They bark like crazy, telling their master that strangers are coming, and Ștefan feels sorry for the scare that seeing a dozen riders will give the old man. The dogs run down barking. They show their vicious white fangs and raise their hackles to make themselves look bigger, and they seem ready to kill until they get close enough to catch Ștefan's scent. When they do, they break into sharp cries of joy and leap at his horse, trying to lick him.

Ștefan dismounts to hug them, but they're too wired to stay put. They run around in circles, barking up a storm and striving to jump out of their skins.

The hut's door screeches open, and an old man limps down the hill holding his axe. "Don't you dare touch my dogs, you bastards!"

"Uncle Vasile?"

The man freezes in place.

"Ștefan? Is that you?"

He drops the axe and shuffles closer. He opens his arms to hug him, and tears run down the deep creases that the years carved into his weather-beaten skin.

"You're alive! And you've grown so big! Look at you! You're almost a man now! How long has it been?"

"Almost two years."

"Good to see you, Ștefan. And who are these?"

"This is my cousin Mircea, the son of Vlad Dracul. And his men."

"Where are you going? Are you at war?"

"No. We just came to see you. And find out if you've got any news."

"About what?"

"About Lena."

"She's…"

As if summoned, a woman runs down the path towards them. Ștefan can't believe his eyes.

"Lena? Is that you?"

It's got to be her, even though she's half a head taller than him. She's a grown woman now, and she's beautiful. Wherever she's been, these two years didn't harm her any. Her beauty glows like a torch in the darkness, and Ștefan can't take his eyes off her.

He hugs her, and her new curves make him dizzy. She's soft and warm and smooth, and she smells like honey and lavender. Her scent alone is enough to cut him at the knees.

He holds her hands and steps back to look her up and down.

"Is this really you?"

Her laugh is unchanged. It's crisp and clear, like the bells on the sleigh horses at Christmas.

"Sure it's me. How are you?"

Ștefan shakes his head to make sure he's not dreaming, when a hand grabs his shoulder.

"Aren't you going to introduce me?"

"I'm sorry, Mircea. I forgot. Lena, this is my cousin Mircea of Wallachia."

"The friend of my cousin is my friend. I'm so glad to meet you, Lena. I've heard so much about you from this little buck."

Mircea takes Lena in his arms and he kisses both her cheeks, like friends do. But he doesn't let go. He holds her close for what feels like forever, and she doesn't seem to mind. And when he finally lets go of her shoulders, he holds onto her hands and stares into her eyes like the world stopped.

The moment lasts until Ștefan can't take it anymore. He steps between them and breaks the spell.

"I'm glad to meet you too, Mircea."

An awkward silence follows as they all pretend they didn't see it, this thunder that struck out of the blue. They walk up the hill to the sheepfold, which is unchanged: small, smoky, and smelling like sheep. Lena brings out the crusty bread she baked this morning. She cuts it into thick, heavy slices and tops it with *caș*, sweet fresh sheep's cheese, and honey.

The old man pours his rough home-made wine into cups.

"To your bright future, kids. And to Moldova and Wallachia. May they long prosper, and may the good God give you both courage, wisdom, and luck to lead them well."

"To your health and your kind words," Mircea says, touching his cup to his.

They drink and eat and laugh, but it all tastes like ashes to Ștefan whose world just got upended.

That night, as he lays by the campfire wrapped in his cloak watching the million blinking stars, Ștefan knows nothing will ever be the same again.

Life as he knew it is over.

CHAPTER 24

THE RIVALS

The three days it took Ștefan and Mircea to get back to Târgoviște couldn't have been more awkward. They barely speak to each other, and avoid each other's eyes. It's like their deep friendship has vanished.

Ștefan feels like his soul died. He's hurt and empty and angry at what Mircea did. And what's worse is that Mircea did nothing. It's just who he is: tall, dark and handsome. Also strong, self-assured and almost eighteen. Next to him, Ștefan knows that he's skinny and wanting.

Mircea is also the heir of Wallachia's voivode, while Ștefan is the just the son of Bogdan, a Wannabe Maybe Someday to be Voivode of Moldova. Mircea leads armies into war. And he was no older than Ștefan when he sat on Wallachia's throne, while his father, Vlad Dracul, struggled to keep his head on his shoulders in Edirne. No wonder Lena was smitten. What woman wouldn't be?

But none of that makes Ștefan feel better. In the blink of an eye, he lost the love of his life, his best friend, and every hope for the future. His thoughts are bitter, and his soul scorched.

The tension gets thicker and thicker as they close in on the court of

Târgoviște. Mircea tries to chat about the weather, the landscape or the people, but Stefan barely answers. It's awkward, and Mircea can't take it anymore.

"I'm sorry, Ștefan."

Ștefan doesn't answer. What is there to say, other than "I wish you dropped dead?"

"I'm sorry, but I can't help it. I've never met someone like her. She's like the full moon lighting the dark sky. My heart melted when I saw her. There is nobody like her, for me. I want her to be mine forever. I need her to be the mother of my children. My life is empty without her."

"Mine too."

"Oh, Ștefan. You are way too young to settle. Have you ever been with a woman?"

Ștefan shakes his head. He's never been with a woman and doesn't want to. He knows the one woman he plans to be with. But it's not looking good.

"You are so young. You have so much to see and learn, Ștefan…"

"And you're what? All the way to seventeen?"

Mircea looks at him, his eyes heavy with pity, and speaks softly.

"I am a man. I've been with women. I led troops into war. I led a country. At your age, four years is an awful long time. I know you don't feel that way, but it's true. You have a lot of growing to do."

Ștefan bites his lips but doesn't answer.

"Either way, it's not for us to decide. It's up to her. If she wants you, she'll say no to me. If she doesn't, then there's nothing you or I can do. It's her call."

"But she's just a woman! What does she know?"

Mircea bursts into laughter. He laughs so hard he tears.

"Oh, Ștefan. What do you know about women?"

Ștefan thinks about the women he knows. His mother, Doamna Oltea, always praying. His wet nurse, Lena's mother, always working and caring for Lena and him. The women at Moldova's court, shuffling around on their pretty shoes, trying to catch the men's gaze.

"They look pretty. They fund churches and pray. They make children and feed them. What else is there to know?"

Mircea chokes with laughter. "You have a lot to learn, my friend. Who made my father take you to the court of Târgoviște?"

"Doamna Cneajna."

"Who made sure you were sent to the sheepfold, whether or not the old man liked it?"

"My wet nurse."

"Men make life as we know it. Women make men as we know them. In Wallachia, we have a saying: The man is the head of the house, but the woman is the neck. She turns him towards where he needs to go."

"We have the same saying in Moldova."

"It's not up to either of us. It's up to her. I can't win her if she doesn't want to be won. But whether I do or I don't, we're still friends, cousins and allies."

Ștefan's soul is a charred emptiness of sorrow and humiliation. He's been dreaming about Lena for years. Ever since they ran from the posse, he's never had a day without wondering where she was and what happened to her. And now, when he found her alive and more beautiful than ever, she's no longer his girl, and his heart breaks.

CHAPTER 25

EDIRNE PALACE, AUGUST 1445

It's summer in Edirne, and the brutal August sun baked the earth into a crust. Even the palace's famous roses have languished, despite the water from Arda's fresh stream joining the lazy Tunca to keep the gardens alive. But the gardeners had to ration the water and leave some for the market gardens supplying the palace with its daily produce, so the roses look worse for the wear, Radu thinks.

But at least nobody talks about war any more. No one but Mehmed, who's obsessed with Constantinople, and looks day and night for a way to break through those impregnable Theodosian walls. And the more he thinks about it, the more impossible it looks, and that keeps him busy.

That leaves Radu feeling kind of lonely. He's going on with his school and his poems and he's still playing his rübap, but he misses their time together. Today he's feeling particularly forlorn, so he decides to go see Ali. He knows the eunuch isn't keen on visitors to the little kitchen where he brews his potions, but Radu hasn't seen him in ages, and he longs for someone to talk to.

He opens the door to find Ali stirring some foul-smelling potion, as usual. The eunuch smiles when he sees Radu, but he doesn't look well.

His eyes are red and tired, and his face is even narrower than usual. And there's an edge to him Radu hasn't noticed before.

"How are you, Ali? It's good to see you."

"Thank you, my prince. How have you been?"

Radu looks around for a place to sit, but there's none, so he sits in the doorway.

"Lonely, to be honest. And bored. Not much happening these days."

Ali laughs.

"That's a good thing, my prince. We're not even one year out of the last war."

"Yes, and Mehmed is thinking of another one already."

"Is that so? Who's he going against this time?"

"Constantinople, who else? He works day and night on a plan to break through their walls, and that keeps him busy. That, and his new girl. He's so busy I hardly ever see him."

"Don't you have other friends at the palace school, my prince?"

"None other than you."

"I'm honored."

"You shouldn't be. I'm nothing to brag about."

He sits, racking his mind for something interesting to say as Ali keeps stirring his potion.

"What are you cooking this time?"

"I'm working on a potion for a friend."

"Is he sick? One of the Transylvanians?"

"Yes. He's got a bothersome skin problem that comes and goes. I'm trying to make something to help him, but I can't find one ingredient. I've been trying to tweak it and replace it with another plant, but I have had little luck."

"Skin is a nuisance," Radu says, scratching a bug bite. "Especially in this heat. I can't stop sweating and scratching. I wonder how the poor furry animals manage. Like the dogs and... hey, did you hear about the werewolf?"

Ali stops stirring. "The werewolf?"

"Yes. They say there's a werewolf roaming around the castle. A couple of the stable boys said they saw him under the last full moon. They got so excited they organized a posse to catch him next time there's a full moon, but I don't know when that is."

"Next week. I didn't know they had werewolves here."

"Of course they don't. They don't have them anywhere. It's just one of those bedtime stories mothers scare their kids with to make them behave. Werewolves don't exist."

"If so, there will be nothing to catch."

Radu laughs. "Of course not. But it's funny to see them all get ready with fishing nets and crossbows and lances and plan who will keep watch where. There's even a team of janissaries who'll go outside the gates, just in case he manages to jump over the walls. They'll wait for him on the hunting grounds."

"Aren't they afraid of him?"

"Sure they are. But they think that if they're together, there isn't much danger."

"I see. What will they do with him if they catch him?"

"I wouldn't imagine they thought that far. They'll probably lock him until the morning to see who he is, and then put a stake through his heart? I think that's the way to kill werewolves. That, or a silver arrow. Or was that for vampires? Maybe the werewolves, they just burn them alive?"

Ali's face turns a pale shade of green.

"But there'll be nothing to it. They'll have a great old time staying awake and chasing shadows, then go tell the others how brave they've been."

Ali says nothing. He just holds onto the wooden spoon and stirs that stinky potion like his life depends on it. He looks terrible, and Radu worries.

"How's the validé treating you, Ali?"

"She's good. She's happy that Mehmed likes the new girl, so she hasn't much to complain about other than Çandarlı Paşa. She doesn't like him much."

"That makes two of us," Radu says. "That old coot always tries to stir something up. Now he keeps bugging Mehmed with a cockamamie story of some Burgund galleys sailing up the Danube to attack the Ottoman outposts. And of course, he says my father is involved. He's always up for stirring trouble, that one."

"Is Hunyadi part of the deal, too?" Ali asks.

"Of course. Isn't he always? There's no trouble coming from the Rum that doesn't have Hunyadi front and center. He's supposed to meet them at Nikopolis on Saint Mary's day."

"How do you know?"

"Oh, I heard Çandarlı Paşa telling Mehmed, trying to get him to forget about Constantinople. Like that's going to happen."

Ali stirs silently, and Radu feels like maybe it's time to go. The eunuch is busy. But Radu worries about him.

"Are you sure you're OK, Ali?"

"Sure."

"Would you... would you and your friends maybe like to meet in my room?"

Ali's smile is all the reward he needs.

"Tomorrow after third prayer? I can send word to the boys."

Ali nods. Tears flow down his cheeks, dripping into the potion. Radu laughs.

"Be careful. You don't know what those tears will do to your potion. What if they make him grow fur instead of healing his skin?"

They laugh, and Radu leaves, happy that he got to see Ali. And maybe helped him a little.

Then a thought crosses his mind: How come Ali hasn't heard about the werewolf? The whole palace talks about nothing else, and Ali always knows everything about everybody.

CHAPTER 26
SESSIZ

Ali pours the chilled potion into a flask, corks it and heads back to the sarayi. God knows she did her best to find the blue omag, the wolfsbane root she needs for Kemal's potion. She looked for it high and low, but since Lena's failed escape, she never got out of the castle; and since Hüma has no urgent need to kill anyone these days, she found no excuse to take off.

So Ali ended up using wolf's paw seeds instead. She used twice as much as the recipe required, but she's anything but sure that the potion will work. And there's nothing else Ali can do to prevent Kemal from turning into a werewolf under the next full moon. It was bad enough the first time, when he went into hiding for the night and had to find some half-baked explanation of his absence for his roommates; but now, when the whole palace is getting ready to catch him?

She wonders where she could lock him up for the night, somewhere nobody can find him. But nothing comes to mind unless... unless she finds a way to put him in jail? But even then, the guards would see him and...

"Hello, Ali. How's your day going?"

It's her new friend Gülbahar, and she's even prettier than she was when she arrived. No wonder, with all the baths, massages, and good food. And her new peace of mind, now that she knows her brother is safe and cared for.

The little boy the validé named Sessiz, Silent, looks happy too. A big smile lights his face when he sees Ali, who takes care of him whenever Gülbahar is busy.

The two of them have invented their own sign language, and Ali can't help but wonder at his ingenious ways to communicate. He can ask for food or water, can say when he is tired or upset, and can even tell her how much he loves baklava. As a game, Ali started teaching him to count, read and write, and the boy learns everything with astonishing speed. Sometimes Ali wonders how he would have been if he wasn't deaf and mute, but there's no point in wondering. Life is what it is. He'd probably be working on his uncle's farm, and have a harder life than this.

"I'm good. You?" Ali asks. "How about you?" she asks Sessiz, ruffling his hair. The kid laughs, and Gulbahar smiles, but she looks worried.

"I wonder if you could take Sessiz for an hour or two? The validé wants to teach me the Ottoman Empire's rules of correct behavior and the purpose of a woman's life. Sessiz would be good for a while, but he gets bored sitting there doing nothing when he can't even hear her, and then she gets impatient."

"Of course." Ali signals Sessiz to come, and he lets go of his sister's hand and runs to hug Ali.

What are we doing today? Sessiz signs, lifting the palms of his hands to his sides.

"I don't know." Ali shrugs. "What would you like to do?" she asks, pointing at him and showing him her palms.

Read? Sessiz signs, opening his hands like he'd open a book.

Ali nods, and the boy laughs with excitement.

Gulbahar sighs. "Oh, Ali, you're so amazing. I don't know what I'd do without you."

"It's my pleasure. I love spending time with Sessiz. He's such a lovely boy, and he reminds me of my younger brother."

"I didn't know you had a brother."

"That was long ago. And far away. This is here and now."

"Do you miss your home?"

"I don't. I didn't like it much when I was there. How about you?"

"I don't miss home. It was a terrible place. But I miss…"

"Yes?"

"When the sultan's men found us, we were with a boy."

"Vlad."

"Yes."

"You miss Vlad?"

"He was good to us."

"Vlad?"

Gülbahar nods, and runs to the validé, who doesn't like to wait.

Ali has a hard time wrapping her mind around the thought that someone could miss Vlad. She's never met him, but she's seldom seen everyone agreeing on the same thing: Vlad Dracula, the Prince of Wallachia, is one of the meanest creeps who ever shadowed the earth. From the stable boys to Mehmed, and from the pigeons to Radu, everyone thinks that Edirne Palace is better off without Vlad, whose anger, hate and savagery poisoned everyone's air.

Even so, this nice young girl misses him, and says he's a good man. How can that be?

She remembers Mama Smaranda's words: Good and bad are often hard to tell apart. Good people do bad things and bad people do good things, and life is complicated.

She takes Sessiz's hand and leads him to the Cihannüma Pavilion, where the sultan's library is next to the masjid. The top floor octagonal room has windows overlooking the Edirne Palace, and its many shelves and low tables are loaded with the most precious books of the empire.

The guards watching the door recognize them and let them in. Ali picks her favorite book, a massive leather-bound tome describing every plant in the Ottoman Empire and its properties. She studied it cover to cover, looking for a something to replace the wolfsbane, but she found nothing but pictures of pretty flowers. Sessiz will like that.

The boy isn't reading, not really, not yet. But he loves touching the pages, smelling them, and following the intricate illuminations with his fingers. His mind is thirsty for knowledge.

"Look at the roses," Ali says, showing him the glorious profusion of red roses in one of the precious Chinese vases in a corner. She picks one and puts it in his hands.

"*Gül.* Rose," she says, opening the book to show him the picture of a rose. She says it again and again, and the boy watches her lips saying it.

Then she shows him the written word. *Gül.*

The boy follows the letters with his finger, imprinting them in his mind.

He turns to Ali and smiles. He's got it.

"Huu," he says.

CHAPTER 27

GIURGIU, SEPTEMBER 1445

The Danube runs slowly near Giurgiu. After rushing over almost fifteen hundred miles from the Black Forest to pour out its heart in the Black Sea, crossing countless countries, bathing hundreds of cities and gathering the water of dozens of tributaries, the mighty river must be getting tired, Ștefan thinks. So, it slows down to meander around mudflats and circle hundreds of small islands, trying to decide where to go.

Still, this is not the mile-wide mass of brackish water that slips into the Black Sea two hundred miles east. Giurgiu is Wallachia's soft underbelly; it's the sore spot the Ottomans find easy to cross whenever the urge strikes them. Even more so since they captured the fort and can control over who crosses the river and when.

Ștefan stares at the sky. It's pitch dark, so there's at least another hour before dawn, but he can't wait to get going. Today's the day they plan to retake the fort from the Ottomans.

After their success at Turtucaia, the unlikely allies gained more confidence. They also learned to work together, though they still keep apart. While Wallerand de Wavrin's Burgund galleys swing softly with the current in the river like a flock of sleeping geese, the Wallachians camped on the Danube's north shore. No matter where you look, there's nothing but sleeping men. They snore like they don't have a care in the world, but Ștefan knows better. The Wallachians care, but they learned to live with the omnipresent danger. They're never sure if they'll survive another fight and get back home to hold their wives and kiss their children. Here in Wallachia, war is a way of life. You learn to live with it or lose your mind. And Ștefan feels like he's about to lose his.

He lies next to Mircea, who sleeps like a baby. Hard to believe, when the battle is looming, but it's true. He's not faking it. There's nothing fake about Mircea. He's exactly who he shows himself to be.

The day they returned from Berzunți, Mircea went to see Vlad Dracul and took Ștefan with him.

"Father, I want to get married."

Vlad Dracul looked at him like he'd lost his mind. "Married? Why?"

"I fell in love."

Vlad laughed so hard he choked. He laughed like Ștefan had never heard him laugh before. "What does that have to do with anything?"

"I fell in love and I want to marry her."

"What for?"

"To... be with her..."

"Be with her then. You don't need to get married for that. You've done it before. Give her a little money and..."

"She's not that kind of girl."

"OK then. Get her a little house on a plot of land and a cow, and go see her whenever you feel like it," Vlad Dracul said.

"But Father..."

"Is she a princess?"

"No."

"Is she high nobility?"

"No."

"Listen Mircea, I hate to break it to you, but you're not free to marry. You're already married to your job. You're soon to be the Voivode of Wallachia, and you'll marry when we find you a match that will bring Wallachia a worthwhile alliance and further our fight. As a matter of fact, this Transylvanian countess related to Hunyadi is looking for a husband. I didn't think you were ready to marry, but if that's how you feel..."

"Father. My heart is taken."

"What does that have to do with anything? This is not about your heart. Not even about your man parts. You don't have to bed the countess unless you want to — and I wouldn't. They say she's still got a couple of teeth left, but her brains are mostly gone. Still, she'd bring a valuable alliance and she wouldn't even notice when you sneak out to see your other girl."

Mircea stared at Vlad Dracul like he's seen a ghost.

"You're joking, right?"

"Not at all. You're a prince. Princes don't marry for love. That's why they all have oodles of bastards. Like Mircea, your grandfather. And Ștefan's grandfather, Alexandru. We marry whoever will benefit our country, like we're supposed to. Then, on the lonely nights when life gets too hard, we seek love in hidden places to soothe our souls. The next day, we return to our wives and our duty. Marriage is just another one of a voivode's many duties. I should have told you about it long ago."

"But Father..."

"What?"

"How about Mother?"

"Your mother was the daughter of Alexandru the Good, the Voivode of Moldova. She came from the wrong side of the bed, like Ștefan's father did, but she brought a valuable alliance."

"Don't you love her?"

"Of course I do. She's the mother of my children."

Mircea looked crushed, and Ștefan felt sorry for him.

"Ștefan?" Vlad turned to face him.

"Yes."

"That applies to you, too. You're just as committed to Moldova as Vlad is to Wallachia. When it comes time for you to marry, you'll have to listen to your elders and bring Moldova the best possible alliance, whether that means that you need to put off the candle when you go to bed or not. Your life is not your own. Your life belongs to your country."

Unlike Mircea, Ștefan found comfort in Vlad Dracul's words. Instead of scaring him, those words gave him hope.

"That's enough for now. Time to get ready for battle. You boys will take our men and meet Wallerand at Silistra, and I'll come meet you all in Giurgiu. Make sure you keep the Burgunds on the straight and narrow. They don't know what they're dealing with."

Vlad Dracul was right. Wallerand and his Burgunds are struggling. They don't understand the Ottomans' thinking, don't know the terrain, and don't see the weather changing, nor the tricks the Danube plays on them. In this unfamiliar territory, they're like sitting ducks.

But for the prisoner Mircea's men caught, they'd have stepped into the trap the Ottomans set for them at Silistra, where thirty thousand Ottoman soldiers had waited for them in the fortress. That could have been the end of the campaign, of Wallerand the Wavrin, and of his galleys. Thanks to God and Mircea, they dodged that one, but there'll be more. Maybe even today, when they plan to take Giurgiu, the most important fort on the Danube.

If only Wallerand listens to Mircea instead of listening to Cardinal Condulmer, the pope's envoy, that would do them a lot of good.

CHAPTER 28
THE UGLY FORT

Even gilded by sunrise, Giurgiu's fort isn't pretty. Sturdy and ungraceful, its square tower sticks out of one of the Danube's many islands surrounded by four great stretches of stone walls. The corner towers are taller than five men standing on top of each other and fortified with crenels and wooden machicolations, square holes allowing the besieged to pour every kind of misery over their assailants, from rocks to tar and hot oil. Just thinking about this turns Ștefan's stomach.

Mircea's tiny wooden boats have a hard time following Wavrin's galleys. The heavy rains up in the mountains have doubled the Danube's muddy waters. The slow, lazy river turned wild and unruly, so the galley oarsmen grunt as they row, struggling to stay the course, while Wavrin's archers hold their arrows ready. Fighting the current behind them, the tiny Wallachian boats struggle to stay afloat. A gust of wind whips the water, bringing the fall's chill from the mountains, and Ștefan shivers.

But the galleys are finally there. Wallerand's soldiers disembark on the island and look up the river, waiting for the Wallachians to land. The tiny boats are still fighting the current dragging them away when the fort's gates crash open to vomit a whole army of angry Ottomans. The silence is shattered as the sultan's men rush the Burgunds with kilijes, tirpans, and battle axes. Blood-curdling screams split the sky as iron meets iron, arrows pierce bodies and swords slice through chain mail, flesh and bone. The Ottomans are going all-out to finish the Burgunds before the Wallachians land.

Dark with anger, Mircea stands in his boat, holding on to the men on the oars.

"Get ready! Fire!" he shouts.

Thankfully, the Wallachian archers are used to firing on the fly. Before Mircea's words die down, a cloud of arrows descends on the Ottomans like hungry vultures over corpses, and, more often than not, they find their targets.

Between the Burgund's heavy killing swords and the Wallachian's murdering arrows, the sultan's men have no choice but to retreat. They're back inside the fort before the dugouts land - all, but for those who'll never walk again. And just like that, the first battle is over before the Wallachians set foot on the shore.

"Nicely done!" Ștefan jumps out of his boat, his sword ready.

"That was just the beginning. This one will be a hard nut to crack," Mircea says, looking up at the tower hiding the sun.

He's right. Arrows whizz and stones fly out of sling-shots, darkening the sky, coming from behind the walls. Mircea's men step back, but there's no cover. The Ottomans hide behind thick stone walls, while the Christians stand in the open, waiting to get slaughtered.

Mircea shakes his head.

"That's no good. We're too exposed down here. Let's get a wagenburg going."

The Burgunds wonder what he means, but the Wallachians know. They've seen the wagenburgs at work in Varna. They scatter about the island to gather the carts the Ottomans abandoned and tie them together into a rolling fort they reinforce with their shields. In mere minutes, they build a mobile barricade that the archers and crossbowmen can hide behind to shelter from the Ottomans' stones and arrows.

But the fort's walls are thick, and the enemies behind them are protected. No matter how good the archer, arrows won't cut through stone walls.

"Let's bring over the cannons and the bombard," Wallerand de Wavrin says.

His men set to do it, but it's a thankless job. Bringing the heavy weapons from the galley takes them the rest of the day. By sunset, the Burgunds are exhausted and hungry, while the fort is as good as new.

"Now what?" Ștefan asks, watching the sun go down from the Danube's Wallachian shore where they set camp.

"We try again tomorrow," Mircea says, pouring wine from his flask. He raises his cup.

"To victory."

Ștefan touches it with his. His soul is torn between loving Mircea and hating him. He's never seen somebody he'd rather be like than Mircea. That man is Ștefan's hero, except that he's got his eyes on Lena. And that, Ștefan can't handle.

But, by what Vlad Dracul said, his chances of marrying Lena are nil. And Lena won't settle for a house and a cow instead of a ring that would make her Wallachia's First Lady someday. Or would she?

CHAPTER 29

EDIRNE, SEPTEMBER 1445

The melancholic laments of the fourth call to prayer wash over the Edirne Palace from every minaret in the city. The Transylvanians listen to it sitting cross-legged in Radu's room, their faces long, their thoughts gloomy. They're in trouble.

They've been racking their brains for a fix to Kemal's problem, but couldn't find it. The full moon is tomorrow, and Ali found no wolfbane, so there's little chance that her potion will help. They only have one more day to find a solution.

"How about we ask Radu to let us use his room tomorrow night, then we lock you in and unlock you in the morning?" Isa asks.

Ali shakes her head.

"What will we tell him we need it for? Where would Radu go? And how will we explain the wrecked room afterwards? Then there's the howling. They'll hear him, and they'll come to look."

"Do you have a better idea, then?"

"I wish I did."

"Maybe they won't catch him," Isa says. "After all, he's faster and stronger than anyone else when he's human, let alone as a werewolf."

"But what if they do? The whole palace is getting ready for

the hunt. The place crawls with guards anyhow, but tomorrow will be worse. Even those who should go to sleep won't, since every stable boy, cook, and eunuch wants to see the show. And they'll all have bows, swords and arquebuses. Or at least fishing nets."

Kemal sighs. His eyes are bloodshot, and he looks drawn and tired. Ali's heart weeps for him.

"Maybe the potion you made will work," he says.

"Don't I wish," Ali says.

"Me too," Kemal says. "But if it doesn't, I may have to go."

"Go where?"

"Back to Transylvania."

"How?"

"If I make it out of the castle, I'll head north. I'm much faster as a wolf, and I never get tired. I should be way north of Edirne before I return to human form at dawn. Then I'll just hide and take my chances."

Ali and Isa look at each other. The chances for a hunted man to make it out of the Ottoman Empire are slim. And even then, he'll have to cross the Danube, then walk north through the whole of Wallachia before getting to the mountains to pass into Transylvania.

"And how will you get out of the castle?" Isa asks.

"One way is through the gate," Kemal answers.

"It's always locked and guarded."

"Unless we trick them into opening it," Ali says.

"You have an idea?"

"Not yet."

"Another way is over the wall," Kemal says.

"That wall is thirty feet high. There's no way you can jump over it, even as a werewolf."

"Not from the ground. But maybe from a tower?"

"That's even higher. You'll break your neck in the fall. If you're lucky. If you're not, you'll break your back. They'll take you alive, and you'll wish you weren't."

No matter how much they think and talk, there's no solution. And it's time to go.

"I guess I'll just have to hope the potion works," Kemal says as he leaves. "I just want to tell you both that I love you. You're the best friends I could hope for. You've been more of a family to me than my own."

"Shut up," Isa says. "We can't deal with that right now. We'll find a way."

Ali hugs them and goes back to the sarayi. Her work doesn't stop just because her friend is in danger. The validé always needs her for something or other, and she gets miffed if she has to wait.

At the door, she bumps into Gülbahar, who's looking for her. As always, the girl holds Sessiz by the hand.

"There you are! Ali, can you please keep him for a couple of hours? The validé called me."

This one time, Ali would love to say no, but she can't. Taking care of the sarayi women is her job. And Gülbahar is the sultan's favorite.

"Sure," she mumbles, hoping it won't be long. She needs to find a way to save Kemal, and she's running out of time.

"There." Gülbahar hands her a leather-bound tome. "This is his new favorite book. The sultan, in his kindness, allowed him to borrow it, since he's so obsessed with it. Maybe you could look through it with him."

"Sure. What is it?"

"Pictures of the Edirne Castle. A collection of the construction drawings. Sessiz loves the pictures of the gardens, the baths, the kitchens with all their utensils, and especially the secret passages. I've never seen him so obsessed with anything."

"Wow. That sounds great. Sessiz and I, we'll have fun with it. We'll even go check out some of those places in person. Take your time and don't rush back. We'll be all right."

"Thank you, Ali. I don't know what I'd do without you."

"Same here. Let's go check this out, Sessiz. I can't wait."

CHAPTER 30

THE WEREWOLF HUNT

As the sun goes down, the shadows grow longer, and the Edirne Palace gets hopping. It's like every person in the palace is out and about, looking for the best place to hide. The janissaries, the stable boys, even the women in the sarayi are ready for a hunt like no other, since nobody's ever tried to hunt a werewolf.

The janissaries-in-training at the palace school team up in small groups, deciding who'll watch the gates, who'll hide in the gardens, and who'll carry which weapon. They devise secret codes, passwords and signals to communicate that the werewolf won't understand.

"Aren't you worried that he'll bite you, and you'll become a werewolf too?" Kemal asks.

"He doesn't stand a chance. The palace is full of armed people who'll gang up on him wherever he goes. Where do you want to be?"

"I... I'm not sure that's a good idea. I really don't want to get bit. I think I'll just stay in my room and lock the door."

They laugh at him. "Really? You, the Kırkpınar winner? Suit yourself, you chicken. You know the sultan put a prize on his head?"

"No."

"Whoever catches or kills him gets an extra year of salary. Whoever helps gets an extra month."

Kemal shrugs. "Good luck."

The boys leave, and he lies on his bed, waiting for the dusk. Soon now.

When the light starts to fade, he slips out and sneaks to Ali's kitchen, where she's waiting.

"I've got something for you," she says.

"What?"

"Look."

She unrolls a piece of paper with a sketch.

"What is this?"

"It's a map of the kitchens. This is the soup kitchen. And see this?" She points to a circle.

"What is it?"

"It's the sewer tunnel that drains the refuse from the kitchen. It starts in the middle of the floor, under a metal grate, and runs to the Tunca river, a hundred feet away. It looks big enough for you to get through, but that grate is awful heavy. I couldn't lift it, but I think you can."

She unrolls another sheet of paper. "This is a rough map from Edirne to Kronstadt. Once you get to the Tunca, you have two hundred flat miles straight north to get to the Danube near Giurgiu, and out of the Ottoman Empire. The Danube is a mile wide there, so you'll have to find a way to cross. Once you do, you're in Wallachia. If you get in trouble, tell them you have a message from Radu, Vlad Dracul's son. That may help. But otherwise, just head north towards the mountains. Another hundred miles or so, and you should be at the foot of the Carpathians and almost out of trouble. Then just another little push and you're home."

"Thank you, Ali."

Ali nods. Her eyes are so bright he knows she's about to cry. But she doesn't.

"I poured grease all over them so the water doesn't spoil them if they get wet, but I wouldn't trust it. Better look at them now, before you get them in the Tunca."

"If I get in the Tunca. I drank your potion. It was so disgusting I think it might work."

"I sure hope it does," Ali whispers, glancing out the door. The sky has darkened, and the glowing orb of the moon rises behind the palace walls.

Kemal watches it, waiting for his body to change. But nothing happens. Nothing but a stir in his guts, like a terrible itch he can't scratch that makes him want to open his mouth wide and holler.

He bites his lip to keep quiet and watches the moon grow bigger and bigger, calling him.

He doesn't move. His feet grasp the dirt floor and his fists get so tight that his nails cut through his skin, but he stays put, fighting the change with all his might.

One, two, three more heartbeats and the moon floats above the horizon. Her glowing orb is now perfectly round as she smiles, pulling Kemal to her. But he fights her tooth and nail.

CHAPTER 31
A NARROW ESCAPE

But without the wolfsbane, Kemal's will is no match for the pull of the moon. His racing heart pumps cursed hot blood through his veins and a wave of excruciating pain floods his body like poison. His face gets pulled and stretched into a muzzle. His spine bends and twists, forcing him to drop on all fours and watch his hands turn into massive paws ending in dagger-like claws.

He's no longer human. Once again, the moon turned him into this terrible creature he hates, and his soul aches even worse than his body. He hurts too much to be scared, but he's heartbroken that he'll be losing his friends. Whether he dies or escapes, he'll leave them behind in enemy territory to fend for themselves. And he's deeply ashamed.

But, all of a sudden, he can see in the dark. He notices the warm breaths of the would-be werewolf hunters hiding in dark corners, and the black bats crossing the dark sky are as clear as fireflies. His ears can catch a million things he never heard as a human, like the breath of the mouse hiding in the corner of Ali's kitchen, and the trees whispering to each other outside. And the smells! Oh, the smells! The good ones, like mutton and chicken and blood, and the awful ones, like Ali's plants, especially the garlic. He hates garlic. He's not supposed to, since he's not a vampire, but garlic is the refuge of the smelling destitute. Once you smell garlic, you can't smell anything else. Phew.

"I'm so sorry."

Ali's hand touches his shoulder. He licks it and growls, since he can talk no more.

"Does it hurt?"

Kemal nods. Ali's eyes shine, and he knows she's crying. Hard to believe, but she cares for him like no one else ever did.

"Isa should give the signal any minute now. There, let me get you ready." She rolls the maps and puts them in a bag she hangs around his neck. She hugs him, and her tears run into his nose, making him sneeze.

"I love you. Take care. Let us know how you did, if you can."

A blood-curling howl splits the night at the opposite end of the palace. Then another.

Someone screams: "He's here, heading to the gardens."

That's Isa, clearing his way. They watch a slew of werewolf hunters run that way without looking back. Time to get moving.

Kemal glances at Ali one last time, then squeezes through the door to look for the soup kitchen. It's not far, just a couple doors to the left, and it's empty, since every single cook left his work to catch the monster.

Kemal sniffs for the tunnel. It's there, but like Ali said, it starts beyond the heavy metal grate letting the blood and filthy juices from the butchered animals flow down to the cleansing Tunca, which takes them away.

Kemal tries to lift the grate with his fangs, but he can't. The holes are too small for his massive snout, so he can't grab it.

He looks for a tool, and finds the hooked iron bar the cooks used to pick the hot pots from the fire. He hooks the grill, levers the bar over a milling stone and steps on its end. The grill lifts like it's magic. Kemal twists it, and the grill drops on the floor with a clang, leaving the tunnel open.

But will this path work? Can he squeeze all the way through it?

What if it narrows, and he gets stuck? What if there's another grill at the end? If so, he's out of luck. Once he's stuck in the tunnel, there's no way to climb back.

He's still thinking when he hears steps. Someone's coming. Not one. Lots of them. He takes a deep breath, sends a last good thought to his friends, then jumps into the tunnel.

He falls hard. The pit is steep and narrow, and there's a long drop to the river, if that's where it's going. Kemal slides head first, then rolls and twists and bruises as he tries to dig his claws into the walls to slow down. But his claws fail. The tunnel walls are hard as a rock and covered in the slippery slime of many years of discarded grease.

His shoulders ache, his paws hurt, and so does everything else by the time he crashes head first into something. He struggles to his paws, but the pain clouds his senses. His vision turns black and the dark water sucks him in.

CHAPTER 32
GIURGIU, SEPTEMBER 1445

Hiding in the dark marshes of the Bulgarian shore, Ștefan listens to the silence and struggles to make sense of everything that happened. He's not alone, he's with Mircea and a bunch of his men, but the quietude is unsettling. There's no sound other than the birds' chirping and the roaring of the Danube in the distance. Nobody would think that a whole army hides under the weeping willows and the bushes.

They had a few rough days. Wallerand de Wavrin, the Burgunds' captain general, has been walking around with his arm in a sling after being hit by an Ottoman rock. He shouted order after order, acting like he knew what he was doing, even when everyone could see he didn't. He had his men fire the cannons and the bombard over and over until the bombard overheated and blew up, killing two of his people but leaving the fortress unharmed.

He blamed Mircea, of course. "You said we needed to take this fort, and take it fast. There now. Are you happy?"

Mircea looked anything but happy. With his dark eyebrows knitted above his narrowed eyes and his hand on his sword, he looked ready to silence Wavrin for good. But he bit his lip and went back to his men, leaving the Burgund standing. Ever since, they haven't said a word to each other. All communications went through Ștefan, who'd have gladly surrendered the honor.

Then Vlad Dracul emerged out of nowhere, bringing a whole army of fresh soldiers. He looked at the mess, shook his head and took Wallerand, Mircea, and Ștefan aside.

"We need to burn them out."

Wavrin stared at him. "What are you saying?"

"We'll pile wood against the towers and set them on fire. Sooner or later, they'll sue for peace."

The Burgund shrugged, but Vlad Dracul was right. It took the men a whole day to gather a mountain of dead wood and pile it up against the walls. The Ottomans hid inside, throwing rocks and shooting deadly arrows at anyone careless enough to come into their view. They lost three men that way.

But when the pile of wood got about as high as the men could build it, the Ottomans worried. They lowered dozens of burning baskets soaked in oil to set the wood on fire and chase the men feeding the pile away. But they'd waited too long.

Fueled by a lucky gust of wind, the flames rose like the heads of hungry dragons. Minutes later, they'd swallowed the tower, and that was the end. Like Vlad Dracul said, the Ottomans sued for peace.

"Let's let them go," Vlad Dracul said to the Burgunds. "My father built this castle, and every stone in it is worth its weight in salt. Let them go so we can take the castle undamaged."

The cardinal wasn't pleased. "There are hundreds of Ottoman soldiers in there, with good armor and weapons and loot. Our men expect a reward after all their work and all the losses. They won't like to let them go."

But Wavrin has had it. His arm still in a sling, he started limping, too. He looked like he'd rather be anywhere else but in this godforsaken marsh where peasants fight with rocks and fire instead of killing each other properly with swords and halberds, like civilized people. And Vlad Dracul knew the Burgund would do whatever it took to be left alone.

"Have it your way," Wavrin said, heading back to his galley, where his doctors waited to bleed him and give him succor.

"They'll need your written permission to leave the fortress with their belongings and get to the Bulgarian shore," Vlad said.

Wavrin nodded as his people helped him to his galley. As soon as he was gone, Vlad Dracul turned to Mircea.

"Take Ștefan and a thousand fresh men. Cross the Danube three miles up, where the boats are waiting for you. The Ottomans will head towards Nikopolis to join the rest of their army. Hide and wait for them on the other side of the river, then ambush them. I want them all dead but for their subaşı. Bring him back alive. He's the bastard who betrayed me last time and made your brothers into hostages. I want to kill him myself."

Mircea nodded and left. Ștefan followed, though he was deeply troubled. "Are you really going to put the Ottomans through the sword? These men you promised to let go?"

Mircea gave him an icy look.

"I promised nothing. Absolutely nothing. As for Father, he promised to let them reach the Bulgarian shore alive, and that's exactly what he'll do. The rest is up to God."

Mircea headed to his men and chose the best. He ordered the officers to get ready and start west, up the Danube. The men got moving in small groups, then gathered out of sight.

The Ottomans got ready too. They loaded and tied their small horses to each other, head to tail. The first one got tied to the rowboat that carried their saddles. Four soldiers rowed it to the Bulgarian shore, and the horses followed, like they did every time the Ottomans crossed the Danube to set fires, kill women and children, and take slaves. Mircea watched them until they reached the shore, then spurred his horse.

"Let's go."

They rode west to the place of the crossing, where the canoes were already waiting. They loaded the men and crossed the Danube miles ahead of where the Ottomans were crossing downstream. As soon as they landed, they looked for shelter and hid in the green tangle of willows and cattails growing from the rich mud. It was cool in the shadows, but the blood running hot through their veins kept them warm.

Mircea climbed to the crook of an old weeping willow from where he could see the narrow trail the Ottomans had to take and made himself comfortable. Then he turned to Ștefan, sitting on a dead trunk.

"Ștefan, as a leader, you must pay attention to everything you say. Every word matters. Father promised to let the Ottoman soldiers reach the Bulgarian shore unharmed. He never promised to let them get away. That would have been foolish. They'd only come back next year, and the year after that, to plunder and kill."

Ștefan nods, but the thought of killing gives him no joy. The Wallachians sit quietly, holding their bows, arquebuses, and swords, and wait in the shadows. Birds sing, the wind plays in the branches, and happy fish jump in the Danube not far away. One could almost forget that in this peaceful setting, a thousand men are waiting for the signal to kill.

Until they hear the horses.

CHAPTER 33
SLAUGHTER

They aren't loud, the horses, their hooves drumming gently against the hardened earth. But the men are. They shout at each other in the Ottoman language that Ștefan doesn't understand. They let their weapons clatter against their shields, and they laugh like they don't have a care in the world. *What on earth is there to laugh at?* Ștefan wonders.

Then he realizes the men are high with the joy of being alive. They've narrowly escaped the burning fort and the attack of two armies with their heads on their shoulders, their belongings, and their horses. They think it's their lucky day.

They're wrong.

"No prisoners, but spare the horses, and the subaşı," Mircea whispers. "The voivode wants him. And remember that the sooner you kill them, the sooner you'll stop their suffering."

The Wallachians squeeze under the low tree branches, walking low like big cats. They make no noise other than breathing, while the Ottomans' chatter gets louder.

"Now," Mircea screams, jumping off his tree branch and pulling out his sword.

The surprise on the Ottomans' faces would be funny if it wasn't so sad, Ștefan thinks, then he has no more time for thinking. He pulls out his sword and slams it on the head of the first Ottoman he meets, a boy no older than himself. The boy falls at Ștefan's feet, and Ștefan ends his suffering with one hard blow to the neck. A stream of salty blood spurts into Ștefan's face. He wipes the blood out of his eyes and spits whatever got into his mouth, then looks for his next kill.

The Wallachians rush out of the bushes with their axes, maces and swords at the ready. All but the archers, who sit in the trees lining the road to have a better view. On Mircea's order, they release a cloud of arrows into the sipahis, the mounted Ottomans leading the retreat. Arrow after arrow takes down the riders, and the horses run free while the men sink in the mud on the side of the road.

The red-clad janissaries who follow on foot turn the corner and get within range. Within heartbeats, the arrows find them like bees find honey.

"Mind the late ones," Mircea shouts, cutting his way through the Ottomans like a farmer harvesting a wheatfield. "Don't let them go back. We need to get them all."

He's watching the tail end of the column, so he doesn't see the dark sipahi on a gray horse behind him. The Ottoman raises his kilij and aims at Mircea's neck, where his helmet ends but his armor hasn't started.

"Allahu Akbar!" he screams, swinging his blade.

Ștefan's sword sinks into the soft spot of his armpit to come out through his other shoulder, and the sipahi crashes over Mircea.

"Thank you, brother. I owe you one," Mircea says.

They carve their way through man after man, but the archers already did most of the damage. Two hundred Ottomans lay on the ground like dead porcupines, and the Wallachians finish the ones still moving. It's a carnage the likes of which Ștefan has never seen.

Mircea looks around, weighing the state of affairs. "Good work," he says, as two men bring him the subaşı.

The man's eyes are wild, his kaftan bloody and torn, and his voice is breaking. "You promised. You promised to let us go free."

"We promised to let you go free to Bulgaria. You were free in Bulgaria. We kept our promise."

"But why? Why did you do this?"

"You betrayed my father. Thanks to you, my brothers are hostages in Edirne, waiting to be slaughtered. That's why."

"But you're risking your brothers' lives! You're killing them!"

"I did what my father told me to. Vlad Dracul, the Voivode of Wallachia, is their father. He told me to bring you back alive without your men, and that's precisely what I will do."

The men take him away, and Mircea turns to the battlefield, but the battle is over. The Wallachians killed every wounded Ottoman, gathered the scattered horses, and collected all the armor and weapons that weren't too broken to serve.

He stumbles upon a janissary laying on the ground, and the man moans. Mircea pulls out his sword and severs his head with one smooth move. The man's mouth is still praying as the head rolls away from his body.

The men collect corpse after corpse, almost three hundred of them, and line them along the riverbank for anyone on the river to see. They add the severed limbs and heads without bothering to match them: Two heads, three arms, a leg, a hand, another leg.

The smell of blood has already called the vultures and the crows who circle up above, screaming at the men to get away from their food. An impatient crow lands on a bloody head nearby and pecks at an open blue eye.

Ștefan's stomach turns. This is the worst thing he's ever seen, even worse than the battlefield in Varna, and it takes all he's got to not retch.

Mircea comes bringing two horses. The two of them, with a few soldiers, will ride, while most of the people will cross back with the boats.

"Ștefan?"

Ștefan nods, struggling to swallow his saliva.

"I know it's ugly, but we had to do what we had to do. Remember that dead people don't come back to fight. Their deaths saved Wallachian lives."

"That, I get. But why display them like that?"

"For their brothers to see and remember, next time they want to come and fight us. It may not be pretty, but it works. Let's go."

Ștefan mounts the horse Mircea brought for him. It's a beautiful palfrey full of nerve. He didn't like the battle, and hates the scent of blood. He dances on his feet, ready to take off, and Ștefan struggles to hold him. *It must be the subaşı's horse*, Stefan thinks.

"The subaşı?"

"He won't need it anymore. The horse is yours now. My gift, to thank you for saving my life."

"Thank you, Mircea."

Ștefan pats the horse's neck and talks to him to soothe him. The palfrey pricks his ears and snorts indignantly, stomping his hooves, and Ștefan smiles. This is the best ride he's ever had, but he can't help but think that, if he didn't kill that sipahi, Mircea would be dead now. And he'd leave Lena alone.

CHAPTER 34

EDIRNE, SEPTEMBER 1445

Kemal opens his eyes to the darkness. Everything hurts. He can hear water running and smell mud, but he can't place them, since his brain is thick with fog. And he feels strange, as if his body is not his body. He struggles to his feet and looks around, trying to figure things out, then he remembers. He's no longer human. He's a werewolf, and he just escaped Edirne Palace.

He must have made it to the river. He remembers the cold darkness that engulfed him, but nothing else.

He's on a grassy riverbank surrounded by forest. Must be the palace hunting grounds, he thinks. The full moon glows in the middle of the sky, pouring silver light over the water, reminding him to hurry. He needs to make the most of his werewolf strength and speed before dawn, when he'll regain his human shape, and get far enough so they won't find him.

He struggles to his wobbly paws and lowers his head to drink from the river. But he forgets his thirst to stare at the face looking back. His head is huge, black, and furry, and he's got amber burning eyes and fangs the size of daggers. But more than anything, he loves the sharp triangular ears standing on top of his wolf's head. He moves his head

133

to one side, then the other, to check his profile, and what he sees makes him laugh. Not quite a laugh, more of a snort, but it's funny.

He never thought he'd like himself as a wolf, but he does. Not that it matters, since he doesn't have a choice, but it's the first time he's excited about his superpower instead of feeling guilty for it.

Somebody screams, far up in the castle, and Kemal wonders how the hunt is going. They won't find any werewolves up there, which is good, but he hopes his friends won't get in trouble. Everyone at the palace knows that Isa is his best friend. Ali too. In the morning, they'll discover he's missing. At best, they'll think the werewolf took him. At worst, they'll know he's the werewolf. Either way, his time with the janissaries is over.

Maybe his time on earth, too, unless he gets going.

He lifts his muzzle to sniff the air, and just like that, he knows he doesn't need Ali's maps. He doesn't need any map. He knows where home is, like birds do when they travel south every winter, and come back in spring.

He takes a deep breath and leaps forward. His senses tell him he's heading in the right direction, and he's overcome with joy. Tonight, everything is right about the world. He loves feeling his heart pumping blood into his strong, sleek body, his lungs sucking in the air, his paws pummeling the ground. He leaps over bushes, then trees, like he's weightless. He's free, and he owns the earth. He's dizzy with joy.

He runs so fast that the trees and the houses pass by in a blur. He's the wind blowing north and the shadow eating up the distance. He's drunk with speed and high with power, and he's never been happier.

Then he notices the sky fade to his right. The dawn is coming. The full moon, his goddess, is about to fade, and with her, so will his superpower. He'll turn back into an ordinary human, and he does not know where he is or what to do. So, against his every instinct, he slows down to a crawl.

Fields. Trees. Roads.

Mosques.

He's still in the Ottoman Empire. Of course he is. He had hundreds of miles to cover when he started last night, and he has yet to cross the Danube to get to Wallachia. But where is he?

The first rays of sun touch the earth and his power fades. His bones shrink, his vision dims, and he shivers, naked in the morning chill. He's human again, somewhere in the world where he has no friends. He needs a shelter to spend the day until tonight's darkness will give him cover to go north.

Far left, there's a shed in a field. A tool shed maybe? He heads there. The door is cracked open. He steps in.

Garden tools. Two barrels of water. Seeds.

He leans over a barrel and drinks all he needs. And that's a lot. He looks at himself in the wavy mirror of the water. Just like he thought. The wolf's gone, and the man is back, and he's not pretty. He'd rather be a wolf, but he's not, and won't be for another month, until the next full moon bestows her magic on him. He's just an awkward boy whose only friends are far away.

What's worst is that he's naked. How can he possibly make do with no clothes whatsoever? It was OK when he had fur, but now?

He takes the useless bag hanging around his neck and rips it with his teeth to cover his privates. It's not much, but it's better than being naked.

He's about to lie behind the barrels for a nap when the door screeches open.

"Come out. Now."

There's no point pretending he didn't hear them. They'll find him anyhow.

He steps out feeling like an idiot, buck naked but for the sack covering his privates. With a bit of luck, he might get a chance to run away.

But no. A dozen janissaries face him, armed with swords and bows. They wear the red uniform he wore only yesterday. The man who speaks is the smallest. He stands behind the others, but acts like he's their boss.

"Who are you?"

He thinks hard and fast.

"I... escaped. I was a Wallachian prisoner, but I managed to escape."

"Where are you from?"

He can't think of a good answer other than the truth. "Transylvania."

"Why did they take you as a prisoner, then? I thought you two were allies?"

"I told them I was a friend of the Ottoman Empire."

The man laughs. "Excellent. You'll get to prove that. Take him."

The men grab him and shackle his hands and feet, then drag him to a cart. Kemal doesn't know where he's going, but he's pretty sure it's not where he wants to go.

"Where are we?" he asks.

"Varna."

"Where are you taking me?"

"To the port."

"Why?"

"You're embarking on a galley."

"Where am I going?"

The Ottoman laughs.

"Wherever the galley goes. You'll have the very special honor of being one of our sultan's oarsmen, and serve the Ottoman Empire you say you like."

"Why?"

"Oarsmen don't last long, so there's always a need. You look young and strong. They'll love having you."

"How long will I be there for?"

"For as long as Allah, the Wise and Merciful will let you live. Oarsmen only leave their post when they die."

CHAPTER 35

NIKOPOLIS, SEPTEMBER 1445

S tefan shivers and pulls his cloak closer. The harsh wind blowing from Transylvania's mountains reminds him that winter is coming. The Danube heard it too. Every morning, the water's edges are crisp with ice. Not for long though, the ice melts away as soon as the sun shines upon it, but it's a dire warning.

Hunyadi knows it. His stormy face says that much, as he looks up and down the river. His eyes take in Wavrin's galleys swinging in the current like a raft of fat ducks, the Wallachians who, after campaigning for a month, look worse for the wear, and his own squeaky-clean men just in from their comfortable homes.

Vlad Dracul also knows it, as he looks lovingly at his rag-tag army. His Wallachians did the best they could do, and he's proud to be their leader. But winter is coming, and the Danube is fickle.

Mircea knows it too, as he told Ștefan only last night. "After all the delay Hunyadi wanted, we're finally all here at Nikopolis, but it's way too late in the season. There's no way to know how long we've got before the Danube freezes over and strands the galleys."

The only one who doesn't know it is Wavrin. He bursts with joy, blabbering about how they'll finally start the real campaign against the Ottomans. Every fight up to this, like Giurgiu, Russe and Turtucaia, they were just practice. Whoever even heard of them? But now that Hunyadi came, they'll finally go to war against the Ottomans and do the right thing for God, the pope, and their sponsors.

Hunyadi's face darkens, and his proud mustache wilts. He tried to visit Wavrin in his cabin last night, as the Burgund lay in bed with a gout attack caused by too much meat and red wine, but he couldn't get in. His white Milanese armor was too wide for the door to the captain general's cabin. He gave up and went to meet the cardinal, telling Wavrin he'll revisit after he sheds his armor.

But now that Wavrin left his cabin and Hunyadi shed his armor, it's time to talk. They take their seats around the luxurious dining table and watch the servants pour wine in filigreed silver cups.

Grinning from ear to ear, Wavrin lifts his cup to Hunyadi.

"I'm so happy to see you and your men arrive! We're finally ready to start. So, let me tell you what I was thinking. If we're ready to head south tomorrow..."

Hunyadi shakes his head.

"Captain general. We came to Nikopolis as promised, on St. Mary's Day, so we kept our word. But it's now too late to start a campaign on the Danube. We never know for sure when the Danube will freeze, but it won't be long. And the last thing you want is to get stuck in the middle of the frozen river. The Ottomans will come and put your ships to fire. They'll capture every one of you and ask for a huge ransom to let you go. If you can't pay, they'll sell you all as slaves. That's a terrible fate for anyone, let alone noble knights like yourselves."

Wavrin's joy melts. "What are you saying?"

"I strongly advise you to head back to the Black Sea without delay."

"You mean *you're* leaving?" Wavrin asks.

"Tomorrow."

The scowl the captain general gives Hunyadi would rattle a lesser man.

"We came all this way to save your king, the King of Hungary and Poland, but we made no progress. And now you tell us to go back?"

"The King of Hungary is dead. I did my best to save him, but there's only that much stupidity one can overcome. His head is in Bursa. Sultan Murad sent it to them as a gift. I saw the king die, and nothing you can do will bring him back. I'll head home tomorrow and I advise you to do the same."

Wavrin looks at him like he's just sprouted horns. "Really? You think we should go home? After all the time, the money, and the men you had us waste? Go home with nothing?"

"You'll keep your lives and your freedom. That ought to be worth something."

"I can't believe this. What will the pope say?" Wavrin shakes his head and turns to Vlad Dracul. "What do you think?"

"I agree. Hunyadi knows this place and the Ottomans; You don't. You should head home as soon as you can. The Danube might freeze at any time, and you really don't want to be here when she does."

Wavrin sighs, and suddenly, he looks much older.

"It would all have been different, of course, if Hunyadi came in August, as he promised. Almost a month ago. We would have had time," Vlad Dracul says.

Hunyadi's face turns an ugly shade of red.

"What are you saying?"

"That you bided your time and knew damn well what you were doing. You chose to postpone until it was too late. So, you got the honor of the partnership without having to fight."

"I fought the Ottomans as much as you did. And I've beaten them more often than you, who often choose to pay them tribute. In money and blood."

"I always do what's best for my country."

"So do I. Listen, Vlad. I've beaten you before. Many times. But listen: Next time I'm not going to beat you. I'm going to kill you."

Vlad laughs like it's a joke, but Hunyadi isn't kidding.

"You'll have to kill me first," Mircea says.

"Gladly."

Mircea's hand flies to the hilt of his sword, but Vlad Dracul grabs his arm. "Let's go, boys. We wasted enough time here."

On the way home, Mircea tells his father: "I'm sorry, Father, for wasting us all this time."

Vlad Dracul's eyes widen. "Are you kidding? We wasted nothing. We showed the Burgunds and their pope who is reliable and who isn't. You boys got to play at war. And we took Giurgiu. My father built that fort, and it's worth its weight in salt. With it in our hands, we'll show the Ottomans a thing or two next time they decide to cross the Danube to loot. I couldn't be happier."

"And we got all those Bulgarians," Ștefan says.

Vlad Dracul sighs.

"There's that. What the heck are we going to do with twelve thousand Bulgarians who crossed the river, asking for shelter? Half of them are just women and kids."

"But the others are men, ready to fight. And they don't love the Ottomans any more than we do. I think you were wise to offer them shelter."

"I hope you're right. But the Ottomans won't like it one bit."

CHAPTER 36

EDIRNE, SEPTEMBER 1445

Edirne Palace is still in turmoil. The morning after the werewolf hunt was gloomy, since many got hurt. Those who fell chasing shadows are nursing broken limbs and wounded egos. The ones got some mistook for werewolves and shot at, have arrow wounds to nurse. An old man's heart stopped beating after the werewolf jumped at him, some say. A young cook's assistant fell in the kitchen drain and drowned in the Tunca. They found his body two miles down.

The whole foolishness would strike Radu as funny, if not for the deaths. You'd think that learned people like the Ottomans would know better. Everyone knows that werewolves don't exist. The mythical creature the Transylvanians call *vârcolac*, a human cursed to turn into a wolf under the full moon, is nothing but a legend, just like the vampires and the striga.

Thinking of Transylvania reminds him of Ali, and he wonders if the kid is all right. He'd better check on him to see. He heads to Ali's kitchen, but finds it closed and guarded by two janissaries who shoo him away.

"You can't get in here. The empire is investigating."

"Investigating what?"

"The escape of the werewolf. Please keep away."

That's even worse than Radu expected. They're going after Ali? But why? Just because he's Transylvanian? How stupid is that?

He can't resist ribbing them. "Did you find any evidence?"

"We are not at liberty to tell you. Please clear the way."

Ali is in trouble. That's insane. Radu goes to the palace school to look for Kemal. Again, guards shoo him away. "We are investigating. Please stay away."

They've totally lost their minds.

"Where is he?"

They shrug and don't answer.

He goes to look for Isa, but he's missing too. What the heck? This looks like an all-out assault against the Transylvanians. He can't find any of them and can't even find out why. He has to do something, and the only thing he can think about doing is to speak to the sultan.

Mehmed has been hard to find lately. He's always busy in some meeting or another. And even when he's not, he's pretty quick to send Radu away. It may have to do with Mehmed's new girl, Radu thinks, though he can't understand why Mehmed has no more time for him. This time, however, he must see him, so he insists, something he's never done.

Mehmed comes out. His eyes are red, his face drawn, and he looks like he hasn't slept in a week.

"Hi. What's up?"

That's not the welcome Radu hoped for, but he's too worried about his friends to drop it.

"I'm sorry to bother you. This is about my friend Ali, a eunuch in the sarayi, the kid from Transylvania. I can't find him. The guards turned me away when I looked for him."

"Is that the one who was friends with the werewolf?"

"The werewolf?"

"Yes. They say that one of the young janissaries is a werewolf. The Kırkpınar winner. I guess we'll have to repeat that tournament.

Nevermind. They say the eunuch helped him escape. He's in the dungeons."

"Ali? In the dungeons?"

Mehmed shrugs. "The eunuch. And some accountant in the tax department, who they say was his other friend."

"Isa?"

"I don't know. Either way, he's in the dungeons too. I'll see their cases the day after tomorrow."

"But what did they do?"

"Something to help him escape, I think. I don't have the details yet."

"What are you going to do?"

"Depends on what they tell me. I'll do my best to judge them fairly. But what's it to you?"

"I know them. Ali is my friend. He helped me when... when things were rough for me. I'm worried about him. And the others."

"Well, hopefully, they had nothing to do with the werewolf."

Radu loses it.

"There are no such things as werewolves. Nobody has ever seen one. It's nothing but superstition and stupidity."

"Tell that to the viziers. They're all over this like stink on shit. So is everyone else. I wish they existed, though. I'd like to have one. If you can get me one, I'll be glad to employ him and set his friends free."

"Mehmed, can I please see Ali?"

"What for?"

"To tell him he's not alone in the world. That somebody, somewhere, cares about him. Even somebody as useless as me."

"You're not useless, Radu."

Radu shrugs. "I've been useless to you lately. You no longer have time for me, and I understand. You're busy. You have better people to see and better things to do. But Ali doesn't. I want to tell him I'm there for him, like he's been there for me when you... when I was in trouble."

"Radu, you're not useless to me. I love you with all my heart, and

I'm trying to keep you safe, whether or not you understand it. But I'll arrange for you to see your friend."

"Thank you, my sultan."

Radu goes back to his room pondering this mess. Can Kemal really be a werewolf? Did Ali help him escape?

And if he did, so what? That's what one does for their friends. He helped him, Radu, the day he stabbed Mehmed.

CHAPTER 37

INSIDE THE DUNGEON

Hidden deep under the Edirne Palace's luxurious rooms, the dungeons are anything but luxurious. They aren't even clean or warm. Curled on her straw bed in her tiny cell, Ali stares at her old cross. It glows blue, for friendship, with makes no sense whatsoever. She drops the cross and closes her eyes, trying to feel what happened to Kemal. She hopes he made it to freedom, and this all is not in vain.

The guards picked her up in the morning and dragged her to her little potion kitchen. "Is this your place?"

Ali nodded.

"What do you do here?"

"I brew healing potions and make healing ointments for the people in the palace."

"Like who?"

"Like whoever needs them."

"Did you shelter anyone here?"

"No."

"A werewolf?"

Ali laughed. It's not funny, really, but what else can she do?

"No."

"Are you sure?"

She looked at the guard, and from the way they measured her, she knew they had something. She didn't know what — whether it was werewolf footprints or Kemal's dead body carrying something from her — but she knew it was something she'd have to explain. Eventually.

"I'm sure."

They brought her down a set of stairs she'd never seen before and took her underground to the dungeons. That's Edirne's jail, where all those who broke the law wait for the sultan's justice, before ending on the stakes by the gates or in a bag at the bottom of the Tunca. The sultan's justice seldom leaves anyone alive. If you're down here, you're guilty, unless you can prove you're not. So Ali doesn't hold much hope.

But, for the first time in forever, she's got a little time to herself. She's been so busy juggling Hüma's demands, her friends' needs, her plans to reconnect to Kronstadt and worrying about Kemal that she didn't have time to think, really think, about her own fate. What is she doing here? Why? How much longer?

She hugs herself to keep away the chill, and she thinks. She's not a boy, and not a eunuch. She's just a girl struggling to make it through a man's world. And the Ottoman Empire is the ultimate man's world. Here, women are locked and silenced. They're not supposed to be seen and rarely heard.

But what is she doing here?

The Kronstadt link fell apart, but she doesn't owe them much. They fed and trained her and they promised her a better life if she makes it back, in exchange for a life of slavery, deception and mortal danger behind the enemy lines. Here, at the Ottoman Court, she's not only a slave, she's a spy. Not only is she at everyone's beck and call all the time, but she risks her life every day. If they find her, she's dead.

And what for? What is this all about? What is her mission?

She remembers Mama Smaranda's words: "You're here on earth to make the world a better place." That sound nice, but how can she accomplish that? What's she supposed to do?

Well, the first thing would be to not get killed. And the second would be to get free.

Then what? What does she want to change about the world? If there was only one thing she could change, what would it be?

And it comes to her.

If there's one thing she'd like to change, it's the fate of women. She hates to see women being treated as second-class humans, locked and controlled by the men in their lives: their fathers, their husbands, even their sons. She hates to feel inferior to men. Why should she? Just because they have something dangling between their legs and she doesn't? They can surely keep that to themselves.

She smiles, filled with a peace she's never felt. She knows she found her mission, and she's thrilled. She'll make the world a better place for women. She doesn't yet know how, but she's glad she got that far.

Mama Smaranda would approve. Lena would, too.

Ali curls on her side, hugging her knees for warmth, and lets herself drift to sleep, relieved she found her mission. She's here to set the women free.

But first, she has to stay alive.

CHAPTER 38

BERZUNȚI, SEPTEMBER 1445

The forest is peaceful at dusk, and the fall has been gentle this year. Up here, the leaves are turning already, and the morning frost whitens the grass until the sun eats it up, but the days are warm and the evenings soft.

Lena loves watching the river flow. Solitude and silence do good to her soul. Washing clothes gives her time to be alone with her thoughts, and that's precious.

She was overjoyed to come home, and she couldn't wait to show her parents what she brought. Mehmed sent her home with a cart full of silks, goods and money. He wanted her to be safe and self-reliant. With what he gave her, she could buy half the village.

Her parents were stunned. Her mother wiped her eyes, and her father gave her a heavy look. "What did you do to get all this?"

"I slept in the sultan's bed."

His arm went up to slap her, but she caught his wrist first.

"Slept, I said. That's all I did. Not like I had a choice, anyhow. I was a slave. I'd still be a slave, but for the sultan's generosity. And keep this in mind: You will not slap me. Ever again. Or I'll kill you."

Her beloved father stared at her like he'd seen a ghost. And, as a matter of fact, she was. He didn't know what she went through: the escape with Ștefan; the posse catching her, her heart wrenching struggle to save the kid, then being sold to the sultan like a cow. Her father knew none of that, but he felt entitled to slap her for sleeping in Mehmed's bed, because she's a woman, and he's her father. He needed to keep her in line.

He limped away, old, slow, and crooked, and Lena felt bad. He was her father, and she loved him. But he couldn't understand where she'd been, what she did and how she changed, and he never will. At first, she'd hoped that things would get better in time. But they didn't.

Her home is no longer home. Lena is no longer who she was when she left, but her parents don't get it. They expect her to be the child she was, but she's not. When they reminded her of the way things used to be, which is the way they should be, she blew up in their faces.

"I've been through too much. I now know that life is more than milking the cow, looking after sheep and baking bread. Life is struggle and worry and pain. I can't pretend that everything that happened to me didn't happen, or that it doesn't matter."

Her mother shook her head with worry.

"Lena dear, we know worry and pain better than you do. We worried about you for two years, wondering if you were dead or alive. You think that was easy? But now that you're back, you must get back to your life. Our life. And our life is about baking bread and milking sheep. You need to be nice and meek if you want a young man to take you despite everything."

"Despite what?"

"Whatever you did when you were gone. The stuff you brought could buy you a plot of land and a cow, maybe two. That would make a good dowry. But, dowry or not, nobody will want you if you don't behave like a nice, good girl."

Lena's blood boiled with anger. She wanted to yell at her mother and tell her where to put her advice. But, as angry as she was, she knew her mother was right. She chose to return, and her life was here now. If she wanted to belong, she had to fit in.

She tried. She went to see her old friends, but they were busy. They worked on their dowry, weaving sheets and towels and embroidering chemises. Or milked the cows or worked in the fields. They had no time for Lena, and they didn't want her friendship.

Remembering the snubs, Lena bites her lip and slaps the chemise on the rocks even harder.

She goes to church every Sunday, then to the village dance like they all do. But nobody even asks her to dance. The other girls glance at her down their noses like she stinks. They whisper and laugh when she passes by, and they call her the sultan's whore behind her back.

The boys pretend they don't see her. They look the other way and laugh with the girls. But whenever she meets them alone in the forest, as she picks raspberries or gathers wood, they come too close, speak nonsense and try to touch her.

All in all, life at home is not like Lena remembered. She'd never have thought she'd miss the sarayi, but there, at least, she felt safe.

She wrings the last shirt and drops it in the basket with the others. She leans over to wash her face and neck, enjoying the freshness of the water. Oh, how she misses the baths!

She looks around. Nobody.

She takes off her clothes and drops them on the grass. She steps into the river, and the freshness engulfs her. The water is cool, but it feels like silk on her sweaty skin. She washes her arms, her breasts, her legs. She laughs, happy to be alone and clean with the moon alone watching. But it's getting late. It's time to go.

She struggles to put on her chemise, now that she's wet. She's getting her skirts when she hears something in the woods. She stops to listen.

It's nothing. She bends over to pull her skirts again, when a shadow blocks the moon. It's a boy from the village. One of those who has no use for her in public. But they're not in public now.

"Hi, Lena."

"Hi."

"Good to see you. You want some help?"

"With what?"

"With... anything, in fact. You miss your sultan?"

Lena leans over to pick the basket. The clothes are wet and heavy. She lifts it on her shoulder and heads home. Behind her, the boy laughs.

Another shadow cuts her way.

"Don't you know it's rude to leave without saying goodbye? Is that how they taught you to behave at the enlightened court?"

Lena turns away from the path and heads home on the shortcut by the river she seldom uses in the dark. But a third boy is waiting for her there while the other two close in.

"How about we have a little fun?"

"Aren't you all brave? Three of you, attacking a lone girl in the dark. Your mothers should be proud."

"We didn't attack you. We just thought you could teach us some of the things you learned there. And just think: At the court you only had one man for all those women. Here, you have three men all to yourself."

"Men? Please! Go wipe your milk mustaches."

They come close enough to touch her, and Lena remembers that night with the posse, two years ago. There it goes again, she thinks, her blood hot with rage.

The first one grabs her shoulder. Lena turns and smashes the heavy laundry basket in his face. Something cracks and he screams. It's a strange, high-pitched noise, like a cat in heat. He crumbles, and the basket falls on top of him.

The other two reach to grab her. But by now, Lena grabbed the short-handle ax she hid inside the basket. She lifts it above her head like she's ready to split a trunk, then fells it over the shoulder of the closest man, flat side first.

Bones crack. The boy screams and collapses. The third boy steps back.

"Next time I won't use the flat. Don't come any closer," Lena says.

He stares at her, then at his friends. He's about to take off.

"Not so fast, young lover. Stay right here."

He stops and waits as Lena checks that the other two are still breathing.

"Gather the laundry and put it in the basket."

His eyes popping out of his head, he does.

"Take the basket and let's go home."

"But…"

"No but. Grab that basket, otherwise I swear to God I'll crush your skull."

They walk down the village street, and people gather to watch the boy carry the bloody laundry basket and Lena, half-naked, follow him with an ax in her hand. When they get home, Lena's parents stare like they've seen a ghost.

"Put the basket down," Lena says. The boy does.

"He and two of his friends tried to rape me. The others are in the forest, by the river. I didn't kill them, but they need help."

Old men scratch their heads, young kids stare, black-clad women cross themselves.

"You can go," Lena tells the boy. "But don't you ever come near me again."

He runs away as the crowd starts to scatter.

"It's her fault," a woman says.

"Of course. Did you see how she's dressed?"

"She'd better not have harmed my boy."

Lena steps inside and her parents follow, crestfallen. Her mother shakes her head.

"Nobody'll marry her now."

CHAPTER 39

EDIRNE, SEPTEMBER 1445

The Imperial room is brighter than a garden in bloom. Brocade kaftans in rich hues wrap dignitaries sitting on velvet pillows. Janissaries in red uniforms guard the doors, their weapons ready. Blooming flowers in Chinese vases big enough to drown a grown man sweeten the room, overpowering the incense burners. Bright yellow birds in gilded cages call each other over the whispers of the crowd.

It's the day of the werewolf's friends' trial, and Mehmed can't wait for it to be over. The whole palace got discombobulated about this little eunuch he can barely remember. But everyone else apparently does. Starting with Radu, who asked him to spare his friend.

"Please, my sultan. Please. Be kind. He's my best friend."

"I thought *I* was your best friend."

Radu looked at him with his sad blue eyes.

"I used to think so too, my sultan."

He said nothing else, but he didn't need to. Because it's true that Mehmed has been keeping Radu at a distance.

First, he doesn't want his mother to get into one of her murdering rages and have him killed. Second, he doesn't want his father to get mad. Çandarlı Paşa's spies have nothing better to do but watch him,

153

instead of figuring out how to crack Constantinople. If he heard that Mehmed ignored his job for Radu, Father wouldn't hesitate to reclaim his throne, like he promised. And third, because he has Gülbahar. The girl comforts him when Radu isn't around. She looks so much like him, it's uncanny. The girl is soft, lovely, and always ready to please. He's very fond of her and her little brother. The nights he spends with her, he doesn't always need to close his eyes and pretend she's Radu.

But Radu is still in his heart. He loves him and feels bad about hurting his feelings. He'd love to make him happy, but he's the sultan, and has to be just.

"Friend or no friend, if he's guilty, he will have to get punished."

"*If* he's guilty. But what punishment?"

"Helping a slave escape is punished by death."

"What slave?"

"The janissary."

"But if he was a werewolf when he escaped, then he wasn't a slave. It's more like losing a dog. Or one of the horses."

Mehmed stared at Radu in wonder.

"I thought you didn't believe in werewolves."

"I don't. But It doesn't matter what I believe. If you decide that he's guilty about letting a werewolf go, then he didn't let a slave escape. It's more like he lost a pet."

Mehmed sighed. "OK, Radu. I won't kill him."

"Thank you, my sultan. You are generous."

"Though, honestly, if I lost a werewolf because of him, it's much worse than if I had lost a slave. Slaves, I have plenty and I can always get more. Where can I get another werewolf?"

Like that wasn't bad enough, last night Gülbahar started crying.

"What happened?"

"My sultan, my best friend awaits your judgement. Please be patient and merciful with him like you always are with me."

"Your best friend?"

"Yes. Ali, your mother's eunuch. He's a lovely boy, and he's been so helpful to Sessiz. He always takes care of him when I'm… when I'm engaged elsewhere. He's teaching him to read and write and to communicate by signing. I couldn't bear to lose him, and I'm sure he did nothing wrong. He loves you. He'd never do anything to hurt you."

Mehmed did his best to calm her down without promising much. He thought it was over, but this morning the validé summoned him. "I understand you took one of my servants?"

"One of your servants?"

"Ali. My eunuch."

"He's been accused of letting a werewolf escape."

"That's nonsense. Ali would never do something like this."

"Why not?"

His mother stared at him like he's lost it.

"Ali is my faithful servant. He only does what I tell him."

"Really?"

"I need him back."

"We'll see what the trial shows. If he's guilty..."

"I already told you he's not guilty."

"But what if he is?"

His mother looked at him like he was slow.

"I want him back."

"Even if he's guilty?"

"Of course. And I want all of him back. Both hands, both feet, tongue, eyes, nose, everything. You will not maim him."

"Mother, may I remind you that I am the sultan and that it's my job to see that Allah's justice is done?"

"Mehmed, may I remind you that I'm your mother and that I made you a sultan?"

Mehmed left before he said something he may regret. But he can't wait to see this eunuch that all these people who matter to him hold in such regard.

The guards bring the boy. He wears the blue eunuch uniform, but his chestnut hair is a mess with a few straws stuck in it. He's small and thin, and not impressive but for his ocean blue eyes. Those eyes make

Mehmed shiver. He's seen them before, he thinks. There's something about them. And he's unafraid.

Next to him, another boy. Bigger, blond and dressed in green. Must be the tax accountant, Mehmed thinks.

"What's your name?"

"Isa, my sultan."

"Isa, is it true that you helped a werewolf escape?"

"No, my sultan."

"How about you?"

"I'm Ali."

"Did you help the werewolf?"

"No, my sultan."

Mehmed shrugs and looks at Çandarlı Paşa. "Tell me."

"The werewolf left the castle from the kitchens. He crawled through the drain tunnel into the Tunca. The grill had been removed."

"How do you know these boys have anything to do with it?"

"They are his friends."

"So what?"

"We found a clump of dark hair in the eunuch's kitchen."

"Why does the eunuch have a kitchen?"

"Because I want him to."

The valide's voice comes from behind the dark grill between the throne room and the sarayi. That's where the sultan's women sit to watch and listen in without being seen. But they aren't supposed to be heard, either.

Mehmed returns to Çandarlı Paşa. "Where is the clump of hair?"

"It... disappeared when the moon went down."

"You mean you lost it?"

The paşa swallows hard. Mehmed sees his Adam's apple moving up and down.

"You have any other proof?"

"The other one was in the gardens. He screamed he saw the werewolf to pull the crowds away from the kitchen. That opened the way for the werewolf to leave."

"Did you?" Mehmed asks Isa.

"I did."

"Why?"

"I thought I saw him. But then he disappeared."

"Everybody everywhere screamed that they saw him. Even here in the sarayi," Gülbahar's voice says behind the grill.

Mehmed shakes his head.

"Where is your friend?" he asks Ali.

"I don't know."

"Isa?"

"I don't know."

"We could interrogate them to find out, my sultan," Çandarlı Paşa says.

"No!" The validé's voice comes loud and clear, and the crowd snickers.

Mehmed is in an untenable position. He can't afford to look foolish, weak and directed by the women. But can he go against all those he loves?

"Did you know your friend was a werewolf?"

The boys shake their heads, looking down.

Mehmed takes in a deep breath. He stares down at the sea of faces waiting for his justice. Then there's all the others, behind the grill, that he can't see. He stands up straight and thunders over all of them.

"You two have been foolish and incompetent. You had an enemy of the state under your nose and you let him go, instead of informing the crown so we could take mitigating measures. You are both guilty of negligence, ignorance and incompetence. And you will get punished in kind.

"Ali, you will spend one week reading the Quran and praying to Allah to give you more wisdom next time around. We will also cut off your..."

The gasp from the sarayi feels like a blizzard.

"Hair. To the skin. To remind you to grow your knowledge and your wisdom."

"Isa. You're supposed to be incredibly bright, but your lack of understanding of your friend's machinations gives me pause. You will spend a week calculating how many camels, how many men, and how much rice I will need to complete my conquest of Constantinople. Also, the size of a cannon that could break through the Theodosian walls. And the guards will cut off your..."

Gasp.

"Hair too. You should both be grateful. Your hairstyle is terrible. Dismissed."

CHAPTER 40

THE BLACK SEA, OCTOBER 1445

A howling wind from the north whips the waves into a white, foamy frenzy, and the sea thrashes almost as loud as the drums. It's cold, but the storm washed away the stench of human decay of the galley and brought in the salty scent of the sea, and Codru feels grateful.

The one thing he keeps from the werewolf even in his human form is the magic power of his nose. And here, on the galley, that's a curse. In Edirne Palace, everything smelled like roses, cinnamon and incense. Here, everything smells like death, even the living. But not today, and Codru is glad for the relief, even though he's shivering.

He's shackled on the fourth bank of oars of the Deniz Bulut, the Sea Cloud. That's the name of the galley his captors brought him to. He hasn't left his bench since they shackled him to it when he arrived. Eating, sleeping, emptying himself — everything happens right here, with his feet shackled to the iron rings screwed into the deck and his hands on the oar.

He didn't know this kind of life existed. Long ago, when he was just a child, he thought that being a nomad was bad. Later on, he thought the same about being a janissary trainee. Little did he know. Compared to the life of an oarsman in the sultan's fleet, that was just a walk in the park. He's been here for only two days — he marked them with scratches on his oar — but it feels like forever.

There are five slaves on each oar, and thirty rows of oars on the galley. They each work a third of the time, unless they need to hurry. Then, they all pull as one on the rhythm of the drums. And, since they face backwards, they don't even know what they're rushing to. But rush they do, since the whip is always there to remind them they are only alive by the grace and kindness of the sultan who permits them to serve him instead of taking their worthless lives as they rightfully deserve.

Codru glances at the old man to his left, then at the old man to his right. They both pull on the oar with all their might. The muscles in their shoulders shine with sweat and the thick veins of their necks are ready to crawl out from under the sunburned skin like fat blue worms. They don't have an ounce of fat between them, Codru thinks, wondering why the Ottomans don't get younger, stronger people to do this hard work.

"What's your name?" he whispers to the man to his left.

"I'm Galen. You?"

"The Ottomans call me Kemal. But I'm Codru to my friends."

"What did you do to get here?" Galen asks.

"I found myself in the wrong place at the wrong time. You?"

"I bedded the wrong girl."

"Really?" Galen doesn't look like he's into that kind of sport. "Why was she wrong?"

"She was my boss's daughter. He found out and tricked me, then sold me to the Ottomans. That's how I ended up on this accursed galley."

"How long have you been here?"

"Four hundred and thirty-two days. But who's counting?"

Galen spits to his left, and the wind carries it to the man behind him, who swears at him in protests. "Same to you, you prick," Galen says, and spits again. "Got to keep the sons of bitches in line."

"How old are you, Galen?"

"Twenty-five."

"Twenty-five?"

"I don't look young, do I? You won't either, before too long. Living chained to this damned wooden bench for month after month, under the sun and the rain, won't do much for your looks. The guy whose place you took was Milos, a Hungarian. He was thirty. He lasted two years."

"What had he done?"

"He fought for the wrong side. They caught him in one of the sultan's battles with Hunyadi."

"Does anyone make it out alive?"

"Not that I've seen. They say you may have a chance if the galley gets captured by the sultan's enemies. Or the pirates. But if it sinks, we go down with it. If it burns, we burn with it. This floating coffin is our life."

Codru digests what he hears, and he's not liking it one bit. He turns to the neighbor to his right.

"What's your name?"

The man looks through him but doesn't answer. Galen does.

"He's Drago. He's about to be gone. A week ago, he stopped speaking. That's how it starts. Then they stop eating and drinking. Then they stop rowing, and they die."

"Next row!" the paşa says, and Galen drops the oar. They're off for a while. They have time to rest, eat and drink while the row behind them gets to work, then the next one. Codru stares at his hands. They're frozen, swollen, and covered in blisters.

"Rub the mutton fat from the soup into your hands. It will protect you from the spray and keep the salt out of your wounds. Your hands will get worse before they get better, but they'll toughen up eventually. Unless they get infected, and then you die," Galen says, stretching his legs as far as his shackles let him.

When the cook brings him his bowl of thick mutton soup and his hardtack, Codru rubs the congealing fat into his hands. It doesn't feel good, and he's so hungry he wants to lick it off, but he resists the temptation and bites off a corner of his hardtack to soften it in his mouth instead. He dips the rest of his hardtack into the soup and eats it, then drinks what's left in the bowl. When he's done, he's just as hungry as when he started.

"Grab Drago's bowl and hardtack. He doesn't need them."

Codru feels awful, but Drago isn't eating. He doesn't even seem to notice when Codru takes his food away to replace it with his empty bowl.

He shares it with Galen, and that makes him feel better. He's got something in his stomach, some grease on his hands and maybe a new friend. Better than when he started this morning.

"Where are you from, Galen?"

"Constantinople, where else? The blooming queen of the world. Have you been there?"

"No."

"You should, some day. If you make it out of here. That place is like no other on earth. No wonder the bloody Ottomans drool after it and tried to take it dozens of times. The golden city of the East. Its cathedral, Hagia Sophia, is like no other church on earth. It's painted with gold, and the relics are mounted in gold and it's nothing but darn gold and emeralds and..."

Suddenly, the heavy drums burst into a frenzy, like pummeled by a hailstorm.

"Everybody to the oars. Pull now. Everybody!" the captain shouts.

The beat of the drums is so low-pitched that Codru hears them in his stomach rather than his ears. Faster and faster, they pull and pull until the galley glides over the water like a white swan, cutting through the waves. For once, the wind blows in the right direction, billowing the square white sails and pushing the boat so fast the oarsmen have trouble keeping up.

"Faster," the captain says, and the drums speed up into a frenzy, like a maddened heartbeat.

"What the hell?" Galen mumbles.

They pull and pull and pull on the oars, feeling their back muscles rip from their joints, even Drago, who stares into space but keeps the rhythm.

Codru's heart is about to burst.

"What's happening?"

"See the white spots behind us? Those two, next to each other?"

"Yes."

"That's a cutter with two sails. Probably a pirate ship. They're after us, and they're flying with the wind. If you think we're fast, they're three times faster. If they catch us…"

"You said that if they catch us, they'll set us free."

"Only if we aren't dead. They have to take the galley first."

"Why are they chasing us?"

"They're pirates. They want our cargo. Gold, silks, furs, whatever our bloody cargo is. Well, not ours. The sultan's."

The cutter is now close enough for Codru to see the men. They hold grapples, matchlock arquebuses and bows.

They shoot a warning shot at the galley. The first load goes through the sails. So does the second. But the next one gets an oarsman two rows ahead of Codru, and the one after that hits Drago. Galen was right. Drago died, even though not the way they thought.

A fire arrow gets stuck in the sail, then another, and another. Heartbeats later, the whole deck is a feast of hungry little fires devouring everything around them. The men scream and try to run, but they can't, since they're shackled. A burning arrow misses Codru's shoulder and falls near his feet. He steps on it to kill it, burning his foot. He'd like to check his wound, but there's no time. Another burning arrow buries into Galen's shoulder, setting his shirt on fire. Galen screams and tries to pull it out, but he can't, so Codru grabs it with both his hands and pulls it out. The arrow's still burning as it flies overboard. Galen's shirt is on fire, so Codru slaps him to kill the flames, but his sleeve catches fire. He rips it off and throws it into the sea.

The janissaries respond to the fire with fire. The cannons fire again and again. They hit the cutter's mast, which breaks with a thunderous noise and falls across the deck, crushing a bunch of men. Their comrades leave their posts and jump to help them, and the pirate ship loses speed and gives up the chase.

The janissaries step to kill the fires and the galley wobbles like a drunk. The oarsmen struggle, since the dead fell over the oars, preventing the others from rowing. The wounded are screaming, covering the drums. The janissaries move from row to row, unshackling the dead and throwing them overboard, and reassigning the others to get the galley back in business. It's slow, tedious work. By the time Drago's body splashes in the water, the night has fallen. Galen is hurting, but alive. Codru's hands are worse than ever from putting out the fire burning Galen's back.

The janissaries move to the next row.

"Thank you," Galen says.

"For what?"

"For helping me."

"That's what we do."

"Not here. But from now on, we will."

CHAPTER 41
FULL MOON

Winter is coming. The mornings are colder and colder, and the seas rougher every day, even though they've been going south for ages. Twenty-five days, to be precise. Codru marked his oar at sunrise every day, ever since the day they shackled him to the galley. He doesn't need to, since he can see the moon every night and watch it wax and wane, but having a count gives him some sense of control. Like he has a say in what's about to happen.

And happen it will. The full moon is coming tonight. He's about to become the first werewolf rowing a galley in the history of werewolves.

Things will never be the same after tonight. Tomorrow he'll be free or dead.

"What are you thinking of?" Galen asks, pulling the oar on the rhythm of the drums.

"I was wondering where we are."

"The Aegean Sea. We left the Black Sea, we crossed the Bosporus Strait, then the Dardanelles. We're about to wander between Greece's thousands of islands as we head south towards the Mediterranean."

"How do you know all these things?"

"I used to be a merchant on these seas, before my dick-brain turned me into an oarsman. I crisscrossed these waters more times than you can count, trading incense for silks, silks for pepper, pepper for gold, and so on."

"Tell me about the islands."

"They're beautiful. Blue skies, green hills covered with grapes and silver-green olive trees, ouzo, retsina, wine, and hot-hearted women. What's not to like?"

"Are they big?"

"Some are. Some aren't. Some are inhabited. Some are not. There are thousands of them, as I said."

"Are the people Greek?"

"Yes. And Albanian. And Ottoman. And some Genoese. Some Venetian, too. All sorts."

"How do you say 'help' in Greek?"

"*βοήθεια.*"

"*Voithia?*"

"Sort of. But why do you want to know? Planning to escape?"

Codru laughs. "Of course. Want to come?"

"No, I love it here. Whatever you do, don't go to Lesbos."

"Why not?"

"It's held by the Genoese these days. Those bastards are almost as bad as the Ottomans. If they catch you, they'll sell you back to the Ottomans. Or to someone else."

"Understood. I'll avoid Lesbos at all costs."

The dusk is near as their shift ends. Codru eats his last hardtack softened in the gray mutton soup, and looks up. The sun is almost on the horizon, to his right. Far to his left there's a shadow that might be land. Or not. It could be a cloud or a patch of fog or a ship. Who knows? He can swim as a werewolf, but he doesn't know how fast and how far. If he makes it off the galley alive.

The sun sets and the darkness grows around them, hiding the boat and the men into a dark gray haze broken here and there by torches. It's dark enough that Codru can't see the third row of oarsmen ahead of him, when the moon rises like a glowing silver queen.

His bones ache as the moon pulls him apart to change him. His face turns into a muzzle, his wolf's nose takes over, and the smell of the galley suffocates him. He can see Galen's every eyelash, as the Greek sleeps with his face resting on the oar, and can hear every one of his heartbeats.

His fingers shorten into toes as his hands thicken into paws and grow dagger-like claws. He drops the oar and lifts his muzzle to sniff the air. A hint of smoke hits his nose, telling him that somewhere, not too far, there are humans.

He tracks the wind, which feels good. Now that he's covered in thick fur, he's no longer cold. But the question is: can he get rid of the shackles?

He lifts his left leg. His foot is no longer a foot, but a strong hairy paw. He tries to pull it out of its shackle, but it won't come. He tries again, but his paws are as big as his feet, and they won't slide out of the iron grip. Not even if he skins them alive. He's trapped.

He hears Galen's heartbeat quicken as the Greek opens his eyes and sees him, no longer human but still shackled next to him. The man gasps.

"I knew it," he whispers. "I knew there was something about you."

Codru looks him in the eye.

"What are you waiting for?"

Codru glances at his feet.

Galen looks down over and sees his paws shackled to the floor.

"You can do this. My grandma told me stories about what your kind can do. Just pull them out and jump off. Swim left, that's where the land is. And it's not far."

Codru takes a deep breath and pulls his feet up from the floor with all his might. The wood cracks and screams as the bolt nailing his shackles to the floor comes out like a bad tooth. And just like that, Codru is free from the boat, though his feet are still bound together. He glances at Galen once more, and he leaps.

"*Voithia*. Remember. *Parakaló Voithia*."

Codru flies for ages before splashing into the dark water. The cold sea embraces him, then sucks him in, pulling him deeper and deeper. His bound legs and the weight of the shackles are no help with swimming, but he struggles until he reaches the surface and takes a thirsty breath.

He paddles in place to get his bearings. To his left, the galley floats between him and the shore, ablaze with the light of the torches and alive with screams. Janissaries holding matchlock arquebuses and bows lean over the sides, looking for him, so he dives again and swims under the ship to clear his way to the land.

He comes out again when he's hurting for air. He sniffs the shore and swims to it with all his strength, but it's not easy. He never realized that his back paws do most of the work when he's a werewolf, but he sure found out now. He moves so slow it feels like he sits still.

A scream from behind, then another. They saw him.

An arquebus fires. Then another.

Codru dives again, but before long he must come up for air. He breaks the surface and takes a breath just as a bullet hits him in the shoulder, making his right foreleg useless.

He howls in pain and dives before they hit him again, wondering if he'll have enough strength to get back to the surface. He's shackled, tired, and hurting, the most wretched werewolf there ever was. His lungs burst with need, so he paddles back up for air. He fights his urge to take a breath, but his lungs have a mind of their own. They draw a breath just before he hits the surface.

Codru coughs, sputters and chokes. He glances back to see the galley far behind, then forces his exhausted, hurting body to push forward to the shore.

Then something slams into his head, and he sinks into darkness.

CHAPTER 42
LESBOS

Codru opens his eyes to a sandy beach. The fine white sand is scattered with pink seashells and the air smells like algae and salt. A faraway wind brings a whiff of wood smoke. Someone, somewhere is cooking, and his mouth waters.

He glances at himself to see that he's back to being a human, naked of course, but for the shackles on his legs and the deep gash the bullet left in his shoulder.

His head still hurts after hitting an anchored boat. And he's half frozen, hungry and exhausted, but he's lucky the water carried him to the beach instead of back to the galley.

This place is beautiful, even in the gray morning light. The sea, bluer than blue as far as the eye can see, graceful beach trees leaning over the white sand, rustling their delicate green leaves, and way behind, a conical mountain glowing purple against the pink sky.

But Codru is not in the mood to enjoy nature. He needs food, warmth, and shelter, and some way to get rid of his shackles, but there's nothing like that here. And the galley may be still looking for him. Any moment now, a boat full of armed janissaries may land here to take him back.

He stands up and waits for the dizziness to pass, then shuffles to one of the beached fishermen's boats, looking for a tool to get rid of his shackles. But there's nothing but oars and fishing nets.

He turns to the next one.

"Lie down."

Codru looks up. It's a child in rags, his dark hair a riot of curls falling on his face, his mouth unsmiling, his eyes sharp. He can't be older than eight, but his hands hold the matchlock steady.

"Listen, kid..."

"Lie down now or I'll shoot you."

Codru lies down.

"On your belly."

He rolls on his belly, wondering how hard it would be to jump and grab the kid's arquebus. A piece of cake, really, if he was still a werewolf. But he's not. And he's shackled and wounded, so he plays it safe and waits.

"Who are you?"

"Codru. You?"

"Nikos. What are you doing here?"

"I... fell off a galley."

"Ottoman?"

"Yes."

"Are you one of them?"

"No. I'm a Christian."

"Catholic?"

"Orthodox."

"Orthodox? Really?"

The kid steps closer to look at him, and Codru sweeps his feet from under him and grabs the arquebus. Suddenly, things have changed. The kid sits powerless. And ashamed.

"Where are we?"

The kid gives him a side look. "Lesbos."

Lesbos. He had to find the one island Galen warned him about. Just his luck. Codru sighs. Then a child with a gun. "Where is your home?"

"My home?"

"Yes. Take me there."

The kid rolls his eyes and stands, leading the way to a tiny whitewashed house sitting high on the slope between terraced vineyards and green meadows. "Here."

"Who lives here?"

"Me. And mom."

"Anyone else?"

"The cat."

The calico doesn't like him. She puffs herself up to get big, and hisses and spits like he's a dog sniffing her kittens. She can still smell the wolf in him.

The mother is too sick to care. Pale and thin, she lays in her bed mumbling things Codru can't understand and speaking to people he can't see.

"How long has she been like this?"

"Three days."

The kid shrunk. His bravado's gone, now the gun changed hands. And his mother is too sick to care. It looks like Codru's main enemy in this place is the calico. "Where's your father?"

"He died last winter."

"You have any brothers or sisters?"

The kid shakes his head, then grabs a cup to give his mother some water. The water runs down her chin to her chest as she speaks to the voices, unaware of her son. She's flushed, sweaty, and nothing but skin and bones. She looks like she'll die soon.

Codru touches her skin. Her cheeks are burning, and she moans like she's in pain.

"I'm sorry, Nikos. Your mother doesn't look well. Why don't you hug her? That may give her solace. Relief, I mean," Codru says, seeing the kid's blank look. "That may make her feel better."

Nikos squeezes in the narrow wooden bed next to her and holds her, and the woman softens.

"Nikos? Is that you?" she whispers.

"Yes, mom. It's me."

But from the faraway look in her eyes, Codru knows she's not looking at her son.

"What was your father's name?" he asks.

"Nikos. I was named after him."

"Oh, Nikos, I missed you so much," the woman said, hugging her young son like he's a lover.

"Hold her. That will help," Codru says, and goes to look for a tool to remove his shackles.

There's a rusty file in the tool shed by the house. He sits on the floor and works on his shackles until his arms feel like they'll fall off. He snaps the chain once more, and the link gives. Thank God. He's still got the shackles, but he's free of the chain.

He cracks the door open to look outside. The sea, endless and blue, blinking at him. Green hills, covered with olive trees and vines. The sun getting ready to bake the earth into a crust.

The little white house is surrounded by a poorly tended garden. He goes from tree to tree, looking for the white willow Ali taught him about, for fever and for pain. He finds one by the stream behind the house and picks some bark to make tea.

He heads back to find the kid sitting on the floor. The woman lays quietly. She's finally asleep.

"How do we make a fire?"

Nikos takes him to the kitchen. The embers are alive, under a thick layer of ashes, so he gets a fire going with some kindling. Codru picks up a pot and boils the willow bark into a pungent green liquid.

"Honey?"

The kid points to a jar on the shelf and Codru sweetens the tea and gives it to the kid for his mom. Moments later, he's back with his cup empty.

"Now what?" the kid asks.

What? Codru doesn't know. He needs to go back to Transylvania somehow. But first he needs to understand where he is. And he can't just leave this kid with his sick mom. He needs to find someone to look after them.

"Do you have any aunts? Uncles? Grandparents?"

"Mom and pop eloped to be together. I don't have anyone. But you."

Codru sighs. He tries to understand how he ended up responsible for a sick woman and a kid that has nobody but him, and he fails.

CHAPTER 43

EDIRNE, SPRING 1446

Edirne Palace's throne room is almost empty. Devoid of the people hiding the marble floors with their rich kaftans and filling the air with their chatter and heavy perfumes, the place looks even larger. The birds in gilded cages on the walls have it all to themselves, but for the sultan's podium and the few scattered brocade pillows where the dignitaries are seated, at an appropriate, deferent distance from Mehmed's throne.

Dressed in a kaftan worth its weight in gold, the sultan sits worrying his amber prayer beads, pretending to listen to Çandarlı Paşa and wondering how upset his father would get if he executed him. He's ready to be done with him. Ever since Mehmed took the throne almost two years ago, the grand vizier has been nothing but a thorn in his side.

Mehmed knows that his other viziers agree. They're all young, enthusiastic and ready to fight, unlike this old fogey who's afraid of his own shadow. And today he brings bad news again.

"My sultan, our source in Buda tells us that the Diet of Hungary is about to designate Hunyadi as sole regent and governor of Hungary."

"So what? He's been doing the exact same thing for years, being a pain in my ass with his armies. What difference does this make?"

"Right now, he's still subject to the decisions of the Hungarian Diet. He can't start a war or make any important political decisions without them. Once he's regent, he'll be as good as a king. The King of Hungary is only four years old, so Hunyadi will run Hungary for decades."

"Listen, Çandarlı Paşa. We've all seen what Hunyadi can do. First, we crushed him in the Battle of Varna, and he ran away like a beggar, leaving his king's body behind. Then he ran with the tail between his legs last year, after the skirmishes on the Danube. Why are you so obsessed with that old-timer? Maybe because you're the same age?"

Mehmed's friend, Zağanos Paşa, bursts into laughter. The grand vizier shoots him a venomous glare.

"I'm old enough to have seen plenty of battles, unlike some young whipper-snappers who shall not be named, and who take their inexperience for courage and their ignorance for instinct. Hunyadi won against us just as often as he lost, often with fewer soldiers. And don't forget it was Sultan Murad, may Allah keep him healthy and young forever, who led our army in the Battle of Varna. It's we, old-timers, who win the wars."

"I can't wait to see you lead our armies in the assault against Constantinople. That's a battle worth winning. I'd like to get ready to start the Constantinople campaign this summer."

"But, my sultan..."

"Within a week, I expect you to bring me a plan for the campaign. Where do we start? How many soldiers do we take? And so on. Please have it ready for me by Saturday."

"But my sultan, we need to deal with the janissaries first. I told you they are ready to revolt..."

"I've been hearing that for months. What is it this time?"

"They didn't get paid for months. And when they finally did, the silver acki had gotten smaller, so it's worth next to nothing against the Genoese ducat. They're angry and they demand a raise."

"Why is the acki smaller?"

"This year we had an extra lunar month, so we had to give the janissary an extra month of pay, but our tax revenue stayed the same. Then we had to rebuild half of Edirne after the great fire last year. We rebuilt a mosque and the baths, and helped the thousands of families who lost their houses in the fire. That's why the treasury is empty."

"And this is my problem how?"

"If we have no money to pay the janissaries, then we have no money to start a campaign against Constantinople."

Mehmed struggled to keep his cool. "Get money, then."

"From where?"

"You're asking me? I am your sultan, not some damned tax accountant. Raise the taxes. Do whatever you have to do."

"But my sultan..."

"Enough. Anything else?"

The grand vizier sighs. "One more thing."

"What?"

"Our source at Hunyadi's court..."

"The housekeeper? What about her?"

Çandarlı Paşa glances at Zağanos Paşa, and the guards in the room. He doesn't want to talk, not here and now, but Mehmed has no more patience. He's about to cut the grand vizier's throat if he doesn't get out of his face soon. He caresses the handle of his sword. Çandarlı Paşa sees it, and sweat beads sprout on his wrinkled forehead.

"Either speak or leave."

"She says... She says Hunyadi has a high placed spy at the court. Somebody very close to you, who's aware of every move you make."

"Who?"

"I don't know."

"What do you know, then?"

"He communicates with Hunyadi through a connection in Kronstadt."

"Anything else?"

"No. Except that it's a kid."

CHAPTER 44

KRONSTADT, SPRING 1446

With its snow-capped peaks, mysterious dark forests smelling like pines, rushing streams, and blue lakes colder than ice, Transylvania is nothing like Moldova.

Sitting in the back of her horse-drawn carriage, Lena stares out in wonder. There's a village once in a while, tiny houses at the foot of the mountain gathered around a white church watching them like a dog watches his sheep, but they're few and far between.

Lena traveled for days now, but she didn't see many fields. Just green pastures rolling down the hills and blooming orchards with pink apple trees. This is not like Moldova, where the wheat and oat fields stretch as far as the eye can see, with barely an old tree here and there as a milestone. Moldova to her is like summer, whereas Transylvania is winter. Beautiful, dark, and scary.

The daylight's almost over when the cart stops in a forest that looks like it never sees the sun. It's dark and unmoving and silent like a tomb.

The old trees seem to live in three seasons at a time. Bright-green buds unfurl along the twisted branches, speaking of spring, while the red leaves set the ground on fire wherever the snow has melted. A few steps further, two tree stumps covered in bright-green moss lean towards each other, joining their low branches like lovers holding hands.

But the strangest thing is the little cottage made of tree trunks loosely fitted together, standing on four crooked stilts. The old thatched roof is steep enough to shed the snow, and the tiny square windows are covered with stretched pig bladders to let in the light but not the rain. A few lacy green ferns flutter on the top like a feather in someone's cap, and a riot of purple petunias hug the walls, sweetening the air with their fragrance.

The little garden is surrounded by a fence made of spiked tree branches saying "stay away," but the gate is cracked open. Lena pushes it and steps in to find herself face to face with a smiling black dog.

She opens her hands for him to smell. He looks in her eyes, then licks her face like he knows her. She hugs him, and for no good reason, tears come to her eyes.

"Come in, Lena."

The woman in the door is like none Lena has ever seen. She's tall and willowy, and she looks like she floats, with her gauzy skirts and long black hair fluttering around her even when she's still. Her sparkling golden bracelets jingle as she opens her arms, and the gold coins in her necklace catch the last rays of the sun.

"Have we met?"

"Not yet. I'm Mama Smaranda, Ali's grandmother. Welcome to my home."

Lena bows to her in the Ottoman fashion, but Mama Smaranda grabs and hugs her, kissing her cheeks one after another, like old friends do.

"Ali's friend is my friend. Welcome to my house."

"Thank you. What's her real name?"

Mama Smaranda's eyes widen.

"Ana. She told you, then?"

"I told her. It won't be long before she can't fool them anymore. I just happened to see it first. She sends this."

She hands Mama Smaranda Ana's note. Mama Smaranda reads it, then hides it somewhere in her ethereal clothes.

"She needs help."

"She does."

"Can you think about a way I can send something back to her?"

"None right now, but I'll keep thinking. What happened?"

"Her connection broke. The messengers who went back and forth pulled out after the Battle of Varna. Hunyadi's men have been too busy to find others, so Ali got stranded."

"Can you help her?"

"I need to think. Are you hungry?"

Lena nods.

Mama Smaranda brings out a round bread as big as the wheel of a cart. She cuts thick slices and tops them with glistening slices of white fresh sweet cheese. She puts a pot of honey on the table and turns to the fireplace to make peppermint tea. A fluffy black cat with golden eyes comes out of nowhere and jumps onto Lena's lap.

"Hello, you," Lena says, scratching her behind her ears. The cat purrs and pushes herself into her hands.

Mama Smaranda's eyebrows rise.

"That's a first. Unlike Negru, this one doesn't like anyone. Gigi barely tolerates Ana."

The cat ignores her, in typical cat fashion. She proceeds to fall asleep on Lena's knees, and the girl eats, careful to not disturb her. The bread is crusty and warm, the cheese is sweet, and the honey is dark and tastes like the forest. Lena wolfs down the food feeling very much at home. They all welcomed her, Mama Smaranda, the dog and the cat. None of them seems to judge her or wonder why she's here.

"Why are you here?" Mama Smaranda asks.

"I... I didn't know where else to go. And I promised Ana that I'll bring her message to you."

"But why should you go anywhere? Didn't you just get home after two years? Weren't you glad to be back?"

Lena's eyes widen. "How do you know?"

Mama Smaranda smiles. "I know things about people. That's my job. One of them."

"I was glad to be back. All the time I was away, I couldn't think about anything else but how to escape and go back home. But my home wasn't like I remembered it."

"Your home wasn't, or you weren't?"

"I wasn't. I no longer am."

"How so?"

"I can't... I can't keep worrying about what people think, and live my life to please others, who judge me without knowing what I've been through."

"What did your parents say?"

"I think they were glad to see me gone. I'm an embarrassment to them."

"What will you do?"

"I don't know yet. I'll figure it out."

"Why don't you stay with me for a while? Nobody will bother you here, and you'll have time to think about your future."

"Will you teach me some of the things you taught Ali... I mean Ana? Healing herbs, and potions and such?"

"I will. And I'll help you understand people. But most importantly, I'll help you understand yourself. It's a useful skill."

CHAPTER 45

EĞRIGÖZ, SPRING 1446

The sun rises high over the fort of Eğrigöz, and the shadows are as short as they get, but it's still cool up here in the mountains, even though the snow is finally gone.

This is Vlad's outside time. Regardless of the weather, every day at noon, the guard unlocks his cell door and takes him out to see the light of day for an hour.

He's got nowhere to go, but the four armed guards never take their eyes off him, even though this whole place is nothing but sheer cliff. It's too steep even for the mountain goats, everywhere but west. And that's where they sit, watching him with their bows ready.

The Eğrigöz prison makes the Tokat fort look grand. It's built on a narrow rocky peak only a few hundred feet wide to thwart any attempt to escape. Even worse, Vlad is the only prisoner here. Hard to believe, but he misses the others' screams. They told him he wasn't alone. Here, there's nothing but silence and gloom, twenty-three hours a day. Then the sheer cliffs looking over the precipice for an hour.

But this is not the time to think. It's time to work. Every day, Vlad makes the most of his hour outside. He carries boulders and throws them, jumps and runs in place until he's out of breath, to keep his strength. He needs to be ready, should there ever be a chance to escape.

While he's locked in his cell, he reads about the Ottomans so he'll know how to fight and destroy them as soon as he gets out. The guards brought him books of history, philosophy, languages, and strategy, and they'll give him more if he asks. At first, he thought it strange that they allowed him to learn. But then he realized they didn't expect him to get out. Ever. They think he'll rot in here.

That's why they gave him the books. To keep him busy, and to say they provided him with an education, like they promised Father. They even got him a teacher to direct his studies.

Kir Daskalos is an old Greek historian who enjoys talking to Vlad. They discuss everything, from the advantages of battle axes over swords to the value of philosophy in national identity. The man is small, crooked and almost blind, so he can't read any more, but he doesn't need to, because he already knows everything. So Vlad asks him questions about the books he reads, and Kir Daskalos answers, then recommends other books that his jailers get for him.

All in all, this place wouldn't be so bad if he knew what's going on at home. And if they let him train with his weapons. But they won't allow him even a wooden sword.

Ignoring the four pairs of eyes watching his every move, Vlad pants, grunts and sweats as he jumps from a high rock, then climbs it again, and jumps again, until he's so winded he needs a break.

Before they take him back, he snatches a sharp rock and hides it in his sleeve. It's not much of a weapon, but it's better than nothing. And it will help with the one pleasure he's got left: killing rats.

They're everywhere, and they're not hard to catch if you're patient. But they have nasty claws and sharp teeth you don't want to get close to.

The first rat he caught by accident. He threw his food bowl at him, and the bowl rolled and fell upside down, catching the rat underneath. The rat squeaked and scrambled as Vlad held the bowl down, thinking about what to do. He lifted it just enough for the head to squeeze out, then stepped on it, choking him to death. It was fun, but not as much fun as when he learned to tie a noose around their little necks and hang them up to watch them die.

Unlike humans, the rats are not heavy, so they don't break their necks in the fall. That's why they take a long time to die, and they fight, contorting their little bodies in the most amazing ways. That was fun until Vlad thought about flaying them. But he doesn't have a knife, and he's not ready to do it with his teeth. The rock will have to do.

Back in his cell, he lies in wait, looking forward to his next victim. But it's a slow day. No rats. So he's glad when the guard lets Kir Daskalos in.

The old man takes the chair, and Vlad sits on his straw mattress while they talk about the Ottoman Empire. Today they're talking about the interregnum.

"After the Battle of Ankara in 1402, when Timur Lang defeated Sultan Bayezid and took him captive with his son Mustafa Çelebi, his other four sons fought for succession until they brought the empire to the brink of collapse."

"I know. My grandfather, Mircea the Elder, supported his son Musa. He even gave him his daughter Arina in marriage to strengthen their alliance."

"But that didn't work for him, did it? He backed the wrong horse. Musa lost, and Mehmed won. He became Sultan Mehmed the first, and he didn't like your grandfather supporting his opponent. He threatened to make Wallachia a province of the Ottoman Empire, like Greece and Bulgaria and so many others. He only relented when Mircea agreed to pay a tribute of three thousand gold pieces per year, plus the devşirme. Your father's still paying that tax, isn't he?"

Vlad's heart aches, like every time he thinks about devşirme. Bad enough to pay tribute, but children? He doesn't even like children, but, for some reason, that irks him no end.

"Anyhow, we were talking about the interregnum. It lasted for eleven long years and brought the Ottoman Empire to the brink of destruction. That's why Sultan Mehmed decided that, for the good of the empire, he had to secure the throne for his şehzade, Murad. He blinded his nephew Orhan, his brother Suleyman's son, and paid the emperor of Byzantium, Manuel Paleologus, to hold on to his own brother Mustafa Çelebi."

"Did that work?"

"Of course not. Manuel let him go as soon as Mehmed died. He wanted more war, to prevent our sultan, Sultan Murad the Second, to take the throne, and hoped to weaken the empire even further. But Murad won. He caught and hung Mustafa like a common criminal, then marched on Constantinople and mounted a siege. He couldn't take it because of the Theodosian walls, but he took most of the Byzantine Empire. These days' Byzantium is just a shadow of what it used to be."

"Was that the end of the Interregnum?"

"Oh, no. As soon as Murad lay siege to Constantinople, his younger brother, Küçük Mustafa, only thirteen at the time, tried to take the throne with help from the Karamanids and the Byzantines. But Murad caught him and had him executed. And that was the end of that."

Listening to him, Vlad has a flash of inspiration. The best way to destroy the Ottomans would be to do it from the inside. Have them fight each other, then finish whoever's left while the empire is still weakened and torn.

But how can he cause a civil war? Mehmed is Murad's only son.

For now.

But Murad is still a sultan, isn't he? And he's young enough to have more sons. Also young enough to take back the throne, if he chooses.

But why would he?

To save the empire.

From whom?

From Mehmed.

Why?

Because Mehmed did something so horrific that he can no longer be sultan, therefore Murad must go back to take his throne.

What did Mehmed do?

Nothing. But he doesn't need to do anything. Murad only has to think he did.

This got complicated, but Vlad knows in his heart that this is the way to destroy the empire. He just needs to work out the details.

This gets him so excited that he takes forever to notice that Kir Daskalos seems a bit off. He's slower than usual and looks worried.

"Are you OK?"

"Sure. I got you a book. Read it very carefully after I'm gone. I'll quiz you on it tomorrow."

The guards let him out, and Vlad opens the book. It's an old tome on Anatolia's geography, with drawings of its mountains, rivers and villages. Nothing exciting, Vlad thinks, looking for Eğrigöz.

He finds a folded loose sheet with a map showing the shortest route from Eğrigöz to Constantinople, and it's not part of the book. It's marked with scribbled Greek words showing the garrisons, the forts, and other places to avoid on the way.

Vlad's heart quickens. Kir Daskalos gave him an escape map.

CHAPTER 46

EDIRNE GARDENS

As soon as spring turned into summer, the palace gardens exploded into bloom. The air is heavy with the scent of roses, jasmine, and lilies. Birds romance each other in the green canopy and the countless fountains murmur softly, cooling the air.

This has got to be the most beautiful place on Earth, Radu thinks. The beauty around him gives him solace, and he gets back to the Persian poem he's been writing. The poem is about joy and pleasure, but he's not in the mood. Right now, his heart is heavy with melancholy and sadness. Last spring, he was here with Mehmed. They were always together. Now he's always alone.

He struggles to capture the joy of nature's rebirth and put it on the page, but what really moves him is the sadness of the old tree that didn't bloom this spring, the call of the lonely bird that no one answers and the dead butterfly he found on the path. *We truly only see with our heart,* he thinks, when someone touches his shoulder.

"Why the long face?"

It's Mehmed, smiling at him like he used to. He sits next to Radu and puts his arm around his shoulders, and, suddenly, all is fine with the world.

"How are you, my friend?" Mehmed asks.

"I'm OK. You?"

"Me too. I miss you."

Radu doesn't know what to say. *Why don't you ever have time for me then,* may not go over well. He settles for the truth.

"I miss you, too."

Mehmed has the grace to blush.

"I've been... busy lately. I'm sorry. But I needed to talk to you. How are your Transylvanian friends?"

"OK, I think." Radu hasn't seen Isa in ages, and Ali's always busy. And she's been kind of weird lately. Preoccupied and anxious. Like she worries about something.

"I think they're missing their friend," he says.

"The werewolf?"

Radu knows werewolves don't exist, but he will not argue with Mehmed about that.

"Kemal."

"I had some disturbing news from Çandarlı Halil Paşa, who never has anything but bad news. Only this time it's worse. His source at the Hungarian court told him that Hunyadi has a spy here. A kid, he says, connected with Kronstadt."

Radu's heart skips a beat. The only Transylvanians he knows of at the Edirne Palace are Ali and his friends. It can't be them. Unless it's Kemal, who escaped. But if it's him, they're all involved.

"Could he be saying this just to annoy you?"

"That's what I think. I can't see those kids being spies. Not even the one who escaped. But I can't be sure."

"What will you do?"

"I don't know. Çandarlı Paşa wants to interrogate them. You know what that means. Under torture, people will confess to anything, even to things they didn't do. And they're never any good afterwards. I'd rather not to go there. First, because I think it's just Çandarlı Paşa's crap. I don't want to give him the satisfaction. Second, both my mother and Gülbahar will poison my life if I do anything to your friend Ali. He's well connected, you know."

"I didn't know."

"Besides being your friend, he somehow made himself so useful to the harem women that they all swear by him."

Radu nods.

"I wonder if you could talk to him. Not directly, but just see if you can get him talking. I don't believe Çandarlı Paşa, but I can't really ignore him."

"But, my sultan, what do you want me to say? Ask him if he's a spy?"

"Not exactly. Find out about his beliefs, his hopes, what he's working towards. That kind of thing."

"Like schmooze him and see if he brags about sending state secrets?"

"Something like that. To be honest, Radu, I'm not sure what I want. Beside Çandarlı Paşa to be gone. And the janissaries to leave me alone. And to be... to spend more time with you."

Radu sighs. "Why don't you, my sultan?"

"Radu, I care about you. Very much. It's true that I'm busy. But there's more than that. My father warned me that as a sultan I'm not supposed to have... close friends. My mother doesn't like our friendship either. She wants me to spend more time with the women."

"Gülbahar?"

"Yes. And others. I'm worried that my friendship puts you in danger. The more time I spend with you, the more worried I am about bad things happening to you. But please believe me when I tell you I love you, whether or not I'm with you."

Radu shrugs. "I'll speak to Ali."

CHAPTER 47
A LOUSY SPY

Radu drags himself to Ali's kitchen, wondering what to say. Then he wonders if there's any point in wondering, since Ali always reads his thoughts. The chances of him getting something out of him without Ali noticing are just as good as the chances of him sprouting horns. He may as well wing it. He knocks and opens the door.

Ali is stirring into a steaming cauldron while mumbling some silly words, as usual. His face glows with sweat, and whatever's left of his chestnut hair is obscured by sweat and darkness, bringing up his amazing blue eyes.

"Hi, Ali."

Ali jumps back like he got caught, then sighs with relief as he recognizes Radu.

"What are you working on?"

"The validé wants a potion to help Gülbahar get heavy with child, and that's one thing my grandmother never taught me. The women who came to see her usually wanted to get rid of an unwanted child. Or not get with child at all. I've been struggling with this for days, but I'm not doing well. I hope she doesn't get one of the deaf-mutes to tie a sack around my head and throw me in the Tunca."

"I thought she was your friend and supporter."

"Sure. Until I fail to deliver. Then, I'm a goner."

"How's Isa?"

"I haven't seen him in a while. I hope he's OK. Why?"

"It must be hard for both of you with Kemal... gone. You must miss him. Unless you know where he's at ..."

"I have no clue."

"I thought so. Are you happy here, Ali?"

"Happy?"

"Yes."

Ali stirs her potion, looking befuddled.

Radu wonders if the eunuch even knows what happy means. "Would you rather be somewhere else?"

"Like where?"

"Back home."

"With my mother?"

"Yes."

"No. I'd rather be anywhere else than with my mother. Even here, failing to make Huma's potion, and wondering if she'll get me killed. So, I guess I'm happy here."

Radu walks around the room, staring at the plants hanging on the walls.

"Are you happy here, my prince?"

"Sometimes. I'm happy when you and Mehmed have time for me, but at times it gets very lonely."

Ali looks down, feeling guilty, but there's no need. Radu understands that, unlike him, Ali has work to do.

"Mehmed cares about you. Very much."

"I don't understand that. You'd think he'd find some time for me. But he's always busy."

"He's the sultan, and he has so much and so many things to worry about. But I know he loves you and thinks about you."

"Thanks, Ali. He stopped by to talk to me today. He... he's worried about you."

"About me?"

"Yes. Apparently, the grand vizier's spy in Hunyadi's court says there's a Transylvanian kid sending information to Hunyadi via Kronstadt. Mehmed wonders if you know anything."

Radu feels like an idiot. This isn't what he was supposed to say. He was supposed to finesse Ali and read his soul. Instead of that, he just laid it all on the table.

Ali's limpid eyes stare at him.

"What do you think, my prince?"

"Of course not. I know you're faithful to the sultan. This is all Çandarlı Paşa, trying to make trouble for Mehmed. That's what he does, all the time."

"Of course. Thank you for supporting me. I hope the sultan understands I'm not an enemy. Maybe you could help with that."

"Of course. I'm your friend. I'll tell Mehmed that I can vouch for you with my life."

"Thank you, my prince."

As he leaves, Radu sighs with relief that he's done with this awkward conversation. What a silly idea, to think that Ali would be a spy. He's just as faithful to the sultan as he is.

As he walks through the enchanting gardens, thinking about their conversation, Radu realizes that Ali never actually said he's not a spy. Nor did he say that he was faithful to the sultan. He didn't say much of anything, really, except that he'd rather be anywhere than home with his mother.

Radu did all the talking and found out nothing at all. He wonders what he'll tell Mehmed. What else, besides the fact that he vouches for Ali?

Nothing else comes to mind.

CHAPTER 48

LOOMING DANGER

It's still warm, but the low sun throws long shadows that creep quietly around Ali. She's in the palace garden, studying the plants, pretending to look for herbs for Hüma's potion, but what she's really doing, is wait for Isa.

They haven't met since the trial. They waited to let the storm pass, but now they need to talk. The grand vizier's suspicion may be the last straw. First Codru's escape, now this. It may be time to run. If they can.

Ali kneels to take a better look at a small blue flower she's never seen here. It looks just like its sisters in Mama Smaranda's garden: small, shy and milky blue. It doesn't look like much but its name is forget-me-not.

"You and your plants."

It's Isa. Her heart thumps with joy at being near him. Oh, how she longed to be with somebody who cares about her, somebody she doesn't need to pretend to or to lie. She's so tired of hiding and lying; her whole life is a lie, every moment of it, from pretending to love the sarayi, Hüma and the sultan, to having to pee standing and binding her budding breasts every morning to make sure they won't give her away.

He hugs her so tight it cuts her breath, then holds her at the end of his long arms to look at her. He grew so much he's almost a head taller than her, and looks different without his long golden hair, but his smile hasn't changed. He's still her old buddy, who gave her his food and had her back whenever she got in trouble.

"How are you?" he asks.

"Better now that I've seen you. You?"

"Me too. You look better without hair, you know," he says, and she smacks him across the back.

"You don't. You're the same doofus you've always been."

He laughs and hugs her again. "Oh, how I missed you, Ali."

She sighs. "I had to speak to you."

"Me too. I'm glad you arranged for our meeting, otherwise I would have had to. What's up at your end?"

"Çandarlı Paşa's spy at Hunyadi's court found out there's a Transylvanian kid spying for Hunyadi. The grand vizier presses Mehmed to interrogate us, so Mehmed sent Radu to feel the waters. Radu supports us, but that won't stop them. They'll soon start asking questions. I think it's time we bolt."

"How?"

Ali shrugs.

"Anything else?"

"Isn't this enough?"

"Anything about Codru?" Isa asks.

"I heard a rumor that one of the sultan's galleys in the Aegean had a rower escape. They say he turned into a werewolf and jumped overboard. They shot at him, but I wonder..."

"I do too. If they had him, they'd bring his head and nail it to the palace gates by the ears to show everyone what happens to those who don't obey the sultan. I don't think they got him, alive or dead. He's there, somewhere. We'll find him some day."

"If we're still alive," Ali says.

"Of course. Trust you to stick to the essentials. I got news from the mother-ship."

"The mother-ship?"

"Yep. Kronstadt. First, they got all our messages, including the one about Rózsa."

"How do you know?"

"We have a new friend. He arrived last week, with the last devşirme and the news."

"Seriously?"

"Yep. His name is Karim. He's from Sighișoara," Isa says.

"What's the news?"

"Rózsa sent the grand vizier another message, explaining how she got it wrong. It wasn't a Transylvanian at all. It was a Serb. She sent his name and his data to the grand vizier. He should get it any day. Unless he got it already."

"You mean..."

"Yep. She's playing for us now. We should be safe."

Ali tries to digest the idea that they aren't in immediate danger and don't need to flee. It's hard, since she's been brooding over this for ages.

"What else?"

"We're not in immediate danger, but Mehmed is. Did you hear the screams and see the smoke?"

"No."

"The janissaries are revolting and they want to depose the sultan. They set thousands of houses on fire in Edirne. Also, the market and a mosque. The sultan is on his way out."

"Why?"

"The janissaries hadn't gotten paid in months. When they finally did, the Ottoman silver acki had been devalued by eleven percent. The silver coins are lighter than they've ever been, so they're worth little against the Genoese ducat. It's like they worked for free half the time, and they're livid. The grand vizier told them it's all Mehmed's fault, so they are all incensed. The sultan's days are numbered."

"Would they kill him?"

"I don't know, but they want Murad back. They love Murad for a hundred reasons, the same ones they hate Mehmed for. And Çandarlı Paşa is spurring them."

"What does this mean for us?"

"I don't know. You're the smart one. You tell me," Isa says.

"If Murad returns, he'll send Mehmed away. To Manisa, or somewhere else in Anatolia. Mehmed would take Gülbahar and Hüma. And, since I belong to Hüma, I'd go with her. But you're working for the Ottoman administration, so you'd stay here. That means we'd be apart, with no way to communicate."

"We need to do some thinking. Find a connection, or find a way to stay together."

"But we'd be more effective if we could get news from here and from Manisa, too."

"We would, but there's no way. Manisa is weeks away by horse. We'd have no way to stay in touch and keep it under wraps. We'd be all alone."

Isa's words hit Ali straight in her heart.

"Yes. We'd be all alone."

"Can you see any other way?"

"If Hüma doesn't take me... or if she dies... I could stay behind. We'd be together. I don't know."

"Neither do I. Let's wait and see."

He hugs her again and this time, his hug lasts longer than she's used to. But he's her best friend, so she softens into his embrace. He whispers in her ear.

"If we ever make it out of here, and even if we don't, I want you to know I love you. You are my soul mate. I want you to share my life and bear my children."

Ali's heart skips a beat. Children?! Now that's one thing she doesn't need. And even if she did, bearing his children? Oh, no. She loves him too, sure she does. But not that way.

CHAPTER 49

HOW MUCH FOR YOUR EUNUCH?

The hammam's air is hot and steamy. Intoxicating scents of jasmine and rose swirl in the haze, bringing pleasure and wellbeing to the glistening bodies lying on the marble slabs or cooling in the pool. The voices are hushed, their movements languidly slow, and the water fountains sing softly, but there's a strain in the air telling Ali that the ladies in Sultan Mehmed's harem are not at ease.

She brings a silver tray loaded with lemon and rose sherbets, chilled with snow brought on the backs of pack horses all the way from Anatolia's mountains. The chilled drinks are worth their weight in silver, but that's just what these ladies are used to: Hüma Hatun, the validé, Mara Branković, Sultan Murad's fourth wife, and Sultan Mehmed's favorite, Gülbahar Hatun. They lay on the warm marble slab, letting the skilled hands of the masseuses soften and beautify their bodies. Hüma, white and full-bodied, with a cascade of flame-red curls falling to her waist; Mara, her curvy olive-skinned body glistening with sweat; And Gülbahar, her slim youthful body the color of acacia honey.

They chat like old friends, but something in the air raises the hair on Ali's neck. The place smells like fear.

"Have you heard from Sultan Murad lately?" Hüma asks Mara, like she doesn't much care one way or another.

But she cares. After snubbing her when he came to Edirne after the battle of Varna, Sultan Murad took only Halime Hatice with him, leaving Hüma and Mara behind. Mara may not give a rat's ass, but Hüma is consumed with jealousy and livid with anger.

"I did, in fact." Mara's voice is low, rich and heavily accented, like a mouth-watering piece of baklava loaded with honey and heavy with pistachios.

"What does he say?" Hüma asks, her voice shrill with impatience.

"He says he'll see us before too long. He heard he's needed here. He regrets having to leave his comfortable retreat in Manisa, but he has no choice other than doing his duty. His only joy in returning is to see us, his dutiful wives, he says."

"Bloody old coot," Hüma says.

Deafening silence. That's not the kind of language anyone — let alone one of the sultan's wives — uses to talk about him, and here even the walls have ears. One never knows who to trust, and the only safe thing is to trust nobody.

Hüma feels the weight of the looks converging on her.

"I'm not talking about my beloved Sultan Murad, of course. May Allah grant him a long and fruitful life in prayer and meditation. I'm talking about that old coot, Çandarlı Paşa. I bet he's the one who asked him to come back. That's why our beloved Sultan Murad considers leaving his retreat to return."

The women sigh, much relieved they don't have to turn Hüma in. Insulting the grand vizier is par for the course. The sultan is God-like and infallible, while Çandarlı Paşa is just a cranky old man with bad breath. They can say whatever they want about him. Who cares?

"Sultan Mehmed himself worried about the janissaries' revolt," Gülbahar says, then blushes as the two older women stare at her.

"He worries that Çandarlı Paşa will use it as an excuse to disturb Sultan Murad from his peace and prayer and persuade him to come back."

"That's unfortunate," Mara says, turning on her side. "I'm sure he's much happier there, and we're much… we're managing fine without him."

Hüma glances at her sideways.

"What will happen to us if Sultan Murad returns?" Gülbahar asks.

"Whatever Sultan Murad says. Sultan Mehmed will most likely go back to Manisa, or wherever his father sends him, if Sultan Murad retakes his throne. That means that wherever he goes, you, Gülbahar, will go with him. As for Hüma and I, we'll do whatever our beloved husband tells us to. That's the fate of the women in the harem. They have no say about what happens to them. The men, guided by Allah in his infinite wisdom, will decide what's best for us."

The women talk, and the expensive cold drinks are getting warm. Ali pushes the tray forward, offering it to them.

Hüma grabs a lemon sherbet. Mara grabs a rose one.

Gülbahar looks at Ali.

"What will happen to Ali, then?"

Hüma shrugs.

"She'll go with us wherever we go. You belong with Mehmed. Murad will probably keep that whore Halime Hatice here and send me away with Mehmed to Manisa. Or wherever. Either way, Ali comes with us."

Gülbahar smiles at Ali.

"Wonderful. I wouldn't want to leave him behind."

Ali sighs.

"Not necessarily." Mara touches the cold silver cup of sherbet to her cheek. "That feels wonderful. Have you tried it, Ali?"

Ali shakes her head.

"It's wonderful. Here, just try it." She brings the cold cup to her lips, takes a deep sip, then offers it to Ali. "It's the elixir of gods. Or their representatives on earth. Give it a try."

Ali shakes her head. "I don't deserve it, my lady. I'm surely not anyone's representative on earth."

"Try it, Ali. For me."

Ali can't think of a way to avoid it, so she brings the cup to her lips. She barely touches it and hands it back.

"Oh, no. Empty it and think about love."

Ali sighs. Like she didn't have enough to think about. Love is nowhere on her agenda, but what can she do? She brings the cup to her lips and sips. The cold drink reminds her of drinking water from half-frozen streams in Transylvania. But this isn't water. It's a potion, scented with roses, enriched with honey, and touched by the curvy lips of the temptress of the sarayi.

The drink may be cold, but it spreads wonderful warmth inside her. Ali's hands shake as she sets the empty cup on the tray.

"How was it?"

"Amazing, my lady. Thank you."

"My pleasure." Mara's slanted eyes look deeply into Ali's, probing her soul. Ali's blood bursts in her cheeks and her mouth goes dry. Mara smiles.

"Hüma?" she asks.

"Yes."

"What would you like for Ali?"

"What do you mean?"

"I like him. I'd like to buy him from you. Though, of course, he's not yours. Like us all, he belongs to the sultan. But if he was yours, what would you want for him?"

"He's not for sale."

"Of course not. But if he was, what would you want for him?"

Hüma stands up and the servants rush to wrap her in soft white towels.

"Ali is not for sale."

"I have the priceless emerald bracelet Murad gave me as a wedding gift. The emeralds, a dozen of them, are as big as the one in your ring. Trimmed with diamonds. I guess the sultan was trying to impress my father, Serbia's despot."

Hüma's breath comes out ragged. She's blowing mad, both from

Mara's insult to the most valuable thing she owns, and from the challenge.

"He's not for sale."

As she leaves, Mara shouts behind her:

"I'll ask Murad, then. Let me know if you change your mind."

CHAPTER 50

LESBOS, SPRING 1446

Winter on the island of Lesbos is nothing like winter in Transylvania, where it gets so cold that a man's piss clicks as it hits the ground. Here, it barely ever freezes. Snow is as rare as hen's teeth, but the wet cold wind cuts through your clothes into your bones. It would stink to sleep outside, but, thankfully, Codru doesn't need to. This whole winter, he's been living with Nikos and his mom. After three days of honey-sweetened willow bark tea, the woman's fever went down, and she came back to her senses. The day she got out of bed, Nikos started looking at Codru as if he was sent by God, inhaling his every word and following him everywhere.

Then it happened. One day, Codru went fishing and Nikos followed him.

"What are you doing?"

"Looking for worms to bait the hook to get us some fish for dinner."

"Why don't you fish in a boat, like everyone else?"

"I don't have a boat."

"How did you get here?"

"I swam."

"From where?"

"From a ship."

"What happened to the ship?"

"It sailed away."

"Didn't they see you fall off?"

"They were busy."

"With what?"

"Wow! Look at that!"

"What?"

"A big fish."

"Can we get it?"

"No. He's gone now. Why don't you hold on to the fishing pole while I prepare another one? Watch for the float, and tell me if it's moving."

The kid grabbed it and went quiet, staring at the piece of soft wood Codru had tied to the line for a float. It wasn't great, but it was the best he could do to help feed them.

They had flour, feta, honey, and olives. And the vegetables Nikos's mom had pickled before she got sick. But that wasn't enough to last them through the winter, even though Codru fished, brought in wood, and picked the forgotten grapes from the neighbors' vineyards. Not enough for a growing kid, a convalescing woman and a hungry werewolf.

And the full moon was coming.

"The float is moving."

Codru dropped the second pole to help Nikos. His hands itched to grab the pole, but he didn't.

"Hold on to it until it settles, then pull it up gently."

The kid was too good for his age. He held until the pulling stopped, then stepped back and waited for the fish to get settled before bringing him ashore.

Codru watched proudly as Nikos brought in a plump, glistening sea bream.

"Well done. Your mother will be so proud."

They had grilled fish with lemon and olives that evening, with crusty hot bread baked by Nikos' mom, and retsina.

Codru didn't know what to make of the retsina. It was golden-yellow and looked like wine, but it smelled like a church.

"What is this?"

"It's Greek wine. We seal the bottles with pine resin, and the wine borrows the aroma. You'll get used to it."

The first glass tasted weird, but the second one was easy. By the third, Nikos was asleep, and Codru was happy.

He looked at the woman seated across the kitchen table and found her beautiful. In the flickering light of the candles, her dark eyes were mysterious and her narrow face glowed like dark honey. Her eyes smiled as she refilled his glass.

"What's your name?" he asked, realizing he didn't know, since Nikos always called her Mom.

"Athena. Yours?"

"Codru. You have such a beautiful name. What does it mean?"

"It's very common. Here, most first-born girls are named Athena, after the Greek goddess of wisdom. Parents hope they'll grow up wise and strong like her. They need to. Here, the boys' lives aren't easy, but the girls always have to struggle."

"It's got to be hard to be a woman."

"It is. Unless you have a man. And even then, it's not easy. It was good to have you here."

"Thank you. I'm grateful for your hospitality."

Athena poured more of the golden wine smelling like incense.

"Where are you going next?"

"To Transylvania. That's where my... people are."

Athena's amber eyes looked into his above her glass.

"Are you married?"

Codru laughed. "God no."

"Engaged?"

"Of course not."

"In love?"

Codru remembered the girl sitting in a bear trap in Edirne's hunting ground. She was beautiful, but she wasn't real. Neither was he. He was just a werewolf looking after a friend's friend.

"I don't think so."

Athena set down her empty glass and put her hand over his.

"Then let's enjoy tonight. I have nobody. You have nobody. But tonight, I have you, and you have me. Let's make the most of being alive today, in case tomorrow never comes."

She opened her chemise. Her olive skin glowed like gold in the flickering light of the candle, making his mouth go dry. His breath caught in his throat as she pulled him to the ground.

They lay, facing each other, on the sheepskins in front of the fireplace. She kissed the palm of his hand, then licked it in a growing spiral, and Codru's groin grew into a beautiful ache.

"I never..." he whispered.

She laughed softly and covered his mouth with hers. Her soft lips touched his, then her hungry teeth nibbled on them, quickening his heart.

"You will now," she said, slipping her tongue inside his mouth and turning him inside out with her touch.

She kissed his cheek, then the ugly scar his mother gave him the night he became a werewolf that nobody had ever kissed. She planted a row of soft kisses down his neck to his shoulder, then laid her cheek over the black curly hair on his chest.

"You are beautiful," she said.

Codru's heart skipped a beat. Nobody had ever called him beautiful.

Her soft hand slid down his stomach towards the throbbing ache between his legs. She touched it gently and laughed.

"And you are ready."

She cupped it with her hands and tasted it, and Codru's mind flew to some place it had never been. *If this is wrong, I don't want to be right*, he thought, before he stopped thinking and let himself fly.

CHAPTER 51

TIME TO GO

But was months ago. Now the spring has come, and it's time for Codru to go home. But it's hard, because he loves both Nikos and his mom. As he lays with her head on his shoulder, he wishes he could stay here with them. But he can't. He must help his friends and accomplish his mission. And there's more.

Athena hugs him closer. "Why do you have to leave? Why can't you stay here with us?"

"I can't. I have to go home."

"Why?"

"You know why."

His callused hand traces the soft curve of her breast and caresses her cheek. He'd like to imprint them in his memory forever.

Her tears glisten in the moonlight, breaking his heart, but he has to leave on the next full moon. Lesbos is not a big island, and a werewolf roaming the hills under the full moon couldn't go unnoticed.

The first night with a full moon, he'd brought home a pig. Athena didn't ask any questions. She butchered and cooked it, and she shrugged when some neighbors stopped by, asking if she'd seen a wolf.

Some even talked about a werewolf, but most thought it was just an old wives' tale.

They ate well that month.

The next night with a full moon, he'd returned with a sheep. Athena studied the sheep's throat, bloody and shredded by fangs, then stared at him.

He said nothing.

When the neighbors came asking again, Athena had her own questions. "Where was the wolf? What was it like?"

"Humongous. With fangs like daggers and eyes glowing in the dark. Didn't you hear it?"

"I didn't."

"That's strange. Some people said they saw it roaming near here. Next month we'll get a posse together and kill it," the men said.

Codru shuddered.

That night in bed, Athena touched his chest, running her hands through his curly black hair, then studied the old scar on his neck. "Is it you?"

"What?"

"The werewolf."

Codru wished he could lie.

"It's me."

That night, she made fierce love to him. She loved him like it was the last time. The same the night after, and the night after that.

That was four weeks ago. Now that the full moon is coming, he has to go.

"Where will you go?"

"I need to get back to Transylvania."

The following morning, she took him to a mountain overlooking the sea and the lands beyond it, far north.

"Lesbos is now Genoese, but that island there is in the Ottoman Empire. Are they still after you?"

"I hope they think I'm dead."

"If they catch you, they'll shackle you again and put you on one of their galleys. The only way out would be to pretend you're one of them. They don't enslave their own."

That evening, he kissed Nikos goodbye.

"Where are you going?"

"Home."

"When are you coming back?"

"I don't know."

"Before the winter?"

"I don't know."

"I'll be waiting for you. I'll be there, by the boats, where I found you on the first day."

Codru hugged them, then headed to the shore, feeling their eyes following him. Oh, how he wished he didn't have to go. But there was no other way. Here, there was no place to hide.

With a heavy heart, he sat alone under the olive trees, waiting for the moon to rise and change him into a werewolf, giving him the strength to swim across the sea, and thought about Athena's words:

"I'm... late."

"Late for what?"

"You know."

His heart froze. It had never crossed his mind that she could get heavy with child, though it should have. He knew how children got made. But he somehow never thought that could apply to him.

"What will you do?" he asked.

"I don't know. I guess I'll just do my best."

She sighed, then gathered the courage to ask. "The baby. Will he... will he be like you?"

Codru's jaw fell. "You mean..."

"Yes."

"I... don't know."

Athena sighed.

"I guess I'll find out."

He hugged her tight, this woman who loved him even though she knew what he was, and may carry his seed inside her. He would have given anything to stay, but he couldn't. He kissed her and whispered: "I'll be back."

The white orb of the moon rose from behind the seas. The ache in his bones became unbearable as the moon pulled him and stretched him into his werewolf self.

He stepped into the water, wondering if he would ever return.

CHAPTER 52

EĞRIGÖZ, SPRING 1446

The spring has finally embraced Eğrigöz. As the days grew longer and the sun stronger, the barren mountain took a new life. The birds call, looking for love, the ash trees burst in pink blooms, and even the guards look happy to be out and chat to each other, taking their eyes off Vlad for short moments.

For weeks now, he's thought about nothing else but his escape. He's been so absorbed with planning it, he almost forgot about the rats. But he needs help.

Kir Daskalos does his best. Vlad's father, Vlad Dracul, promised him a comfortable life without worries if he can get his son back, and Kir Daskalos would love to retire in a sunny spot with a little vineyard and a view of the sea. But that takes more than a teacher's meager pay. He'd love to help, but it's a long way between giving Vlad a map, and pulling him out of Eğrigöz, then whisking him six hundred miles away to Târgoviște.

"We'll have to bribe the guards," Vlad says.

Kir Daskalos glances at the door. Today's guard, Amir, is a graying man with a deep scar on his cheek. He marches in front of Vlad's cell, glancing in every once in a while.

"Which guard?" Kir Daskalos asks.

"All would be best. But it's risky, since any of them could talk."

"Expensive too. I'm still waiting for the gold your father promised, but the guards won't move on promises. We'll have to have the gold in hand."

"I think Amir would be the best, then. He's not as brain-washed as the others, and he's old enough to be ready to settle."

"What makes you think he won't sell you?"

Vlad shrugs.

"Why would he?"

"To save his neck. If you escape, they'll kill every single guard. After they torture them, of course. Me too, if they catch me."

Vlad remembers Tokat. For a split second, he wishes he was still there with Şevlet Paşa interrogating prisoners. But he's not there. He's here, in Eğrigöz, and he needs to get out.

"I'll work on the guards. You work on the money. Father should arrange for a horse, close by, and for safe houses on the way out."

That evening, Vlad hangs out by the door. "Amir?"

"Yes?"

"Are you married?"

The guard keeps marching.

"Of course."

"How many wives?"

"Four."

"Kids?"

"Three sons."

"Any girls?"

Amir shrugs. "I lost count."

Vlad laughs. "You're a lucky man. Three sons, four wives, and you've lost count of your daughters."

"Allah has been good to me."

"Surely. Do they live here?"

Amir glances at him like he's crazy. "Here? Where?"

"Are they in Edirne?"

"Bursa."

"Nice house?"

"Nice enough."

"You see them often?"

"Not enough. I have to work."

"Have you considered retiring?"

"If I retire, who will pay for the girls' dowries and the women's jewelry and the boys' horses? Thanks to the sultan, they have a good life. But I have to work for it."

"There may be ways…"

Amir glances at Vlad. "Like?"

"There should be a way to reward a brave man like you. You're so much wiser than the others. And more experienced. You should be captain and get the money and the honor you deserve."

"Next year, they said."

"But they said that before, didn't they?"

Amir's eyes narrow. "How did you know?"

Vlad doesn't know. But it's easy to see the man hates his job and thinks he deserves better. Don't we all? It's easy to play on his ego, and sell him hope.

"They said that last year. And the year before that."

"I'm sorry, Amir. There may be ways to get what you deserve. And revenge, too. That's even sweeter than money."

After that, Vlad kept working on Amir day after day. He learned the names of his children, and the name of the lovely village near Bursa where he dreams of having a farm and a few sheep. He listened, learned, and nurtured Amir's dreams.

So when Kir Daskalos finally brought the gold, Vlad got so drunk with joy he could barely wait for Amir.

When he finally arrived, Vlad showed him the green velvet purse… "This is enough for a farm with sheep and horses. And for your daughters' dowries."

Amir weighed the purse in his hand. He opened the bag and glanced at the shiny golden Genoese ducats, then bit one to make sure it was gold. He nodded and opened the cell door, waving Vlad out.

Vlad stepped out cautiously. He looked right and left. Nobody. He rushed down the dark tunnel heading out until he reached the gate. It was wide open, but something was stuck in his way. A stake.

He looked up. Kir Daskalos's head, his blind eyes still open, stood impaled on the stake, smiling at Vlad with his five yellow teeth.

Behind him, the agha and the guards are smiling.

"It may be enough for the farm and the dowries, but not enough for my head. There isn't enough gold on earth to buy me another," Amir says, handing agha the purse. The agha smiles.

"You're a wise man, Amir. And you, prince, are lucky. Your head is safe for now until we hear from the sultan. Back to your cell. No more teacher, no more books, no more outside privileges."

Vlad's soul goes dark with anger. As the door slams shut behind him, he looks for the sharp rock he saved for his rats. Now, more than ever, he needs a release.

But his rock is gone.

CHAPTER 53
EDIRNE

The validé's dazzling quarters would put to shame any palace on earth. Everything the eye can see or the hand can touch is beautiful, rare, and precious. From the white marble floors, veined with pink blushes and spotted with delicate purple bursts, carried on the back of camels from thousands of miles away, to the gold-embroidered red silk pillows, there's nothing like this in the world.

Still, the validé is in a funk. Her green eyes are brewing a storm, and her delicate eyebrows meet above her nose like a hawk taking flight. Hüma Hatun is not happy, and her only son can't help but notice it.

"You called me, Mother?" he asks, after kissing the soft hand dwarfed by her massive emerald.

"Yes. We need to talk."

Mehmed crosses his legs to sit on one of the pillows scattered on the thick Isfahan carpet.

"Not here."

She's in one of her moods, Mehmed thinks, wondering what it is this time. He barely spent any time with Radu, and he takes Gülbahar to his bed on most nights. He even took a couple of other women she sent, just to keep her happy. But it's still not good enough.

"Let's walk." The validé claps her hands, and her little eunuch, Radu's friend, rushes in. He's easy to recognize, with the chestnut shadow barely covering the pink of his scalp, and his eyes like deep lakes.

"My yashmak."

Ali brings it back moments later. Hüma covers her face and heads out, and Mehmed follows her through the labyrinth of corridors to the gardens.

The spring turned into summer. The evening air is imbibed with the scent of a million roses and lilies. Mehmed takes in a deep breath and can't help but smile, though he knows nothing pleasant is about to follow.

"You heard the news?"

"Which news?"

"About your father."

Mehmed's heart skips a beat. What news about his father can incense his mother so? He shakes his head no.

"He wrote to Mara — to Mara! — to tell her he's coming back. He thinks he's needed here."

Mehmed's blood heats to a boil.

"It's got to be that old weasel Çandarlı Paşa! When he complained about the janissaries' revolt, I told him to take care of it. So he called Father back."

"Most likely."

"I'll kill the old bastard. This is the second time he's talked to Father behind my back."

"And it won't be the last."

"I'll take care of him. He won't do it again after swimming in the Tunca with a bag around his head."

"And what good will that do, now that your father is on his way back already? It will only make him angrier. Don't do it."

"So, what do you want me to do? Sit and watch the bloody coward betraying me?"

"You need to refocus. Çandarlı Paşa is no longer your problem. Now that he's talked to your father, things are out of his hands. The damage is done, and cutting off his head won't solve anything."

"It will make me feel better."

"Is this what it's all about? Making you feel better?"

Mehmed wishes he could see her eyes beyond her veil. "What do you mean?"

"You are the sultan. Behave like a sultan. What would you do if your great uncle Orhan escaped Constantinople and came to take your throne?"

"I'd raise an army and go to war. And I would, once and for all, destroy those filthy Greeks who call themselves Romans. I'd take Constantinople."

"And how is this different?"

Mehmed's jaw drops. He stares at his mother.

"What are you saying, Mother?"

"Somebody is coming to take your throne. What should you do?"

"You've got to be kidding. Are you saying I should go to war against Father?"

"It's your throne. It's not just your right, it's your obligation to protect it. You swore on the Sword of Osman."

"From Father?"

"From anyone who tries to take it."

CHAPTER 54

THE PRICE OF A THRONE

Mehmed's jaw falls. He stays quiet as his brain struggles to absorb the enormity.

"But Mother, Father gave it to me. He put me on the throne."

"Exactly. So it's yours now. Therefore, it's no longer his to take back whenever he feels like it."

"And how exactly do you see this working?"

"I don't think he'll bring a lot of men. But even if he comes with the whole Anatolian Army, you still have more men. And we have Edirne. And the Sword of Oman. You are the sultan. I don't think he'd even try to fight. If he sees you're not willing to go peacefully, he'll just go back to Manisa, his meditation, and that whore Halime Hatice Hatun rather than start another interregnum."

"Mother, if that's what you think, you don't know Father. If he's coming back, he's doing it to save the empire. I don't know why he thinks he needs to, but I'm sure it is so. He doesn't want to be sultan. He'd rather meditate and read the Quran. But no matter what, he'll do his duty. He'll fight if he needs to fight, and he'll kill me if he thinks that's what he needs to do. If I raise an army, he will fight."

Hüma shrugs.

"OK then. You still have the bigger army, and you're a great leader. You have a good chance of defeating him."

"Mother, I have zero chances to defeat him. He's older, wiser, and a better leader than I am. His men love him and would die for him. Even worse, *my* men love him and would die for him. Once they see his tughra, they'll leave me like I've got leprosy. You understand? There's no way on earth that I can win a war against Father, even if I wanted to. And I don't."

"Why not?"

"It's his throne. He gave it to me, then he came to bail my ass out at Varna and went back. If he's coming back to take it, I will step aside."

"Do you even understand what that means?"

"That he'll be the sultan?"

"That you won't. He's young enough to live another thirty years. He can have another dozen sons. Once you're no longer sultan, any of his sons can take the throne when he dies. Or even before. He can give it to another, like he gave it to you. Then you're nothing. Less than nothing. You're the governor of Manisa. And how about me? I worked hard to put you on this throne. I did things that shall not be mentioned so that you can be sultan. And now you're ready to give it up without a fight and make me lose my status as validé? I'll get to be, once more, behind Halime Hatice Hatun. She's always been his favorite, and she's still young enough to make him another son. Do you understand this?"

Mehmed sighs.

"I'm sorry, Mother. I understand you're not happy that I won't fight for the throne. Please believe me when I tell you that I don't stand a chance to win. Not one. And if I fight and lose, you'll still lose everything. Your beautiful clothes, and the slaves, and the jewels. Everything. Including me. Because Father won't have a choice but to execute me. He will have to set an example, and he will. There's nothing we can get by going to war against Father. Nothing but death."

Hüma stays quiet for a long time, and Mehmed hopes she gets it.

"So maybe a war is not a good idea," she finally says.

"It surely is not."

"But there are other ways."

"Other ways to what?"

"To keep your throne."

"I hope so. I'll speak to Father and see why he's coming back. Maybe I can even get rid of Çandarlı Paşa. Father won't be pleased if he sold him a bunch of lies."

"Maybe. Or maybe we need to find more... definitive ways."

"To what?"

"To keep you on the throne."

"What are you saying, Mother?"

"People live. People die. Sultans too. It's a long, dangerous trip from Manisa to here. Things can happen. Accidents."

"Are you talking about..."

"I'm not talking about anything. I'm suggesting you may have a few of your most faithful men to go meet your father on his way and make sure he's safe."

"My men?"

"Of course. You are the sultan. Not me. I have no men, and even if I did, nobody would do it for me. What do I have to give them? I'm just a woman, locked within the bounds of the harem. But you... You are a young sultan, and you can promise anything to those who earn your trust. Ambassadorships. Lands. Money. Anything. You just need to find the right person and offer the right thing."

"Mother?"

"Yes."

"Don't go there."

"Where?"

"If I ever hear you suggest something like this again, I'll have no choice but to tell Father. How do you think he'll take it?"

"Not well, I guess."

"Then don't mention this to me ever again."

"I won't. But don't forget what I told you. You have the means. You only need to have the will and the courage."

"That's enough!"

Mehmed turns around and leaves. He's so angry he can't see straight, so he's not sure if he saw a shadow moving in the bushes, or he just imagined it. His heart in turmoil, he stomps away without looking back.

CHAPTER 55
TÂRGOVIȘTE, JUNE 1446

It's a stormy day in Târgoviște. The angry dark sky spits thunder after thunder, and pukes a deluge of rain that whips the castle and sneaks in through the leaks in the roof. The court of Târgoviște isn't that old, but it was built in a hurry. Between harvesting crops and fighting the Ottomans, the Hungarians, and whoever else was invading Wallachia at the time, the roof had to wait.

Sitting in the banquet room, which is also the throne room and even the state dining room, depending on the occasion, Ștefan stares at the steady stream of water darkening the thick stone in the corner, pretending he can't hear Mircea argue with Vlad Dracul. They're fighting like Ștefan hasn't yet seen them, though he's been here for years.

Mircea's red in the face like he's been tending a bonfire. His fists are tight and his knuckles turned white as he leans across the massive table separating him from his father.

"What do you mean you'll return the Bulgarians? You promised to give them shelter. Twelve thousand people who left their country and their homes because you promised them a place to live. They left with nothing but the clothes on their backs, and now you're going to send them back to the sultan? Where is your word?"

Sitting at the other end of the table, Vlad Dracul seems tired and old. His eyes are sad as he looks at his incensed son.

"Listen, Mircea. I wish I didn't have to do this, but I need to make peace with the sultan now that Hunyadi is after us. I know he's coming. Our Wallachian merchants got arrested in Kronstadt, so it's just a matter of time until he crosses the border. We can't fight both the sultan and Hunyadi at the same time. You have to choose your fights."

"But why choose the sultan? Hunyadi is a Christian, like us. We fought together at Varna. If you have to choose, why not choose him?"

"I don't get to choose, Mircea. Hunyadi made up his mind already. Now that the Estates of Hungary made him regent, he's more powerful than he's ever been, and he's working to consolidate his power. That's why he's looking to set himself up with neighbors that suit him. He backs Ștefan's uncle, Petru Aron, for the throne of Moldova, and he's grooming my cousin Vladislav to be his puppet here, in Wallachia."

"But Father…"

"No but. Please listen. Hunyadi will try to get rid of us as soon as he gets a chance, but right now, the Ottomans are weak. They aren't even sure who their sultan is. The janissaries have revolted, and Mehmed is so obsessed with Constantinople that all he wants from us is peace. We'll get good terms if we sue for peace, and they'll back us when Hunyadi comes. Which will be soon."

"But Father, the Bulgarians…"

"Forget about them. They're the least of our worries. We have our Wallachians to worry about. And what's even worse. I'll have to give back Giurgiu."

Mircea jumps to his feet.

"You can't be serious. I took Giurgiu."

"WE took Giurgiu. You may have held the sword, but those were my men."

"So where do I fit in with all this, Father? You make decisions without consulting me. I go into battle, but they are your men. What am I here for?"

"You're here to learn. Soon enough, you'll be making the hard decisions and you'll have some youngster screaming in your face that you're nothing but an old coward, while you're doing your best to keep your country safe. You learned to fight, and you're a good fighter, but you haven't yet learned how to rule. There's a big difference. Fighting is about defeating the enemies. Ruling is about keeping them away."

Mircea shakes his head.

"That may be, but there is right and there is wrong. Returning twelve thousand people who trusted you to be decimated by their worst enemy, that's wrong. Returning the hard-fought fort in Giurgiu to the Ottomans, that's wrong. The people killed in that fight will roll in their graves."

Vlad Dracul shrugs.

"Probably not. Most of them have no graves. They fed the fish in the Danube. Please, son, get off your high horse and get real. Wallachia is a tiny country. We're just the bloody battlefield between two empires that don't give a rat's ass about us. We're nothing but their playing field: they come when it suits them, they leave when it doesn't. God put us here, where the west and the east collide, and said: 'This is your place. Take care of it.' So we do the best we can. We're like tiny crickets watching the birds fight the frogs. We're not strong enough to worry about morals and ethics. Our business is to not get eaten, and we're doing all right. Look around. The Bulgarians, the Albanians and even the Greeks no longer have a country. We do. Our job is to take care of it."

Mircea shakes his head. "Seriously? That's the best you can do?"

"Yep. I hope you can do better."

"I don't think so. I'm not interested in crawling through the dirt like a worm, hoping nobody eats me."

Mircea storms out, slamming the heavy door. Vlad Dracul sighs.

Ștefan shrinks in his chair, pretending he doesn't exist, but his uncle knows he's here.

"How are you doing, Ștefan?"

"I'm good, thanks."

"This must be hard for you. I know you and Mircea are close."

Ștefan nods. That was true, of course. Before Lena.

"Still, everything I told him is true for you. Just like us, Moldova is a tiny country stuck at the frontier between the cross and the crescent. It's not easy being us, but we do our best with what we have. That's why we have to always weigh our priorities. I'm sorry about the Bulgarians, and I'd give a lot to not have to send them back, but I have no choice. They'll have to meet their fate, like we'll have to meet ours, and hope for the best, which seldom comes to be."

Ștefan sighs, his soul heavy.

"But, on a happier note, I have news for you. Bogdan, your father, is well, and wants you back."

CHAPTER 56
BURSA, JUNE 1446

The Ottoman Empire's first capital, Bursa, has a special place in Sultan Murad's heart. The old city may lack the glitz and glitter of the Edirne Palace, but the mosques and monuments built by the first Ottoman sultans, their tombs, and the tombs of their many wives and children, bring Allah's blessing over the people of the city, which is a place of love and remembrance, and Murad loves it.

He sometimes wishes the capital was here rather than Edirne. Edirne is a young city. Barely a couple of hundred years old, still struggling to make a name for itself. No sultan was ever buried there, and he won't be the first. He wants to be here, in Bursa, near Aladdin, his favorite son, with his many dead babies and his ancestors. That's why he'll make sure that his will is recorded and respected. When the time comes — maybe soon — he wants it to be ready.

He sits cross-legged on his pillow in the greatest room of the sultan's palace in Bursa, staring at the viziers he asked to witness his will. They look uncomfortable, but he couldn't care less about their comfort. He's only worried about their willingness to enforce his will, should it prove necessary.

"But my sultan, you are young and well. There's no reason to worry about your death," says Çandarlı Paşa.

Murad frowns.

"That's so not worthy of you, Çandarlı Paşa. You called me back from my retreat to retake the throne. Do you really think there is no danger?"

Çandarlı Paşa blushes.

"I have no reason to believe that your son would try to hurt you, my sultan. He respects and cherishes you. I think he understands that if you come back, it is for a good cause."

"So, he'll be delighted to see me back? And his mother?"

Çandarlı Paşa shrinks and kowtows.

"Sorry, my old friend. I know you mean the best. And so do I. But I must be ready. It will give me peace of mind to know that, should I find my death instead of my throne, my last wishes are known and recorded. That's why I want to sign my will before I proceed any further."

"But why insist on this peculiar arrangement? You deserve so much better! Why get buried in a tomb of uncovered dirt exposed to the elements, when you could have the finest craftsmen sculpt the rarest marble and build you a mausoleum like no other? You deserve it, after three decades of victories and building the Ottoman Empire beyond anyone's dreams."

"I deserve nothing. I'm here to make the word of Allah into truth. I tried to do that, with moderate success. The one thing that matters to me is that the empire is safe, and that Allah gets the praise he deserves. That's why I want to have a gallery for the disciples to read the Quran and memorize it day and night. I also want to be near my son Aladdin, his sons, my daughters, and all those dear to me."

The paşas, all of them, kowtow and sign his will, but their eyes are veiled with sorrow. They're not happy to think about his death.

Neither is Murad. He worries about what will happen to the empire and to his son after he dies. But more than anything, he feels guilty.

He dropped the whole weight of the Ottoman Empire on the

shoulders of his twelve-year-old son, who was utterly unprepared for the magnitude of the task. If being a sultan was too much for him, how on earth could he ever imagine that a young kid could do it? Just because he was tired of politics and fighting, and he foolishly thought the empire was safe.

He was wrong — he knew it when they called him back for Varna. Even so, he left Mehmed in charge and left again, just because he was too tired to fight. And now the kid is in trouble again. Allah only knows what he'll do when he sees his father at the gates, ready to take back the throne.

And he has no other son but Mehmed.

That night he asks for Hatice Halime to be brought to his bed. Not because he wants sex — sex is the farthest thing from his mind — but because he needs an old friend to talk to, and he has no older friend.

They've been married for over twenty years. They've had good days and bad. But she made him the best son he could hope for. He was so gifted that Allah claimed him for himself, so they're both still mourning Aladdin.

She's already waiting when he gets to his bed, and her loving smile warms his heart. He drops his armor and kaftan and squeezes under the silk sheets by her side, and she envelops him in her loving arms. She's not as young as she used to be. Neither is he, but for a man, it doesn't matter. Her skin is soft and tired, and the wrinkles run deep around her golden eyes. But her embrace is love, and her sagging breasts are home, unlike the virgins they push on him at every stop. He's beyond proving anything to anyone. He's old and tired and he needs a friend.

"I want to be buried next to Aladdin. Thank you for giving me the best son I could hope for. I miss him every day and every night, and I know you do, too."

Hatice Halime bursts in tears. She sobs so hard she can't talk.

"I'm sorry, baby," he says, hugging her tight to absorb her heat and her love. "I'm so sorry this happened to our son."

"Hüma," she chokes, her brown eyes full with tears. "It's Hüma's doing. I know it."

He draws her close, his heart aching for her. She's probably right, but only Allah knows. He, at least, has another son. And a bunch of daughters. She's got nothing. Nothing but the pain.

"I'm sorry, my love. So sorry. How would you like to have another son?"

She gasps, and he thinks he said something stupid, until she draws him close. Very close.

"Yes. Please. There's nothing on earth I want more."

He pulls her close, kisses her eyes, and rejoices in the scent of her womanhood and her happy submission. Loving her is his privilege and his duty. As he takes her, he feels like a lucky man.

CHAPTER 57

EDIRNE, JULY 1446

July in Edirne is not for the weak. Neither are the long dusty roads devoid of shade, the heavy sky melting over them, nor the merciless sun. The horses' hooves clatter like hammers on the rock-hard dirt that hasn't seen rain since this spring. It's been a long way from Bursa.

It's not over yet, but it's close, thank Allah, Murad thinks, watching Edirne castle's walls dance in the heat above Tunca's narrowed blue ribbon. He's about to find out if he has to go to war against his son, or if they can build the empire together.

He gathers his men around him, preparing for an attack. He grabs the bejeweled hilt of his kilij and spurs his white stallion forward.

The gates are closed, and Murad's heart skips a beat. The heads popping over the walls watching them aren't good news either. There's no trace of Mehmed, though he must know they're coming. That's a bad sign.

He sighs and prays to Allah to guide him for the good of the empire and have mercy on him and his son, just as the palace gates open. Cheering crowds erupt to greet him, and Murad's heart is torn between joy and hurt. He's delighted that his people love him and want him back, but he's heartbroken that in the two years of being sultan Mehmed hasn't earned his people's trust and love. He wonders why.

Murad rides in through the tall gates, nodding to the adoring crowds that cry with joy to see him back. Their love is touching and painful. They'd die for him, but they're glad to be rid of Mehmed, and Murad wonders where his son's rule went wrong. The kid is young, handsome and fierce, while he's old, tired, and in much need of rest. Still, these people welcome him like they've never seen a better sight, and that's bitter-sweet. Why don't they love Mehmed?

Somewhere in the depths of his mind, he still wonders if there's a quick way to fix this so that he can return to Manisa and live his last years thanking Allah for his gifts in prayer and meditation.

The palace door opens. The janissaries stand to attention on both sides of the wide steps, their red uniforms catching the eye, their hands on their swords. Mehmed is there, waiting in the open door. He's taller than Murad remembers him, and he holds his head high, but his pale face and tired eyes speak about lack of sleep and worry.

It's got to be hard for him, Murad thinks. He's been sultan for two years. And now, suddenly, his father came back to take his throne. It's an enormous loss of face for Mehmed, and Murad does his best to smooth things out.

He dismounts, steps on the first step, and opens his arms.

Mehmed stares for a moment, then walks into his hug, his eyes moist with tears. They embrace in full sight of the palace, and the crowd erupts in deafening cheers.

"Thank you, Father," Mehmed whispers.

Murad tightens his hug one more time, then lets go. Side by side, they climb the stairs into the palace. They stop in the door to wave one last time, then head in.

The throne room is packed with dignitaries welcoming the sultan. The first, of course, is Çandarlı Paşa, who drops to his knees in front of Murad and kisses his hand in submission.

Murad pulls him up into a hug.

"Good to see you, old friend."

"Good to see you, my sultan. We're glad to have you back."

Mehmed throws him a venomous glance, then steps aside, while Murad greets the many richly dressed paşas and aghas, dignitaries and ambassadors, many of them old friends he hasn't seen since he left.

"It's good to see you all," Murad says, his melodious voice resounding through the tall marble room. "Thank you all for being here. Sultan Mehmed and I will see you all tomorrow, after we have time to consult. Now I have to go see my ladies."

"About time you did," a low, heavily accented voice comes from behind the screen separating the throne room from the sarayi. Murad laughs, and so do the others. They all know it's Mara, even though they've never seen her.

Murad turns to Mehmed. "See you in the study in an hour?"

Mehmed nods. Murad turns to the sarayi.

"Father?"

"Yes."

"It's been a long trip. Don't you need some refreshment?"

"Not right now. I'll go see the old girls first."

"Then..."

"Yes?"

"Take nothing from anyone unless they taste it first."

Murad's eyes widen. "Seriously?"

"Just to stay safe."

"Of course. I won't." He looks at Mehmed. "She took it badly?"

Mehmed shrugs.

Murad nods and goes to see his women. He's not surprised that Hüma wants to kill him. She's a wildcat, that one, and she doesn't take kindly to being spurned. He's not concerned about Mara — she's happy to be left alone — but Hüma is a different bird. He'll have to be very careful. And, more than anything, he'll have to keep Halime Hatice safe. Hüma will stop at nothing to get rid of her. Halime Hatice was right; she must be the one who had Aladdin killed, he thinks, and his heart darkens with anger.

But there's good news too: Mehmed warned him, even against his own mother. His son is loyal and steadfast, no matter what the issues with his governance are. That's a foundation he can build on.

But Çandarlı Paşa was right. From the way his people received him, he knows they don't love Mehmed. And if they don't love him, they won't die for him, no matter how brilliant his plan or how worthy his cause. Because people don't dedicate themselves to causes and plans; they dedicate themselves to the leaders who inspire them, and channel the power inside them — for the good, or for the bad.

Mehmed needs to learn to inspire his people.

CHAPTER 58

EDIRNE, SEPTEMBER 1446

Radu lays in bed in his little room at the palace school. It's so hot that his chemise, soaked in sweat, sticks to him like a second skin. Summer should be over by now, but this year, it just won't let go. It's September already, and the days have been getting shorter every day, but the sun's been working overtime. The mornings bring a little relief from the heat, but the evenings swelter till after midnight.

Radu plays with Sari. Out of a handkerchief filled with straw, he tied with a string, he made a fake mouse good enough to fool the cat. Radu throws it, then pulls it back before she can catch it, and Sari loves the game almost as much as she loves catching real mice. Whenever she gets it, she rolls on her back with the mouse in her mouth and scratches it to death with her hind paws.

Radu laughs and pulls the mouse away. Sari gives a battle scream and leaps, just as the door bursts open.

It's Mehmed. He's flushed and sweaty too, and his red curls are stuck to his forehead. And he looks flustered as he stares around the tiny room like he's looking for something.

"I heard you... I thought you had someone here."

"No. Just me and Sari. And you."

"I'm sorry I burst in. I just heard someone scream, and I got worried."

Mehmed studies him with a strange expression, and Radu realizes that his wet silk chemise leaves nothing to the imagination. He blushes and pulls on his kaftan, despite the sweltering heat.

Mehmed laughs.

"Don't do it on my account," he says.

Radu blushes and mumbles something.

Mehmed sits on the bed next to him.

"I came to say goodbye."

Radu's heart skips a beat. He barely ever gets to see Mehmed these days, but knowing he's close soothes his heart.

"To say goodbye? Are you leaving? Or am I?"

"I am."

"Where?"

"Back to Manisa."

"Why?"

"Father... Sultan Murad came back to take his throne. He says I have more to learn before I can be a good sultan."

"Learn what?"

"Everything. Especially how to deal with people."

"But you're wonderful with people!"

"Father doesn't think so. Neither does Çandarlı Paşa. Nor do the people. Did you see them welcoming Father back?"

"Sultan Murad is their hero. He's been their sultan for over twenty years, and he won battle after battle. You've been sultan for only two years, and you're still so young!"

"That's what Father says. He says that he'll take care of the empire while I endeavor to learn and become the best sultan I can be."

"When will you come back?"

Mehmed shrugs. "Whenever he tells me to. Or if he dies."

The words hang heavy in the tiny room. Radu waits for more, but nothing comes.

"Can I come with you?"

Mehmed shakes his head.

"I wish. I asked, but Father said absolutely not. You're not only my friend, you are a prince of Wallachia and a valuable guest of the empire. You need to be treated like an honored guest, he said, and he promised your father to give you the best possible education he can provide in all matters. I said that we could study together. He laughed."

Radu bites his lip to hold back his tears.

"Who's going with you?"

"I'll take my tutors, and Mother. And Gülbahar."

"Good. Then you won't be lonely."

"I'll be lonely, if I'm without you. Will you write to me?"

"Of course."

Radu's eyes fill with tears. There he is, alone again. He misses Mehmed already, and he's not even gone.

"I have a gift for you," Mehmed says.

He hands Radu a long package wrapped in the finest Chinese purple silk. Radu's heart isn't into it, but to please Mehmed, he unwraps it. It's a splendid dagger, with a bejeweled hilt and sheath. The handle is silver, filigreed in lacy arabesques holding smooth nuggets of amber surrounded by pearls. He pulls the dagger out of its sheath to see the blade. The ripples frozen into steel show it was made in Damascus, the finest steel ever made.

"It's beautiful, thank you."

"You recognize it?"

"No."

"This is the dagger that you... that I got stabbed with, that night before Varna."

Radu's face catches fire. He forgot the dagger, but that night he'll never forget. They had wine to celebrate Mehmed's first battle, and then more wine. Mehmed... acted strange. So strange that Radu got so scared that he stabbed him to get away.

"You remember?"

"I do."

"I'm sorry I... pushed myself on you. And thank you for accepting my apologies and accepting to be my friend after that."

Something strange stirs in Radu as he remembers that night. He felt scared, confused, and trapped, but there was more...

"I have to go."

Mehmed takes his hand and brings it to his heart.

"I'll miss you, my friend, and I'll think about you every day and every night."

"Even when you're with Gülbahar?" Radu jokes.

"Especially when I'm with Gülbahar."

Mehmed takes Radu into his arms. His rough cheek rubs against Radu's, and his mustache tickles his ear as he kisses his cheeks, first one, then the other. He lets go, but Radu pulls him closer, inhaling his scent of leather, horse, and man. He presses his body against Mehmed's muscled body from head to toes.

Mehmed draws in a sharp breath and tightens his grip. And that's good, since Radu's knees have softened and he's feeling dizzy. They stand together, their hearts beating against each other, for what feels like forever, until Sari meows, looking for attention.

Radu has never seen a more beautiful face than Mehmed's. His flushed cheeks are wet with tears, and his green eyes are full of love. He cups that beloved face in his hands and kisses him on the lips, softly first, then more and more demanding, until Mehmed's mouth opens and Radu's tongue sneaks inside it, exploring him, tasting him.

Mehmed softens in Radu's embrace until Radu lets go. Mehmed steps back, looking stricken. He glances at Radu one more time, then turns around and leaves.

"I love you," Radu says to his departing back.

That night he doesn't sleep, but he dreams about what could have been.

CHAPTER 59
HÜMA'S PARTY

This is Hüma Hatun's last night in the sarayi, and she's throwing a party.

There's never been a more miserable host, Ali thinks, watching Hüma's frozen face and her swollen red eyes. But Hüma wants to leave with her head held high, and pretends she can't wait to be gone.

Nobody believes it, of course, but that doesn't matter. They're too polite to show it. So they talk about Hüma's upcoming life in Manisa, at the freedom she'll enjoy, as the governor's mother, and at the wonderful time she will have, while they laugh at her behind her back.

With her foul moods and red-hot anger, Hüma hasn't been an easy validé. Nobody is sorry to see her leave, not even Mara, who's the closest thing she's got to a friend. They can't wait for Sultan Murad's mother, the old Emine Hatun, to be back and lead the sarayi with wisdom and kindness. Emine Hatun stayed in the harem for Mehmed's reign — where else could she go? But she kept a low profile, reading her Quran, praying to Allah, advising the young women and watching. Even now that she's back in power, she acts like she's grateful to be invited to Hüma's party.

And it's a party like no other. The food is even better than the food

at Mehmed's coronation — after all, Hüma had nothing to prove at the
time. Huge silver platters loaded with the best of everything fill the air
with mouth-watering aromas: roasted whole lamb stuffed with
rosemary and garlic, served with mint sauce; plump chickens with
yellow saffron, sultanas and mint; dolmas, stuffed grape leaves with
rice, raisins, pine-nuts and onions flavored with parsley and basil;
warm baklava dripping with butter and honey, and sweet cataifs made
with noodles finer than hair, soaked in milk and honey and flavored
with lemon peel and crushed pistachio nuts, and too many other
things to count.

There's music too: three eunuch musicians sit in the far corner,
playing their rübaps, along with a woman whose sultry voice is known
all over the empire, even though nobody outside the sarayi has ever
seen her face. There are so many flowers there's barely enough room to
sit around the food, and Hüma's precious birds sing like they know
something's coming.

And, to top it off, there's the wine. There's a wonderful sweet white
wine from Murfatlar and harsh reds from Wallachia to cut the grease
of the meat, and retsina, resin-scented wine from Greece. To Ali's
knowledge, that has never happened before in the women's quarters,
but by the way the old girls drain cup after cup, that doesn't bother
them one bit. Cheeks brighten, eyes sparkle, and the laughter gets
louder and louder. Their clothes seem to get in the way as the wine
heals hearts, softens brains and loosens bodies.

After a few cups, Hüma's frozen face softened. Relaxed, she looks
like a queen in her green brocade kaftan and gold-embroidered
Chinese silk shalwars. Her neck, arms and ears are heavy with gold,
and the wine flushed her cheeks and brightened her eyes. She looks
like a happy twenty-year-old, but they all know she's not.

The wine and the gifts helped ease her pain. Everyone brought
her a gift to be remembered by, and now there's a pile of precious
silks, perfumes, and jewels in front of her. There's even a bird of
paradise in its gilded cage, and other amazing gifts not for the mere
mortals.

Emine Hatun, who'll be Emine Validé starting tomorrow, brought Hüma a precious Quran.

"It was illuminated during the reign of Osman I, may Allah forever take care of his soul. There's none like it. I hope it brings you solace and rekindles your faith."

"Thank you, Mother. That's generous of you."

Hüma drops the old tome on top of the growing gift pile and leans to kiss the hand of the old woman. She has no bitch with Murad's mom. It's not her fault that things turned out as they did. Still, Hüma would rather have a flask of good old poison than the book of Allah, Ali thinks.

Mara follows. Her sinuous body moves with the grace of a lynx as she presents her gift to Hüma.

"I'll miss you, Hüma. We've had our differences, but I will miss your spunk, your dedication, and your hunger to win. This is the most valuable thing I own, but since nobody ever sees it, it doesn't do me much good. I hope it brings you joy."

She drops a bracelet made of emeralds as big as pigeon eggs at Hüma's feet, and Hüma stares at it in disbelief. This must be the bracelet she offered for me, Ali thinks, staring at the trinket that's supposedly worth more than her.

Hüma glances at Mara, then back at the bracelet.

"Is it…"

"Yes."

"Thank you, Mara. I should forever be in your debt. But I won't."

The women wonder what's coming.

"I have a gift for you. And it's just as special. Maybe more. Ali?"

Ali drags herself out from the shade of the curtains where she's been watching over the women, which is her job. Being the center of attention is not her thing.

"Mara, this is my precious gift to you. Take Ali and be kind to him. He still has a lot to learn, but he's very special. But, mind you, he's only on loan. I need him back when I return."

Ali is floored. After all her struggle to decide what to do about this

move, the decision was made for her. She'll stay here with Mara —
which is another challenge.

Mara glances at Ali, then at Hüma.

"Are you sure? I know you love the boy."

"You love him, too," Hüma says. "He's yours starting tomorrow."

Hatice Halime Hatun stands up. She must have had a cup or two,
since her heavy-set body wobbles a little as she turns to Hüma. Hatice
Halime, Sultan Murad's first wife, is older than all the other women
here but Emine Hatun, and the years haven't been kind to her. Hard to
believe she's still Sultan Murad's favorite, despite all the young women
fighting for his attention, but she is.

"I also have a gift for you, Hüma," Halime Hatice says, her low voice
pained.

Hüma doesn't meet her eyes.

"My son, Aladdin, was a wonderful boy. And a good man. He was
healthy, loving and strong. He was his father's joy and hope."

Hüma nods.

"He had two sons. One was eighteen months old. He'd just learned
to walk. The other was just six months old. He wasn't crawling yet.
They all died within one night, the three of them. Someone strangled
them in their sleep. My only son and his two sons. That's when my life
stopped."

Hüma looks around for somebody to stop this, but nobody moves.
The woman's pain hurts them all, and there's no dry eye in the room,
other than Hüma's.

"I know you killed them. You killed them to make your son sultan,
though he wasn't ready. And, for a while, you succeeded. But now he'll
go back to Manisa, where he belongs, and thank Allah, the merciful,
you're going with him. Edirne Palace will be better off without your
venom. But, as I said, I brought you a gift. It's the gift of knowledge."

Every breath in the room froze in wait.

"I'll tell you your future. You'll never return to Edirne. Never. You'll
die far away, and nobody will remember your name, or who you were.
Your tomb won't bear your name, only that of your son. You'll die

without knowing if your son will ever become sultan, and you'll never again taste the fruit of your poison.

"As for your son, he will die poisoned by his own son, like he deserves. He got his throne by murder, and he'll lose it by murder. But you'll be dead and forgotten by then. That's my gift to you, Hüma. Enjoy."

The silence is deadly as Halime Hatice waddles out of the room.

"Crazy woman," someone says, trying to make Hüma feel better.

But Hüma is white as a ghost. If she thought the party started badly, she didn't know nothing. Sobbing, she falls into Gülbahar's arms as Mara brings a wine cup to her lips.

Hüma's party is over.

CHAPTER 60
SECRET MISSION

But for the flicker of the candles by the door, Hüma's bedroom is dark and quiet. Lights and shadows dance on her tearful face as she sits up in bed under her silk sheets, while Ali massages her feet and Gülbahar brushes her hair to help soothe her. Ali's lavender and verbena potion helped stop the sobs and the screaming, but her tears are still running.

Hüma blows her nose in her perfumed silk handkerchief.

"She said that Mehmed will die poisoned by his own son," she says, looking somewhere in the dark like she's trying to see the future. "But that can't happen. Never since Osman Ghazi, the first sultan, has a son killed his father. That cannot happen to my son."

"Of course not," Gülbahar whispers. "Don't listen to her. She's just an old woman crazed by the death of her son. She doesn't know what she's talking about."

"She's not that old. Barely thirty-one. And she's a witch. What she said, that wasn't a prophecy. It was a curse."

Gülbahar shivers. "Why do you think she's a witch?"

"How else do you think she kept the sultan tied to her for almost twenty years? Did you look at her? She's old, wrinkled and fat. It's surely not her looks, so what else can it be other than witchcraft? Eleven years ago, when Murad married Mara, he sent Halime Hatice to Bursa, and I hoped we got rid of her. But she bewitched him from afar. Only months later, he sent Mara away and called the old witch back."

"I'm sorry, Mother. You and I, we'll take care of Mehmed. We'll make sure that nothing bad happens to him."

"Except that I'll be dead. But never mind. Go to bed, Gülbahar. Go get some rest. We have a long trip starting tomorrow."

"You too, Mother."

"I don't have time to rest. I only have tonight to get everything in order."

"But..."

"Go."

Gülbahar sets down the brush and heads to the door. Ali follows.

"Not you, Ali. I need you. Come, sit here."

Ali sits on the pillow by the head of the bed. She's never sat in Hüma's presence, since pillows are for important people, not for servants like her. But boy, do they feel good, she thinks, sinking into the soft wool and allowing her tired feet to rest.

"Ali, you already know that I'm leaving you here with Mara. You know why?"

"Are you unhappy with me?"

"Nonsense. Just the opposite. You've been a faithful servant, and I'm very pleased with you. I'll leave you behind just because I trust you. You'll be my eyes and my ears at Edirne Palace. You understand?"

Ali nods.

"I need you to watch Halime Hatice and Murad. I need to know if they are well or they get sick, and I absolutely need to know if she gets pregnant. It won't be hard to find out. They'll make a huge fuss over it, like the future şehzade is about to be born."

"Yes."

"And I want you to send word to me."

"How?"

"As soon as I get to Manisa, I'll send back a man with a cage of pigeons. He'll look after them and show you how to attach a message to their leg and let them go. They'll fly back to Manisa and get the message back to me in less than a day. Much faster than on land."

"I understand."

"Ali?"

"Yes?"

"Should the sultan fall ill and die while I'm gone, or even Halime Hatice Hatun, I will be devastated, and I will mourn for them like a dutiful wife should. I'll tear my hair and cry and scream. But I'll set you free. I'll let you go home, like Lena did, with a cart full of gold and silver. You'll have enough money to have your own home and your own servants and live like a prince for the rest of your life. You understand?"

Ali nods. She refrains from pointing out to Hüma that she can't set her free. Ali belongs to the sultan, like all the women, the eunuchs, and every other slave in the palace, and not to Hüma. But pointing that out seems unwise.

"Go now. And not a word to anyone about what we discussed."

"Yes, my lady." Ali heads to the door.

"Ali?"

"Yes?"

"Be careful with Mara. She's... different. Be careful around her."

CHAPTER 61

TRANSYLVANIA, SEPTEMBER 1446

By September, Transylvania's short summer is over. The leaves started turning in August, and up in the mountains the green canopy turned into reds and golds that stand up against the deep blue sky, pleasing the eyes and soothing the soul.

Lena straightens her back and stops to rejoice in the beauty. They're deep in the forest, gathering plants for Mama Smaranda's ointments, lotions and potions. Most of the summer herbs are already gone, but Smaranda already gathered what she needed. The fall is the time for the fruits, nuts and seeds. It's also time to prepare for winter, which is long and relentless. The unprepared, from crickets to humans, won't live to see the spring. Nor will their offspring, because up here in the mountains, life is harsh, and it favors the strong.

"See this?" Smaranda points to an unimpressive purple flower, smaller than Lena's fingernails, shaped like a tiny tulip. "This is the fall crocus. There are few more deadly things in the forest."

Lena stares at it with new respect. "You mean one of these could kill a man?"

"It takes more than one, but yes. A good strong concoction will go a long way to settle old grievances and get some impatient heir their early inheritance. It's also poisonous for cats. Strangely enough, some things that would kill a human are harmless for cats and dogs, and the other way round."

Mama Smaranda picks them carefully and puts them in her basket. Lena studies her thoughtfully.

"You know, Mama Smaranda, I wonder why you're not rich. You have all this valuable knowledge. You can cure people's pain, get rid of unwanted babies and kill the undesirables. That's got to be worth a lot to many people."

Smaranda's eyes crinkle in a smile. "How do you know I'm not rich?"

"You live in a tiny hut in the forest with a dog and a cat. You eat bread and cheese and honey and drink tea. You wear the same clothes, over and over. That's not what rich people do."

"What do rich people do, Lena?"

"They wear brocade and jewelry and have servants to work for them and eat fancy foods and drink wine. They live in houses made of marble and sleep between sheets made of silk. They ride fancy palfreys and wear gold to impress their neighbors."

Smaranda laughs so hard she chokes.

"You're right. That's what rich people do. Or at least those people who want to look rich. What does rich mean to you, Lena?"

"It means you get to do what you want, when you want, and no one can stop you. You can go wherever you please and be whoever you want to be. That's rich to me."

Smaranda nods. "So why do you think I'm poor?"

Lena stares at Smaranda. She's wearing the same clothes Lena met her in and she seldom eats anything else but bread and cheese. But she never has to ask anyone what she should do and when. She wakes up when she's ready and goes to bed when she's ready and she doesn't seem to care about what anybody thinks about her.

"I don't know. I just think you're different. It's like the rules don't apply to you."

Smaranda nods. "Very good. As far as I'm concerned, the rules are made to be broken. Wisely. So, Lena, what do you want to do with yourself?"

Lena leans over her basket, adding another herb she doesn't need, just to get to think about it. "I don't know. I spent months trying to think about it and nothing came to mind. It looks like there's no future for me."

Mama Smaranda nods as she picks another fall crocus. "If you had a choice, where would you see yourself in the future?"

Lena stares into space, trying to conjure some sort of inspiration. But nothing comes to mind.

"Would you like to get married and have children?"

Lena's eyes widen.

"Of course not. What for?"

Smaranda laughs, and her laughter is clear and bright like a bell.

"Well, that's what women are for. Ask your father, your mother, and your best friends. There is no other use for women. They are meant for breeding."

"Like sheep?"

"Pretty much."

Lena shudders. "Not me."

"So, what are you here for?"

Lena shrugs. She can't think of her plot in life. Other than knowing that it's not breeding.

"Is there any other purpose but breeding?"

"Well, those who nobody wants, or they don't want anyone, go to a monastery. You could become a nun. You could pray, garden, care for the sick, and then pray some more."

"Pray for what?"

"Pray for God's forgiveness."

"God's forgiveness for what?"

"For your sins."

"What sins?"

"Any sins. Your greed and your lies and fornicating and your coveting something that belongs to others."

"I didn't do any of those."

"Well, you're a woman, so you're still subject to the original sin. Adam and Eve were chased off the Garden of Eden thanks to Eve. You're still redeeming her sin."

Lena gives Smaranda a rotten look. "Didn't Adam have a choice?"

"I guess."

"So, how is this my sin?"

Mama Smaranda laughs. "Sorry, Lena, religion isn't one of my better skills. But the point remains. Do you want to join a monastery?"

"Will they tell me what to do?"

"At all times. Starting before sunrise. And ending never."

"No thanks. Any other ideas?"

Smaranda shrugs. "Not really. Women are either wives and mothers, or nuns. Unless they are whores, but nobody ever talks about them."

"Who are they?"

"They're women who relieve men of their burden in exchange for money."

"Like…"

"Yes. They open their legs to let men live unencumbered by unfulfilled sexual needs."

"No thanks. It wasn't that much fun with the sultan. I can't imagine doing it for a living."

"Then what? You don't want to get married and have kids, you don't want to be a nun, you don't want to be a harlot. What do you want?"

"I'd like to travel the world. Meet new people. Learn new things. Sail the seas. Climb mountains. Breed horses. And dogs. And fight in a war. I'd like to make a difference."

Smaranda laughs. "What you're saying is that you'd rather be a man. No woman I know does those things. Except for making a difference. We all can make a difference every day, from the queen to the humblest peasant. When we're big, we can make a big difference for many people. When we're small, we can make a big difference for a few people."

"Is there a way you can turn me into a man? Do you have a recipe for that? Or if not a man, at least a queen?"

"I wish. Speak about getting rich!"

CHAPTER 62

MARRY ME

It's been days and days, but Lena's soul is still in turmoil. She hasn't yet found her place in this world that has no room for people like her, who don't fit the mold, and she's lucky to have Smaranda, who doesn't care about what the world thinks. Mama Smaranda showed her the many uses of her herbs and taught her to read and write in Wallachian — which is Romanian, just like the language in Moldova — and encouraged her to think about her future. But nothing came to Lena's mind.

It's early evening as they sit sipping mint tea by the fireplace, waiting for the stew to be ready. Negru brought a hare today. It was dead by the time he dropped it on the porch, and all Smaranda's magic couldn't bring it back to life.

"We can bury it, and let the worms feast, or we could make a stew, and be thankful. What do you think?"

"Are you kidding? He's dead already. We may as well make the most of him."

"That's what I thought," Smaranda said, hanging the rabbit on a hook behind the house to dress him. "If you were an animal, you'd be a cat. You always land on your feet."

"Is there any other way?"

"A few. Some folks land on their heads. Very unwise."

They sit by the fire waiting for the old hare to cook, when Smaranda raises her head to listen. Lena listens too, but she hears nothing. She takes another sip of her mint tea and pets the cat when Smaranda turns to her. Her eyes are wide, and her voice so low it's like she's speaking in a dream.

"He's coming."

"Who?"

"Your future. He's on his way right now. He doesn't know what he's offering you, besides his hand. But he will give you something nobody else can."

"Like what?"

"The freedom to do what you like."

"That must come at a cost."

"Doesn't everything? Are you ready?"

Lena shrugs. "I was born ready."

"That's a good thing. Think carefully before you say yes or no. Both have massive consequences."

"Should I listen to my heart?"

Smaranda laughs. "Should you?"

"Probably not. I should listen to my judgment."

A knock at the door.

"Who's there?"

"Mircea."

Mircea. Who's Mircea? Lena wonders. Then she remembers. It's Ștefan's cousin. Good-looking boy, though kind of gloomy. But hard to ignore.

The young man at the door is tired but handsome, with moody eyes, long dark hair and shoulders that barely fit through the door. He looks at her with hungry eyes, but doesn't touch her. He drops on a knee instead.

"I came to ask for your hand in marriage."

Lena's heart skips a beat. Smaranda was right. As always.

"Why don't you come in?" Smaranda says. "Are you hungry?"

The man nods. Smaranda offers him a chair, then brings a barrel of wine Lena didn't know she had. She spikes it and pours wine into three cups, but gives Lena a warning look as she grabs her cup. Lena sniffs it, tastes it, and sets it on the table.

"Who are you, young man?" Smaranda asks.

"I'm Mircea, Wallachia's voivode's oldest son. I'm also Ștefan's cousin and friend."

They knock their cups, and Mircea drains his.

"Does your father know you're here?"

Mircea hesitates. "Not exactly. But he knows about my affection for Lena."

"What does he think of it?"

Mircea looks down, the wind out of his sails.

"Not much, I'm afraid. He thinks that if I'm looking to get married, I should choose someone like Hunyadi's sister and bring Wallachia a valuable alliance."

"Why aren't you, then?"

"She's almost three times my age. And I don't love her."

"How old are you?"

"Nineteen."

Smaranda fills the cups again.

"Life isn't easy, is it? Not even when you are a voivode's son." She checks on the stew and stirs it again. "I think we're close to ready."

She brings out the bread they baked yesterday and cuts thick slices.

"I know this isn't the kind of meal you're used to, but this is the best we can do. We're just ordinary people, living ordinary lives."

"Thank you for having me," Mircea says, and for a moment his eyes focus on Smaranda rather than Lena. "I'm thankful for your hospitality."

Smaranda sets the slices of bread on wooden plates and drowns them in the hare stew that smells like rosemary and garlic. She sets the best pieces on Mircea's plate, and they eat, talk about the weather and sip on their wine, until Smaranda stands.

"I'm done for the night. Why don't you, young people, go out to walk and talk? Wake me up if you need me. Good night."

Lena and Mircea walk side by side along the moonlit paths, and Negru follows them closely. It's dark, quiet and weird, and Lena looks for something to say.

"What kind of things do you enjoy?" she asks.

"Food, and wine, and…"

"And what?"

He stares at her like he means business.

"And fighting. I'm sorry if that's a problem, but I'm not a friend to the Ottomans."

"Neither am I. That's one thing we have in common."

Mircea says nothing. Lena goes quiet, too. She doesn't know what to say or to ask. Nobody ever asked for her hand, though, long ago, she hoped Ștefan would. She remembers her mother's words, the night she beat up the boys who tried to rape her.

"Nobody's going to want her now."

She was wrong, Lena thinks, grateful to this silent, awkward boy who proved her mother wrong. They keep on walking without touching, but Lena can't help but be aware of his strong, male body. Her heart skips a beat when his warm hand takes hers.

"Why are you looking to get married?" Lena asks.

Mircea stares at her like she's lost her mind.

"I'm not. In fact, getting married may even get me out of Father's will and disinherit me, my children, and their children. I came because I can't get you out of my mind. I've never met anyone like you. I was so smitten that I hurt my best friend's feelings. I know Ștefan cares a lot about you, but I couldn't help it. I had to come and see you, even though my father disagrees and my best friend is mad. I don't even know what I can offer you. If God wishes it, I may become Wallachia's voivode someday. Or I may die next week. But I came to offer you my life, such as it is, my future, as God will shape it, and everything I am. It may not be much, but it's all I've got."

Lena sighs. "I'm not like other girls."

"I know. That's why I'm here."

"I don't like to be told what to do."

"Neither do I."

"I... I've never been with a man."

He stares at her. "I thought you'd spent long months with Mehmed?"

"Not in that way."

He kneels in front of her and touches his lips to her hand. "That makes me very glad. I will be patient."

Lena shrugs. "OK then. Let's get married."

CHAPTER 63

TRANSYLVANIA, OCTOBER 1446

Codru stops to check the direction and catch his breath. He looks ahead at the forbidding white peaks separating Wallachia from Transylvania. These are the southern Carpathians, the tallest and most fearsome third of the wooded mountain ring that gave Transylvania her name — the country between forests. And they're standing in his way.

Down in the plains it's still the fall, but the mountains are already white. The higher Codru climbs, the redder the leaves, the colder the nights, and the closer the winter.

He's been heading north for months now, and it's been an arduous journey. It started with the swim from Lesbos across the Aegean Sea. He somehow lost his way, and the moon set, leaving him a naked human in the middle of the sea. He swam and swam, fighting the cold seeping into his fragile bones, the exhaustion in his every muscle, and the deep despair in his heart. The sea tossed him around until he lost the desire to go on.

"Why fight?" the sea whispered. "Where do you think you're going? And why? You left Athena and Nikos, and you'll never see them again. You left Ana and Ion behind long ago. For all that you know, they're both dead because of you. What do you think you'll find in Transylvania that's worth fighting for?"

He didn't listen. He steeled his heart and pushed forward, spluttering and coughing and keeping his eyes on the horizon looking for land. But there was none.

His wish to live set with the sun. He'd lost all hope, but he kept on paddling when his arms got too tired to swim, floating when his legs became useless, always fighting the sea that sucked him in.

"But why?" the sea asked. "What's there worth fighting for? Why don't you just close your eyes and breathe me in, and you'll finally rest."

The temptation was overwhelming. Why not, indeed? Why not give up?

But he couldn't. He promised Athena and Nikos to return someday, and promised Ana and Ion to see them again. He had to keep his promises. That was all he had left.

The fisherman found him when the black sky faded to blue in the morning. A burly man in a small fishing boat picked him up in the middle of the sea, miles away from the shore. He took him to his home, clothed him and fed him. And Codru stayed.

They went fishing night after night until the next full moon forced him to flee north again. It's been months now that he's been pushing to get home, but it was an awful long trip. Through the Ottoman Empire, then Greece, and Bulgaria, and then Wallachia, that puzzling country that's so much like Transylvania, but it's not. And here he is, at the bottom of the mountains, just as winter is coming. Even down at the feet of the Carpathians, the ground bears a thin white dusting, and the snow will be way deep at the top, making it impossible for a lone man to pass.

But, thank the lucky stars, there's a full moon tonight.

The moon's power molds him into his wolf self as soon as the sun goes down. His white goddess pours her magic into him, empowering him to run home.

His paws eat up the distance as he runs north through the mountains like a storm wind flying across the sky. He takes a leap, then another, then a hundred more, until his nose tells him he's getting close. He's not sure why, since the wood smoke smells the same, and so do the sheep, the cows, and the villages. It's got to be the pines, he thinks, breathing in their incense. More than any other place, Transylvania smells like pines.

Heartened by knowing he's close, he flies like an unleashed blizzard over frozen stream beds, across the dark forests alive with strange things, and through the narrow pass some long-gone river cut through the mountain's rock. He leaps and climbs and bounces, clawing his way through ice and snow, again and again, until he can't do it anymore.

The mountains are just too much. Too high, too cold, too foreboding. He's not yet at the top, but he's exhausted, and the moon has started going down. Before long, he'll be just a drained, naked human, and this frozen mountain is not a good place for a defenseless human to be.

He raises his muzzle to the moon and cries out his despair. He can't help it; he can no longer keep his sorrow inside. The howl bounces from peak to peak, like the whole mountain crawls with desperate werewolves.

Someone howls back. Codru's heart skips a beat. Is it the echo? No. Somebody answered.

He howls again and gathers the last of his strength to push on. His heart racing, his paws burning, his lungs ready to burst, he leaps over boulders and claws his way up the rock to the top, until he catches sight of meadows and rivers down below.

The howl returns, closer now. Codru flies towards it like an arrow.

And there it is. Negru, his friend, is racing to meet him. Or is he?

They stop to greet one another like dogs do, with bared teeth, stiff legs and raised hackles. They sniff each other's butt, then the snouts. It all checks out, so they jump and roll and bark like puppies, overjoyed to be together again. But the sun is about to come up. It's time to go.

They run and run through the enchanted forest all the way to

Smaranda's old house in the woods. Negru barks, and two women come out. They stare at him, but they look neither angry nor afraid. And that's the last thing the werewolf sees before the moon sets, leaving him a naked human.

He shivers and covers his man parts with his hands, while Negru leaps around him with joy. The women come closer.

"Codru?" Mama Smaranda asks, her eyes shining with tears. "Are you back?"

The girl studies him from head to toe. He struggles to cover himself, but she doesn't seem to care. Her smiling blue eyes take everything in.

"Are you the werewolf?"

Codru nods.

"Really? You look much more impressive on four paws, if you don't mind my saying. What's your name?"

"Codru."

"I'm Lena. I think we met before. Remember the bear trap?"

He does. He also remembers the girl, who is like no girl he ever met. Not that he met that many.

"I do."

"Thanks for saving me," she says.

"My pleasure," he mumbles.

"Let's go inside," Mama Smaranda says.

She opens the door and steps in. The girl follows, then Codru shuffles in, still struggling to cover his privates.

"Why do you keep hiding them? I thought you men were really proud of those things," Lena asks.

Codru shrugs. "Only when there's a use for them, I guess."

"Like sticking them in some girl's parts?"

Codru chokes. This isn't the kind of conversation he's ever had with a girl, including Ali — not that Ali is a girl. And he can't think about an appropriate answer. Fortunately, she doesn't dwell on it.

"How's Ali doing?"

"I... don't know. I left Edirne quite a while ago, and haven't heard from them since."

"Well then. Isn't it time to be back?"

"To Edirne?"

"Where else?"

"For me? Or for you?"

Lena's eyes widen, then she laughs. "Good point. Let's think about it."

They eat fresh bread with cheese and honey and wash it down with mint tea. They talk about Ali and Isa and the Ottomans and about Codru's amazing journey. And, for the first time in many years, Codru feels at home. It's like heaven, to be back, and not need to hide who you are. He's out of the Ottomans' reach, and Mama Smaranda can keep him human.

That night he curls on the sheepskins in front of the fire, thinking about Ali and Ion, wishing they were here and hoping they're alive.

He thinks about going back to Edirne, but there's no way. It took him almost a year to get here, and it was hard. Time and time again, he barely escaped a gruesome death. He can't do that again.

But Ali and Isa are still there.

He sighs and pushes the thought away for the night. He'll think about that tomorrow. But the one face he can't get rid of is Lena. The girl inhabits his dreams.

CHAPTER 64

EĞRIGÖZ, SPRING 1447

It's dark, damp, and cold in Vlad's cell in Eğrigöz. The steam of his breath condenses into glittering rivulets that run down the gray rock, working themselves into stalactites and stalagmites. He's been here so long he's building a cave with his breath.

He doesn't know how long, since days and nights here are all the same. He hasn't seen the light of day since he tried to escape and stumbled upon Kir Daskalos' dead smile. Ever since, he's been locked in his cell inside the mountain. The only thing he's kept count of are the rat tails.

Hunting rats is the one thing keeping him alive. He's caught one hundred and twenty-one of them. Sometimes he gets one, sometimes two, sometimes none. Either way, he's been locked in here for an awfully long time.

Long enough to lose his mind. Sometimes he can't remember why he's here. Other times, he can't remember where he is. And, every once in a while, he's not quite sure who he is.

But the rats keep him sane. Almost. They give him something to fight, a way to pass the time, something to cry about, something to laugh. Since the Ottomans took his walks, his books, his teacher, and everything that made his life a life, he has nothing left but the rats.

He's gotten good at this. He can anticipate their movements, and can guess if they'll go forward or retreat. He even knows what they'll think before they think it. Every day, he has nothing to do but hunt. Every night, he has nothing to do but hunt. He has nothing to do but hunt.

And kill. He's gotten good at that, too.

But, more than anything, he has become the master of suffering. He's learned how to skin them alive, watching their little whiskered faces shiver with pain. He's learned how to make them suffer, breaking their every bone, and how to remove their entrails, one by one, while they're still alive. He's obsessed with their pain. He inhales it. If there was such a thing as a chief rat torturer, nobody could compete.

He sits with his back to the wall, watching the little hole in the corner where they usually come from. He hears something, and his focus heightens. The empty bowl is ready. He holds his breath to make no noise. And waits. Patiently. He has all the time in the world.

Nothing.

But he doesn't give up. Some are more cautious than others, the rats. The old ones are the worst. They're cautious and cunning. They think ahead.

He knows they're old since they're so ugly. Young rats are fat, shiny and curious. And easy to grab. The old ones are scarred, with bald patches, thin whiskers and broken tails. They're not curious, they're cautious and almost impossible to catch. They seem to know he's there even if he stops breathing. Vlad feels proud of himself every time he catches an old rat.

A shadow in the corner. Vlad holds his breath and tightens his grip on the bowl, ready to pounce.

The shadow grows into a small triangular head, moving left and right. He's blinded by the meager torchlight, and his whiskers shiver as he sniffs, reading the smells.

Vlad waits, holding his breath. He's ready, but he's got to let the rat come all the way out before throwing the bowl, otherwise the slightest noise will send him back into his hole. You can't catch half a rat under the bowl — you need to have him covered and step on the bowl before he shakes it off and vanishes.

He's almost out, but for the tail. He's getting cocky, sniffing the ground, looking for the crumbs Vlad left there for him.

One more inch. Vlad takes a slow, deep breath and gets ready to leap.

The key clanks in the door.

The rat disappears like he's never been there, and Vlad's bowl catches only thin air. He's livid as he turns to glare at the guard standing in the door.

"What do you want?"

The man opens the door even wider and nods to the passage, calling him out.

"Out? What do you mean out?"

The janissary shrugs, holding the door.

Vlad is to come out of this cell that he hasn't left in God knows how long, and he's terrified.

"Why?"

The janissary doesn't answer.

Vlad's heart quickens. He's afraid to get out. But they'll drag him out, if that's where they want him, no matter what, so he steps out into the low tunnel in the rock with its uneven, slippery floor. He shuffles cautiously towards the brightness outside.

The sun blinds him. He stops and closes his eyes, waiting for them to adjust. The guard waits behind him.

When the swirling stars behind his eyelids fade into black, he opens his eyes to the endless green of the hills facing him beyond the cliff, only three feet away.

Are they going to push him over? Is this it?

"Now what?"

The guard nods to the stone stairs hugging the cliff going up. Vlad sighs. His legs shrunk after months of disuse, and he's so weak his whole body shakes as he climbs. He takes the steep steps slowly, one by one, until there's none left, and stops at a heavy wooden door. Another guard waves him inside.

He shuffles in. There's a small hallway, then a wide room. The walls are the same bare rock, but a large rust-colored carpet softens the floor. Tall candles stand in the corners and a small fire dances in the fireplace, bringing warmth and light to the austere room. This must be the main room of the castle, Vlad thinks, feasting his eyes on the flames.

Sitting on a pillow by the fire, the paşa nods. His sharp eyes inspect Vlad from head to toe, and his eyes narrow.

"How are you?"

"Alive."

"That's what I hoped for. How is your health?"

Vlad shrugs.

"I see. Well, we'll have to build you up and strengthen you first."

"For what?"

"For the journey."

"What journey?"

"You'll find out when necessary. In the meantime, you'll get a room in the fort, decent food, and an opportunity to stretch your legs and exercise a little. I know you haven't done that in a while."

Vlad sighs. It doesn't look like they'll execute him tonight. And right now, that's all that matters.

"But the first thing you'll do is take a bath. You really, really need it," the paşa says, wrinkling his nose.

Vlad nods. He'd love a bath. He can't remember the last time he had one. But first, he needs to know.

"Why did you let me out?"

"The sultan's order."

"Really? Mehmed let me out?"

The paşa smiles. "No. The sultan. Sultan Murad."

CHAPTER 65

EDIRNE, JUNE 1447

After struggling to make up her mind over a few long, wet, muddy weeks, spring finally turned into summer. The long cool mornings gave way to unrelenting heat, and the sun broiled the grass to ugly brown. The scorched earth is so hard that the horses' hooves sound like hail. But Vlad's long journey is finally over.

The trip from Eğrigöz to Edirne took weeks, and all because of him. After the months he spent locked in his cell, he couldn't ride long hours, day after day. They had to slow down to let him rest, again and again. But they somehow made it back to Edirne, and for once, Vlad is overjoyed to be back in this place he used to hate.

They never told him where they took him, but Vlad recognized the slow-moving Tunca, tucked between the Edirne hunting grounds and the market gardens with golden lemons and red cherries peaking between the leaves, and his heart filled with joy. He's back to Edirne, to people and gardens and the good life instead of locked in a dungeon skinning rats. Unless they throw him into another cell.

But the guards took him straight to the janissaries' hammam. He almost cried when the servants took his filthy clothes, laid him on the marble bench and poured hot water over him. He luxuriated in the skilled masseurs scrubbing him clean and working the kinks out of his muscles. They washed off the weeks of sweat, dust and dirt with lavender-scented soap, then rinsed him off and scrubbed him again, until all the misery got rinsed off his shoulders. Then, when he was all clean, they let him sink in the pool of cooling water, and he lay there thinking.

Why did they bring him back? To set an example of what happens to traitors? Has Father defaulted on his oath, so they brought him back for a public execution before they send his head back to Father? But then why would they bother to bathe him first? And wouldn't it be easier to execute Radu, who's already here, than cart Vlad all the way from Eğrigöz?

But maybe Radu isn't here. Vlad has been jailed for so long he no longer knows anything about anything. He doesn't even know why Murad is the sultan instead of Mehmed. Did Mehmed die? For all he knows, Radu may be dead too. Ever since Kir Daskalos died, he had no news from the outside world.

Oh well. One way or another, he's about to find out, so he may as well enjoy this moment. He rests his head on the marble edge, closes his eyes, and drifts into a sweet daydream. Sophia. Her smile, her eyes, her softness. Their kiss. He misses her like he's never missed anyone, not even Father. He wonders what happened to her and her brother, but he's not sure he wants to know.

He thinks about home. About Wallachia, about the scent of the heavy blooming roses Mother turned into sweet preserves, about the warmth of her embrace. He seldom thinks about Mother, because thinking of her makes him feel even more lonely. But he hasn't forgotten her smile and her hands that smelled of freshly baked bread when she touched his hair, and his eyes swell with tears. He splashes water on his face, glad no one can see him.

Something touches his shoulder, and he startles. But it's just the bath attendants who came to rinse and brush his overgrown, tangled hair. They dry him off with soft rose-scented towels, as he lies on the marble slab, staring at his legs. They're still dark and hairy, but they no longer look like his legs. They got so skinny that his bony knees look huge. Those dratted months in the cell wasted his muscles and stole his strength. He's never been big, but he's always been strong and lean. No more. These days, he's just the shadow of who he used to be.

They dress him in shalwars, a fine linen chemise and an embroidered kaftan, then add a necklace that Vlad knows well, since it used to belong to Father. It's made of Wallachian gold coins, and it's heavy. But why would they deck him like that?

To send a clear message: This is Vlad of Wallachia, and he's here to die. So that's it.

Vlad sighs and looks back at his life. He's not even sixteen; he killed a few men, a horse, and a hundred twenty-one rats. He kissed a girl once, but he never bedded a woman.

Thinking back, he can't help but wonder if he misplaced his priorities. Maybe he should have done less with his sword and more with his weapon. But it's too late to wonder.

The guards take him down a maze of stone corridors, dark but for the sizzling torches burning in iron rings on the walls. They head deeper and deeper inside the castle, and Vlad wonders if that bath was just an extra touch of cruelty meant to make his new incarceration even harder. Why not? He sure learned a lot about suffering in Tokat, but there's much more to learn.

He follows the guards, thinking about what he did and what he could have done. Should have done. And only one thing comes to his mind.

It's not his escape — he had to try. That's a prisoner's job. It's not trying to kill Mehmed either — he was just an ignorant kid, and he thought killing Mehmed would weaken the Ottomans and save Wallachia. Stupid, of course, but he didn't know any better.

The one thing he regrets is roughing up his brother. He's been beating on Radu since before the kid was old enough to walk. He's always been jealous because of his looks and the smiles he brought to people's faces. He'd have liked him to be ugly and dark. And he somehow thought that if he only kept at it long enough, he'll get Radu to change. To stop speaking softly, tearing up whenever he got upset, blushing, and acting like a girl. Vlad thought he could make a real man out of him.

But he didn't realize that Radu didn't choose to be who he was; he was born into it. God made Radu that way, just like he gave him blue eyes and golden hair. Being girly is not Radu's fault, just like Vlad's dark hair and green eyes are not his fault. Nor is his love of rats.

That's the one thing I wish I could change, Vlad thinks, as the guards stop at a small wooden door deep inside Edirne castle's belly.

CHAPTER 66

CHANGE OF FATE

The guards step aside and wave him in.

Vlad steps in cautiously, ready for a trap. The room is clad in white marble but otherwise unadorned. And it's barely big enough for a cot, a bookshelf, and two sitting pillows.

Sultan Murad, dressed in white from his pearly turban to his upturned slippers, sits reading the Quran, and he's alone. There are no weapons in sight. Nothing but books and candles.

The sultan raises his eyes and pushes the Quran away.

"Thank you for joining me, Prince Vlad. Please sit."

Vlad scans the place looking for hidden killers — though why would Murad need a hidden killer? He can kill whoever he wants whenever he wants; no one would tell him no.

"How are you doing?"

The sultan's eyes are strange. They're dark yellow, the color of amber, like those of a preying cat. His eyelashes and eyebrows are so dark they make his eyes seem transparent as he stares at Vlad like he looks for the truth inside his soul.

"I'm managing. How are you?"

The sultan nods, as if that's the answer he's waited for.

"Me too. I'm doing my best, but sometimes that's just not good enough. Does that ever happen to you?"

Vlad nods. This isn't the reception he expected from the leader of the Ottoman Empire. He studies him carefully. He doesn't look old, sick, or troubled. But he's odd.

"How are you feeling?"

"OK. You?"

"I'm all right. Listen, Vlad. I thought it was time we talked and cleared the air. I sent you to Tokat for trying to kill Mehmed. Honestly, I wanted to kill you, but Mehmed stopped me. So, your Tokat sentence? You deserved it."

"I did."

"I'm glad we agree. A while later, you escaped from Tokat. That cost us a few lives, and you almost made it to the border. Our men caught you and brought you to Mehmed's justice, and Mehmed sent you back to jail. Not to Tokat, but to Eğrigöz."

Vlad nods, wondering where this is going.

Murad claps his hands.

"Talking is thirsty work."

Two slaves come in, loaded with platters of snacks, fruit, and wine. They pour wine into two exquisite golden cups and serve them.

Murad sniffs the cup, twirls it, then sniffs it again. He takes a sip.

"This wine is from Wallachia, from Dealu Mare. Your home country. I must confess I'm partial to the Moldavian wines — the Murfatlar, and the Cotnari, but this red won my heart." He drains the cup and signals the servants to fill it again.

Vlad can't remember how long it's been since he's had wine. He sniffs the cup, sips, and empties his cup. The wine goes smoothly and warms him inside, softening the ache in his shoulders.

"Then you tried to bribe a guard to flee Eğrigöz, but he sold you out instead. To punish you, they took away your privileges. It must have been hard."

The sultan empties his cup. Vlad too. He's missed wine more than he thought. It tastes like home, and it warms his heart. May as well make the most of it. They refill his cup and Vlad sips again, staring at the man in front of him. The sultan.

Strangely, he's never thought about Ottomans as being people. To him, they're nothing but a scourge on his country and his people. A disease overcoming Wallachia. God's punishment for whatever unknown sins.

But now Murad behaves like a human being and treats him like an equal.

"I think your punishment was well deserved. Do you agree?"

Vlad nods, and the sultan smiles.

"I'm happy we agree. Now that we cleared the waters, let me tell you why I brought you back, even though we both agree that you deserved your punishment. I brought you back because of your father. Have you heard about him lately?"

"No."

"I happen to know that Hunyadi is planning a campaign against your father. Soon. After being named Hungary's regent. Hunyadi has more power than ever before, and he intends to use it. To protect Hungary, he wants to put his puppets on neighboring countries' thrones. He already controls the Hungarians and the Transylvanians. He's looking to have his new brother-in-law, Petru Aron, take Moldova's throne. To make sure he stays loyal, Hunyadi had him marry his sister, even though he's just twenty-five and she's fifty, if a day. After that, the only other neighbor he needs to replace is Vlad Dracul, who has been our faithful ally, much to Hunyadi's chagrin. And he'll do that this year. Your father will have a hard time fighting him. Alone, he can't win."

Vlad knows about Hunyadi. He's supposedly half Romanian, therefore should be like a brother to Wallachians and Moldavians, but he never acted like a brother. Hunyadi fought Father too many times to count, and often won.

"He's been grooming your cousin Vladislav, the son of your great uncle Dan, to take your father's throne, and he'll give him an army to invade Wallachia. But that doesn't suit us.

"We don't want a strong Hungary under Hunyadi, buffered by their friendly allies all around. That's why I decided to help your father. But to keep his throne, he needs the boyars to reject Vladislav and support him. That's where you, Vlad, come in. You know the people and the language, since you're one of them. That's why I've brought you back. I remember your passionate defense of your country, and can't think about anyone better suited to help your father. I want to send you back to Wallachia."

CHAPTER 67

MANISA, JUNE 1447

The shadows grew long and the sun's strength faded by the time Mehmed turned Rüzgar back towards Manisa, with a wide grin on his face.

His beloved falcon, Güzel, caught two hares he'll have cooked for dinner. His mouth waters when he thinks about having mutancana, his favorite dish. They like to make it from lamb, but he prefers hare, which is not as gamey, and goes well with the shallots, the almonds and the figs flavored with sumac and thyme. With rice pilaf, of course.

What a great day! This morning, he cantered through the shady forest, then slowed down to listen to the birds and look for game. He hasn't had to deal with business the whole day, which makes it a good day in his book, even if the afternoon turned hot and dusty, so he's dirty and covered in sweat. He can't wait for his bath, then dinner, then a lovely restful night with Gülbahar in his arms.

He loves that girl. The day he kept her for himself, he mostly did it to irk Vlad — he saw the way he looked at her, and heard from the guards that Vlad never took his eyes from her on the long trip to Edirne. He wanted to make him suffer.

But her softness and kindness bring him joy. He enjoys her

company more than anyone else's besides Radu, and he feels lucky to have her. He dismounts and leaves Rüzgar with the stable boys, then heads to the hammam for his bath. But a guard stops him, bowing deeply.

"Our lady, your mother, asked for you."

"Now?"

"A while ago."

"I'll see her after my bath."

The guard doesn't look happy. Mother will give him hell for failing to bring Mehmed over, but so what? Mehmed is no longer a child to run to his mother the moment he's summoned. He wants to clean himself up first, though he wonders what this is about.

Mother has something to tell him, and that's rarely good news. It's either something he should do, or something he should stop doing. And it's never what he wants to hear.

He sighs and relaxes, glad that Adel, his old masseur, came with him to Manisa. He always knows where and how hard to push to soothe his sore muscles and get rid of the knots. This is beyond knowledge. It's an art. It took Adel years to learn Mehmed's body.

When he's done, he reluctantly lets the servants help him dress. He'd rather stay and chill a little longer, but no good will come from letting Mother wait. She's got to be in a state already.

He finds her sitting in her bedroom with a young woman massaging her feet.

"Good evening, Mother. You look as beautiful and young as ever. How did I get so lucky as to be your son?"

Mother's face lightens up. She almost breaks into a smile, but recovers quickly. She waves the girl away so they can talk, but the girl takes her sweet time. She's pretty, this one, with lustrous dark hair falling to her waist, red lips and slippery blue eyes that gaze at him a touch too long.

"I'm glad you managed to carve some time out of your busy day to stop by."

"I have no bigger pleasure," he lies.

"How was your hunt?"

"Great. Güzel got two hares. We'll have them tomorrow for dinner."

"Good. Hare is lean and healthy. Gülbahar will like that."

Mehmed nods, wondering when did Mother start worrying about what Gülbahar likes. Even he hardly knows what she likes. She always says that she likes whatever he gives her, or whatever he wants her to do, and never complains. The closest she ever got to complaining was when Sessiz, her deaf-mute brother, had trouble communicating. She wanted Ali.

"I wish Ali was here. I miss him terribly," Gülbahar said.

"Why isn't he here?" Mehmed asked.

"Your mother, in her kindness, gave him to Mara Hatun."

"To Mara? Why?"

"I think she really fancied him. And your mother is so generous."

"Mother? Not that generous. She liked him pretty well herself, and she knew how useful he was to you. I'll ask her," he said, but he forgot. Now he remembered.

"Mother, why did you give Ali to Mara?"

Hüma Hatun stares at him like he lost his mind.

"What does that have to do with anything?"

"Nothing. I just wondered."

"Wonder about the things that regard you. Like Gülbahar."

Mehmed's heart skips a beat.

"What happened to Gülbahar?"

Hüma smiles, happier than Mehmed has seen her in ages.

"Nothing bad happened. Just the opposite. We have wonderful news. Gülbahar will have your son this winter."

"My son? How do you know?"

"She missed her bleeding for the second time. I wanted to be sure before we told you. Now we know. She's with child."

"How do you know it's a boy?"

"What else can it be?"

"A girl, maybe?"

"Nonsense. Allah didn't bless us for nothing. There's no point in having a girl. You can have a few later if you want, once your succession is secure, but for now, nothing but a son will do."

"I hope He heard your order, Mother, and He complies," Mehmed jokes, but Mother is not amused.

"I got you another girl."

"What for?"

"To bed. She's beautiful and untouched, of course. She's a fast learner, this one, and she's got lots of spunk. She's Venetian, a luscious blue-eyed brunette. You saw her. She's the one who was massaging my feet."

"I don't want her. I want Gülbahar."

"Didn't you hear what I told you? She's with child."

"So what?"

"What's the point in bedding her? She can't get any more pregnant than she is. You need an empty womb to plant your seed."

"I don't want to plant my seed. I want to feel comfortable and at home. You should be happy you finally got what you've been waiting for."

"I am. But one is not enough. Besides, what if it's a girl?"

"You just assured me that Allah took your order for a boy."

Hüma shakes her head.

"Stop this, will you? Gülbahar is pregnant. She's out. Not only because she can't get pregnant again, but because your bedding her might interfere with her pregnancy. Women don't share their husbands' beds when they're pregnant, to keep the baby safe. Got it? Enough of that. I'll send you Gülşah tonight. Now, on a different subject. Have you heard the news from your father?"

Mehmed shakes his head, too annoyed to speak.

"Of course not. You were out hunting, and you wouldn't want the empire's business to ruin your day. That Hungarian vulture, Hunyadi, is agitating again. He's about to replace Vlad Dracul with a man of his choice, and that means that the peace on the Danube is about to be broken. Your father called young Vlad back from Eğrigöz."

"What for?"

"To groom him as the next Voivode of Wallachia, of course, once Hunyadi dispatches his father."

"Why Vlad? Radu's there."

"Radu is too young and... soft. He may be the back-up, if Vlad doesn't make it."

"I wish Father would let me bring him here."

"That's precisely why he won't. Bad enough that you spend your days riding and hunting..."

"Mother!"

"What? You don't think I know that the Genoese ambassador has been waiting for two days to see you, but you've been too busy with your horse and your hawk? You think the ambassador doesn't know? How do you expect to make friends and build alliances if you treat foreign dignitaries like that?"

Mehmed shrugs. "I didn't think he knew. And he smells bad. They all do."

"Of course. Because they don't wash. That's why you have to expand the empire. To civilize the world. And make them bathe."

Mehmed laughs. "Are you saying that my role in life is to make the world smell better?"

"Among other things. After taking Constantinople, of course. Remember?"

Mehmed remembers. He's been dreaming about that for so long. Then Father retook his throne and sent him to Manisa, and he went back to being a carefree child. But Mother is right. Hunting for hare won't help him take Constantinople.

He sighs. "I'll see the ambassador tomorrow."

CHAPTER 68

EDIRNE, JUNE 1447

Seen from high above, the Edirne gardens look like a priceless Isfahan carpet glowing in the setting sun's golden light. They're bright and fragrant, and there's no better way to appreciate the exquisite design with its intricate geometry and the interplay of shapes and textures. The flowerbeds complement each other in color, shape, and perfume. That's why the orange roses sit next to the purple petunias and the red poppies are tucked inside a thick green border.

Standing between them, the water fountains chill the air, soothe the ears with their soft murmur and entice the singing birds. Whoever designed these gardens, I hope they got to see them from up here, Radu thinks, looking for a more comfortable spot in the ancient plane tree, the one said to have risen from Osman's breast.

This tree is his friend. This is where he finds shelter when the real world misbehaves, like when he stabbed Mehmed. He sat here for three days until the cold and the thirst forced him down to face a well-deserved death. But he was lucky. Mehmed forgave him and even chose to be his friend. But that was long ago. Radu hasn't seen Mehmed in a year.

That's why, when he heard the bad news, the one thing Radu could think to do was to run here and hide. And this was the first place he thought of.

But now that he had time to settle, he wonders why he got so upset. For all that he knows, it may not even be true. It might just be someone's idea of a good prank, but Radu doesn't think so.

One of the Serbian boys told him that Vlad returned to Edirne. He said he saw him arrive, but that's not likely. Vlad's been gone for years; he must look different. He's got to be a grown man. How would the boy recognize him?

And if he's back, so what? Radu should be happy to have his brother back. Especially since Mehmed is gone, and he's been so lonely. But Radu has few good memories of Vlad. As a matter of fact, he can't think of any but the bad ones. Vlad killing Yellow. Vlad killing the dove. Vlad beating him. Vlad trying to kill Mehmed. Every memory he's got of Vlad is of his hate, rage, and inflicting pain.

Still, that was years ago. Vlad has been through so much since. Radu too. Neither of them are who they used to be. Maybe they could start over and treat each other like brothers.

And he may not even have to deal with him. Sultan Murad may throw him in jail, or even execute him. Unless he sends him home. The sultan must have a plan. There's got to be a reason he brought him back after all this time.

Radu feels guilty that he's less worried about Vlad getting jailed or even executed than about having him around. As far as Vlad going back home, he's not so sure. Maybe because he'd like to go home himself? Not much at court gives him joy since Mehmed left. Sure, his books, his rubab, and his art give him pleasure, but he's lonely. The other boys don't care about these things. They're all obsessed with horses, hunting, and fighting, which Radu doesn't care for. He joins them once in a while to pretend he's one of them, but he's not. He knows it and they do too. As for going home, he's not so sure. He'd rather go to Manisa and see Mehmed. But he can't.

He takes out Mehmed's last letter. He always carries them with him, because they make him feel loved and give him strength. He reads them until they fall apart, but by then he knows them by heart.

Dear Radu,

I hope you are well. It's hot here in Manisa. I imagine it must be hot in Edirne as well. I went hunting yesterday and Güzel got two hares and a bird. Remember the old hare she lost when we went hunting together and I got upset that you smiled? I'm sorry I was mean to you. I miss you.

Things are good here. My mother is finally happy. Can you guess why? Yes. Gülbahar will have a baby this winter. We all pray to Allah that it's a boy. My mother fusses over her so much — what to eat, what to do, what not to do — that she leaves me alone. Except that she doesn't let Gülbahar come to my bed any more — she says it's unnecessary, now that she's with child, and that it's not good for the baby. She pushes other women on me, instead of leaving me alone, but none of them is like Gülbahar and none of them is like you.

Love,

Mehmed

Radu wipes a tear and sticks the letter back into his sleeve, then looks down.

Movement at the gates. Two guards come out, flanking a man. That's Vlad. He's too far for Radu to see his face, but there's no mistake: The greasy dark hair, the stiff back, the head held to one side like he doubts what you're saying. It's Vlad all right. The Serbian was right.

Radu sighs.

Oh well. It is what it is. Vlad is back, and there's nothing he can do about it, other than wait to see when and where he'll show up to corner and harass him, like he always does. Unless Radu makes the first move. He could go find him and get over that first awkward encounter, establish the battle lines and move on.

Radu shrugs. He may as well be done with this, and move past the dread of what's coming. Get over it, he tells himself, and climbs down the plane-tree to look for his brother.

CHAPTER 69

OH, BROTHER!

His palms sweating, his heart racing like crazy, Radu steps in front of the guards flanking Vlad. They step aside when they recognize him, letting him face his brother.

This close, Vlad is nothing like he used to be. He's always been lean and wiry, but now he looks downright frail. These last years carved his face into a narrow, angry mask, and his lips have all but disappeared under his new thick mustache. The only thing left unchanged are his sharp green eyes. They're still the color of poison.

"Buna seara, frate. Good evening, brother," Radu says.

Vlad's eyes widen. He looks him up and down, then stares at him like he's a ghost. "Radu? Really? Is this you?"

Vlad steps forward, and Radu resists the urge to run. He tightens his fists and digs his heels into the ground, ready to fight. What he's not ready for is Vlad closing his arms around him in a brotherly hug like they never shared before. He kisses Radu's left cheek, then the right, and steps back, holding his shoulders to see him better.

"Radu! Unbelievable! Look at you! You've grown taller than me! And bigger. And you're just as handsome. How are you doing, brother?"

Vlad is right. In the years they've been apart, Radu grew like a weed, thanks to the good food, rest, and exercise, while Vlad seems to have shrunk. He looks so sickly, he'd be pitiful if it wasn't for the fire in his eyes that hasn't faded one bit.

"I'm good. Not much changed here. How about you?"

"Oh, am I glad to be back! And I'm thrilled to see you. But we have too much to talk about to do it here. They're taking me to my new digs, wherever they are. Care to come?"

Radu nods. He has nothing better to do, so he may as well be done with this.

Vlad's new quarters are in the palace school, and they're spectacular by dormitory standards. He has a bedroom and his own living room, furnished with a thick blue carpet woven with orange birds and green vines, a carved wooden chest, and even a fireplace.

"This is way better than my bedroom," Radu says, wondering what made the sultan give Vlad such a grand place.

"Better than my cell, too, for sure," Vlad says. "Except for the rats. I quite enjoyed the rats, and it doesn't look like I'll have any here."

That's got to be a joke, Radu thinks, so he lets it pass.

"Tell me about you," Vlad asks.

"Not much to say. School, sleep, school again. That's it."

"Mehmed?"

"In Manisa."

"Why?"

"Murad said he needed more training."

Vlad nods. "How do you feel?"

Radu shrugs. "I'm fine. Tell me about you."

"It's a long story. But I'm back now."

"I can see that. How come?"

"Do you know what's happening at home?"

"No. I haven't heard anything in a while."

"Murad said Hunyadi is preparing to go to war against Father. He wants to replace him with a puppet in order to better secure his border.

Murad thinks Father will need all the help he can get, so he brought me back."

Radu's heart skips a beat. He's been here all this time, but Murad never spoke to him about what's going on in Wallachia, let alone ask for his help. He called Vlad back instead. Radu wishes he didn't care, but he does. A lot.

"So, what will you do?"

Vlad shrugs. "Murad says that it will depend on the boyars. Their council decides who will be voivode. If they choose to stand with Father, Hunyadi can't get rid of him. The sultan wants me to go to Wallachia and talk the boyars into sticking with Father rather than accepting Hunyadi's pretender."

"Who's that?"

"Vladislav, one of the Dănești. He's our great cousin."

"So, what are you going to do?"

"Damned if I know. I need to think about it."

"Why does Sultan Murad want to send you there for this?"

"Who else?"

"Why didn't he just send a messenger to Father to tell him? And let him convince them?"

Vlad rubs his chin. "Murad says that Father and Mircea have ruffled a lot of feathers. They've accused some boyars of treason and confiscated their lands. That's why they're all up in arms. He thinks there's too much bad blood between them to work things out, but I've been gone for so long that they might listen to me. He wants me to act as his envoy and explain to them that the Ottoman Empire is their friend, unlike that treacherous snake Hunyadi. Murad will forgo a year of tribute if they listen and leave Father be."

Radu's heart is torn. He's worried about Father and Mircea, but he can't imagine Vlad acting as a peacemaker. He has never seen anyone less prone to peace. But that doesn't sound like the right thing to say.

"But I thought you hated the sultan. And the Ottomans."

"Sure I did. I still do. But when Wallachia and Father are in trouble,

I'll do whatever it takes. And if it takes being friends with the Ottomans, I'll do that."

"How are you going to go about it?"

"I'll cross the Danube and head home. I hope to see Father, Mircea, and Mother."

Vlad's voice cracks when he talks about Mother, and Radu feels sorry for him. Mother always loved him best. He's not sure if he's happy or sad that Vlad is going back home, and he isn't. But he's relieved that convincing the boyars to support Father did not fall to him. He wouldn't know how to do that.

"Mother will be so happy to see you," he says.

"Not more than I'll be to see her. I miss her terribly. Father and Mircea, too. But I'm so glad I found you," Vlad says, hugging Radu again like he means it.

Radu submits to the embrace, though he could do with less closeness.

"I'm glad you feel that way," he whispers.

Vlad looks him in the eyes, and his green eyes are wide and honest. "Listen, Radu, I know I haven't been the best brother. I've been mean, and I harassed you and called you names."

"And you beat me."

"And I beat you."

"And you killed my dog."

"Yes. I did plenty of things to hurt you, I know. But I'm really, really sorry. When they brought me back, and I didn't know whether I'd live or die, the one thing I wished I could change was being a better brother to you. Out of all that I did, that's the one thing that kept me awake. I want to do better. Will you give me a chance?"

Radu nods, his eyes full of tears, and hugs him back. He's happy about this unexpected truce. Still, deep in his heart, he wonders how long it will last.

CHAPTER 70
WALLACHIA AUGUST 1447

The journey from Edirne to Târgoviște is not long. Not hard either, once you cross the Danube with a good horse under you and a hundred janissaries watching your back. Nothing like the scorching misery of the dusty roads of Anatolia, whether towards Tokat or Eğrigöz. Here, the oak forests are shady and cool, the fields heavy with the next harvest, and the rivers cold and clear, with water just as sweet as Vlad remembers it. This is his Wallachia, and he's high with breathing the air of his home. He was just a child when he left, but he hasn't forgotten the sway of the cattails in the marshes, the song of the nightingales, or the mouthwatering smell of fried pork. He's overjoyed to be home.

But things are no longer the same. The small villages are grayer, and the garden plots surrounding them are drier and poorer. But, more than everything, the people have changed.

Many years ago, when he and Radu left their home for sultan's court, everyone along the way stopped to bless them and looked at them with kindness.

"Look at those wee ones. They're Vlad Dracul's sons. He's sending him to the Ottomans as hostages," an old man said.

The black-clad woman next to him shook her head. "Poor kids. They don't even know what awaits them. I hope they come back some day."

The man shrugged. "I do too. But you've got to give it to Vlad Dracul for putting his own sons on the line to stop the war. It couldn't be easy."

"It's not easy for us either," another man said. "Every other year, they come to take our crops and steal our children. So what if the little princes will grow up in Edirne? They'll live in luxury, not like ours. Our boys get brainwashed and trained to fight their own brothers, and our girls get sold to birth the Ottomans' children. I don't feel one bit sorry for those two."

The woman glared at him. "Come on, Nicolae, don't be daft. Rich or poor, they're just children torn off from their mother's breast, and their heads are at stake. You can't hate on them. I'll pray for their health and safety."

That was then. Now that Vlad is no longer a child, he sees no kindness in any of the eyes that look at him. Even less so when they glance at his janissaries.

Old women with black scarves tied under their chin stand behind the wooden fences and watch them with worried eyes. The half-naked kids standing in the open doors stare at them with round eyes, but don't smile either. And the old men leaning on their rakes and their shovels spit to the side when they think no one sees them.

Vlad wonders why.

CHAPTER 71

TÂRGOVIȘTE, AUGUST 1447

The Târgoviște royal court parties like they don't have a worry in the world. Red wine flows like water, and the cups get filled before they're empty. The long heavy table made from the trunk of a three-hundred-year-old oak bows under the weight of platters. Lying like a king in the middle of the table, a whole golden-brown steamy suckling pig holds an apple in his mouth. He looks askance at the wild partridges with mushroom sauce and the fried fish stuffed with lemon and garlic. A bowl of deer stew, simmered in red wine for hours, sits next to the lovage-flavored sour soup thickened with sour cream. And so much more, the best delicacies Wallachia has to offer, now that her beloved son is home.

Vlad stuffed himself. Since Muslims don't touch pork — to them it's unclean and unhealthy — Vlad hasn't had suckling pig ever since he left home. He ate so much he had to loosen his belt.

"Have a bit more; you're way too skinny," Mother says, tempting him with a golden piece of crispy skin.

"I can't. I'm about to explode."

Mother ignores him, of course, and sets another morsel on his plate. Vlad smiles, even though he doesn't want it. But it's wonderful

286

to be home and feel loved. He missed that even more than he missed pork.

"I wish Radu was here too. Wouldn't it be wonderful if we could be together again?" Mircea says.

"The little one must have grown a lot," Mother says. "Has he changed?"

"Not a bit. He's taller than me, and wider, but he's just as handsome as he's always been."

"Why didn't you bring him too?" Ștefan asks.

"He couldn't. Radu is a hostage for my good behavior," Vlad Dracul says. "The sultan let Vlad come, but he couldn't let them both go."

"Why not? Not like you're going to kowtow to Hunyadi," Mircea says.

"I wish," Vlad Dracul says. "But it wouldn't help. Hunyadi's mind is made up. He wants to get rid of me and plant Vladislav on the throne; it's just a matter of time until he comes to kick us out. He already sent his puppet to Kronstadt, so he can be close when the time comes."

"When do you think that will be?" Vlad asks.

"In spring. This summer's over, and it would be insane to start a war with winter coming. Hunyadi is smarter than that."

"But what if he does? Are you ready?"

Vlad Dracul shakes his head.

"Not even close. The peasants are still working the fields. I can't pull them away before the harvest, or the country will starve. And the boyars have been busy lately. Too busy to have time for me. Whenever I ask them to come, I get nothing but silly excuses. One sprained his back while riding. Another one's wife fell sick. The other one's roof is leaking. Like he's going to get up on a ladder to fix it himself. No. I bet they changed sides, and they decided to back Vladislav. Whatever he and Hunyadi promised, the boyars sold themselves, and I can't rely on them if the war starts. Even worse, I'll have to watch my back. They wouldn't hesitate to catch me and hand me to Vladislav. And that goes for you too, boys. Be careful."

Mircea wipes his mustache with an embroidered cloth. "I'm always careful."

Hard to believe how much Mircea has changed, Vlad thinks. He's a grown man now, and Wallachia has never had a better soldier. He's Father's right hand. Even more, he's his best general. He led the Wallachian army at Varna and conquered Giurgiu. Vlad can only hope he'll be as good as him some day.

That evening, Mircea invites Vlad to the stables. "Want to see the new foal I started training?"

"Sure." Vlad follows him.

Ștefan stands to join them, but Mircea shakes his head. "I'll show it to you later."

Stefan sits back, looking forlorn, and Vlad wonders why.

The two boys watch the stable hand bring the foal. He's a splendid black stallion with a white star on his forehead and legs as long as a spider.

"He's beautiful. He'll look just like Mehmed's Rüzgar when he grows. What's his name?" Vlad asks.

"*Furtuna.* Storm."

"What a perfect name for a worthy horse," Vlad says.

"Isn't he? But Vlad, I didn't bring you here to show you the foal. I wanted to talk to you privately. I needed to tell you something that Father and Mother don't know. Ștefan doesn't know either." Mircea looks away, chewing on his mustache like he's trying to decide whether or not to trust Vlad. He finally spits it out.

"I got married."

"Married? To whom?"

"A girl. Her name is Lena. She's Ștefan's milk sister."

"Why not tell Father and Mother?"

"She's just a common girl, and Father didn't give me permission. He said that I could only get married if brought a valuable alliance to the country. Marriage is not about love, he said. It's about duty and making children. He even suggested that I asked for Hunyadi's sister's hand, but I didn't. So, Hunyadi gave her to Petru Aron instead, and now he's after us. Maybe we wouldn't be here if I had."

"Too late to worry, brother. That's water under the bridge. You did what you could," Vlad says.

Mircea sighs. "You're right. Either way, I married Lena in the fall without telling Father. I kept waiting for a better time to tell him, but the better time never came. And now that the war is coming and anything can happen, I needed someone to know. Will you take care of her if I don't... if I can't?"

"I'll take care of her as if she was my sister," Vlad says.

"And if she's... if she's with child?"

"I'll take care of him as if he was my own."

"Thank you, brother. That gives me peace of mind."

"Where is she?"

"Near Kronstadt. Vlad, there's one more thing."

"What?"

"She's... Ștefan loves her too. That's why I couldn't bring myself to tell him."

CHAPTER 72

EDIRNE, SEPTEMBER 1447

The long summer is finally over. The evenings are soft, but the mornings are getting chilly in Edirne. Ali shivers as her thin slippers touch the cold stone path from the kitchens to the castle. The sun isn't up yet, but the sky started pinking to the east and it's almost time for the Fajr Salaah, the dawn prayer.

It's been a year since Sultan Murad sent Mehmed back to Manisa with Hüma Hatun, Ali's mistress. That's why Ali is now serving Mara Branković, Sultan Murad's fourth wife, and life hasn't been the same ever since.

Where Hüma was moody, Mara is calm. Where Hüma was fierce, Mara laughs. Hüma was passionate about power. Mara loves life. She loves good food, good wine, good jokes, and beautiful people. Women, of course, since there are no men in the harem other than the sultan.

The whole sarayi is still asleep when Ali tiptoes to Mara's bedroom with the silver tray for her breakfast: a slice of juicy red melon, a piece of fresh white cheese, ten glistening black olives, and a pot of mint tea. She sets down the tray to open the door when she hears soft voices and laughter from inside.

Who can be in Mara's bedroom before sunrise? Ali doesn't want to know, and yet she does. Should she just leave? She knocks softly, hoping they won't hear.

"Come in."

The room is dark but for the two fat candles by the bed. Mara, her eyes half-closed, lays between the silk sheets the color of butter with her long dark hair spread over her pillow.

She smiles at Ali.

"Good morning, Ali. Have you met Zambak yet?"

Zambak, her head resting on Mara's shoulder, her blonde curls tangled with Mara's dark, smiles too.

"Of course. The sarayi is a small place, you can't help but bump into each other. We met the other day in the hammam."

Ali nods, her throat suddenly dry. Zambak, which in Ottoman language means lily, is the new girl in the harem. The validé bought her from the Anatolian slave traders just months ago. She's still in training, but everyone knows she's meant for Sultan Murad's bed. Emine Validé has been working hard to help secure Murad's succession, but he rarely wants women in his bed. And when he does, it's always Halime Hatice Hatun, who's getting too old and too fat to have children.

That's why the validé brought some fresh blood in the harem, a few choice girls to wet Murad's appetite. Ali knows this. What she doesn't know, is what Zambak is doing in Mara's bed. But she has an idea.

"I brought your breakfast," Ali says, avoiding Mara's eyes.

Mara laughs. "I know. Why don't you just set it down and join us?"

Ali's breath catches in her throat. "I... I wouldn't dare, my lady."

"Why not?"

Ali has never had sex, but she knows what sex is. She also knows that the women in the sarayi are not supposed to have sex with anyone else but the sultan. Whatever Mara and Zambak are doing in that bed is forbidden. And if that's bad, having a eunuch lie with the sultan's ladies is inconceivable. If they get caught, they'll all lose their heads. The eunuch first, since his job is to guard the women, and make sure that such things don't happen. Ali's duty is to report this to the chief eunuch, who would report it to the validé and the sultan.

"I don't think the sultan would approve," Ali says.

Mara gives a dismissive look. "Whatever the sultan doesn't know won't upset him. And we aren't about to tell him, are we?"

Ali shakes her head. "I'm sorry, my lady. I can't."

"Oh, well, be that way. But if you change your mind, we'd be happy to have you."

Mara turns to Zambak. She kisses her pink ear, then caresses her cheek, her neck, her rounded white shoulder. She pulls down the sheets to uncover a firm white breast with a tip like a rosebud. She leans over it to touch it with her tongue, and Zambak sighs.

Mara's hand pulls the sheet even lower, uncovering Zambak's flat stomach and her long slim legs with a bunch of blonde corn silk between them. Mara's mouth glides down the creamy skin to the navel, then further down towards the corn silk. Her hand caresses it, then nests in the secret spot between the girl's legs, and Zambak moans like she's hurting.

Ali wants to leave, but she can't. She's mesmerized by the soft play of Mara's fingers under the corn silk. It's like she plays an instrument. The instrument is the girl, who shivers like a strummed guitar, opening her legs further to make room for Mara's hand. Mara teases her, her touch softer than a butterfly's. The girl complains, then grabs Mara's hair and pulls her head between her legs. Mara laughs right there, and her laughter makes the girl tremble. Mara lifts her head and looks into Ali's eyes. Her lips are red and moist and her half-closed eyes glazed with desire, and something happens inside Ali that never happened before.

"Are you sure you don't want to join us?"

Ali shakes her head and tries to move her leaden feet towards the door, but they won't listen. She watches Mara lower her head between the girl's legs and sees the corn silk raise to meet her. Mara blows over the heated flesh, then tastes it with her tongue, then sinks her mouth into it like she's sucking on a juicy peach. The girl sighs and mumbles as her hands grasp Mara's head to pull it closer.

Ali's face is on fire. She's so dizzy she can hardly stand. She forces herself to walk away and touches the door just as the Muezzins' call for the morning prayer joins with the melody of Zambak's pleasure.

CHAPTER 73
FOUND FAMILY

After running out Mara's door, Ali wandered around for ages. She didn't know where she was going, but she needed time to think this through.

She'd heard about men lie with each other — it's even in the Bible — but women? She'd never heard about something like that, and her world just turned upside down.

Women aren't supposed to like sex. They're supposed to tolerate it for the sake of their husbands. And if they get tricked into it for the pleasure of their lovers, they get stuck with the consequences. But she's never heard about women enjoying sex, let alone with each other!

Even worse, seeing the two women enjoy each other stirred something inside her she didn't know existed. For a moment, she even wanted to join them, damn the consequences. Something stirred deep inside her, and now she's terrified. Is she a monster? Is she abnormal? Will God, in his anger, strike her dead?

She touches her silver cross, looking for an answer, but for once, the cross has nothing to say. The stone is blank and clouded like her soul and won't tell her anything.

There's nobody here to ask. If she was home, she could ask Mama Smaranda, who knows everything about everything. But here? She barely dares to think about it, let alone tell someone. So she walks and walks, looking for an answer, until she feels a touch on her shoulder. It's Radu, looking at her with worried eyes. "Are you OK?"

No. She's not OK. Ali is anything but OK, but she can't tell him what she's seen.

"I... I had some bad news."

"What happened?"

"My... my grandmother is not feeling well," she lies.

"I'm so sorry. Tell me about her," Radu says.

"There isn't much to tell. She's... I love her very much, and I miss her." Ali's eyes fill with tears, and Radu looks even more worried.

"Of course you do. Come, let's go to my room and talk."

He grabs her hand and pulls her. Ali would like to be alone, but she can't shake him off. Still, it's nice to have somebody who cares, even if she told him a lie. Well, not entirely. She sure misses Mama Smaranda.

Once in Radu's room, he sits Ali on his bed, then catches the cat and sets her in her lap.

"There. I always feel better when I pet Sari."

Ali laughs, but petting the purring cat surely helps. The kid is so kind! "Thank you, Radu."

It's the first time she called him by name, instead of "prince."

"Of course. I'll do anything to help..."

The door slams open and a man bursts in. He's short, lean and dark, with a thick black mustache and striking green eyes. He grabs Radu in a bear hug and lifts him off the floor.

"I'm back. So good to see you, brother!"

"Good to see you, too. How was your trip?"

"Fruitless. I had no luck with the boyars. Most didn't even want to see me. And the few who did had no interest in anything the sultan offers. Father thinks they've all sold out to Hunyadi and his puppet, and it's only a matter of time before they invade. He thinks they'll have war in spring."

"I'm sorry to hear. How is he? And Mother?"

"They are well. They both miss you and send their best wishes. Mircea too. And our cousin Ștefan."

"Ștefan? He's there, too?"

"He's been there for the last couple of years, apprenticing with Mircea. He fought with him at Varna and Giurgiu. You wouldn't recognize him. Remember he used to be this scrawny little blond kid, and now... but then it's the same with you."

Ali realizes they forgot about her. She coughs, and they turn to her and stare.

"I forgot. Vlad, this is my friend Ali. He's from Transylvania. Ali, this is my brother Vlad."

Ali nods.

Vlad studies her carefully from head to toe.

"You are...?"

"I'm in the sultan's service. Mara Hatun's service, in fact."

"Are you a eunuch in the sarayi?"

"Yes."

"I wonder... I wonder if you met a girl who came to the sarayi a couple of years ago. Her name is Sophia. She has a deaf-mute brother."

"I did, indeed. A lovely girl. The validé changed her name when she came to the sarayi, as is the custom. Her new name is Gülbahar."

"How is she?"

"She is well. She's in Manisa now, with Sultan Mehmed. She's his favorite and expects his child this winter."

Vlad's face turns whiter than snow. For a moment, he looks about to faint. He gasps, then goes quiet.

"Are you sure it's the same girl?" Vlad finally asks.

"I'm sure. She's a good friend of mine. She told me about you. How you saved her and her brother and hired a boat to help them flee. She cares about you and remembers you fondly."

Vlad sighs. He suddenly looks old and sad, nothing like the fire-spitting demon Ali heard about. He's just a heartbroken young man, and Ali feels sorry for him.

"Would you like me to send her your regards, should I get a chance? Tell her you are well?"

Vlad shakes his head. "There's no point. Why bother her? Whatever's done can't be undone. I hope she has a good life. But thanks for offering. You are kind."

Radu nods. "He is a treasure. Ali is my best friend here. He helped me through a bunch of tight spots, and I can always rely on him when I need help."

"You are honoring me, my prince. I didn't do much, but I'll always be here if you need me," Ali says.

She heads to the door, but Vlad stares at her like he's missing something. "Ali, have we met before?"

"Not that I know of, my prince."

"It's strange. I feel like I've seen you before. Or somebody very much like you. Do you have an older sister?"

"No."

Vlad nods with uncertainty, and Ali leaves, wondering who she's taking after. Because she knows, even though Vlad and Radu don't, that they are cousins. They're all the grandchildren of Alexandru cel Bun. And so is Ștefan.

CHAPTER 74

TÂRGOVIȘTE. NOVEMBER 1447

The fall is past its peak in Wallachia. The glorious reds, greens, and yellows of the trees' canopy crumbled to the ground in a pile of wet leaves. The brown fields are barren, waiting for the snow, and a nasty rain falls in tiny cold needles, soaking Mircea's tunic and chilling him to the core. Wallachia's not pretty in November, but then no place is. But Mircea doesn't care about pretty as he stands in the watchtower with Ștefan, looking towards the mountains.

A lone rider gallops from the north as if the devil chased him. And that's bad news. The north used to be safe, but now, with Hunyadi's growing spite, Transylvania isn't safe anymore. Even less so than the south, where Murad offered them support and shelter.

The rider reaches the gates and crumbles down into a heap. Two stable boys help him back to his feet and drag him inside.

Ștefan heads down the stairs, taking them two at a time. Mircea follows with a heavy heart, remembering Smaranda's warning. Last month, he sneaked out to visit Lena. He lied to his father and said he was going hunting, then declined Ștefan's offer to join him.

Ștefan looked hurt. "But why?"

"I just need some time for myself," Mircea mumbled, hoping his father wouldn't ask him any questions. But Vlad Dracul helped.

"Ștefan, young men need some time on their own. They need... privacy. You'll understand as you get older."

Father knew Mircea was going to see a girl. He just didn't know which girl, nor did he know that she was his wife.

When he opened the door of the little hut in the forest, Smaranda looked at him and shivered. Lena jumped in his arms, happy to see him, but Smaranda's eyes were in turmoil.

She didn't talk much while he was there. She left them alone in the hut the whole night — she said she had herbs to collect, but there are no herbs to collect at the end of October up in the mountains. Only dead leaves and snow.

Then, when he got ready to leave in the morning, Smaranda sent Lena on an errand and caught his hand.

"Be careful, Mircea. Very careful. I foretell terrible things are going to happen to you in... ten days or so. Don't trust anyone and get ready for badness. You may defeat it, but it will be hard."

Mircea's heart froze. He stared into her stormy eyes that mirrored the sky.

"What should I do?" he asked.

"Whatever you always wished you could do, but never got around to. Do it now. Don't wait."

A chill went through Mircea. He wanted to ask her more questions, but Lena returned with the jar of preserves she'd gone for, and he couldn't. But he knows Smaranda thinks he'll be dying. Soon. And today is the tenth day, on the dot, since that day.

Mircea follows Ștefan down the steps to the council room, where Vlad and Ștefan are questioning the messenger. The man is bloodied and pale, and he pants as he speaks.

"Vladislav and his men are coming. They're close, less than a day behind me. Don't trust anyone, she said. Somebody you hold close is about to betray you."

A chill goes down Mircea's spine, hearing him echo Smaranda's words. "Who is she?" he asks.

But the messenger can't talk anymore. His eyes glaze, and a bloody foam flows out of his mouth. He shakes and drops to the ground. His breath comes out in a rattle as he chokes on his tongue, and it hurts to watch.

Ștefan looks away, but Vlad doesn't budge as the messenger takes in his last breath. Then it's over. He lies on the floor staring at the stone wall, finally at peace.

"Well, then." Vlad turns to Mircea. "Hunyadi's coming. With Vladislav. And an army, of course. They'll be at the gates by the morrow."

"They weren't supposed to be coming before spring," Mircea says, then wishes he'd kept his mouth shut.

Vlad gestures with his chin.

"That's Hunyadi for you. Not only does he do the stupid thing, but it works for him."

"Not this time. We'll close the castle gates and get together an army."

"How? If we close the castle gates, we can't even send a messenger."

"We'll send the messenger first, then lock the gates."

"OK. Ștefan, whatever happens, Hunyadi has no beef with you. You don't need to be here. We can spare a horse and a few soldiers to get you out of here, but we have to do it now."

Ștefan shakes his head.

"No, Uncle. You and Mircea are my family more than my real family. I haven't seen Mother or Father in years. I'm not going anywhere. I'll stay with you, and I'll do my best."

Flooded with guilt, Mircea averts his eyes. He still hasn't told Ștefan he married Lena, and now is not the time.

By sunrise, ten messengers have left throughout the country to gather an army. The peasants finished harvesting, so they should be able to grab their bows, axes and their horses and come. But will they?

Mircea isn't so sure. Why should the men leave their homes and risk their lives for the Drăculești? After all the years Father sat on Wallachia's throne, they still pay tax in wheat, coin, and children. It's a sad day for a country when people hope their daughters grow ugly, and their sons are too short or have too many fingers. But that's where Wallachia is, since the Ottomans only take the best. Hunyadi must have promised to stop the devşirme. But he lied.

By sunset, the gates are locked, and they're ready to go, or to stay, fight and die. Whatever God in his mercy chooses for them.

Mircea, the commander of the guard, decides.

"Stefan, you stay with Father, whatever happens. Look at this. It's the map of the southern exit, and no one knows it. The men who built it died long ago. You go through the tunnel in the floor of the banquet room, then..."

"They're here. They're at the gates. Hundreds of them. All armed and ready," a guard shouts.

"Just make sure everything is locked and bolted. Open nothing before talking to me."

"The west gate! The west gate is opened, and the soldiers are pouring in."

"That can't be. The west gate is..."

"Guarded by our faithful vornic's men. Maybe not so faithful, after all," Vlad says.

Mircea's heart skips a beat. That can't be happening. He glances out through the tall window. It is happening. The gate is open, and Hunyadi's men are pouring in.

"Time to go, Father."

"I can't leave you here."

"We have no time for that."

Mircea signals Ștefan, who grabs Vlad Dracul's arm and pulls him to the banquet room.

"Head south. The sultan will help you if you make it to the Danube," orders Mircea.

"And you?" Vlad asks, tears brightening his eyes.

"I'll do my best. I'll see you there. Or on the other side, whichever way God chooses. Father and Ștefan, I love you both, and I'm sorry for everything I did wrong."

They head to the throne room.

"Bolt the door," Mircea says. He waits to hear the bolt screeching closed, then grabs his sword and bow, ready to fight.

But there's no point in fighting. Hunyadi's men are just walking into the castle. The Wallachian guards have left their posts and fled, and he's alone. Charging them would be foolish.

I should have fled with Father, he thinks, but it's too late. The sound of heavy boots and the clatter of swords gets closer. They're at the door.

Mircea slams shut the last bolt of the heavy wooden door to buy himself some time, then heads to the watchtower. The stone steps are steep, slippery and narrow, and the ceiling is too low to stand upright. To get up there, they'll have to come after him one by one. He can kill a lot of them before he tires and buy time for Father and Ștefan to escape.

CHAPTER 75
A RISKY ESCAPE

Mircea struggles to breathe as he runs up the last three steps to the top of the watchtower, then flips the heavy wooden hatch and bolts it behind him. That should slow them down, he thinks. That hatch won't be easy to break from below, and it's the only way up here. He drops to the ground to catch his breath, wondering what happened. How the heck did they open that gate?

There's no other way but treason. The vornic turned to the other side. Hunyadi and the Dănești offered him something he couldn't refuse, so he sold himself. And to think he was Father's childhood friend!

Mircea sighs and gets up. It's not big, the tower, just thirty feet across or so, but it's almost a hundred feet tall, raising high over the surrounding plains. But for the darkness, he could see for miles and miles around. But the sunrise is close. Soon enough, he may see Father and Ştefan ride south from the small copse of ash trees that hide the tunnel's opening. They'll find fresh horses there, and a few faithful men.

Maybe. These days, faithful is hard to find.

In the graying light of the morning, he looks around for an escape. It's now or never, and the chances are slim. It's a long jump to the ground. That's not an escape, but a fast death. Faster than any they'd give him if they caught him, since they'll want to set an example. To put God's fear into people's hearts, they'll do things to him they won't dare mention in confession. The thought makes him shiver and reminds him he hasn't confessed in a while. He's been too busy.

But God knows.

Mircea checks his sword and dagger, then heads to the northeastern corner of the tower and steps on the stone with the rust patch. The fake stone lifts, and he takes out the bow, the arrows, the water flask and the rope ladder he stashed there long ago. They all look good. He looks for the best place to drop the rope. The southwest side is the hardest one to see, since Hunyadi's men are coming from the north, and the sun is rising in the east. He takes off his red velvet tunic that makes him easy to see, keeping on his linen chemise and brown breeches.

Something cracks. They're tearing through the hatch.

It's now or never. He can wait for them to break through, and take them one by one until he runs out of arrows, then cut them with his sword until he runs out of strength. That could take hours. But when he's done, unless he's dead already, they'll catch him and punish him for everything he's ever been guilty of.

Or he can try to escape.

He can slide down the rope, hoping nobody sees him, and escape. He may snatch a horse somewhere and get away. Or not. But at least he'd have a chance, albeit slim.

Mircea sighs, remembering his last night with Lena in Smaranda's bed. Thinking of her makes him smile even now. That girl is everything he hoped for, and more. She's a wildcat, full of spunk. He's never felt more alive than when he made love to her, not even when he won a fight.

"Come back," she said, resting her cheek on his shoulder after they'd made love.

He inhaled her scent of lavender and honey and traced her face and her neck with his finger, hoping to carve them into his heart forever.

"I'll do my best."

"I hope your best is good enough. But if it's not, what would you like your son to be named?"

He choked, his eyes swimming in tears. "Are you..."

Lena nodded, caressing his chest with her soft hand.

"You want him named Mircea, after you?"

"How do you know it's not a girl?"

"Are you crazy? After all this trouble?"

"Call him Vlad. After my father."

"Then you'd better be there for the christening," she said. "Otherwise, he'll be Mircea."

Mircea looks around once more. There's nobody on this side of the castle. They're all at the vornic's gate, or rummaging through the castle, and up here, breaking the hatch. The sun isn't yet up, and the morning fog shields the fields in a forgiving mist. It's now or never.

Mircea drops the long rope ladder and scales the wall as fast as he can, though he's encumbered by his weapons: he's got the bow and arrows and his sword and his dagger. It's a lot, but he couldn't decide what to drop. Three more steps and he's on solid ground.

He glances left and right. Nobody. But there's the wide moat he has to cross, and there's no way to do it unnoticed. And they must be close to breaking through the hatch, so they'll also see him from above.

The only way out is the way they came in. He needs to get through the vornic's gate.

He skirts the walls, heading to the traitor's gate until he's close enough to see it. It's almost empty. They must be all inside, busy with the loot. Three steps ahead, a lone guard leans against the wall, watching the road.

That's Mircea's chance.

He sneaks behind him, grabs his greasy hair to pull his head back and severs his windpipe with his dagger before the man can whisper. He sets him on the ground and dons his mantle and his shield, making himself look as Hungarian as he can, then steps out through the gate like he owns it.

"Hey, you!"

He turns around. A Hungarian soldier with his bow at the ready.

"Who are you?"

"Me? You're talking to me? You? You'd better tell me what that is!"

The soldier stares.

Mircea bristles. "What's that, I said?"

He points to a coffer that somebody must have dropped in their looting.

The man shrugs.

"Go get your captain!" Mircea yells.

The man leaves, and Mircea hustles down the wide path to the city of Târgoviște. Wallachia's capital is big, with plenty of streets, houses, and churches to hide. And the merchants may give him shelter. He keeps a steady pace, though his heart races and his palms sweat with fear, until he's put some distance between himself and the castle.

At the town's edge, he stops, wondering whether to go forward or turn left and head to the forest when someone calls him.

"Hey! Who are you?"

The man doesn't look like a soldier. He's not a peasant either. His linen tunic is cinched with a buckled belt, and he's wrapped in a fur-trimmed cloak, like most of Târgoviște's merchants, who got rich from Vlad's peace. The man can't be against him — why should he be? Hunyadi's army will most likely loot their places and destroy the town, so he should be an ally. The only one he's got.

"I'm Mircea, Vlad Dracul's son."

The merchant nods and brings his horn to his lips, calling to the others. They rush in droves from everywhere and surround him.

Mircea knows he's lost. But he doesn't know why.

"Why? My father was good to you. Why did you do this?"

The merchant shrugs.

"Do you know the price Hunyadi placed on your head?"

"No."

"It should please you to know that it's even higher than your father's. Hunyadi really wants you, and he wants you alive. Next time — should there be a next time — you should think things through more carefully."

CHAPTER 76
INTO THE DARKNESS

A dozen men bind his hands and blindfold him, then drag him away. He can't see where, but he hears the wind rustle the dead leaves and smells the earthy aroma of the mushrooms and the musky dampness of the forest. A deep chill goes through him as the sharp November rain seeps through his thin chemise.

He catches a whiff of pine — not many of those here in Wallachia — which reminds him of communion, and of his son who's yet to be born.

He promised Lena to be there for the christening if she named his son after Father, but it looks like he won't. He won't make it to the christening, nor to the birth, nor to anything else. For him, this is the end of the road. It's time to make peace with God — which is hard — and with himself, which is even harder.

He takes in another deep breath, inhaling the scent of the pines, then they push him down and he stumbles and falls to his knees. Somebody rips off his blindfold.

A camp fire stoked by two men. Sitting around it on fallen logs, the boyars stare at him with stormy faces, and the Târgoviște merchants surround them.

There's no sign of Hunyadi, his protégé Vladislav, or their soldiers. The invaders left the locals to do the dirty deed, and Mircea wonders why these people he thought were his allies hate him so.

"How does it feel to sit there waiting for your fate, young whippersnapper?" a fat boyar asks.

"Better than being old, fat, and impotent. How does it feel to be you?"

The boyar shoots him a deathly glare while others chuckle.

"We gathered here to bring God's justice over this sinner," someone says, and Mircea recognizes his father's vornic's grating voice.

"This man and his father, Vlad Dracul, sold our country to the sultan. Thanks to them, we've been paying the Ottomans ten thousand golden coins every year. Plus wheat, wine, sheep, and honey. Even worse, they took Wallachia's best children, leaving our peasants struggling to harvest our crops and leaving us short of soldiers. This man and his father sold our country to the infidels, and they both deserve deaths that shall be remembered forever by anyone who ever thinks about doing the same.

"In their insatiable hunger for power, Vlad Dracul and Mircea even sold their own kin. Mircea's brothers Vlad and Radu are at the Ottoman court to this day. They're getting brainwashed into becoming Ottomans to continue their family's horrible legacy and keep Wallachia enslaved. That's why no death can be too cruel for this man and his father."

The others yell and clap and nod. The fat boyar raises his hand to ask for silence.

"You heard the charge. Do you have anything to say?"

Mircea's mouth tastes bitter. He spits to the side. "My father and I fought the Ottomans, and the Hungarians, and the Poles, and every other single nation who tried to subjugate our country for as long as we lived. You, boyars, did nothing but set one pretender against another and extract privileges from each, while watching Wallachia go down in flames. You ought to be ashamed of yourselves. You betrayed your country over and over, and this is just your latest betrayal. But mind my words: you will live to regret it. We, the Drăculești, the Sons of the Dragon, have no better goal, no higher hope, no more important interest than those of Wallachia. We lived for it, and we're ready to die for it. But if I die, and if my father dies, my brothers shall one day return to avenge us. You'll live to regret this, and you'll regret it soon. I just wish I was here to see it."

The vornic laughed. "You won't see it. You won't see anything, in fact. Starting now."

He nods to the people stoking the fire. The men take out two white-hot pokers and head to Mircea.

His heart freezes. This can't be happening. They can't do this to him! Something like this has never happened in the history of Wallachia, Mircea thinks, his mouth dry, his heart beating to break his chest.

But it is.

A dozen strong hands grab him and push him to the ground. A sharp rock jabs him in the back, cutting his breath, then the smell of hot metal fills his nose. A raindrop sizzles as it drops on a poker.

Mircea struggles to break free, but the hands holding him are too strong and too many. They push him down and laugh, keeping him there.

The red-hot pokers come closer and closer. His heart races, urging him to escape, but there's nowhere to run. He smells the hot metal and feels their heat near his face, then his world turns inside out.

The pain is like nothing he's ever felt before. Inside his crazed brain, lights chase each other. It's like his eyes are on fire and he's watching them, feeling them, and wishing he was dead instead.

He hears a scream, then another and another, before he understands it's him. The pain in his eyes burns his brain and his heart. He looks inside his heart for Lena's face, but all he sees is the fire eating him alive.

"How's that?" the vornic asks, but Mircea doesn't answer.

"The good news is that you won't suffer long. Well, not too long. I always thought that people should have a chance to think before they die. To help them prepare to meet God. There are so many questions: What did I do wrong? How could I have done better? What should I have done instead?

"Most people don't get to ponder before looking into Our Father's eyes. Well, you won't be looking, but you'll be standing with Him, nevertheless. I decided to be generous, and give you time to get ready. I hope you make the most of it."

Mircea can't listen to what he's saying, other that he'll have time to think. But that's good, since his thinking right now isn't what it ought to be.

They grab him and drag him somewhere — he doesn't know where, but he can still smell the forest. Then they push him into a pit. He struggles to his feet and takes a step, but there's nowhere to go. He's surrounded by walls on all sides, just a few feet apart, so close he can't stretch his arms.

He feels them with his fingers. They're not walls, it's just earth, smelling like dead leaves and dirt and worms. He's still struggling to understand when something drops on him, like rain or snow. But it's neither. It's crumbly and heavy. He touches it, smells it, and breaks it between his fingers. It's dirt, falling over him like snow.

He hears a shovel bite the dirt. He tries to pace, but he stumbles. The ground under him is uneven, and the soil piled on him pushes him down. He drops to his knees, and more dirt keeps coming, covering him. He pushes it away, but more comes down. The moist clay is everywhere, covering him, weighing him down, choking him.

Mircea struggles to breathe, but it's getting harder and harder. He gasps, forcing his brain to understand what's happening.

They buried him alive. That's why they said he'll have all the time he needs to think.

Mircea's breathing gets heavier and heavier. He struggles to hold on to his reason, but his sanity is fading. As he heaves, choking in his tomb, he sees Lena's lovely face, and she's not happy.

He won't make it to the christening.

CHAPTER 77
A WEREWOLF'S MISSION

Wallachia's marshes are unlovely in December, unlike Transylvania, where the mountains in winter are a thing to wonder. There, snow covers the bare fields, the naked trees, and even the ugly little huts with a thick, sparkling white blanket, turning the world into a wonderland. Fluffy star-shaped snowflakes fall slowly like white feathers, sticking to your lashes and melting on your tongue like a dream of water. And you can't but smile at the beauty, Codru thinks.

Not here. Here, December is nothing but mud and cold wind and a sharp nasty rain seeping into your boots and chilling your bones and your soul, making you shiver and grumble and sputter.

Even the great Hunyadi's famous mustache droops limp along his tired face. His temper matches it, hanging by a thread. Thankfully, after all these months at his side, Codru has learned to stay out of his way until Hungary's hero gets over his bile.

When he finally came back to Transylvania after years in Edirne and his painful journey back, Codru didn't know what to do with himself. Smaranda and Lena didn't need him. They didn't have room for him, either, though they never said it.

"What should I do?" he asked Smaranda.

"What would you like to do?"

"I'd like to know what's going on with Ali and Isa."

"Then go to Kronstadt to the burgomaster. If anyone knows, it's him."

Codru didn't really care to see the burgomaster, but he had no better plan, so he did.

The mighty Kronstadt Castle looked small and dark. So did the guards, who didn't recognize him — no wonder, after all these years. He was just a kid when he left, and now he's a grown man.

The burgomaster received him in the old banquet hall. The place seemed plain and drab after Edirne Palace, where everything glittered and sparkled. Even the burgomaster had shrunk. His dark hair had turned white, and his thin face looked frail and worn, but the eyes measuring Codru from his head to his toes were still sharp as steel.

"How can I help you?"

Codru looked for a sign of recognition, but there was none. "I'm Codru. I came back."

"Codru?" The burgomaster's face lit with understanding. He took a step closer to see him better. "Are you? Really?"

Codru nodded, but the burgomaster didn't seem convinced. "Who won the pork chop?"

"Ion. But they called him Isa now."

"What was your teacher's name?"

"Professzor Geza."

"Why did he slap you and send you to work without dinner?"

"Because I called Ali a stupid girl."

The burgomaster smiled and wrapped him in a bear hug. "I'll be darned! I had heard about your escape, but I must admit, I didn't think I'd see you again after all this time. I was sure you perished somewhere on your way back. I'm so glad it isn't so! Welcome back, Codru. Tell me about your trip."

Codru told him about the Tunca, the sultan's galley, the winter in the Greek islands and his spring with the fisherman. The one thing he left out was that somewhere in Lesbos there might be a tiny werewolf waiting for him. The burgomaster listened to the end.

"Isn't that something? So, what do you plan to do now?"

Codru shrugged. "I don't know. What can I do?"

"Our promise stands. We promised you a home and land and money, and they're certainly yours if you want them now. But if you're not ready to settle, I have another offer for you. Through all your travels, you've gained precious knowledge that no one else has. You lived in the Edirne Palace, trained with the janissaries, roamed the Ottoman Empire, rowed on the sultan's galley. You know more about Ottomans than anyone else but the Ottomans themselves. It would be sad to waste such precious knowledge.

"I have no doubt that Transylvania's voivode would be pleased to have your counsel. I'd like to send you to his court in Buda. You'd be in the thick of things, you'd know everything that happens and you could help your country. Hunyadi is a powerful man, and he's growing more powerful each day. As Hungary's regent, he directs everything and everybody in the empire. If he's pleased with you, he might even grant you a nobiliary title, propelling you into the Transylvanian elite. That's more than I could ever do, and it beats owning a house and some sheep — not that there's anything wrong with that."

That got Codru thinking. If he went to Buda, he'd get a chance to meet new people and face new challenges. But he'd have to leave Lena.

Not that she'd care — Smaranda said that she was promised to some Wallachian boyar, so she's out of his league. But he'll miss her.

Still, he had no purpose there other than chopping wood, carrying water, and hunting for food.

The burgomaster read his struggle.

"And one more thing: with Hunyadi, you'd find out what's going on with Ali and Ion. That's where their connection goes," he said.

What else could Codru say but yes?

CHAPTER 78
WALLACHIA ON LOAN

That's why now, almost a year later, Codru pushes his horse to slog through these damn muddy Wallachian marshes in the freezing rain behind Hunyadi and Vladislav, the freshly minted Voivode of Wallachia, looking for Vlad Dracul.

They took Târgoviște a few days ago. Since that, they've searched high and low to stop Vlad Dracul from reaching the border; the last thing they want is to have him cross the Danube into the Ottoman Empire and come back with an army. And it's been no fun. They're all tired, wet, and grumpy, especially the famous white knight, who stopped being white a while ago, and is now dripping mud and ill-humor.

"We should go further south," Vladislav says. "It's been three days. He's got to be closer to the Danube."

Hunyadi nods. "Not a bad thought. Why don't you do that? As for me, I'm done. I'm going home. You have the boyars and their men, and I'll leave you another couple thousand men for now. That should suffice. Vlad left with only a few guards, and there's no way he can resist once you find him. Spread your men along the Danube to make sure he can't cross, and, sooner or later, he'll show up. But I've had it."

"Of course. I'll take it from here."

"Good. You do that. But there's one more thing. You can't do to Vlad what you did to Mircea. Something like that should never happen again. What happened to Mircea has stained your legacy forever. Mine too. God knows I hated that arrogant, snot-nosed kid, and I wanted him dead. But he was a good general and the son of a voivode and he got treated worse than a common criminal. That will not do. Someday your reign will be over, and whoever comes after you will look at your children and remember what you did to Mircea."

Vladislav's weak chin juts forward and his eyebrows rise, making him look like an old turkey. "I didn't do it. Those weren't my people. They were the burghers of Târgoviște."

"And your boyars. Your army. Who do you think will get the blame for this? Listen, Vladislav, I'm all for putting the fear of God into the enemies' hearts. But we are knights, nobles and Christians, and we have to abide by our rules. We must comport ourselves with dignity and honor at all times, with those we like and those we don't. Yes, I wanted Mircea dead. He deserved to die. But he didn't deserve what happened to him."

Vladislav hangs his head like a scolded child. "I understand."

"I hope you do. Because, let me remind you, you're not the only one craving Wallachia's throne. Thanks to your grandfather Mircea's high spirits, there are more pretenders to that throne than hungry fleas on a mangy dog. I toppled the voivode once, and I can do it again. And again. I got you this throne, and I can take it back from you. I'm only lending Wallachia to you, you understand?"

Vladislav nods, his face burning.

Hunyadi glances at Codru and spurs his horse. "Let's go home."

Codru calls his men. As the head of Hunyadi's personal guard, he leads five hundred elite riders whose task is to protect Transylvania's voivode at all costs. He follows, but not too close, to give Hunyadi time to chill.

But Hunyadi's not interested in chilling. He wants to talk.

"You know Vlad Dracul's children? The two that are still hostages at the Ottoman court?"

"I do."

"Tell me about them."

"The eldest, Vlad, is a fighter. He's small, mean and wiry, and he'll stop at nothing to get what he wants. He was only twelve when he tried to kill Mehmed in a play-fight. Murad sent him to jail in Tokat, but he escaped. They caught him and sent him to Eğrigöz. He's a spitfire, that one."

"How about the other one?"

"Radu the Fair? He's four years younger, and a nice kid. He's a good friend of Mehmed and my friend Ali. Radu is into poetry, music and flowers rather than fighting, and he's terrified of his brother. Those two couldn't be more different from each other."

"Which one would make a good Voivode of Wallachia, in case our friend Vladislav doesn't deliver?"

"Depends on what you're looking for. What do you want from a Voivode of Wallachia?"

"I want him to resist the Ottomans and stand against their aggression. I want him to stop them when they want to come north and keep Hungary safe. For a while, I thought about taking Wallachia and incorporating it into the kingdom, but decided against it. Too much work. I'd rather use it as a buffer against the Ottomans. But I need a voivode that will comply with my wishes and be faithful to me."

"Vlad then. But if you want him to be faithful to you, you'll have to be faithful to him. He won't be grateful that you put Vladislav on Vlad Dracul's father's throne. Nor that you allowed Vladislav to kill his father and brother."

"Yes. Well, it is what it is. It's too late for Mircea, but I hope Vlad Dracul fares better."

CHAPTER 79

BĂLȚEȘTI, WALLACHIA, DECEMBER 1447

The five tired riders are quiet. The sun has already set, and the moon hid behind the clouds, giving them barely enough light to see the road south towards the Danube.

They're making slow progress, and the cold got into their bones. After three days of riding under the merciless rain, their clothes are soaked, their horses tired, and their souls all but frozen.

Vlad Dracul looks worse than the others. Ștefan's tired too, and so are the guards, but the voivode lost his light. He slouches in the saddle as he keeps riding like he doesn't know what else to do.

"We're doing good," Ștefan says, with a pep he doesn't feel. "Only a few more miles, and we'll find a warm place to spend the night and have something to eat. And maybe even some wine."

Hearing about food and wine, the guards perk up a little. They could all do with some refreshments and a bit of rest, even the horses, who've lost most of their spark. They keep going until the rain stops and the clouds scatter, uncovering a glowing white moon that shows them the way. But the mud, the tired horses and the hopelessness make it slow going.

A village would be good right about now, Ștefan thinks, with a fire to warm them up and dry their soggy clothes. But, as far as the eye can see, there's nothing but marshes and mud.

"We've got to be close," Ștefan says with a joy that doesn't reach his heart. He's wet and tired too, and his soul is heavy. He thinks about Mircea, who stayed behind to cover their escape, and wishes he was here. What happened to him? Staying behind was a brave, selfless plan, the sort of thing a hero would do, but was it wise? Wouldn't it be better to have Mircea here, with his fearless determination to keep them going? Ștefan can't do it anymore. He's at the end of his rope, and the guards are too. And Vlad Dracul no longer cares.

"It doesn't matter. It's too late now," Vlad Dracul says, in an odd, toneless voice.

"Too late for what?"

"Too late for anything."

"Why?"

"They'll catch us. And Mircea's dead."

Ștefan shudders. He can't be. Not Mircea. He fought and always won, ever since he was a kid. He can't be dead.

"No, he's not. He'll catch up with us any moment. Either here, or on the other side of the Danube."

Vlad Dracul's weary eyes and his hunched shoulders tell Ștefan what he thinks about his encouragement. "Why don't you just leave me and go, Stefan? I can't go any further," he says.

"Sure you can! Just think about the kids. Vlad and Radu. You haven't seen Radu since he was a child..."

"And I won't see him again. Listen, Ștefan, you're a great kid, and you'll make a fine soldier and voivode one day. You'll make your father proud. Also Mircea, and me. But one thing a leader should never do is lie to himself. It's OK to lie to your enemies, it's even expected. But rarely lie to your friends, and never, ever lie to yourself. This is it for me. They'll be here any moment. Hunyadi won't risk letting me escape to return with an army. That's why he attacked in the fall. He knew I'd be ready by spring, so why wait? Now listen to me. Leave me and go. I have nothing left to live for, but you do. And once they get me, they won't look any further, so you'll be safe. Return home to Moldova, but be careful. It's hard to tell your enemies from your friends."

"I can't leave you here."

"Yes, you can. I don't need your death weighing on me. I'm guilty of enough deaths already."

Ștefan shakes his head, then he hears the horses.

Vlad Dracul was right. They're there. It looks like a hundred of them, galloping behind them, outlined by the silver moon. And they're only five.

No. Not five. Only two. The guards disappeared without a trace. They are alone.

Deep terror freezes Ștefan's heart as the riders surround them. Vlad Dracul turns to them and straightens, his weariness gone. He's every bit the brave knight and proud voivode he's always been.

"I wish you'd listened and left when I told you," Vlad says. "Now be quiet and let me do the talking, for whatever that's worth."

Ștefan nods. They wait side by side as the riders surround them.

"Drop your weapons."

Vlad throws his sword and his dagger to the ground. Ștefan bites his lip but does the same.

The talker, a thin man with a pockmarked face, glances at Vlad, then looks at Ștefan.

"Who's the kid?"

"My nephew, Ștefan of Moldova."

"He's lying," someone says. "That's got to be his son, Mircea."

"He's not. Mircea's dead."

The words hit Vlad Dracul like a hatchet. He wavers and tightens his hands on the reins. Ștefan's heart hollows.

"How do you know?" Vlad Dracul asks.

"I was there," the man says.

"How did he die?"

"He died like a warrior. That's all you need to know. He was a brave man."

"Let my nephew go. He'll do you no harm; he's not a contender to your throne. And he'll spread the word that I am no more, giving you peace in your reign."

"What's your name, boy?"

"Ștefan Mușat."

"Ștefan Mușat, you can tell the world that Vladislav of the Dănești, the Voivode of Wallachia, has spared your life. Now go."

Ștefan can't move. He can't leave his uncle to die alone.

"Go, Ștefan," Vlad says.

Ștefan turns to Vladislav. "May I wait? To close his eyes and say a prayer?"

Vladislav nods and signals his men. Two of them help Vlad Dracul off his horse. The voivode is so weak he'd fall if they didn't hold him, but he finds his balance and looks around him once more.

He kneels in the mud and crosses himself: first up, then down, then left and right in the Orthodox manner, then leans to kiss the ground.

"I'm ready."

The longsword catches the moonlight, its silver blade a blur as it cuts through the air. One slash, and Vlad's head rolls to the ground while the kneeling body shudders, then drops on its side in the mud.

Ștefan kneels by the head and picks it up with shaky hands. He closes the eyes and makes the sign of the cross over it, then sets it on the ground at the end of the neck, making it look like Vlad Dracul was still whole, but for the red around his throat. He whispers the Lord's Prayer, then kisses the hand of the man that treated him like a son.

"Thank you, Vlad Dracul. Your sons and I, we'll never forget what you taught us. And God willing, one day we'll avenge your death. And Mircea's."

Then he mounts on his horse and heads home to Moldova.

CHAPTER 80

DEMOTIKA, DECEMBER 1447

Thanks to Allah the merciful, Demotika happens to be right on the way from Manisa to Edirne. And thanks to Sultan Murad, who spent time, money and care building it, the new hilltop castle is brand new and shiny, instead of the dusty ruin it used to be. The floors have thick carpets and soft pillows, the kitchens could feed a whole army, and the new hammam smells like lavender and jasmine and hisses with hot water.

Still, the imperial room is not big enough to contain Mehmed's worry. His heart racing, his sweaty hands closed into fists, he paces up and down the marble floor waiting for news from the sarayi. And the news takes its time.

Last month, when his father called him back to Edirne, Mehmed didn't know what to think. What was it this time? Had he done something to deserve his father's wrath? Was he calling him to execute him?

Probably not. If Sultan Murad wanted to kill him, he wouldn't ask him to come back. He'd either send the janissaries to take him back, or he'd have had him strangled right there, in Manisa. He wouldn't wait weeks for him to return.

Murad must have something different in mind. A new war? Maybe he's sick and needs help? Unless he's trying to teach him something? Mehmed doesn't know what it is, but he knows Father wouldn't call him back without a reason.

Oh well. He'll tell me when he's ready, Mehmed thought, and told the servants to get packing.

He'd thought Mother would be overjoyed to return to Edirne. But he was wrong.

Hüma Hatun glared at him with her hands on her hips, her long red hair burning around her like a flame.

"Why?"

"I don't know. I just know Father asked me to come back."

"What for?"

Mehmed shrugged. "I don't know. If he wanted me to know, he'd have told me."

"Of course. And if you wanted to know, you should have asked. That's why Allah gave you a tongue, so you can speak and ask questions. And that's why he invented pigeons, to send them back and get an answer. But no. Not you. You're too busy hunting and prancing around to ask."

"He wants me back, and that's that. How does that make a difference, Mother?"

"First, we'd know for how long. Does he want you back just to talk, in which case you'd be back in Manisa in a few weeks, or does he want you back as his co-sultan, in which case you'd never be back? Should we pack and join you, or should we wait here for your return?"

Mehmed got it. "I see. How about you pack and go with me, and then we see what happens?"

His mother looked at him like he was dim-witted. "You forgot Gülbahar is about to give birth? Would you like her to give birth to your first-born son on some Anatolian dusty road on the way to Edirne, like a peasant, and hope they both make it? Or would you like her to get the best care of the best midwifes in the Ottoman Empire so she can give you a healthy son?"

Mehmed bowed. "I'm sorry, Mother. I hadn't thought about that."

"You haven't thought about a lot of things. Thinking doesn't seem to be your strong suit."

Mehmed blushed and did his best to swallow his anger.

"We'll pack and go, all together. We'll get the best midwife of the empire to travel with us. We'll also have Akşemseddin, should things not go as planned. Gülbahar has another six weeks to go. By that time, we should all be safely in Edirne and have the baby born in the sarayi. How does that sound?"

His mother shook her head and glared at him. There's more frustration than love in her angry green eyes, since her devotion has already transferred from her son to the baby growing in Gülbahar's belly. Once she decided that he'll be a boy and the next sultan, she stopped cutting Mehmed any slack. It's odd to be cut off from her affection he used to take for granted.

Even worse, she was right. No matter how slowly they crawled and placed pillow over pillow in Gülbahar's cart to soften her ride; no matter how much honey and quieting herbs the midwifes fed her to delay the birth, she went into labor days before they reached Edirne.

But thanks to Allah, they were near Demotika, so Gülbahar didn't have to give birth in the cart or in some dirty caravanserai along the road. Still, Mehmed felt like a dunce for dragging her on this trip.

She's now in the Demotika sarayi with Mother, the midwife, and the women, but he can hear her bloodcurdling screams. And every one of them stabs his heart like a knife. For almost two days, he's walked back and forth over that floor until he started wearing a path in that marble, but it's not over.

He knew birthing children took a while, but this is getting ridiculous. He sighs and drains another cup of harsh Greek wine. That's all he had to eat or drink since this started, and he thanks Allah for the wine that keeps him going and numbs his worry.

The door opens. Akşemseddin, his face clouded, steps in.

"I'm sorry to say that I have no good news, my sultan."

Mehmed's heart skips a beat. "What are you saying?"

"The baby's too big. She's a little one, your favorite, and the baby has trouble coming out. She's worked hard, but she's losing her strength. The midwives fed her honey and even wine, but she's getting weaker and weaker."

"Are you saying she's dying?"

The doctor shrugs, avoiding his eyes. "Not yet, but..."

"What can you do?"

"Not much. And what we can do, it's not pretty."

"What is that?"

"If the baby doesn't come out soon, she will die. The baby too. We have to get the baby out, one way or another."

"What other way is there?"

"We can... we can cut the baby inside her. He might be dead anyhow, after all this. We could take him out piece by piece."

Mehmed's heart freezes. Akşemseddin, the Ottoman Empire's best doctor, talks about chopping his baby into pieces so that Gülbahar can live. The thought of it makes him sick, and he leans against the wall to stay upright until he musters enough strength to speak again.

"Will she live, then?"

"Maybe. Maybe not. We don't know. Only Allah, in his endless wisdom, knows. She may live, or she may not, but she'll probably never have another child."

Mehmed wipes the sweat off his brow with his sleeve. "Is there any other way?"

"It hasn't been done in forever. And it's terribly risky. But..."

"What?"

"We can cut her belly to take out the baby that way. That's how Julius Caesar, the Roman Emperor, was born. If the baby's still alive, he might make it. If he's not..."

"How about Gülbahar?"

"Nobody has ever lived after this. She'll die, but she'll probably die anyhow."

Mehmed grabs another cup of wine and drains it. His soul is a storm and his heart poisoned with anger. How could Allah the Merciful allow this to happen?

He's so mad he can't see straight, but most of his anger is for himself. Mother was right. He shouldn't have dragged Gülbahar on this journey that he doesn't even know the reason for.

"I need to see her."

"But, my sultan, you…"

"I need to see her. Now."

CHAPTER 81

HARD LABOR

A woman opens the door. She stares at Mehmed like he's crazy, but he doesn't care. He pushes her aside and strides in. He needs to see Gülbahar alive one last time, if that's all there is.

The small hot room is crowded with women who move aside to let him pass. Propped in her birth chair in their midst, Gülbahar is whiter than snow. She's so small and frail she looks half-dead between the two women holding her up. One is the cheeky Venetian; the other is one of the girls Mother sent to his bed after she denied him Gülbahar. They're both haggard and tearful as they struggle to hold her up, since she's too weak to sit.

The midwife, an elderly woman dressed in black, kneels between Gülbahar's legs, where dark blood pools on the white marble floor. Her face darker than a moonless night, Hüma Hatun sits watching. She sees Mehmed, and her angry eyes blame him.

Mehmed kneels by Gülbahar and takes her freezing hand. He calls her, but she won't open her eyes. Her head droops forward, like she's too weak to hold it. She's barely breathing, and the only proof that she's still alive is the blood dripping out of her.

Mehmed's brain darkens with rage.

"Why is she seated? Lay her in her bed."

"She needs to sit. The birthing chair will help her give birth, and the walnut wood will bring fortune and health to the baby," Hüma says.

"I don't care. Can't you see she can't sit? Lay her down. Now!"

The women rush to do it, and lay the girl between the pearly sheets. Mehmed sits by her side and touches her pale cheek.

"What's going on?" he asks the midwife.

"The baby is too big. It won't come out," the midwife says.

"Well, take it out somehow."

The midwife glances at him like he lost it. She shakes her head and walks to the screen separating the sarayi from the next room, where Akşemseddin waits to share his wisdom and advice. As a man, he's not allowed to see a birthing woman, let alone touch her.

"What else can we do?" the midwife asks.

"Bend her knees as far as they go, to straighten the curve of her spine. That may give you another half-inch of room. Then push low on her belly, just above the lowest bone, to squeeze the baby out."

The midwife instructs the two women. They grab Gülbahar's slim ankles and pull them up, bringing her knees by her ears. The midwife lies her hands on Gülbahar's belly and pushes on it with all her weight. The girl moans, since she's too weak to scream.

All of a sudden, the baby's head pops out between her legs.

Gülbahar screams. The women gasp. Mehmed leans closer.

The little face is flat and purple, with tight-shut eyes covered in a white waxy coating and a sprinkling of red hair.

"The head's out!" Hüma screams. "Praise Allah, the head's out."

"Twist it gently to release the shoulder," Akşemseddin says from behind the screen.

The midwife cups the baby's cheeks and twists the head left, but nothing happens. The baby's stuck, half in and half out, and won't come any further.

White as a sheet, the midwife turns from Gülbahar to the screen. She can't pull out the baby by the head, or she'll break his neck. But what can she do? Most babies slip out easily after the head is out, but not this one.

"It's stuck!" she gasps.

"Mehmed? Can you hear me?" Akşemseddin says.

Mehmed stares from his baby's purple face to the white face of his mother. They both look dead, and he's never hurt like this.

"Yes."

"We may have to hurt the baby to get him out. But he may be dead anyhow. And if he's not coming out, he'll be dead for sure. And so will she."

"Do what you must. I need her alive."

"Get your hand inside her," Akşemseddin tells the midwife. "Find the upper shoulder, stick your fingers under it and pull it out, even if you have to break his collarbone."

The room gasps. Hüma jumps to her feet like her seat caught fire.

"Remember that this is the next sultan you're talking about. The Ottoman's hope, blood of the blood of Osman, the empire's builder, and Murad's grandson, the man who..."

"We all know what Father did, Mother. But this child has a father too, and that's me. Do whatever you have to do — anything — to get him out. Now!" Mehmed roars.

The women fall to their knees.

"Get up and get working. Now!"

The midwife leans over the little blue head sticking out between Gülbahar's legs. She's passed out, thank Allah, so she hasn't heard them. The midwife reaches her shaky hands towards the baby's head.

"Slide your fingers around his neck first and make sure the cord isn't wrapped around it. If it is, release it gently," Akşemseddin says.

The midwife slides her trembling fingers alongside the baby's neck. You'd think they'd slide easily, with all that blood and slime, but they don't. She finally gets them in, and the sweat drips off her forehead on the baby's head.

"The upper shoulder?"

"Yes. Slide your three longest fingers into his armpit and pull the shoulder out."

The woman sighs and does it. She pulls with all her might, and the shoulder pops out. A heartbeat later, the baby slides out like a slippery fish. The tiny purple body lies silent and unmoving on the white sheets.

The women gasp and surround him, but Mehmed has no time for him. He kneels by Gülbahar and whispers in her ear. He tells her how he missed her, and how they'll make up for the lost time. He tells her that her baby will grow to be the empire's pride, and she'll be validé someday.

He doesn't believe any of it, of course, since she's as good as dead, but he wants to give her something to live for. And if she dies, he wants her to die happy.

But she doesn't seem to hear him, and she doesn't move. Her eyes are closed, her skin paler than the sheets, and her chest's barely moving.

The midwife rubs the baby dry. She slaps its feet, then turns him upside down and squeezes him like a lemon to get the bad juices out. Nothing happens.

She grabs him by the ankles and slaps his bottom, hard.

And just like that, the baby sneezes like a cat, then coughs and screams.

The room screams even louder. Everyone rejoices in this miracle of life. The women laugh, sob and cry as the baby's blue face turns white, then pink. He screams louder and louder, cursing the hands that rub, shake, and squeeze him.

Gülbahar's eyes open, and her smile melts Mehmed's heart.

"Is it a boy?" she asks.

Mehmed doesn't know, nor does he care, but Hüma does. Despite the protocol saying that the midwife should call the baby's gender, she can't help herself.

"It's a boy, thank Allah and his endless kindness. It's a big baby boy and the Ottoman Empire's next sultan."

Gülbahar's smile lights her weary face. Her eyes glow with pride, watching the baby as the women fuss around her. They wipe the sweat off her brow, rub her hands, and pour honey into her mouth, gazing at her like she's the most beautiful thing they've ever seen. Because she is, Mehmed thinks.

"What will his name be?" Gülbahar asks.

Mehmed studies the baby, looking for his name.

He's clean and dry. The midwife wiped off the blood and the goop and washed him, then salted his skin to remove the bad smells and dripped honey into his mouth to make his words forever sweet. She tied and cut the cord, swaddled him into clean silks, and handed him to Mehmed.

Mehmed gazes at his son, wondering who he'll take after. Will he be sweet like Gülbahar? Fierce like Mother? Ambitious like him? Or patient like Sultan Murad?

He looks into the baby's eyes, wide open as he contemplates the world around him, and smiles. Mehmed doesn't know who this baby will become, but Allah has told him his name.

"His name is Bayezid. He'll be one of the greatest sultans ever and make us all proud. You, Gülbahar, and you, Mother. And Sultan Murad. And me."

As if he heard him, the baby screams a piercing scream that shakes the walls, then goes back to studying his father's face.

Mehmed smiles and touches his cheek.

"Your voice will make the world tremble someday, my son. From the north to the south and from the east to the west, people will shudder when they hear your name. Like your forefather Bayezid Yıldırım, you'll take the world by storm."

CHAPTER 82

EDIRNE, JANUARY 1448

Radu doesn't know what's going on, but he's sure it's not good news. He rushes down the hallways to the throne room, wondering what it is this time. He hasn't done anything that he knows of. Maybe Vlad? But then why call him?

Ali's face looked somber when he came to summon him.

"Sultan Murad wants you now."

"Why?"

Ali shrugged.

"Will I be coming back?"

"I think so."

"If I don't, will you please take care of Sari? She doesn't have anyone else."

Ali's eyes reddened. "I will. But you'll come back. I'm sure."

That helped a bit, since, to Radu's knowledge, Ali has yet to be wrong, but his heart still thumps inside his chest when he gets to the throne room.

The sultan sits on his podium, alone but for the guards, worrying his amber prayer beads. He nods and points to a pillow. Radu sits and waits.

He listens to the silence. Today, like never, the throne room is quiet other than the murmur of the fountains meant to cool the air and hide whispered secrets from curious ears. To quiet his mind, he follows the intricate design of the rich Isfahan carpet. A rust-colored field covered with entangled green vines and scattered octagonal purple flowers and triangular birds...

It feels like forever until rushed boots clatter outside. It's Vlad, flushed and dusty from fighting someone somewhere. From the look in his eyes, he's just as bewildered as Radu, but he's ready to fight, even if he doesn't know what he's fighting for.

The sultan points to the other pillow. His back stiff, his fists closed, Vlad sits like a lynx, ready to pounce.

Does he ever relax? Radu wonders. Vlad fights like he breathes. To him, life isn't worth living unless there's someone to fight. Thank God it's not me these days, Radu thinks.

The sultan looks from one to the other. His face is somber and his eyes sad.

"I'm sorry, but I have bad news for you. It's about your family."

"Mother?" Vlad asks.

"Mircea?" Radu whispers.

The sultan looks at them kindly, which is even scarier than when he's mad.

"I don't know about your mother. I'll try to find out. But your brother Mircea died. He died like the hero he's always been. I just wish he was on our side in Varna and Giurgiu. He was one of the brightest young generals I ever met. Sadly, he is no more."

Radu chokes. "What happened?"

"When Hunyadi became Hungary's regent, he decided to surround himself with faithful neighbors to protect his borders. Your father refused to fight us, so Hunyadi brought your uncle Vladislav with an army and had him challenge your father to Wallachia's throne. He bought the boyars, who bring most of the Wallachian army. The boyars and Târgoviște's merchants caught Mircea."

"What happened to him?" Radu asked.

The sultan clears his voice. "Nothing good, I'm afraid. Mircea stayed behind to let your father flee. The Saxon burghers from Târgoviște blinded him with hot pokers, then buried him alive."

Radu bends over to retch. The sultan averts his eyes.

But Vlad needs to know more. "What happened to Father?"

"He tried to escape, but he didn't make it to the Danube. They executed him in the marshes of Bălteni."

Radu struggles to understand, but he can't. He tells himself that Mircea is dead and Father is dead, but the words make no sense. His brain can't get that.

Vlad does.

"So, Father's dead; Mircea's dead; Mother's missing; Wallachia is in the hands of Hunyadi's puppet. And we're here."

Murad nods, watching Vlad intently. "That is an accurate and succinct presentation of the situation. I couldn't do better myself."

"Now what?" Vlad asks.

"That's why I brought you here. To discuss your plans for the future. What would you like to do?"

Radu's jaw falls. What would he like to do? Ever since the day he was born, there's been someone there to tell Radu what to do and what not to. Nobody ever asked him what he'd like.

"You mean we have a choice?" Vlad asks.

"Of course. I'm really sorry that your father and your brother perished, but they died as the Ottoman Empire's faithful allies. Your father didn't break his oath. That's why he died. Therefore, you two are no longer the empire's hostages. You're both free to stay or go as you please and do whatever you choose from now on."

The thought is too much for Radu, since he's never been free to do what he wanted and go where he pleased. But not for Vlad.

"Where can we go?" he asks.

"Wherever you want. You could go to Moldova, but I wouldn't advise it. Moldova is in as much turmoil as Wallachia, and I lost track of which of your uncles sits on the throne for the moment. You could also stay here — you both are the Ottoman Empire's honored guests while you decide what you wish to do about your future.

"Or you could go to Wallachia, but I wouldn't do it without an army. Vladislav and the boyars will think you came for revenge, and they'll kill you."

Radu sighs. The options overwhelm him, though there really aren't that many. Go to Wallachia and get killed, or go to Moldova and get killed, or stay here.

"How can I get an army?" Vlad asks.

The sultan smiles.

"I hoped you'd ask. It just so happens that we aren't at war for the moment. I might be able to spare... four thousand janissaries..."

"Ten thousand," Vlad says.

"Friends shouldn't fight friends about little things. Say I gave you seven thousand. What would you do with them?"

"I'd avenge my father and my brother. And take the throne back."

"How?"

"I'll put the God's fear in the boyars and make them regret the day they were born. And I'll show Hunyadi he's fighting the wrong man."

"Vlad Dracula, I like the way you think. But that is an aspiration, not a plan. How precisely would you go about defeating Vladislav?"

Vlad's eyes are burning, but he doesn't speak.

The sultan smiles again.

"See, my young friend, that's where experience is priceless. Your years in Tokat and Eğrigöz strengthened your character and your resolve, but they didn't teach you how to lead an army. But we can work on that.

"I'd like to offer you an officer position in our army. Our best men will train you in troop management, strategy, tactic, and all the other topics a general must master. Then, when you're ready and the time is right, we'll look at sending you back to Wallachia. What do you think?"

Vlad nods. For once, there's something resembling a smile on his face that seldom smiles.

"I'm in."

"How about you, Radu? What would you like to do?"

What would he like to do? Only one thing comes to mind.

"Can I go to Mehmed?"

CHAPTER 83

EDIRNE, SPRING 1448

It's been a while since Radu got to spend time with Ali, since he's been too busy with his training. Not his choice, but both Vlad and Sultan Murad insisted he should get the same training as Vlad — just in case.

"In case of what?" he asked.

"In case I don't make it. If I go back and they catch me, they'll treat me like they treated Mircea. If so, you're our only hope for revenge. And the last Dracula to fulfill Father's promise to Wallachia," Vlad said.

Radu laughed.

"If you don't make it, no way can I."

The sultan shook his head. "I wouldn't be so sure. Vlad has his strengths, and you have yours. They're different, but not less important. And you both have weaknesses you need to overcome."

"Like what?" Vlad asked.

"What do you think?" the sultan asked.

Vlad shrugged.

"How many friends do you have, Vlad?"

Vlad shrugged again.

"To be a leader, you need to inspire your people. They need to trust you and love you enough to die for you."

That got Vlad thinking. Radu too.

"How about me?" he asked.

"You want to know your weaknesses?" the sultan asked.

Radu shook his head. He didn't need anyone to tell him his weaknesses — he's heard about them since the day he was born. "My strengths," he whispered.

"You're kind, and patient, and loving. And very handsome," the sultan said.

Radu blushed, and Vlad snickered.

"What does handsome have to do with anything in a man?"

"More than you'd think. Either way, I want you both to train and learn and work towards becoming worthy leaders for your country," the sultan said.

That settled it, even though Radu would rather spend time with Mehmed, or draw, or play the rübap. Or even play with Sari.

But he did his best and went through drill after drill and lesson after lesson, learning how to be a worthy officer of the Ottoman Army. He suffered through countless boring lessons of strategy and tactic, studied history's greatest battles, classic and modern weapons, the greatest sieges, and whatever else they shoved his way. But now that Ali came to visit, he pushes the book to the side.

"Hey, Ali, do you know the difference between tactic and strategy?" Radu asks.

Ali sits on his bed, petting Sari. "I don't."

"Neither do I. And they've been cramming this in my head for two days."

"It's easy," Vlad says, entering the room. "Strategy is what you're trying to achieve. Tactic is how you do it. Strategy is the aim. Tactic is the tool."

He drops his sword and dagger to his side, crosses his legs, and sits on a pillow. He's all sweaty and dusty, after whatever he's been up to. Radu hands him his cup of sherbet. Vlad drains it.

"Thank you, brother. Would you happen to have some wine?"

Radu shakes his head. "I don't, sorry. But I have more sherbet."

Vlad shrugs. Radu fills his cup and Vlad drains it again.

"Where are you coming from?"

"Sword fight. And lance. I'm not bad with the sword, but the lance? I'm not big enough. But I did the best I could."

"I'm sure you did. I've never seen anyone work as hard as you."

"I do my best. I just fear it's not good enough."

"Good enough for what?"

"Good enough to take back the throne and avenge our father and our brother."

"If you aren't, then nobody is."

"That's what I'm afraid of."

Radu shrugs. "Sorry, brother. I'm just not like you."

"I know."

"You're not like him, but you're better in many ways," Ali says.

Vlad laughs. "Good to see you, Ali."

"Thank you, my prince. It's good to see you."

"Have you… by any chance… heard any news from your friend? Sophia?"

"Gülbahar is doing well. It appears she had a difficult delivery, but she birthed Mehmed's firstborn son, Bayezid. Both she and the baby are well."

"Good to hear," Vlad says, his face puckered like he swallowed something sour. "I'm happy to hear she is well. Speaking about babies. I just remembered something. Believe it or not, our brother Mircea got married last fall, and asked us to take care of his wife if anything happened to him. And of his baby, should there be one."

Radu's eyes widen. "Mircea? Married? To whom?"

"A girl from Moldova named Lena. Ali, you may know her. She was in Mehmed's sarayi for a couple of years, then he released her. You know her?"

"I know her well. How is she?"

"I don't know. I haven't met her yet, but I will. He was so smitten he married her against our father's wishes. He didn't tell anyone, not even our cousin Ștefan, his best friend. He seems to have fancied her, too."

"Isn't life complicated?" Radu says. "I never met her, but Mehmed held her in high regard. She's got to be a special girl."

"That, she is," Ali says.

Vlad contemplates her thoughtfully. "Ali, you come from Transylvania?"

"Yes. A small village near Kronstadt."

"Have you ever met Hunyadi?"

"Never."

"But you know about him."

"Who doesn't?"

"Would you like to go back?"

"To Transylvania?"

"Yes."

Ali's face runs the gamut of every emotion, from joy to fear.

"I'd love to. But I can't."

"Why not?"

"I belong to the sultan. I can't just leave."

"What if I take you back?"

Ali's eyes narrow.

"How?"

"If the sultan sends me back with an army, I could ask him to let you go with me. I need somebody who knows about Transylvania to help me against Hunyadi and whatever he brings my way. I'm thinking that if the sultan gives me a whole army, he'll let me have a eunuch?"

"Maybe. Ali's mistress, Hüma Hatun, is very attached to him, and she won't be glad to see him go," Radu adds.

"But she's not here, is she? So she has nothing to say."

"Mehmed's mother always has something to say. And I heard they're coming back soon," Radu says.

"Then I'd better ask before they do. What do you think, Ali?"

"It sounds interesting...."

"What's the problem? Is it about Isa?" Radu asks.

"Who's Isa?"

"Ali's friend. He's in administration."

"I don't know that I can get them both. But I can always try."

"Thank you, prince. Let me think about it."

Ali leaves, his face in turmoil. The brothers glance at each other.

"What's wrong with him? I thought he'd be over the moon," Vlad says.

Radu doesn't know, but he's worried. And he'd really hate to see Ali go.

CHAPTER 84

EDIRNE, MAY 1448

Ali sits on a window ledge in the sarayi, hugging her knees, and watches the gardens below. The window, like all the others, is shaded by a wooden grille, and it overlooks the rose gardens in bloom. It's almost dusk, and the roses went nuts. Their intoxicating scent mixes with that of the blooming white lilies and wafts in with the warm spring breeze. There's plenty of beauty to soothe one's soul, but Vlad's words got to her, and it would take more than the flowers' scent to bring her peace.

Go home. What would she do if she went home?

She'd hug Mama Smaranda and Lena and play with Negru and eat cozonac and go fishing. She'd roam the woods and learn about healing herbs and people from her grandmother who never went anywhere but is still the wisest person she knows. She'd live in the little hut in the forest that scratches its roof with its feet whenever the squirrels burrow in. And she might buy a cow and some sheep, if the burgomaster keeps his word. But they said five years, and she hasn't been here for five years. Not yet. So, they may not.

But, more than anything, she'd be free. She wouldn't have to lie and hide or drink bitter herbs to forgo her monthly curse and stop her breasts from growing. She wouldn't wake up every morning wondering if today's the day they'll expose her, behead her, and skewer her head on a stake to set an example for all those who'd ever try to deceive the sultan. She could just be a young girl called Ana, living her life.

But here, she's where things happen, where the powerful people make the world spin. Sure, she carries trays and runs errands and is everyone's servant, but she gets to make a difference. She sends home vital news, like last time, when she told them about Bayezid's birth. Or before, when she sent word that Murad recalled Mehmed. She loves the thrill, even though she knows that if they catch her, the punishment is death. A bad one.

But Radu said that Hüma Hatun may be on her way back with Mehmed. Hüma, with her murderous moods, killer jealousy and never-ending spite. Hüma, who thinks Ali's potions can make people fall in love, get heavy with child, or die, when Ali is the most pathetic witch there ever was. She's lousy with potions, she sucks at curses, and she couldn't spin a spell to save her life. The only thing she's good at is lying. And reading people's souls.

Ali hasn't missed Hüma one bit, even though Mara is a challenge too. After that time with Zambak, Mara never again called her to her bed, but Ali knows the invite is open. Mara's half-smile, her come-hither eyes, and the way her fingers touch Ali's whenever she hands her a cup, tell her that the invite is still on.

And it's hard to ignore it. The one thing that kept Ali from taking the bait was knowing that in that kind of closeness, there's no way to hide that she's not a eunuch. She saw what Mara did to Zambak. Saw it? She felt it in her bones. There's no way she wouldn't notice.

But a strange thought crosses Ali's head. What if Mara knows already?

That's silly. If she did, she'd have screamed it at the top of her lungs and have Ali crucified, but she didn't. Still, something beyond reason tells her Mara knows.

Ali shakes her head. That's nonsense. And has nothing to do with anything. The question is: should she stay or should she go?

Then there's her best friend Isa, who's been gathering information about the sultan's army and finances. If she leaves, he'll be all alone. She can't abandon him.

Though he's been a pain in the ass lately. Last time they met in Radu's room, Isa grabbed her and kissed her on her mouth. She had to knee him in the groin to get him to let go. He'd gasped and bent over like she'd maimed him, but he'd deserved it. He remembers her since she was a girl and thinks she's available, but she's not. If she had to choose between sharing a bed with Isa or with Mara...

But that's not important right now. This isn't about bed sharing. It's about her plans for the future. Where does she want to be?

She doesn't know. But what she knows is that she doesn't want to be a woman in a man's world. Even being a eunuch is better than being a woman. Anything is better than being a woman.

Ali sighs. She decided. She won't go back. Not yet, if she can help it.

Finally at peace, she gets back to her tasks: bringing drinks to the women, getting them afternoon snacks, checking that everyone behaves, and reporting to the chief eunuch. That's her daily life, and it's better than many.

She gets chilled drinks from the kitchen and takes them to the hammam where the ladies are preening themselves, hoping that Sultan Murad will seek their company. They chat and laugh, laying on the white marble slab. Ali sets the drinks near them, then turns to head back.

"Ali?" Mara calls.

"Yes, my lady?"

"You know my friend Halime Hatice, Sultan Murad's favorite? Her son Aladdin was the most endowed şehzade who ever saw the light of day."

Ali bows deeply. "We met, of course, but we have not been introduced. I am not worthy."

Halime Hatice Hatun smiles a polite smile, blurred by the steam, and looks kindly at Ali.

"Hüma Hatun is returning, and I bet she'll want you back. I know she's fond of you. But I thought I'd recommend you to Halime Hatice. If she asked Sultan Murad, he might assign you to her service. You could serve her, rather than Hüma. Would you like that?"

Ali is befuddled. She dreads serving Hüma, but Huma is Mehmed's mother, and soon she'll be the validé again, with power over everyone in the sarayi. It would be foolish to upset her.

"My mistress, Hüma Hatun, has been very kind to me," Ali says. "I wouldn't dream about asking for a different assignment."

Mara turns to Hatice. "I told you he's worth his weight in gold."

Hatice smiles, her round face kind.

"I'll see what I can do," she says, then drains her sherbet.

CHAPTER 85
COMING HOME

Edirne's short spring is over, and the sun is still high. The summer's merciless heat sets the dust dancing, and it bakes the muezzins in the city's many minarets into a sleepy torpor before the evening call to prayer.

Thank Allah we made it, Mehmed thinks, holding Rüzgar back. The stallion smells the stable, and is eager to gallop through the last mile to the gate, but that won't do. Sultan Mehmed's retinue needs to maintain its decorum, even if he's sultan in name only, and he's here at his father's pleasure.

Mehmed's reception is nothing like Murad's, a couple of years ago. Merchants and peasants glance over, bow politely, then go about their business, unworried about Mehmed's comings and goings. They don't give a rat's ass about why he came or what he does.

Boy, is he glad the women stayed behind. Mother would be spitting mad about the lack of interest in him and his arrival. And if they didn't fuss about little Bayezid, she'd take that as a personal insult. She thinks everyone should worship him like he's the rising sun.

At the gate, Mehmed dismounts, pats Rüzgar's neck and hands him to a stable hand, then follows the guards taking him to his father.

He didn't fail to notice that Sultan Murad wasn't waiting for him. Not that he holds that against him — Father has waited for him for months. Then Gülbahar's baby came and brought even more delays. If he'd been waiting at the gate all this time, Father would get nothing done, and he has plenty to do.

Still, it doesn't feel good. It feels a little like he's breaking in, though he's here at Father's request — and, once again, he's glad that Mother isn't here.

Sultan Murad is in his study. Dressed in white from the top of his snowy turban to the tip of his upturned rafiqs, he sits cross-legged under the window, reading the Quran, as usual. Mehmed bows deeply before sitting on the pillow offered him, hoping for no bad news.

"Thank you for coming, Mehmed."

That's just being polite. Not like he had a choice. He bows again, waiting for Father to speak.

"Congratulations for your son. I hope he'll lead the Ottoman Empire further, when you and I are gone, and bring it to further greatness. I understand that his birth was not easy."

Mehmed nods.

"Birth and death — neither is easy. And they often go together. But I'm glad that your favorite survived. I'm even gladder that your son survived."

"Thank you, Father. I'm glad too."

"But this is just the beginning. You'll have many more sons to ensure the Ottoman Empire's future. You're young and strong, so there should be no problem. We'll get you a wife worthy of your upbringing. I've been looking."

"Thank you, Father. You are too kind. But I don't need a wife. Mother keeps me supplied with an endless number of girls, only too willing to birth the Ottoman Empire's next sultan."

"I bet she does. That's Hüma for you. She's never seen a challenge she didn't rise to. She should have been a man, that one. Her beauty is meant to cheat you into thinking that she's just an ordinary woman, but there's nothing further from the truth. She's a wild one, and she'd like to rule the world. But I'm sure you noticed."

Mehmed nods, waiting for his father's further wisdom.

"I'm glad you didn't bring her here. If I were you, I'd send the women back to Manisa. The farther they are, the less they'll bug you and cause you trouble."

"Why am I here, Father?"

"You're here to learn. I look forward to returning to my quiet days in Anatolia, so I want you to be ready. And we're about to have another big fight with that damn Hunyadi and the rest of the Christians. After we crushed him in Varna, he's been licking his wounds and preparing. I think he's ready to come back again. We need to crush him once and for all and be done. That's why I wanted you here.

"We'll work together. You'll get to learn a lot about war. Just as important, it will give our men a chance to know you and learn to respect and fear you. You'll have to earn their trust so you can become the great sultan I know you will be. I want us to partner in this fight."

Mehmed bows deeply. "Thank you, Father. I am honored. When, you think?"

"Sometime this year. Hunyadi has overextended himself. First, he took Wallachia for Vladislav, then he took Moldova for this Petru that nobody ever heard about. Seems to be another one of the dozen bastards Alexandru the Good left behind.

"You know, Mehmed, looking at the Christians makes me wonder about the wisdom of our harems. We lock up our women to ensure their children carry our ancestors' blood. But look at the Wallachians and the Moldavians. They produce oodles of kids from all these women, then pick those they like and ignore those they don't. They don't even have to remember their mothers' names, let alone watch them fight like wildcats in their own harem. I could sign up for that."

Mehmed smiles. He knows Father is talking about Hüma, who's always been a thorn in his side.

"Anyhow. I brought you so we can fight together what I hope will be my last big battle. If we crush Hunyadi, we'll reestablish the safety of our borders, and we'll plant our own man in Wallachia. Vlad is almost ready, and he's fearsome."

"How about his brother?"

"Radu? He's a lovely boy, but not a fighter. He doesn't even want to be. He'll be happier here, being your... friend."

CHAPTER 86

SMEDEREVO, SERBIA, SEPTEMBER 1448

The summer is over. The mists of the fall enshrouded Serbia's low plains in a silent veil of secrecy. Especially here, near Smederevo, Đurađ Branković's new capital, where the Danube is just a stone's throw away. The sunny days are still warm, but the early mornings have turned chilly.

Thankful for his long fox-trimmed mantle, Codru cinches his belt a little tighter. He glances at the men fussing around the fires or tending to the horses. They don't look happy, but then they seldom do these days. He shrugs and walks to Hunyadi's blue silk tent that's splattered with brown mud from the men's boots and horses' hooves after a whole month of sitting in camp.

"Regent?"

"Come in, Codru."

Hunyadi is up already. Dressed in a blue velvet tunic that's grown tight at the waist, he scratches his head, staring at a map like he expects it to enlighten him. Codru sure hopes it will, since he doesn't know what they've been waiting for.

"Everything's all right."

"The Serbs?"

"It's like they don't exist. They never come close."

Hunyadi shakes his head.

"I wish those lousy cowards would come out and fight like men instead of leaving their houses and fields open to plunder and burn. I'd feel better if I could fight them face to face. But that old two-faced coward Đurađ Branković told them to stay away. What sort of man lets an army torch their way through his country without a fight? And he calls himself Serbia's despot!"

Codru shrugs. "I guess he took it to heart when you said you'd catch and kill him. He'd rather stay alive."

"Not for long. Sooner or later, I'll get my hands on that fool. He calls himself neutral, but I know he's rooting for Murad. The old dog is stupid enough to believe that Murad will let him keep his country if he wins."

"You don't think he will?"

"Are you crazy? The Ottomans are a bunch of hungry land grabbers. They took the whole of Anatolia and most of the Byzantine Empire, and that wasn't enough. So they took Greece, Bulgaria, and Albania, other than the wild mountains in the north that Skanderbeg managed to hold on to. As soon as he has no more use for Branković, Murad will swallow Serbia like it's a cherry, and spit out Branković like its pit. You'd think the old coot would know better, after Murad blinded both his sons and jailed them, even though he gave him his daughter for a wife. And a beautiful one that one was. Have you met Mara Branković?"

Codru laughs. "As a lowly janissary, I didn't get to bump into the sultan's wives in the sarayi. But I've heard of her. She's quite the star in Sultan Murad's sarayi."

"I bet. Well, Mara or no Mara, Branković played the wrong card. If I win, I'll crush him and put him through the sword. If Murad wins, sooner or later he'll put him to pasture and install some paşa in his place, then build mosques from the bricks of their churches and have the muezzins' call to prayer replace the church bells, God damn them both. And the pope, who gave me no help but prayer. What do I do with prayer? I need soldiers and weapons and horses."

"With God's blessing we should…"

"Don't get me going on what God can do with his blessings. I'd rather have a few cannons or another ten thousand men. Speaking about that, how are the men?"

"They're growing restless. We've been sitting here for a month, and they've had nothing to do but raid the nearby villages. And there isn't much left to raid."

"I know. I've been waiting here for the other armies — Skanderbeg's, and the Germans. The Wallachians under Vladislav the Second are ready to cross the Danube further east. We'll join them on our way. Same with the Albanians. We're heading south tomorrow."

"Where are we going?"

"To Kosovo Polje. The field of the black birds. We'll wait there for the Albanians."

"Kosovo? Really?"

"You know your history, don't you? The great Battle of Kosovo in 1389? They say that the Ottomans won it, but that's crap. The Ottomans lost way more men than the Serbs — and they even lost their sultan. Murad the First's tomb is still there, on the battlefield. Would you call that a win? Kosovo is a lucky place for us, especially if we get there first so we can choose our setup."

Codru isn't convinced, but who is he to advise the greatest general of Christianity? Though he lost the Battle of Varna two years ago. But everyone said the Christians lost because of King Władysław's youth and lack of discipline. He didn't obey Hunyadi's orders and rushed ahead into the Ottoman's trap, losing not only his life but also half the aristocracy of Poland.

"How many people will we leave behind?"

"None. We all go."

"So, we'll separate later?"

"No. We need to destroy Murad once and for all. I need every single man I have. I only have thirty thousand all together. He'll probably have twice as many. I'm not leaving anyone behind."

"But if we lose..."

Hunyadi turns red and thunders: "I said nobody stays behind! Understood?"

"Yes, regent."

Codru heads to the door but Hunyadi stops him. "How many supply carts do we have?"

"Two thousand, including those for the cannons."

"Make sure we take enough water. Once we leave the Danube, we never know when we'll find water. And supplies. Have the men do one last raid today, gather whatever they can find in the villages and take it. And set fire to everything else."

Codru nods. He heads out as fast as he can and bumps into Baron János Székely, Hunyadi's brother-in-law and right hand. The baron grabs him by the sleeve and pulls him away from the tent.

"How is he?"

"Not happy. But at least he said we're leaving tomorrow. Today we get ready."

Székely glances at the tent, then walks away with Codru. They weave their way between tents, fires, and horses, all crowded in this little place for weeks now. This camp has been here for too long. It doesn't look good, and it doesn't smell good, Codru thinks, glad to be leaving.

Székely sighs.

"I hope we don't do a repeat of Varna, or he'll run out of brothers-in-law."

CHAPTER 87

KOSOVO POLJE, OCTOBER 14, 1448

It's a glorious day as Murad and Mehmed ride side by side towards the infamous Kosovo plains. The sun shines, and the sky bluer than blue brings up the gold and red of the leaves. A soft breeze caresses their cheeks and fills their noses with the bitter scent of the fall.

Mehmed has never felt closer to his father. In the weeks it took them to ride the hundreds of miles from Edirne, they had hours and hours to talk. And talk they did. Not only about the upcoming battle, but about so many things they'd never talked about before. Mehmed is grateful for the time they got to spend together.

"Why Kosovo Polje?"

"You know what that means?"

"No."

"The field of the black birds."

"Why?"

"Because of the crows. They say that in 1389, after the last Battle of Kosovo, the battlefield was black with the crows gathered to eat the flesh of the dead. Not a lucky place for the Serbs, no matter how they still brag about that battle. Nor the Albanians. They lost then, and they'll lose now. I'm just surprised that Hunyadi chose it, because it suits us well. Branković was right: Don't approach him. Let him get far from his base so he can't sustain his supply chain. Then cut him from meeting Skanderbeg, he said."

"How come the despot didn't go with Hunyadi, like he did before? Is it because of Mara?"

Murad laughed. "Oh, no. Đurađ Branković doesn't care a spit about Mara. He gave her to me to tie me to his interests, not the other way round. He knows that my life at home will be endless misery if I touch a hair of his head. Mara Branković is her father's shield, not mine."

"So then, how come you blinded her brothers?"

"I didn't have a choice. Those two were a couple of cowardly traitors who hid behind her skirts. They betrayed me, and I couldn't let that go. Not only would I become everyone's laughingstock, but then any worthless fool would think they can betray me without fear of punishment. I had to do it. If they weren't her brothers, I would have killed them both. I should have, anyhow, but I couldn't bring myself to do it. She's a good woman, Mara, and she's very fond of you. She's the one woman in the harem you can trust, besides your mother. You're like the child she's never had."

"How come she never had children?"

Murad shrugs. "A sultan has two kinds of wives. The wives he takes because of politics, to forge valuable alliances for the empire, and the wives he takes because they gave him sons. I married Mara for her connections and I treated her right, but she didn't care to have children, and I respected her choice."

"How about Halime Hatice Hatun?"

"Halime was the daughter of İzzettin İsfendiyar Bey, the ruler of the Candaroğlu Beylik. I married her and gave my sisters Selçuk and Sultan to her brothers, Ibrahim and Kasım, to forge an alliance against the Karamanid Türkmen. Those weasels blocked our expansion to the east, and are still a thorn in my side to this day. But our alliance still holds."

"Were you happy with her?"

"Very much so. Halime Hatice turned out to be a wonderful woman, and gave me a wonderful son, Allah keep him by his side forever. Unlike Mara, Halime lives to have children."

"How about Mother?"

"Your mother was stunning, charming, and very ambitious. I was very lucky that she gave me you."

Mehmed's eyes burn. Before now, Father never told him he felt lucky to have him as a son. He always knew Aladdin was Father's favorite, and he knows he couldn't compare, so his words bring joy to Mehmed's heart and tears to his eyes.

"Thank you, Father."

"What for? That's the truth. You're still learning and growing, but you'll be a wonderful sultan someday soon."

They ride in silence for a while, then Murad asks: "Have you studied the maps?"

"I did."

"What do you think?"

"It depends on where they are."

"Where would you be if you were Hunyadi?"

"I'd be up on the crest, looking down at the plateau. Near Murad's tomb."

"Any reason to not be there?"

"There's no water."

"And?"

"And they're cut off from the south, where Iskander would come from."

"But if Skanderbeg comes, he'll fall in our back, so that's actually an advantage."

"Skanderbeg won't come."

"How do you know?"

"Because if you thought he'd be coming, you wouldn't have us take this route and expose our backs. You know he isn't coming."

Murad smiles. "How do I know?"

"Because... because you made it happen?"

"How?"

Mehmed racks his brain for an answer. And the answer comes loud and clear.

"Branković. You set him up. How?"

"I had Đurađ occupy the mountain passes at the border between Serbia and Albania with his army. It'll be a piece of cake to plug in Skanderbeg's men until we're done with Hunyadi."

Mehmed looks at his father, wishing he was half the general he is. One day, maybe.

"How would you deploy?" his father asks.

"We should deploy wide. We have at least twice as many men as Hunyadi, so the wider we deploy, the thinner they'll have to be."

"Good. What else?"

"You'll be in the center, behind the janissaries and the azabs. Ahead of them we'll have the fortifications and the cannon dugouts. We'll sit the Rumelian sipahis and the akinji on the left, and the Anatolians on the right. We'll assemble the wagon fort behind and leave the light cavalry in reserve to send it wherever it's needed."

"Very good. And where will you be?"

"With you?"

"Not this time. It's time you tried your wings. You'll be leading the right flank with the Anatolian troops."

Mehmed's heart skips a beat. He's half excited and half terrified.

Murad senses his fear. "What are you afraid of? Are you afraid of death?"

"No."

"Then what?"

"I'm afraid I'm not good enough and I'll let you down."

"Then don't."

CHAPTER 88

KOSOVO POLJE, OCTOBER 19, 1448

The morning's still young when Codru steps out of his tent to check the fading sky. Today is his first battle day, and his heart pounds in his chest. He's terrified he'll let down his men and disappoint Hunyadi, who made him the head of his personal guard over men twice his age and with way more experience. He hopes he won't turn out to be a coward. And he wonders: If I die, will I turn into a werewolf? Or will I just die like everyone else and stay dead?

Their men are ready. They assembled an enormous wagenburg on the very top of the hill for their defense. The monster rolling fort is big enough to protect their whole army if needed — hundreds of carts tied together with chains and loaded with cannons. More cannons sit between them — the long-barreled ones that shoot even further. The left flank is the cavalry, under Székely's command. The right flank is the Wallachian light cavalry, all eight thousand of them, under Vladislav the Second.

Unlike the armored Hungarian knights dancing on their palfreys, the Wallachians have no armor. Mounted on nimble ponies, the peasants-turned-soldiers dressed in quilted coats and tired leather armor glare at the Ottomans with grim determination. It's not hard to see they're not here for the glory.

Mounted on his stallion, his white armor mirroring the sun and his mustache stiffer than ever, Hunyadi himself will lead the center's eight-thousand-strong infantry.

They are ready.

Codru looks across the uneven marshy field where the fog twirls like steam. That's where the Ottomans are spread into a perfect half-moon, their arrangement so precise it looks like a woven prayer carpet. And God help, they're just as many as a carpet's many-colored threads. They've got to be at least twice as many as us, Codru thinks. That's why Hunyadi left no troops behind and risked having the Ottomans cut his retreat. If he plans to destroy them with an all-out attack, he needs every single man he's got and more.

Front and center are the bright red janissaries. They're right behind the fortifications and the cannons sitting in their dug-outs, but they're too far to recognize, thank God. With a heavy heart, Codru wonders which of his friends will fight today. Not long ago, they were almost like brothers. For years, they shared the same bread, the same dormitory and the same bawdy jokes. Just like him, they came to Edirne as kids through no will of their own. They grew up with the Ottoman Empire as their home, and the sultan as their father. For them, courage and loyalty to the sultan are primordial duties, right there with faith and love for Allah. And he'd be there too, if he hadn't escaped. He'd be on the other side, looking up at Hunyadi's army and planning his demise.

But he's not. He's the head of Hunyadi's guard, and his job is to keep the great man alive, no matter what else comes to pass.

Mehmed's tughra flies high above the Ottoman's right flank, and the Wallachian eagle with the cross in its beak flies over Vladislav's army in Hunyadi's right flank. Codru's heart skips a beat. This is just like that first field fight lesson when Vlad tried to kill Mehmed. Codru fought on Vlad's side against Mehmed and Radu. And he lost.

But there's no time for silly memories. Hooves clatter behind him, and Codru turns to see Hunyadi, sitting tall on his chestnut stallion.

"Are we ready?" he thunders.

"Yes," the men answer as one.

Hunyadi glances down the hill at Murad's army. They're so far they look unreal, like a faraway garden in a riot of colors, with their tughras flying and their swords catching the sun.

All of a sudden, the silence splinters. As always when they go into battle, the Ottoman assault starts with the noise. The cymbals clatter, the trumpets blare, and like a furious storm, the thunder of dozens of drums rattles the earth, shaking the enemy's guts. Sixty thousand swords strike sixty thousand shields, daring the Christians to attack them, and sixty thousand voices call as one:

"Allah u Akbar! Allah u Akbar! Allah u Akbar!"

Hunyadi bites his lip. He's been through this a hundred times and still doesn't like it. He knows it frightens his men.

"Left and right: let's go."

The flanks charge as one, the Wallachians on the right, the Hungarians on the left. The earth trembles, pummeled by the horses' hooves. Ten thousand men and ten thousand horses gallop downhill, eating up the distance. Ten more breaths, five more, three more. One more.

Ten thousand hearts beat as one.

"For God! For the cross! For the country!"

They raise their swords, ready to fight, but the Ottoman flanks fold like wet paper. The riders' speed takes them forward, and both the right flank and the left cut through the Ottoman defenses like hot knives through butter. The sultan's orderly flanks scatter like shattered glass under the Christian's hammer, and Codru's heart leaps with joy.

Like his men around him, he screams and beats his shield in applause. Hunyadi's men are so happy they can't stay put, and the horses share their excitement. The whole hill dances with joy.

Codru grins. He glances at Hunyadi, but he doesn't look pleased, and Codru wonders why. He looks back at the battlefield where everything changed in a heartbeat. The scattered Ottoman flanks reformed around the Christians, and they're cutting through them like sickles through ripe wheat.

The battle turned to slaughter. Both Christian flanks are getting decimated. Men scream and horses fall, drowning in their own blood. The Ottoman sipahis and akinjis are about to destroy Hunyadi's army before the battle has properly started.

The Christians struggle to escape. Those who can ride back uphill to Hunyadi's camp. But most don't, since the Ottomans grip them tighter and tighter. The Christians fight with all their might, but their bravery can't make up for the vastly superior Ottoman numbers. One by one, riders and horses fall under the murderous kilijes or yield to the killer arrows, and the Christians' hopes die with them. This is not a battle, it's a carnage.

CHAPTER 89

THE BLACK CROWS' FIELD

His fists tight, his heart racing, Mehmed watches the battle with bated breath. He's burning to join it, but he can't. He's Sultan Mehmed, and his father's general, not some silly sipahi who can't resist getting in trouble. He struggles to hold back a snorting Rüzgar dancing on his hooves, maddened by the smell of blood, eager to join the battle, and watches his Anatolian sipahis swarm Hunyadi's left flank like a hive of killer bees.

Unlike the Hungarian knights, armored steel towers of bravado mounted on massive destriers, the Christian's light cavalry is a just bunch of wiry men in chain-mail and leather armor riding nimble mountain ponies. They pursue his sipahis like hardworking ants, and his men are having trouble.

The force of the Ottoman offensive has stalled. Not only are they no longer advancing, but they're hardly holding on, overwhelmed by the Christians' ferocity. Those men fight like demons possessed. Their maces break bones, their spiked clubs crush skulls, and their sickles harvest lives like it's going out of style. They're the Wallachians, Mehmed thinks, and he finally understands where Vlad gets it from.

One sipahi steps back, then another. Suddenly, the promise of victory turns to doubt, and the daring offensive becomes a defensive. Things are not looking good.

Mehmed turns to glance at his father, but Sultan Murad is busy with his other flank, and Mehmed knows it's up to him.

"Insha'Allah," he whispers, and tightens his knees to spur Rüzgar.

The stallion jumps into the thick of the fight like a hungry fox into a flock of chickens. He rears, neighs, and shows his long yellow teeth, ready to bite, as Mehmed pulls out his kilij and screams the battle fight.

"Allah u Akbar!"

"Allah u Akbar!" ten voices answer. Then a hundred more.

"Allah u Akbar!"

Mehmed blasts forward. His kilij takes a life of its own, seeking the enemy. A mace descends over Mehmed's head, but the arm holding it is no match for Damascus steel. The mace rolls in the dust with the fist holding it. An arrow whizzes by his ear, barely missing his eye, and Mehmed spares a grateful thought for Allah. Out of nowhere, a battle axe comes down too fast to stop, but Rüzgar rears and the man falls under a sipahi's blow.

The fight smells like blood, dust and so much gun smoke that Mehmed's eyes water. But it doesn't smell like victory. Emboldened by his lead, his men went all out, but they're still running thin. There are more sipahis on the ground than there are on the horses, and those left are tired and bloodied. They won't last long unless something changes, Mehmed thinks, when a huge fighter in chain mail armor, on a courser even bigger than Rüzgar, charges out of nowhere, and Mehmed stops thinking. It's all about muscle memory and lightning-fast reflexes.

The giant lifts his long broadsword above his head for the cut of wrath. Mehmed prepares to meet him with a thrust. The giant roars and the broadsword falls like Allah's fury. Mehmed's kilij blocks it halfway with a cut from below, stopping its momentum.

The man wrenches his blade around and aims at Mehmed's leg.

Mehmed parries with a hanging guard and tightens his knees,

spurring Rüzgar forward to fall upon his opponent. The man's horse rears, and he lifts the broadsword again for another cut from above.

Mehmed charges in. His kilij catches the broadsword's blade halfway down and he twists it upwards toward the man's face. The broadsword slides to the side as Mehmed's kilij finds the soft spot under the chin above the armor and slides through it like butter, coming out the other side.

A stream of hot blood hits Mehmed's face, blurring his vision. He wipes his eyes as the man falls sideways and his horse drags him away.

He was a brave man, Mehmed thinks, wiping the blade of his kilij on a dead soldier's chest and slipping it back into its scabbard.

He looks around. While he was fighting, his father worked his charm again. The Rumelian sipahis from the left flank came around to breathe much-needed life into Mehmed's Anatolians. Together, they made short work of those wild Wallachians, and the fate of the battle changed again. Allah's faithful are winning.

Mehmed glances at his father, hoping he didn't see him jump into the fight. And sure enough, Murad's eyes are glued to Hunyadi, who watches the battle from the hill by Murad the First's tomb.

Seeing both his flanks demolished, Hunyadi can't take it anymore. He raises his sword to give the signal, and his heavy cavalry, the pride of Hungary, bursts forward in a furious gallop.

A thousand proud destriers leap forward, mounted by a thousand brave knights. Their silver armors shine in the sun and the colorful flags on their lances fly high as their killer wave rolls like God's hammer towards the Ottoman center.

Hooves thunder, men scream, metal clangs against metal, drowning the ruckus down the hill. The killer wave rolls downhill so fast that Mehmed is afraid to blink, gathering speed, and nothing can stand in their way.

The sultan's brave azabs raise their long, curved tirpans and their halberds to stop them. Stabbed from underneath, horses scream and fall, rolling over their heavily armored knights. But the heavy armor is too strong to break and the horses too fast to stop, so, heartbeats later, the azabs too are down in the dust.

The janissaries raise their bows. On Sultan Murad's command, a cloud of arrows darkens the sky, seeking the Christians like bees seeking nectar. Unafraid and undaunted, the sultan's best fighters stand up to the assault, holding off the Christians.

But their arrows are no match for heavy armor, and their sabers no match for the horses' speed. No ordinary arrow, no matter how skilled the archer can pierce through a breastplate or a helmet, unless it happens upon the soft spot in the armpit or the neck. No saber can stop a ton of horse and man and armor crushing you into the ground, and the janissaries join the azabs in the dust.

Their momentum is unstoppable. The tide has turned, and the battle is again the Christians' to lose.

Mehmed takes a deep breath and glances at his father. Mounted on his proud white horse, Sultan Murad looks up at Hunyadi like he's challenging him to come over. But Hunyadi stays put.

Mehmed turns back to the fight. After thrashing the azabs and crushing the janissaries in the Ottoman center, Hunyadi's heavy knights own the field. They look like victors, but the Ottomans' fortified carts crammed with archers cut their further advance.

They stop to catch their breath, and raise their flags to salute Hunyadi, congratulating each other for their victory, but it's too early for that.

On Murad's sign, the scattered janissaries regroup and surround them, cutting their retreat. They attack not just them, but their horses, whose chest is armored, but their back end is not. Unlike the knights in their Venetian armor, the horses are an easy target for lances, arrows, and kilijes.

Horse after horse screams and falls, bringing their riders down. Some get crushed by a ton of dying horse. The others' fifty pounds of heavy armor pin them to the ground. Powerless to get up and fight, the mighty armored knights get slaughtered one by one like giant turtles lying on their back.

It's time to do or die for Hunyadi. Up on the hill, he watches the pride of Hungary get slaughtered. He raises his sword and sends the light cavalry to the rescue.

Men and horses thunder down the hill to join the fight. They're valiant and brave, but not armored. Their leather-padded quilted tunics are no match for arrows and kilijes. They fight to help their brethren, but they fall under the Ottoman arrows, lances and kilijes one by one. They slow down and stumble. They hesitate and stop. And, just as they're getting surrounded, they gallop uphill to their wagenburgs' safety.

The second battle of Kosovo is done.

CHAPTER 90

GRIM RETREAT

The Battle of Kosovo Polje is over.

Hungary's pride, her best and bravest, lay dying in the Kosovo marshes, and there's no saving them. The Wallachians got decimated, and Székely is dead. So are most of the Christian army.

This is a carnage like Codru has never seen, and he stares at the killing field, wondering what to do. But then he remembers he's not here to fight; he's here to protect Hunyadi. And that's precisely what he needs to do, since the Ottomans are closing in. One janissary after another crawls up that knoll, despite the cannons firing non-stop. The barrels are red hot and cracking from incessant firing. The men tied them with ropes to hold them together, but if they don't get to cool, they won't last long.

But the sun is about to set, thank God, and the Christians will have the night to get themselves sorted out before the fighting restarts in the morning. The bloody sky turns black, and a terrible night settles in. It's too dark to fight, so the Ottomans retreated to their camp, but their cannons keep firing. Once in a while, a cannon ball gets too close and spits dirt all over the tired men curled behind the massive wagenburg.

They're all shattered after that horrible day, and utterly exhausted, but too terrified to fall asleep.

The noise won't quit. The cannons are bad. So is the relentless pounding of the drums. But worse than anything is the screaming of the wounded horses, and the cries for help of the wounded men abandoned on the battlefield below. Codru's stomach turns with every scream, and he wishes he could stop their suffering, but he can't. His job is to watch over Hunyadi, who sits drinking wine by the fire without saying a word. He's got to be planning tomorrow's fight, and he doesn't look happy, Codru thinks, waiting for him to speak.

Finally, Hunyadi turns to Codru, his eyes dark with foreboding.

"It's time to go."

"Go where?"

"Home. The Ottomans won, and we lost. Dying here will do no one any good."

Two hours later, they're on their way. It's not pretty. The march north is even less joyous than the journey south had been. Last week, they dreamed of victory. They planned to crush the Ottomans, throw them out of Europe, and reestablish God's reign over every the countries they'd stolen. Greece, Bulgaria, Serbia, Albania, and others were to come back under the cross. With the pope's blessing and God's help, the Christian knights were going to show the faithless warriors what's what.

It didn't work out that way.

They ride north through the night to put as much distance behind them as they can. They hope the Ottomans are too damaged and exhausted to follow them and wipe out what's left of Hunyadi's proud army. There isn't much, since they left everything behind: their brother's bodies, their cannons and even their wounded. Not much to brag about.

They cross a tiny stream and stop to quench their thirst, then push forward through a hundred-year-old oak forest. The full moon comes out of the clouds and strange noises break the night's silence, disquieting the men: an owl's hoot, a soft whirring of wings, a distant howl.

Codru wonders if there are other werewolves here, and breaks into a smile. Would they try to bite him? Or would they recognize him as a brother? Either way, he's grateful to Smaranda's potion for keeping him human, even though, on the full moon nights, his shadow's still that of a wolf.

He rides ahead surrounded by his guards, sniffing for any whiff of danger. It can come from anywhere, since they're on Serbian territory, which is anything but friendly. No wonder. Last week, they plumaged, pillared and set everything on fire on Hunyadi's order, to punish Branković for refusing to fight alongside them. But a week ago they were battle-ready and twenty thousand strong. Now they're just a few hundreds, all at the end of their rope.

"Codru!" Hunyadi calls.

Codru falls back to his side.

"How are the men?"

Codru pauses. God's truth is that the men are exhausted and angry. They didn't expect to lose that battle and waste so many of their comrades. Even worse, they feel guilty about leaving the wounded behind to face a life of slavery, or death. Because, by the laws of war, the captives become the winners' spoils, slaves to use or sell. Ordinary peasants are doomed, but even blue-blooded knights end up serving in the victors' homes, or ploughing their fields. Unless somebody will pay their ransom. If so, with luck, they may get home someday. But most don't. That's why the men are not happy. But that's not what Hunyadi wants to hear.

"The men are doing their best to stay the course, my regent," Codru says.

Hunyadi nods.

"We should be back in Hungary in a couple of days, but be careful until then. That old fox Branković, would know no bigger joy than getting his paws on me. I bet his spies already told him what happened, and he's looking at setting a trap."

"But I thought he wasn't keen to fight. He didn't even show up when we plundered his villages on our way south."

"True that. I wonder why. I wish I'd thought about that sooner. I wonder if he made some deal with Murad."

The path through the old oak forest opens wide to a bare field shrouded in the dawn's fog. The field is bare, but not empty.

In the creepy gray of the dawn, Branković's whole army stands in wait. Emerging from the swirling mist, there are cannons and cavalry and infantry, all ready to fight. But there's no fight left in Hunyadi's men. The men run back into the forest or drop their weapons as soon as they see them, leaving only Hunyadi with Codru and his guards. They're a few dozen men against thousands.

Those are not good odds. Still, Codru will do what he must, hoping his men will follow. But thank God, Hunyadi's tired of the bloodshed.

"Stay here. All but you, Codru. You come with me."

Sitting straight on his chestnut, Hunyadi advances towards the waiting army, with Codru by his side. Two mounted knights come forth to meet them.

The first one is tall and frail. The one behind him is the biggest man Codru has ever met, and his eyes are the color of steel. They're both in armor and armed.

"Good to see you, Janos. I've been looking forward to it." The thin man smirks.

"I wish I could say the same, Đurađ. I guess the news came out?" Hunyadi asks.

"Of course. You lost most of your men, lost the battle and covered yourself in shame by running away and leaving your wounded behind."

Hunyadi's face darkens, but he says nothing.

"On the other hand, I've heard Murad lost even more men than you did, and almost lost Mehmed. Your brother-in-law did you proud."

"What happened to Mehmed?"

"The stupid kid threw himself in battle like a simple sipahi, and your brother-in-law took the challenge. He almost killed him, but

Mehmed was younger and faster. He made it and Székely didn't. But it was a good effort."

"God rest him. He was a good general and a good man," Hunyadi says. "Now what?"

"You look like you need some rest. I'd be happy to offer you my hospitality at Szendrő, my new castle in Smederevo. You'll be cared for and well protected. We'll treat you with the honor you deserve, for as long as it will take you to rest. And for of us two to agree upon some terms."

"What do you want, Đurađ?"

"Don't worry, Janos. I'll ask for nothing you can't afford. Or anything I don't deserve. But why don't we talk it over like civilized people, sitting by the table with a cup of wine, not here?"

Hunyadi nods. He looks years older than a week ago when he put Serbia through sword and fire and threatened to kill Đurađ Branković. That was then. Today, he's the prisoner of a man he despised, threatened and wronged.

The wheel of fate has turned.

CHAPTER 91

EDIRNE, OCTOBER 1448

Edirne Palace is bubbling with excitement. They all know their sultans are fighting somewhere in Serbia, but nobody really knows how it's going, so the rumors are going strong. The kitchen staff, the hammam servants, the stable boys — they all have very special knowledge that they're the only ones privy to: Murad died; Mehmed killed Hunyadi; The Christians were obliterated; Hunyadi is ready to take Edirne. Nobody really knows what happened, but that doesn't prevent them from squabbling with others who know even less.

All but Radu, who has more urgent things to worry about. He's in his room, forcing himself to sit and listen, but wishing he was anywhere else. Vlad has finally gone bonkers.

It started when he came to say goodbye. He hugged him with tears in his eyes.

"Once again, Radu, I'm sorry about all the times I wasn't the brother I should have been. I wish I did better. Anyhow, I came to say goodbye. I'm leaving tomorrow at dawn."

"Where are you going?"

"Back to Târgoviște to take our father's throne and give Wallachia a better future."

Radu's jaw drops. He should have known it, after all the talk and all the training, but he didn't. He was too worried about Mehmed to think about Vlad.

"Really! And how will you do that?"

"Murad gave me five thousand men. He said that's enough, since the whole Wallachian army is in Serbia with Vladislav, fighting alongside Hunyadi. I shouldn't meet much opposition."

"Wow. Good for you," Radu says, aghast to discover he's jealous. But why? Jealous of Vlad? What for?

He doesn't want that bloody throne. He wants the good life here in Edirne, with his rubab, the hammam, and the lovely evening walks in the rose garden. And Mehmed. He has no use for cold gray stone halls, courtyards smelling like an outhouse and bathing in a wooden barrel. Vlad can keep that to himself.

So then, why is he jealous?

Because he's tired of Vlad besting him at everything. Archery, fighting, sword, and hunting. Even strategy and tactics. And now he's bound to be the Voivode of Wallachia while he, Radu, is nothing but a hanger-on at the Ottoman Court. He doesn't want that responsibility for himself, but it hurts to see Vlad get it.

Fortunately, Vlad is too preoccupied to notice his long face.

"There are a couple of things we must discuss, just in case Sultan Murad is wrong and things don't go as planned. First, if I die, you must take over, get an army, take Wallachia, and avenge Father and Mircea's death. And even mine. You'll have to prove yourself to be a real Dracula and make us all proud."

Radu sighs. Suddenly, he's much less interested in being voivode. Better Vlad than him.

"Second, I promised Mircea to take care of his bride and her child, should there be one. If I'm not here to do it, it will fall upon you."

Radu remembers what he knows about Lena. If what he heard is true, she won't need much taking care of. That one should be easy.

"Then there's Sophia. They call her Gülbahar now, but she'll always be Sophia to me. If I live long enough, I plan to liberate her from the harem. I'll do everything in my power to set her free, but if I die, you'll have to do it."

Radu chokes. Now that's downright nuts. Gülbahar is well sheltered in Mehmed's sarayi, and she's not some seamstress nobody heard about. Gülbahar is Mehmed's favorite, his first wife and the mother of his only son. Getting her out would be just as easy as flying her to the moon.

"How about her baby?"

Vlad's eyes widen.

"Her baby?"

"Yes. Remember she has a baby, just a few months old? What will you do about him?"

Vlad shrugs. "I don't know. Leave him here, I guess?"

"You think she'll go anywhere without her baby?"

"Why not?"

Radu shakes his head.

"Listen Vlad, we both have a lot to learn. But one thing I know is that mothers tend to get attached to their babies. I don't think Gülbahar would go anywhere and leave her baby behind."

Vlad ponders for a moment.

"Then take him too."

Radu sighs. There's no point in talking. Vlad wants him to kidnap Bayezid, the second in line to the Ottoman throne, and take him somewhere, hoping that nobody will notice. How insane is that?

Not to mention that Gülbahar might be pleased with her life as Mehmed's wife, and her perspective of becoming validé. What would she say to an offer of leaving the Edirne palace for some hut in Wallachia to hide with her son, so she can be free?

"I'll see what I can do," Radu says.

"Thank you for sticking with me, brother, after all we've been through. If things go poorly, you'll find out. If they go well, I'll send for you."

"Send for me?"

"Of course. I'll bring you back home. We'll be together."

Radu nods, too tired to talk. He doesn't want to go back to Wallachia, and certainly not with his brother. Nor does he want to even think about kidnapping Gülbahar. But it never crossed Vlad's mind to ask him what he wants. Vlad is deranged, but that's not news. And Radu is so befuddled he doesn't even know if he wishes Vlad good luck or bad luck on his endeavor.

The brothers hug and kiss on both cheeks, in the Wallachian fashion, and Vlad turns to the door. He stops with his hand on the doorknob.

"One more thing."

"Yes?"

"Tell Ali I tried. I talked to the sultan about taking him, and he laughed. 'Don't even think about it. Mara Branković has him, Hatice Halime wants him, and Hüma Hatun asked me to send him to Manisa. They all take precedence over you. It will be hard to decide who to give him to, but it surely won't be you,' he said."

Radu nods. "I'm sure he'll understand."

"I hope so. I got her friend Isa instead. He's going with me."

CHAPTER 92

TILL WE MEET AGAIN

It's raining cats and dogs, and Ali can't for the life of her understand why Isa wants to meet her in the garden. The garden isn't pretty at the end of October, and in the rain, it really sucks. But that's what he wanted, so she's here, even though she should be back in the sarayi, reporting the women's behavior to the kapı ağası.

That's her job. She has to watch who gets along, who doesn't, who hates who. The validé needs to know about any problems before they turn into full-blown disasters. Like if two women become too close to each other, which is always, sooner or later, a recipe for trouble. Or if somebody acts funny. Like Zambak.

But Ali is not about to report Zambak, even though the girl's been acting strange. It may be because she's Mara's close friend; or maybe because she got to spend a few nights with Sultan Murad. She must be hoping to be heavy with child, but there's no sign of that. The clerks who record the women's periods and the nights they spend with the sultan reported nothing yet.

Still, Zambak has been bugging Ali. She walks too close whenever they meet, and smiles like they're sharing a secret. And they are: that morning Ali found her in Mara's bed. She told no one, but the memory of that day hasn't left her. Zambak acts like she'd like Ali to share her bed, and that worries Ali.

Oh well. She'll cross that bridge when she gets to it. For now, she needs to see what's going on with Isa. Must be important; he wouldn't risk a meeting for no good reason. She paces the garden, and the small sharp rain soaks her in minutes. She wanders between the tired flower beds and stops by the lonely rose bushes to smell the few flowers left. They're well past their prime, but their scent is sweeter than ever. She shuffles through the wet leaves covering the alleys, wondering where Isa is.

Her heart jumps as a pair of warm hands covers her eyes from behind. That's a game they used to play as children, guessing each other by the touch of their hands, but that was long ago.

"Who is it?"

"The pope. Come on! What's up?"

He lets her go.

"Aren't we uppity today? Did someone spit in you soup?"

He smiles, his warm blue eyes as clear as ever, his long blond hair darkened by the rain sticking to his forehead, and she remembers he's her oldest friend. Her only friend these days. And he rarely asks for anything.

"I'm sorry I'm grumpy. I'm cold and wet, I'm late for my report, and I'm in a bad mood. What's up?"

"I came to say goodbye."

"What? Why? Where are you going?"

"I'm going to Wallachia with Vlad."

"You are? But why?"

"He asked for you, but the sultan said no. All his wives want you, so he can't let you go. But nobody wants me, so he told Vlad to take me."

"What for?"

"Because I'm Transylvanian. He thinks Vlad might need help in case Hunyadi comes at him from the north. Or in case he needs to go after him."

"Seriously? Can't he just get a map?"

"I don't know. I'm thinking he has one. But when the sultan says go, I go. Not like I have a choice."

"You don't. But he does. There's no good reason to take you!"

Ali stomps her foot to the ground, and Isa gapes at her.

"Why are you so upset?"

Ali isn't sure, but she's livid. She's so angry she can't see straight.

"I'm going to be left here all alone."

"You're already alone most of the time. I barely ever see you."

"Yes, but I know you're here. That helps."

Isa laughs.

"I'm honored you feel that way. But I don't have a choice, Ali. And from Târgoviște, I can get valuable information to send home. They'll want to know what Vlad is up to."

He's right, of course. But Ali can't fathom him leaving. They all left, and she'll be here all alone. Codru is God knows where with Hunyadi; Lena is in Kronstadt, with Smaranda; And now Isa too.

She shakes her head. "I can't be here all alone. I just can't."

"You won't be alone. You have Radu. And Mara. And Gülbahar. You have plenty of friends."

Ali gives him a dirty look that needs no explanation.

"I know. They're not like us. But things are complicated. People are complicated. Alliances shift and change. You'll be leaving too. You'll have to. Someday soon, we'll meet again. I'm sorry, Ali, but I don't have a choice."

"I know. I'm sorry."

He catches her in his arms, and his hug feels like home. Until he gets too close and he tries to kiss her on the lips.

She pushes him away and sputters: "Are you crazy? What if somebody sees us?"

"You're right. This is not the time. But someday soon, you'll be mine. I love you."

"I love you, too."

And she does. But not that way. She'll never be his in the way he's thinking. Never.

CHAPTER 93
WALLACHIA, OCTOBER 1448

The fall is way past its peak, and a spiteful cold wind goes through Vlad's clothes like he's naked. That's because here, on the plains of Wallachia, there's no mountain nor forest to hold it at bay. Just fields, barren now, and marshes, and a heavy, sullen sky hanging above like it's about to fall and choke Vlad.

It's been weird to ride north with an army of Ottoman soldiers. After crossing the Danube, Vlad spent long, painful hours searching the marshes around Bălteni for the place where his father had died. But the cattails kept the secret to themselves.

Further north, he searched the oak forests, wondering where Mircea got blinded and buried alive. He looked and looked for his grave, but found nothing.

This whole journey has been filled with sorrow and loss, instead of joy and triumph for reclaiming his father's rightful throne. Vlad seethes with rage. The boyars, those filthy traitors who sold their souls to Hunyadi, deprived him of his father's counsel and his brother's love. Then, they stole his joy of coming home to take the throne he's always wanted.

As God is my witness, I'll pay them back. May they rot in hell forever.

He bites his lip to hold back a tear and pushes further north through bare fields, forests shrouded in fog, and one impoverished village after another.

The people who stop to watch them are all old, other than the half-naked toddlers. Of course. The young ones died in wars, filled the sultan's janissary troops, or went to Serbia to fight alongside Vladislav. White-haired men lean on their rakes, listening to the old women dressed in black who cover their mouths to talk. But most of them say nothing. They've seen so many voivodes come and go that it's no longer a big deal.

"That one's Vlad Dracul's son," someone whispers.

His neighbor shrugs. "Which of them? They say he had many."

"Not that many. Just five. Six, if you count the monk. Plus the girls."

"So, which one is this?"

"Vlad. The third one."

"I thought Vlad was the second?"

"Yes, from the home bed. But there are the others."

Vlad acts like he didn't hear them, but he's deeply perturbed. He's always known he had two brothers. Three princes deserving of the throne. But Mircea is dead, and Radu doesn't want it, so the throne is his. And now there's at least two more? And a monk? Who are they? Where are they?

He pushes the thought to the back of his mind to revisit later. For now, he's got to be careful and look out for traps as he nears the Royal Court of Târgoviște. Vladislav may have gone to war with Hunyadi, but that doesn't mean that he left the castle unprotected.

His heart heavy with worry, Vlad rides ahead of his troops until the road takes a turn. Wallachia's flag, the eagle carrying the cross in its beak, comes into sight.

The wind is strong, and the flag flies high over the Royal Court's watchtower. Vlad's heart fills with awe at seeing the stately castle his grandfather built. This is not the Edirne Palace, which is as big as a city and as richly ornate as the sultan's gold could make it, but it's his. His childhood home, his inheritance, and his destiny. And he'll take it if he has to crush it into dust.

But the gates are closed, and the drawbridge is up.

Effendi Paşa, the janissary commander, stops the troops and comes to Vlad.

"How do you wish to proceed? Send a messenger, or will the cannon balls be message enough?"

Vlad sighs. Sending a messenger would make him look weak, like he begs them to open the gates. But firing the cannons will make him look like an enemy coming to conquer, not Wallachia's loving son returning home. But what else is there?

"I'll speak to them myself."

Effendi Paşa measures him with worry.

"Are you sure? Those archer slits are damn close, and it only takes one arrow... If some hot-headed youth inside there gets reckless..."

The man is right. Vlad knows he's right. But one has to do what one has to do.

"I'm sure."

He steps forward alone, forcing his eyes away from the dark slits frowning at him from the wall.

"Good Wallachians, I am Vlad Dracula, Vlad Dracul's son, coming in peace. I'm here to free you and our beloved Wallachia from Hunyadi's grip. How much longer should our country stand as a buffer between two clashing empires? How much longer will our children waste their lives for the pleasure of two enemies that want them as slaves? How much longer will our fields fatten the Hungarians and the Ottomans while our children starve? I came to put an end to all that. I came to set you and Wallachia free, so help me God."

Nothing happens.

The wind whips the flag and whistles through the towers. A flock of dead leaves twirls madly, heading south. A murder of crows circle high above, screaming curses.

Mounted on his black destrier, Vlad sits as straight as he can muster, staring at the gates. He tightens his fist around the hilt of his sword, forcing himself to not glance at the archer slits, and he waits.

Nothing happens.

A rush of cold sweat runs down Vlad's back, soaking him under his chain mail armor. He feels his horse shiver under him, and knows he's heard it too, that soft fluttering coming from the archer slit to his left. Someone's readying his bow.

He awaits. Nothing happens.

A wave of rage mounts inside him, whipping his heart into a frenzy, boiling his blood and making him see red. The treasonous bastards won't let him in. They let that traitor Vladislav, but not him, Vlad Dracula, Wallachia's son.

He'll give them one last chance, then crush this place into dust.

"I am Vlad Dracula, Vlad Dracul's son, and I came to take my throne. I order you to open the gates."

His fingers tighten around the hilt of his sword once more, ready to pull it up and give the signal for destruction.

The silence shatters.

The gate screeches open, and the drawbridge lowers.

CHAPTER 94
THE THRONE OF BLOOD

The rusty iron hinges screech like they're hurting as the gates open wide. Vlad spurs his mount forward.

The place is so empty it looks deserted. Hard to believe, but Vladislav the usurper must have taken every man he could get to help his puppet master, Hunyadi, defeat the Ottomans. He left the royal court of Târgoviște unguarded.

But, God willing, they didn't defeat the Ottomans. If God is as just as he is powerful, Vladislav's bones are getting cleaned by crows somewhere in Serbia, while Vlad will take the throne that's rightfully his.

There's no other noise but the clatter of his boots on the stone floor as Vlad wanders through the empty castle in search of old memories. There's the courtyard where he and Radu practiced archery with old Gheorghe. And that's the doorstep where he killed Yellow.

Vlad sighs, wishing he hadn't. Yellow was just a useless old dog, but he didn't deserve that arrow. He didn't understand at the time, but now he does. Like Father said, you don't kill for the fun of it. Unless it's rats. You kill for a reason, and Vlad had no reason to kill Yellow other than he could. And he wanted to hurt Radu.

He moves on, wondering where everyone went. Did Vladislav take them? Did they flee when they heard he was coming? But why?

He makes his way to the throne room.

The throne room, Wallachia's seat of power, is the one place Vlad used to fear. But now that he sees it again, it doesn't look like much. Just a dark stone room with a carved wooden chair sitting on a podium. It doesn't even compare with the sultan's throne room. For God's sake, this place is even more sparse than his quarters in Edirne. There, he has rich Isfahan carpets, and carved chests and alcoves and candles and flowers. Here, there's nothing but cold gray stone smelling like mold and spiders guarding their webs in the corners.

But this is where Vlad Dracul taught him about life, death, and duty. This is where Father instilled in him the responsibility for his country and his people. To Vlad, this is hallowed ground, and he knows Father watches him from far above.

He sits on the throne looking out through the narrow slits that show nothing but sky and thinks about Father. How comfortable he was here. How he never worried what was right and what was wrong. He just knew. Oh, how he wishes he was as wise as him.

But he's not. There he is, sitting on his throne and staring into an empty room. He's Wallachia's voivode, and nobody gives a hoot. Nobody even bothered to congratulate him and wish him well. Nobody even seemed to recognize him. Hard to believe, but he's nothing here. Even less than he was in Edirne.

He's still feeling sorry for himself when an old man limps in. He looks at his feet rather than look at him.

"There's someone to see you."

"Who?"

"He says his name is Cazan."

That doesn't sound familiar, but Vlad is so lonely he'd talk to anyone.

"Bring him in."

Cazan is white-haired and wiry, with a face carved so deep it looks like old wood. Like most Wallachian boyars, he wears tall boots, a fur-trimmed hat and mantle, and a wide-belted leather armor.

He drops the long slim bag he brought and bows.

"I'm Cazan, Your Highness."

Vlad nods.

"I used to be your father's advisor. Vlad Dracul was kind to me and my family. He was a good man, your father, and he always tried to do the right thing. Sometimes he succeeded, sometimes he did not, but I always felt lucky to be in his service."

"Glad to meet you, Cazan. What can I do for you?"

The man stands straight and smiles.

"It's the other way round, my voivode. This is about what I can do for you. I brought you your father's inheritance."

He points to the bag on the ground.

"I was with your father the day before he left Târgoviște. I wanted to ride south with him, but he said no. 'Go home, Cazan, and look after your family. But when the time comes, I want you to take care of mine. When my son comes to claim Wallachia's throne, I want you to give him these two things and tell him my last words.'"

"What were his last words?"

"Wallachia isn't mine, and she isn't yours. She belongs to your children, and your children's children. Take care of her as if she'll live forever, because she will."

Vlad's heart melts. He can tell these words are Father's. With the mind's eye, he can see him saying them, and he feels grateful for this gift he didn't expect. But there's more.

"He also gave me this to give you."

The long, sheathed sword is plain and beautiful. The silver blade glows like the full moon.

"This is his Toledo sword. His protector, King Sigismund, gave it to him when he took Wallachia's throne, and he wanted you to have it."

Vlad's eyes burn with tears. His father's legacy fills him with unbearable joy and searing pain.

"Then there's this."

A golden sigil. A twisted dragon biting his tail.

"This is his Order of the Dragon. Your father was one of the few who ever got it. That's why they called him Vlad Dracul, the Dragon. The Order of the Dragon is a select brotherhood of Christian knights who banded together to fight for the Cross. You father left it for you."

Gratitude fills Vlad's heart.

"What's your name again?"

"Cazan, my lord."

Vlad bows in front of the old man.

"Thank you for bringing these to me and thank you for your service. Father was lucky to have you advising him."

"Thank you, my voivode."

"Hereby, on the sword of my father, I swear I shall not find rest nor pleasure in earthly things until I avenge his death. I will kill the usurper with my own hands, so help me God."

"So help you God."

"Cazan, I don't have friends here. Nor anyone I can trust. Can I count on you?"

Cazan drops to his knees.

Vlad picks Vlad Dracul's sword and touches Cazan's shoulder.

"From now on, you will be my *armaș*, my man of arms. You will guard me, advise me, and ensure that my orders are followed. Will you take this job?"

"I'm yours, my lord."

Vlad helps the old man up and hugs him. He hopes against all hope to match his father's wisdom and undaunted courage someday. Wallachia needs the wisest, bravest, and strongest voivode she can get.

But all she's got is him.

AFTERWORD

Thank you for reading Throne of Blood. If you enjoyed it, **please take a minute to leave a review**, and tell a friend. You'll help other readers like you discover this book, and I'd really appreciate it.

To find out what happened next to Vlad, Radu, Mehmed and the three Transylvanians, read **Song of Swords**, the third novel in The Curse Of The Dracula Brothers series. You may also enjoy **Throne of Thorns**, the prequel novella of the series.

RR Jones

ABOUT THIS BOOK

This entire series only exists because of George R.R. Martin's Game of Thrones. Reading it made me itch to write my own GOT, set in my birthplace, Romania, whose history is just as gripping and wild.

But I wasn't ready to write a whole saga spanning countries, decades, and dozens of characters, so I started writing what I knew: the ER. I wrote OVERDOSE, a medical thriller, as Rada Jones MD. That turned into a whole series and inspired another, featuring a cast of heroic bomb dogs in the Afghan war. They're quite a roller-coaster, but they all end well.

When the urge to write my Romanian GOT returned, I started the Curse of the Dracula Brothers series.

Radu, Vlad, Ștefan, and Mehmed were real historical figures you can find in history books. I read all the books I could find about them, researched the Internet, and visited most places to respect the historical accuracy of events and do them justice. I smelled the flowers, ate the food, and drank the wine. I even partook of the hammam and petted the cats - somebody had to do it, after all.

The magical kids are characters drawn from our folklore. The zmeu - the Romanian dragon, the vârcolac - the Romanian werewolf - and the wise witches living in Transylvania's dark forests. They live in our legends, and who knows? They may still roam Transylvania, waiting to return...

I hope you enjoyed Den of Spies, and can't wait to read more. If so, read <u>Song of Swords</u>.

About the Author

RR Jones was born in Transylvania, ten miles from Dracula's Castle. Growing up between communists and vampires taught her that humans are fickle, but you can always trust dogs and books. That's why she read every book she could get, including the phone book (too many characters, not enough action), and adopted every stray she found, from dogs to frogs.

After joining her American husband, she spent years studying medicine and working in the ER, but she still speaks like Dracula's cousin.

When she's not exploring faraway places, she lives with her husband and their German shepherd Guinness in a tiny cabin in the woods. She spends her days writing, hiking, and talking to her imaginary friends.

facebook.com/RRJonesBooks
instagram.com/rrjonesbooks
bookbub.com/profile/rada-jones